The Bonds of Blood

Rob Sinclair is the author of the acclaimed and bestselling Enemy and James Ryker series of espionage thrillers. His books have sold over half a million copies with many reviewers and readers having likened Rob's work to authors at the very top of the genre, including Lee Child and Vince Flynn. Rob began writing in 2009 following a promise to his wife that he could pen a 'can't put down' thriller. He worked for nearly 13 years for a global firm specialising in forensic fraud investigations. Rob now writes full time.

Also by Rob Sinclair

DI Dani Stephens

The Essence of Evil
The Rules of Murder
Echoes of Guilt
The Bonds of Blood

The Bonds of Blood

Rob Sinclair

CANELO

First published in the United Kingdom in 2021 by

Canelo
31 Helen Road
Oxford OX2 0DF
United Kingdom

A CIP catalogue record for this book is available from the British Library.

Print ISBN 978 1 80032 287 5
Ebook ISBN 978 1 80032 286 8

Look for more great books at www.canelo.co

Printed and bound in Great Britain by Clays Ltd, Elcograf S.p.A.

Prologue

'Hey,' she said, her voice soft and smooth, the perfect complement to her luscious, silky skin and her dazzling eyes which were firmly set on him as he idled towards her.

She had sunk down into an armchair, her blonde hair draped over her left shoulder, legs crossed one over the other, bare skin visible all the way up to—

'Terry!'

His name – the simple command – carried a whole weight of instruction. He stopped and turned. Annie, his wife, was sitting in an armchair opposite. Her clothes were more formal than the younger woman's – more elegant – and her face was made up strategically. She'd made an effort and there was no doubt she looked good, despite being a couple of decades older than the woman Terry had been heading for.

The strangest thing was the look on Annie's face. Not as aggressive, or as angry as he'd imagined it would be in this moment. Almost curious.

'Honey,' he said to his wife. 'How about getting me another drink?'

He wiggled the glass in his hand. He'd forgotten he'd had that there. He looked down to it and saw the pint was still nearly full. He took a large swig. The beer was warm and weak.

'Looks like I'm nearly out,' he said, yet despite the large gulp, the glass seemed even more full now, and Annie even more suspicious.

She stood up from the chair as her eyes flitted between Terry and the other woman. Then she walked off. Out of the door. To the bar?

There were still plenty of people left in the sprawling and brightly lit room, but no one other than the leggy blonde was paying any attention to Terry now.

He took another good look around. What was this place anyway? He didn't recognise it.

'Come on then,' she said, her lips moving seductively as she spoke. How did she do that?

She was on her feet, her swaying hips exaggerated as she stepped closer to him. The increased pressure in his already tight jeans was palpable, though he wasn't apprehensive in the slightest about what the other people around him would think. Empty-handed now, he wrapped his arms around her waist as she pressed up against him and tickled his neck with those amazingly soft lips.

'No, not here,' he said, though he realised his words weren't even half-hearted.

'Don't worry, Annie won't mind. She already knows.'

His eyes went wide for a second, but his surprise at her words didn't last long. Sod it. Annie, if she didn't already know, would have to find out somehow, sooner or later. Wouldn't she? Why not now? Why not here? Wherever the hell *here* was.

Where were they?

It didn't matter. Moments later they were enjoying a deep kiss. Her hand reached around to undo his belt.

WHOOMPH.

Terry jolted at the unexpected noise. Where'd that come from? He didn't pull back from the kiss.

WHOOMPH.

Louder this time. A wet, thudding sound. He jolted again. Like he was bouncing.

Whatever.

They were lying down on the floor now, her blonde hair smothering him, their bodies entwined. How could he ever say no to this woman?

'Oh, Terry,' she murmured.

She had said his name… except… no, that was crazy to think.

WHOOMPH.

Even more focused this time. And the thud was accompanied by a murmur. Not a murmur. A moan. A groan. Of surprise. Pain.

And it was definitely Annie…

Terry opened his eyes with a start.

Darkness. Not complete darkness. A shadow moving.

WHOOMPH.

He was in bed. His bedroom.

'Annie!'

Terry sprang upright, or at least he tried to. The blow to the side of his head sent him crashing back down onto the pillow.

The pillow. The bed. His bed. His home. His weary brain was still trying desperately to recalibrate.

SMACK.

Another blow to the head and Terry sank further down.

Wetness. That was the sensation that he felt most vividly. No smell. No taste. Just wetness. The pillow was covered. The sheet beneath him too.

3

WHOOMPH.

Another thwack. The bed jolted. His eyes were still adjusting to the light, but then that big shadow above him moved again. A figure, tall. It moved to the side and a shaft of light broke through from the gap between the bedroom door and the hallway and onto the bed, the glow enough to light up Annie's face. Her face. Eyes bulbous and pleading. Mouth half open in a silent cry for help. The red of blood everywhere.

Her lips twitched. A bubble of blood burst from her mouth, but no words came. The figure brought down the weapon with another almighty clatter. Annie's body shuddered. A helpless exhale of air escaped her lips.

The next moment the figure jumped up onto the bed. The mattress sank from the weight. Terry tried to move but his limbs felt distant. The figure held the weapon aloft. Terry's already weary eyes followed as it hurtled towards him. The only reaction he could muster was to blink his eyes shut as contact was made.

No pain. Not exactly. The weapon was pulled up, and whacked back down again. Onto his head this time.

Onto? No, not onto. *Into*. Somehow he could feel it inside his head.

It stuck. His eyes twitched. His vision blurred. Blood? The figure stamped down onto Terry's belly to yank the weapon free.

'Fuck's sake!'

That voice…

Terry tried desperately to place it, as though it would make a difference now.

The dripping blade of the axe hung over his head for what felt like an age.

Then came down once more.
After that, there was nothing.

Chapter 1

March

Winter had been long and cold, and the temperature outside was still chilly when Dani had arrived at West Midlands Police HQ in central Birmingham shortly after seven a.m. But as Dani stepped out of the revolving doors at nine, and into a block of warm sunshine that had somehow found its way between the tall buildings surrounding her, she wondered whether perhaps spring had finally arrived.

She certainly needed it.

She headed across the road towards and then past Snowhill Station, then further along Colmore Row with St Philip's Cathedral standing proud to her left. She took the turning onto Church Street where a hundred yards down, nestled between two office blocks, was a trendy new coffee shop she hadn't been to before.

As she stepped inside, she was greeted with an industrial-cum-shabby-chic interior, and a big blackboard with some eye-watering city centre prices. A quick glance at the offerings and she realised this cafe was about as unique as the myriad other establishments around the business district. Still, the coffee smelled damn good, and the array of cakes and pastries looked even better.

Dani didn't head to the counter to order one, though. Briana Clark was already seated in the corner of the cafe, two steaming mugs on the table in front of her.

Dani walked over, not sure whether to be pleasantly impressed or perturbed by the fact her drink had been chosen and bought for her.

'I got you a cappuccino,' Briana said. 'It's what you normally have, right?'

It was. At least on the last three occasions that Dani had met the journalist like this, though there was still something about the act of presumption that irked.

'Thank you,' Dani said as she briefly looked around at the near-empty cafe before taking a seat. Briana smiled and pushed a pair of thick-rimmed glasses up the bridge of her nose. With her long, straight, silky reddish hair, her svelte figure but downbeat clothes, Briana reminded Dani of one of those teen movies where the obviously already pretty geek gets bullied, until one day she has the most dramatic makeover ever by taking her glasses off and putting on some skimpy clothing. Then, all of a sudden, everyone likes her and she gets the boy.

Pretty, in an understated and effortless way, was an easier way of putting it.

Dani was jealous.

'How's everything going?' Briana asked.

'Busy. Which is both good and bad.'

Briana didn't seem to know how to take that. Dani wasn't even sure about it. Because of course it would be a good thing if there weren't so many murders in the West Midlands. Wouldn't it?

'How's Jason?'

Dani squirmed a little at the enquiry about her boyfriend, though Briana didn't seem to notice.

'He's fine, thanks for asking. Getting stronger every day. What about you?'

'Oh, Joey's settling in really well at his new pre-school. He'll be ready for the big start in September in no time.'

Dani nodded and smiled as she took a quick sip from her coffee. Hopefully that was the personal talk done with. She wasn't really the personable type. Never had been, and was even less so these days after... no, she didn't want to think about that right now.

'So what can I do for you?' she asked.

Briana shifted uncomfortably. 'I'm guessing you saw the paper yesterday.'

Dani had. There was always a copy in the office of the latest *Birmingham Mail* – the city's evening tabloid – and it wasn't at all unusual for the front-page story to be related to the work of the Homicide team. Even though Dani herself hadn't been mentioned in the story, yesterday's headline had nearly made her head explode when she'd first spotted it. A38 VICTIM'S HISTORY OF VIOLENCE. Not so much a hatchet job as a sensationalist piece of propaganda that was sure to add a ton weight to the defence's position.

'I did,' Dani said.

Briana looked down at the table. 'Sorry about that.'

'It's fine,' Dani said, not really feeling it. 'But it might have been more helpful if you'd held back until after you'd spoken to me.'

'I tried, honestly, but... slow news days, and all that. And I did try to speak to you—'

Dani waved the excuses away. 'It's done now.'

'So...'

'So what?'

'Is there anything else you can tell me?'

8

Dani shook her head, doing a bad job of hiding her agitation. She was trying to remain calm and courteous here. She quite liked Briana. Of all the journalists she dealt with, Briana seemed to have the most common sense, the most decency, and the most favourable view of the Police Force. All of that was why Dani was willing to have these little tête-à-têtes. Well, and because her boss, DCI McNair, had suggested it was about time Dani made and maintained such acquaintances, not just in the press but all over. But whether that was more to help build Dani's profile in order for her to be groomed for higher things, or to help protect McNair when things went wrong, Dani still wasn't quite sure.

She liked Briana. Yet to Dani the relationship still felt so one-sided. What was she actually gaining from this? The problem was, she was naturally wary of any journalist these days. Largely because she herself had had her name and her life dragged through the papers more than once in the past. Most painfully, a few years ago when she'd been caught up in a murder investigation which had ended with her twin brother, Ben, the chief suspect. Ben, who later attempted to murder both Dani and his second wife Gemma, in order to hide his other crimes.

Dani sighed. Briana looked bemused, but how to explain that it remained difficult to spend more than five waking minutes without somehow being reminded of her murderous brother?

Ben was now locked up for life. Dani had suffered permanent brain damage from the attack. She was a traumatic brain injury – TBI – survivor, though her survival had come at a cost. Firstly, in the negative press against her and her family, but most significantly in the permanent changes to her personality caused by the irreparable damage to her frontal lobes. She wasn't the same Dani as before. She was more angry, more on edge, more irritable, more selfish and less empathetic. Though she tried as hard as she could to hide those now-natural traits. Like right now.

'Dani?' Briana prompted.

'Sorry,' Dani said, coming out of her thoughts. 'I can't tell you much, I'm afraid. It's too early.'

Briana seemed genuinely disappointed by that. As though a cappuccino was the surefire way to Dani's heart and soul, and having played her trump card she was now out of ideas.

'Will Clinton Harrison be charged with murder?' she asked.

'He's been arrested on suspicion of murder.'

Briana's perky exterior dropped fractionally with each of Dani's vague and diverting answers.

'A lot of people are saying what he did was justified,' Briana continued. 'That they would have done the same thing in his position. What do you think?'

'That's not for me to decide.'

'But you must have an opinion.'

'And you must know by now I'm not going to give it to you if I don't want to.'

'Which tells me a lot,' Briana said, sitting back in her seat. She looked more confident all of a sudden, like a barrister who'd just cornered a troublesome witness. 'Because plenty of times I've seen you denounce people you've arrested and charged. You tell the press things like *another killer is off our streets*, long before the jury's announced their verdict, before trial even. But you're obviously holding back with Harrison.'

'Because what happened on the A38 was an absolutely exceptional circumstance. And I'm sure you'll appreciate it's barely twenty-four hours after the event.'

Briana held Dani's eye now. A challenging look. Dani didn't appreciate it. This was the first time she'd felt like this with Briana. As though she was under the cosh. Why now? Especially after the friendly set-up.

'And what about Dylan Roberts?' Briana said.

'He's dead. And your paper has already smeared him as being a bad guy who probably deserved it. So what exactly are you asking?'

'Were you aware of his criminal past?'

'Me personally? No. I'm a Homicide detective. Roberts has never been involved in one of my investigations before. But yes, I'm now aware he had a criminal record. Do I think that meant he deserved to be beaten to death? No, I don't. Do you?'

'Me? I… er…'

'You don't know? Then I'm really not sure what the purpose of your headline and your story was yesterday.'

Briana looked a little offended by that. Dani picked up her drink and took a couple of hot mouthfuls, trying to get to the bottom of the cup as quickly as she could. Her tongue and the roof of her mouth stung but she battled through.

'You have something else to get to?' Briana asked.

Dani looked at her watch. She did, but not for forty minutes, though Briana seemed to be giving her an invitation to leave. As though she too had had enough this time.

'Yeah,' Dani said, finishing her coffee at the fourth attempt and doing her best to hide the pain.

'I am sorry,' Briana said as Dani got to her feet.

'It's fine. But please, next time—'

'I'll definitely speak to you first. But… I hope you'll do the same for me too? There's a lot of public interest in this one.'

Dani paused, but then nodded. Perhaps Briana wasn't really asking for much. 'Speak to you soon.'

Five minutes later Dani was re-entering HQ. She still had half an hour before the scheduled meeting with Clinton Harrison and his lawyer. In only a few hours Dani and her team would have to decide whether they were charging him with murder – and if not, with what?

The open-plan office space taken up by the Homicide team was about as busy as ever, with nearly a dozen heads sticking up over the desk dividers. DS Easton – Dani's go-to sergeant and the closest thing she had to a classic partner – spotted Dani as she headed to her own desk and he was soon by her side, looking bright and breezy.

'How'd it go?' he asked.

Dani rolled her eyes in response. 'Are we—'

He held up his hand to stop her.

'Yes, we're all set, but first, Boss wants to see you.'

He indicated over to DCI McNair's closed door.

'Anything I should be worried about?' Dani asked.

'She didn't say. But on the pissed-off scale I'd say she's only about three.'

'Out of—'

'Out of more than three.'

'Good start.'

Dani took off her jacket and hung it on the back of her chair before heading over to McNair's office. She knocked on the door.

'Come in.'

Dani opened the door, stepped inside, then shut it behind her. McNair, glasses perched on the end of her nose, was sitting on the edge of her seat staring at her computer screen. McNair was formally dressed – as ever – in a plain-looking grey suit. Her short but neatly styled brown hair, her glasses and her overly stiff appearance reminded Dani of a stereotypical schoolmistress from years gone by. She was about as strict too. Many referred to her as a ballbreaker. Dani, even though she hated that sexist term, had thought of McNair as that plenty of times in the past, though the longer she worked with the DCI and the more experienced and senior Dani herself became, the more she realised McNair was a strong but fair copper. And the more Dani realised that she was probably a lot more like McNair than she'd ever care to admit.

Dani's eyes rested on the copy of the *Birmingham Mail* on the desk, the paper folded in such a way as to clearly show the front-page headline. Obviously.

Dani looked up from the paper and caught McNair's eye. McNair gave her a look as though she'd spotted her child rooting in the sweetie jar without permission.

'Yes, about that,' she said. 'Come and sit down.'

Dani did so.

'I understand you met with this Briana Clark just now,' McNair said, as she tapped the journalist's byline on the paper.

'Basically, so she could apologise for that,' Dani said, indicating the same.

'A bit late.'

'Which is pretty much what I told her.'

'So you didn't know they were running this before-hand?'

'She tried to speak to me yesterday but we never managed it.'

McNair gave Dani a dubious look, like she wasn't sure whose fault the failed communication was. Neither was Dani.

Then McNair sighed and sat back in her chair.

'And you're speaking with Harrison at ten?' she said.

'That's the plan.'

'His lawyer has no doubt seen the paper by now.'

'It would be weird if he hadn't.'

The office fell silent. Dani got the impression McNair expected her to say something else.

'We'll just have to wait and see how it plays out,' Dani said.

McNair humphed. 'Because when has winging it ever backfired?'

'That's not quite what I meant.'

McNair waved that away. 'Tell me everything you know so far. I was trying to find the footage on here but the damn thing won't let me into anything.'

She slammed the mouse onto the table in retaliation for the computer's apparent obstinance.

'Is it OK if I bring Grayling in?'

McNair nodded.

A minute later DC Grayling – the youngest member of the team, but certainly not the least capable – was hovering over McNair's desk as she set her laptop down for both Dani and McNair to see. Claire Grayling, in her mid-twenties, jeans and a sweatshirt, her hair and general attitude laidback – though not unprofessionally so – was so far removed from McNair in both appearance and attitude that it was amazing they could function effectively as part of the same team. They could, because both were abundantly competent in their roles. Grayling was just far more technologically adept than the boss.

'You were looking for the video footage?' Grayling said. 'We have quite a combination. CCTV from various angles, particularly in the build-up and aftermath, but not so much for the incident itself. Then we have seven mobile phone videos of varying quality and lengths that we've gathered so far. No single video covers everything, though, so it's a bit of a patchwork in terms of trying to look at events from start to finish.'

'Just start with whatever's best,' McNair said.

'Let me try,' Grayling responded. She typed away furiously on the keyboard, opening folders and files. The screen flickered as a combination of videos popped up. Grayling then chose one and hit play. 'This is a good place to start.'

'Where is that?' McNair said, eyes narrowing as she stared at the screen.

'Halton Street. It's just off the A38, not far from Fort Dunlop. About half a mile from… where it happened. This is the first capture we have – or have found at least – of Harrison and his son.'

They watched the five-second clip over and over, Dani with a strange feeling of grim inevitability. Clinton Harrison's older son, Tyler, was twelve years old. He and his dad had been out on what would have been an eleven-mile cycle, but had made less than two.

'Then this one shows Dylan Roberts, approaching the junction just around the corner from there. He's in the blue van.'

'A Mercedes Sprinter,' Dani added.

'And he was alone?' McNair asked.

'Yes,' Dani said.

'Where was he going?'

Dani looked to Grayling. 'It's one of the things we're still trying to piece together.'

Another humph from McNair. 'There's no indication Harrison and Roberts knew each other?'

'Nothing yet.'

'OK, so what next?' McNair said.

All eyes returned to the screen. 'This is less than two minutes later,' Grayling said. 'A little further up the A38, about a mile away from Spaghetti Junction. That's Roberts' Sprinter in the foreground. You can just make out Tyler Harrison on his bike in the left-hand lane, right at the top. Clinton was a few yards further ahead, out of shot.'

Grayling sighed. 'Now this is where it gets more sketchy. The actual incident was in a CCTV black spot, by all of two yards. So we can see the build-up of traffic. We see people on their feet, rushing to the scene. We even see some of the people who were filming on their phones.'

'Any who we haven't tracked down yet?' McNair asked.

'At least four. But no CCTV of the scene itself. Just mobile phone footage of the immediate aftermath.'

'OK, show me.'

'I have to say, if you haven't seen this already, it's…'

Grayling didn't seem to know how to finish the sentence. McNair blinked sombrely at the incomplete warning. If a blink could be such a thing. Dani's heart thudded hard in her chest as the next video opened. She'd seen this one. She wished she hadn't.

Grayling turned the volume up a couple of notches and the shouts and calls and screams – surprise, shock, terror – filled the room. The initial grainy image cleared to show a scene of carnage and horror. Vehicles at a stop all over. The blue Sprinter van took up much of the screen.

Dani's eyes flitted to the bike in the bottom right-hand corner. The child's bike, the metal and rubber torn and twisted almost beyond recognition. The gleaming silver frame, and the tarmac all around, glistened red with blood. The crumpled body of Tyler Harrison lay unmoving next to it. Only his bedraggled feet and legs were in view, the rest of him off-screen. Thankfully. Dani had seen footage from the other angles too. Had seen what was left of poor Tyler. She'd nearly thrown up at that.

There was a shriek of terror from a female bystander and Dani's eyes switched back to the mêlée. Roberts on the ground, himself unmoving now, and covered in his own blood. Harrison, all six feet five of him, musclebound, raging and sobbing and out of control, stood over Roberts as he rained down blows on his victim's head with the heel of his shoe.

One, two, three bystanders tried and failed to haul Harrison away, to no avail, before he eventually seemed to see sense himself.

The video came to an end with only Roberts and Tyler on screen.

'There's another one.'

McNair held up her hand. 'No, I get the picture.'

Her face was paler than before. Like for so many others who'd seen this, Dani wondered if it was the horror of Tyler's death that had affected her so much, rather than the savage beating that had ended Roberts' life. And it was surely the horror of Tyler's death which had led to his father's violent outburst. Wasn't it?

'Paramedics attended Roberts as soon as they arrived on the scene,' Dani said. 'He was still breathing but was dead before they got him into the ambulance. Harrison remained there the whole time, by Tyler's side.'

Dani shivered at her own words. What must the father have been going through in those moments as he held his son's mangled body in his hands?

She glanced to the clock. Ten minutes to ten. She'd rarely been so reluctant to interview a murder suspect before.

'Have we got a clear account of what actually happened to Tyler to prompt this?'

'Four witness statements so far from other drivers, all giving a more or less consistent account,' Grayling said. 'There'll certainly be more to come too. What we've been told is Roberts was speeding on the A38, had been for a few miles along the dual carriageway. It's 40 mph along most of that stretch, with traffic lights every couple of hundred yards. He was said to be driving erratically, cutting in and out of lanes at each set of lights to beat the traffic. But it sounds like the collision was... I don't know.'

'What?'

'Accidental. But potentially still caused by dangerous driving. What we've heard is that Roberts had just pulled into the outside lane, where the Harrisons were cycling. They were only going to be on the main road for less than a quarter of a mile. Roberts was accelerating to go past them when Tyler's bike swerved. It's not clear why. A pothole. A drain cover. The Sprinter nudged the back end and sent Tyler over the handlebars. Roberts did brake, apparently, but… obviously we can't see exactly, but somehow Tyler got stuck under the wheels and…'

Grayling trailed off, but the gory images were ingrained. McNair let out a long and sorrowful sigh. 'And we've just seen the rest.'

The room fell silent for a few moments. Dani's brain whirred.

McNair looked to her. 'We need to keep our emotions out of this. This was a horrible, tragic event, but don't get caught up in that. We have to remain objective. Clinton Harrison killed a man in cold blood. We need to not lose sight of that, even if we think the motive is clear cut.'

Dani and Grayling both nodded.

'We'll look into both men,' Dani said. 'Explore whether there's any connection at all.'

'And I do want to figure out where Roberts was going or coming from in such a hurry. Aside from the Clinton Harrison issue, at the very least there'll be an inquiry into his son's death. Make sure we know exactly what happened. I haven't spoken to the CPS yet, but however much anyone feels sorry for Clinton, from what you've just shown me I don't see how we could do anything other than charge him with murder.'

There was a knock on the door. All three of them turned as the door inched open and Easton poked his head inside.

'Sorry,' he said. 'Talk about timing.'

'What is it?'

'I've just had a call from uniform at a scene in Sutton Coldfield. Suspected double murder.'

Dani's heart raced as all eyes turned to her. Was that at the mention of Sutton Coldfield?

She glanced to the clock again. Five minutes to ten.

'I'm happy to attend on my own,' Easton said, 'but—'

'There's no other DI available?' McNair said.

Easton shook his head.

Dani looked to her boss. Could McNair read her mind?

'You know what?' McNair said. 'Let me and Grayling deal with Harrison.'

Rarely had Dani felt so relieved to be informed of a new murder. What had she said to Briana earlier about being busy?

Moments later, she and Easton were heading for her car.

Chapter 2

'You OK?' Easton said.

Dani waited for the lights to go green, and then put her foot down before answering.

'Yeah.'

'Something's on your mind.'

'You think?'

She gave him a scolding look. Perhaps a bit unnecessary.

'I get it,' he said. 'At least I think I do. Hearing those words together. Murder. Sutton Coldfield.'

'You're reading too much into it.'

She glanced at him again. He didn't look too convinced. And he was partly right. Those dark and harrowing memories of Ben, what he'd done – and the aftermath where Dani had struggled for months to rebuild every aspect of her life – had been brought right back to the fore once more. How could that not be the case on hearing of a murder in Sutton Coldfield? It wasn't as though the town of some hundred thousand people saw a high number of murders, and it would never be the case that she'd hear those words together and not be immediately reminded of her own traumatic experience there at the hands of her murderous twin brother. Ben was, in essence, Sutton Coldfield's most notorious ever resident.

Yet she still lived there.

'It's not just you who has those random thoughts,' Easton said. 'I'm the same. When I took the call, you know what my first thought was?'

'What?'

'What if it's someone I know? My parents. A neighbour. It's natural.'

'Is it?'

The question went unanswered. She knew his explanation was a long way from where her own head had been. Regardless, they were soon turning off Lichfield Road and onto the Four Oaks Estate – a cluster of private roads right next to the expansive Sutton Park – where some of the regions wealthiest people lived. Not a gated community, but not far off it, with tree-lined roads, wide pavements, and tall gates, hedges and walls keeping the large houses mostly hidden from the few pedestrians who came down here.

They arrived at the entrance to Kibble House a few seconds later. Two uniformed officers stood by the open wrought-iron gates, and waved Dani through when she showed her ID. Two marked police cars and an ambulance were parked up on the gravel driveway. The house beyond was large, but not overtly extravagant. Probably five or six bedrooms, a few sprawling reception rooms, half an acre of land, and a couple-of-million price tag. Well out of Dani's, and most people's reaches, but the houses on the estate here were largely owned by local well-to-do corporate types, rather than the mega rich who opted for out-of-town country pads several times the size of this one.

Dani parked her car behind the others, furthest from the house.

'The owners are...?' she said as she shut the engine down, though she didn't make a move to get out.

'Terry and Annie Eccles,' Easton said. 'He runs a few local businesses. Property related mostly. She's a doctor. Or was in the past. They've lived here for fifteen years. As far as we know, they're the victims, pending formal identification.'

Dani took a big inhale of breath, then let out a long and thoughtful sigh. 'OK, let's go and take a look.'

With a set of coveralls each, masks and gloves in their hands, they walked slowly along the gravel, Dani taking in the surroundings. Beyond the huddle of emergency vehicles was a separate double garage with a black Range Rover outside it. Not brand new, but still worth a fair amount. Next to the SUV was a much more run-of-the-mill Kia Picanto. It looked like a baby elephant next to its mother.

Dani nodded over to the cars.

'I presume that's the cleaner's car,' Easton said. 'She was the one who made the 999 call.'

Dani didn't say anything to that. They soon arrived at the open front door where another uniformed officer was stationed. He introduced himself as PC Forrester.

'Who's inside?' Dani asked.

'Just the photographer, PC Ahmed, and the lady now,' he said. 'Paramedics confirmed death and are awaiting instruction. Ahmed's with the lady.'

By which Dani took to mean the cleaner.

'Ledford said he'd be here by midday,' Easton said to Dani as he finished pulling on his mask.

Jack Ledford was the main local pathologist. It wasn't strictly necessary to have a pathologist out to every scene of death, but given what Dani had heard of the nature of the killings here, she'd made that call while they were on the road.

'You were with PC Ahmed as first response?' Dani asked the copper.

'Yes, Ma'am.'

'So you've had a look around the scene already?'

He nodded.

'Will you walk with us?'

A more reluctant nod this time.

'Let's go.'

Dani took two steps into the large but dark hallway before she stopped. She looked down to the tiled floor. Victorian patterned tiles swirled outwards across the space, with walls decked with dark wood. There was little natural light coming in. An old but elegant design.

'The killer's?' Dani said as she stared at the pair of black boots that were neatly arranged on the tiles, and which glistened with still wet blood. There was a trail of red leading off from them, and neat red prints heading back towards the carpeted stairs.

'I think so,' Forrester said.

Dani turned to Easton. 'So the killer bludgeoned the victims, headed downstairs in these, then takes them off before they leave?'

Easton shrugged.

'Barefoot? Or did they have other shoes?'

'We may be able to get something from the tiles to confirm,' Easton suggested.

Dani nodded. 'Still odd though, isn't it?'

They carried on along the hallway. The staircase was off to the left, doorways off to the right. Light murmurs drifted over from the nearest room. Most likely from the cleaner and PC Ahmed. Dani would check on them later.

They moved up the stairs, Dani being careful not to tread on any of the many blood streaks on the mauve carpet. There were also specks and flecks and streaks on the wooden handrail, and on the patterned wallpaper the other side.

'Was there any blood on the cleaner?' Easton asked Forrester. 'From moving the bodies perhaps?'

'Nothing obvious,' he said with a shrug. 'From what I understand she took one look and bolted. She didn't go near the bodies.'

'So we're to presume the blood prints here are from the killer, not from her,' Easton said.

A perhaps obvious point really, but still worth making, Dani felt. Always best to air thoughts in case there was an alternative someone else had.

'The killer fled down the stairs,' Dani said. 'But where did they come in?'

They reached the top floor. Dani followed the blood trail on the carpet until she was standing just beyond the doorway to the master bedroom.

'Shit,' was all Easton said as he came to her side.

Neither of them said anything for a while after that as they both stared at the gory site. Dani was shocked. Horrified. Revolted. But she was also taking in everything she saw.

A man. A woman. Both in the bed. Their bloodied bodies partially under the twisted and soaked-red duvet. The bed was like a bloodbath. Thick and dark streaks of red stained the headboard and the wall, and spread out across the carpet. Boot prints were noticeable on the carpet all around the bed. Smudges were everywhere. From the killer's movements? Their hands?

Dani shuddered. More than once. This certainly wasn't the first time she'd seen the aftermath of such a frenzied attack. The last similar scene to this – victims attacked in their own bed – had been at the hands of a mentally unstable ex-convict named Damian Curtis. The repercussions of his crimes still weighed heavy on Dani, not least because Curtis had at one time, prior to his murder spree, shared a cell with her brother Ben at Long Lartin prison, and had attacked Dani and Jason in their home. Jason was still far from making a full physical recovery as a result of that attack. Curtis was behind bars now. He was so mentally unstable he would likely never be released. This crime had nothing to do with him. Yet was the killer of a similar ilk? Surely nobody of sound mind could do this?

Easton moved around to the right-hand side of the bed, where the woman's sorry-looking body lay.

'Axe,' Easton said.

Dani took a couple of steps his way and looked down to the floor where the bloodied tool lay. A whole host of fresh and grim images flashed in her mind.

'And baseball bat,' Easton said, indicating the second discarded weapon. 'Two killers, weapon each, or one killer with two weapons?'

'One killer,' Dani said. 'There's nothing in the blood marks on the floor to suggest two people leaving. Only one pair of boots downstairs.'

'Probably,' he said. 'So what do you think?'

Dani moved around and closer to the bed now. She leaned forwards, held her breath as she moved her head closer and closer to the man's body, looking all around his hands, arms, torso. She did the same with the woman. Before long the tang of blood and death was stuck deep in her mouth and nose and she couldn't wait for some fresh air.

Not yet.

Dani looked up. The light was on.

'Was it like that when you arrived?' she asked Forrester.

He looked unsure. 'I... er, I think so. I didn't turn it on.'

'We'll need to check with the cleaner,' Dani said to Easton. 'But my thought is they were both asleep when this happened. There's no indication they put up a defence.'

'They could have been drugged,' Easton suggested.

'It's possible. Ledford will tell us that eventually. But looking at this, the brutality... this was quick. The killer came in. Bludgeoned them repeatedly, ferociously. Gave them no chance to wake properly and fight back. Then he – they? – left. And quite casually too. Downed tools. Took off their boots.'

She shuddered at her own words. Easton was staring at her.

'What?'

'Nothing,' he said.

He looked away. Dani turned to leave. She moved out into the hallway then stopped again as her eyes followed the blood down the stairs.

'Any sign of forced entry?' Dani said to Forrester.

He shook his head. 'I checked the doors and windows. Nothing obvious. The house was fully locked up. Well, downstairs at least.'

'Downstairs? So what about upstairs?'

'It's all sash windows. And not new ones. None of them have proper locks. A few have limiters.'

'Some don't?'

'The ones in the main bedroom didn't. Nor the one over there, or in the bathroom. Same in one of the bedrooms. All a bit hit-and-miss, really.'

Dani looked across the landing again to the tall sash window at the far end that was beautifully glazed with coloured glass in the corners. She walked over, treading tentatively, her eyes focused on the carpet underfoot. Nothing there. She reached the window and looked down outside. The window was directly above the entrance. No drainpipes or anything else nearby to make an easy climb.

'The killer could have had a key?' Easton said.

'Possible,' Dani said, but she was already following a different line. 'It was raining last night. There were puddles everywhere first thing this morning.'

'Yeah,' Easton said.

'We'll check those boots for any sign of mud. But the fact is, if the killer got in upstairs, there should be some evidence.' She turned to Forrester. 'The house is alarmed, right?'

She'd spotted several infra-red sensors as they'd walked through to here.

Forrester nodded. 'Yeah. Except the cleaner said it wasn't on when she came in.'

'Would it normally be?'

'She said not. She didn't know if the owners normally set it at night, but she comes over on a Thursday morning, and they never have it on then as Mrs Eccles is often in. Even when she's not, it's daytime so... The cleaner has a key, but she said she doesn't have the alarm code.'

'Even if the alarm was on at night, most likely it was only set downstairs,' Easton said.

'True,' Dani said. 'But if that was the case, it also didn't trip when the killer went down and out through the front door. So either it was never on at all, or the killer turned it off.'

She turned and moved back across the landing. A quick glance in the main bathroom. A nice room. More modern than the rest of the house. Nothing of interest. Dani carried on to the other bedrooms. After a couple of minutes she was in the room furthest from the stairs. A plain-looking room, natural decor, nothing but a double bed, side table and wardrobe. She moved over to the window. The curtains were drawn back. The sash was closed, but the ageing clasp was unlocked. Or had it been forced? It looked like it could have been more than a hundred years old so who knew. A search from the outside might show whether the window frame had been prised open, though there was no indication of that on the inside.

Dani reached down and wiped at the sill with her gloved hand. A small brown smudge was left on her finger.

'Could just be dust and grime,' Easton said.

Dani knelt down and felt around the carpet with her other hand. Its thick pile and dark colour didn't help matters, but there was definitely a couple of small patches of dampness around the window. By the time she'd finished feeling and prodding, the plastic on her fingers was dotted with brown smears and specks of grit.

She straightened up, and looked to the window again. The clasp lock was in the open position. It was so old and twisted that it didn't quite close properly. With her clean gloved hand she pulled up the sash window, opening it a couple of feet with ease. She stuck her head outside and looked down. Paving slabs on the ground below. A metal drainpipe – its black paint aged and cracked – a foot away from her. A smudge of brown on the bracket holding it to the wall. Bootprint?

Dani pulled herself back inside. She took her gloves off and handed them to Easton. 'Put those in a bag,' she said.

She turned and looked out of the still-open window.

'I think this is it,' she said as she stared to the manicured garden beyond. 'This is where the killer came in.'

Chapter 3

Fran Willis was a rotund sixty-something lady with short dark hair and a droopy face. Though perhaps the look today was particularly downbeat because of the circumstances. Dani and PC Ahmed were with Fran in the front sitting room. A relatively small space that was dominated by two floor-to-ceiling bookcases that were crammed with paperbacks and hardbacks of varying age.

Fran was sitting forwards in an armchair, propping herself up with her elbows on her thighs. Perched as though ready to jump up and get to something. Dani and Ahmed were on the opposite sofa. Dani still had on her white coveralls though was now without her gloves, and had also taken off her mask to at least try and make Fran feel a little more at ease for this conversation.

It didn't seem to be working.

'How long have you known the Eccles?' Dani asked.

'Five, six years.'

Fran's Black Country roots came through with each and every word.

'You come every Thursday?'

'Unless they tell me not to. Three hours a week. I normally start about nine.'

They'd already run through what had happened earlier this morning, when she'd walked in to find her employers dead. Dani wanted to move on from that now. She wanted to find out more about the poor people who'd been killed in their own bed.

'Do you know the family well?' Dani asked.

Fran looked put out by that.

'How would I know them well? I clean their house. I don't socialise with them.'

Fair point. Dani let the following silence hang, though, as she was sure Fran would know plenty about them, if she took the time to think, and if she was at ease enough to answer.

'Terry was always busy,' she said after a while. 'I didn't see him much. He was usually at work. That was the first odd thing I noticed this morning. His car was still here.'

'The Range Rover?'

'Yeah.'

'And Mrs Eccles? Does she have a car?'

'No. Weird, isn't it? I do a lot of houses around here, and they all have three, four cars. Just one here. Mrs Eccles was into conversation. Conservation, whatever. You know? She would always walk or take the bus or train.'

Dani nodded. See, Fran did know about them.

'What did Terry do?' Dani asked.

Fran shrugged. 'Eccles Property Services. You know them? I see their vans all over near where I live.'

'Which is?'

'Perry Barr. They run loads of apartment blocks around there. Maintenance and that. See their vans all the time.'

The name was vaguely familiar to Dani.

'But he did other stuff too, I think. I remember Annie talking about a new retirement village Terry was building. Not himself, his company, you know? Not far from here, past Little Aston.'

Dani nodded again as she took in the information. Terry Eccles' business interests would certainly be a key area of scrutiny.

'And Annie?' she asked.

'She's never worked as long as I've known her. Her letters are nearly always labelled to Dr Eccles, though. I think she used to be a GP, but not since I've known her. She does all sorts now. Community stuff. Charity. Some people tell me she's a busybody, but I always thought it was nice that she got involved. And for nothing. No money, I mean.'

She looked down at her feet. Something she'd said had caused a flicker of emotion. Dani saw it often when people talked about the recently deceased. It was easy to forget the moment, to start talking like everything was normal, before suddenly remembering the reality.

'She was one of the good ones,' Fran said. 'I don't really know why they used me at all. This place was always near spotless. Annie said she hated people being in her house if it was dirty. She'd give it a once-over on a Wednesday night before I came. Other people… you should see the state they live in.'

Fran shook her head in disbelief at her own words. Then wiped at her eyes as another well of emotion came to the fore.

'They have kids?' Dani asked, indicating over to the photo frames above the stone fireplace.

'Four. Three boys, one girl. Well, you know what I mean. They're all adults now. Terry and Annie were grandparents. Baby Oscar was born last year.'

'Do you know much about the children?'

Dani already had a DC back in the office in the process of contacting them all, but she was still interested to know.

'Eric is the oldest. He's Oscar's dad. They were here one time with the baby. He must be in his late thirties now.'

Dani frowned. From the information she had, Terry had been fifty-nine, Annie fifty-seven.

'I know, I know,' Fran said, as though picking up on Dani's thought. 'Not normal for these types to have kids so young. Apparently, there's an interesting story to it all. Two young lovebirds. Runaways, shunned by their families. Annie was a teenager when she had Eric.'

'Is it a story you know well?' Dani said.

Fran shot a scathing look now. 'Maybe you should ask the family about that.'

Dani nodded. 'And the other children?'

'Laura is next. I remember they had a big party here for her thirtieth last summer, so there's a bit of a gap between Eric and her. Then Henry. Youngest is Will. He's... twenty-two, -three perhaps.'

Her face soured. At the mention of Will?

'So if you started here six years ago, Will would have still been at home then?'

'Henry too actually. He stayed at home through university. Left here maybe two or three years ago. Will not long after. Henry more voluntarily than him, if you know what I mean.'

Dani thought she did. So Will was the young trouble-maker? Or was it that he was mollycoddled? Both were common in her experience.

Experience? No, she had no mothering experience so who was she to judge?

'Which were their bedrooms?' she asked.

Fran thought for a moment as she looked to the corner of the room, as though imagining the layout upstairs. 'Far left from the landing was Will's. Middle right was Henry's. It's all been made-over now though. You wouldn't know. Thankfully. Those rooms were a right mess most of the time.'

'Perhaps that was why Annie felt she needed a cleaner,' Dani said with a smile.

The smile wasn't returned. The room fell silent for a few moments. Dani's brain rumbled with the information she'd been given. The far-left bedroom from the landing, Will's, was the one she was sure the killer had used to get into the house.

Fran looked at her watch. She'd said herself she was due to clean here for three hours, and there was still a way to go before that time was up, so she surely didn't have anywhere else she needed to be. On the other hand, she'd been sat in this house, with the corpses of her employers upstairs, for plenty long enough already. It wasn't unreasonable for her to want to be anywhere else but here.

'Do you have any idea who could have done this?' Dani asked.

Fran's face tightened in disgust. Anger? 'Of course not.'

'You're not aware of any disagreements the couple had with anyone else.'

'No.'

But then after a few seconds her face twitched slightly.

'I mean, maybe the odd discussion about the neighbours not liking the height of the hedges or something stupid like that, but nothing that would lead to this.'

You'd be surprised, Dani thought, but didn't say.

'Have you noticed if anything is missing?' Dani asked.

On her own brief walk around it didn't look as though anything had been disturbed particularly.

'No,' Fran said, the bluntness in her tone clear. Did she feel like Dani was accusing her of something?

'Is there anything else you can tell me that you think could help?'

'There's nothing.'

They sat in silence for a few moments as Dani held Fran's eye, but the cleaner offered nothing more.

'OK, thank you for your time. PC Ahmed will collect your details in case we need to contact you again.'

'So I can go?'

'Yes, you can go.'

Fran still seemed unsure, so Dani took the opportunity to leave the room first. She was out at the side of the house, half mooching around, half looking for Easton, when she heard a rumbling car engine and looked over to see the Kia crunching across the gravel to the exit. As it reached the gates, another car was just attempting to turn in. An ageing silver Ford Focus estate. Ledford.

Moments later Dani was back inside the master bedroom, going over everything she'd seen, all of her thoughts, with Ledford. He took in everything she said with nods and murmurs of recognition, but few real words, and no eye contact. He really was a curious one. People often asked Dani if she was desensitised to seeing death. To murder scenes. The answer, her answer, was no. Every scene affected her. Every scene took part of her soul. Though, in reality, she must be desensitised at least compared to people who had never before seen such a thing.

Ledford, though? He dealt with death every single day. Was around dead bodies every single day. Dani would hate that job, but after a while, did it all just become normal? Was Ledford's stiff and often frosty manner the reason he'd found a job with the dead, or the result of having carried out that job for so many years?

'DI Stephens?' Ledford said, his voice stern.

She'd been miles away. He was staring at her. The unusual eye contact sent a shiver through her.

'Sorry,' she said.

'I said, there're no obvious signs of any defensive wounds to their hands or arms.'

'You think they were drugged, or incapacitated before they could do anything about it?'

'You know I can't tell you that yet. But with those weapons, any defensive wounds would be obvious. Massive lacerations from the axe, or swelling and bruising from the bat. There's nothing like that.'

'I think—'

Dani stopped there. The voices outside grabbed her attention. Heightened voices. Men. At least one of them not at all happy.

'Give me a minute.'

'I'm fine, really,' Ledford said. 'If I need help, I'll ask.'

Dani turned and rolled her eyes as she headed out. She moved down the stairs. The voices got louder, and more irate, with each step she took. She bounded out of the front door. Easton and PC Forrester were holding back a man. Behind him a woman was cuddling a baby to her chest, the other two uniformed officers from the gate stood by her looking on. Looking like they didn't know whether to get involved or not.

'Let me see them!' the man screamed.

As Forrester shoved him back, Dani caught the man's angry eyes. She recognised him from the pictures in the house. Eric Eccles, the eldest son.

He charged forwards again and both Easton and Forrester grabbed him – more conciliatory than aggressive – to hold him back.

'Mr Eccles?' Dani called as she walked towards them. The woman looked over too. Oscar and his mother? 'Eric Eccles?'

His name seemed to bring a moment of calm, and he shoved Easton and Forrester off. They both stepped to the side as Dani approached.

'Eric?' Dani said again.

'Yeah,' he said. 'You can't stop me seeing them.'

'Unfortunately we have to. The house is a crime scene.'

'They're still in there,' he said, his voice quavering now. 'I know they are.'

'They are. But you can't go in. We'll be bringing them out shortly.'

'In bags. You'll be bringing them out in bags.'

'There's no other way. I'm really sorry.'

He seemed to consider this for a few seconds. His chest rose and fell with deep, heavy breaths. His cheeks were red. His fists were balled by his sides. Dani wasn't sure why but in that moment she was reminded of the interview she should have been in right then. With Clinton Harrison. He too had suffered tragedy. He too had turned to anger in the immediate aftermath. It was far from unusual.

'Eric, I'm really sorry. We'll need you to formally identify your parents at a later point, but right now the best thing for you to do is to come with me. We'll go and find somewhere quiet. We'll talk about this.'

He caught her eye. He nodded.

Then the next moment he charged forwards, barged into Dani and sent her tumbling to the gravel.

Chapter 4

August last year

He watched her with keen interest as she rose naked from the bed and moved over to the dresser unit, each step slow and deliberate. She stopped and gently stroked her hand against the fabric back of the chair. His gaze moved from her to the mirror and she caught his eye. Her knowing smile turned into a laugh and his cheeks flushed even though he was laughing too.

'You can't be ready for more,' she said as she picked up the silky robe from the floor and slipped it over her shoulders.

'If I could, I would.'

She turned back to him. The robe was dangling open, leaving just enough view of… everything.

'Don't you have somewhere you need to be?' she said.

He looked at his watch. His Rolex. The one Annie had got him for their silver wedding anniversary. Not an everyday watch. But then today was a special occasion.

It was ten to ten. 'I have a few minutes,' he said.

He stood from the bed and moved over to her and gently wrapped his arms around her waist. He leaned in for a kiss but she only pecked him before she pushed him off.

'*You* might have time, but I certainly don't,' she said with a coy smile. 'I want to look perfect.'

'You always do.'

He went in for a kiss again but only got another playful peck before she turned and sat down on the chair in front of her cluster of make-up bottles and jars.

'But if you're a good boy, you can have whatever you want later.'

'I'll hold you to that.'

Down below the doorbell rang. There was a barely perceptible clunk as the door was pushed open, then, 'Mum! Dad?'

'They're early,' Terry said, rolling his eyes.

'Just as well you were quick then.'

Annie fixed him a sultry gaze in the mirror. He shook his head and smiled then quickly rooted for his clothes on the floor.

'Coming!' he shouted, then caught Annie's eye again. She was smirking. He thought he knew why. Perhaps a bad choice of word. 'Now that's just childish.'

She shrugged.

'I'll have to shower later,' he said as he quickly got dressed. When he was finished he bent over and kissed his wife on the cheek.

'Love you.'

'I love you too.'

–

The official start time for the party was one p.m., but by twelve thirty most of the family was already there. Except for Will. But he'd be late. He'd make a point of it most likely. Terry wasn't even sure if he'd bother coming at all.

It was only his sister's birthday, after all. Would he really give a damn?

Fifty people had been invited in total. Terry was expecting between thirty and forty, and had been busy prepping the garden most of the morning. The weather was holding out. Just. There'd been a few light spots of rain earlier in the day when he, Eric and Henry had been setting up the gazebo, and getting the all-important bar table set up, but now the thick clouds in the sky were finally revealing tiny glimpses of blue. With any luck there'd be a bit of sunshine at some point.

As long as the heavens didn't open, it'd be fine. An outdoors party, in August in England, was always going to be hit-and-miss. They'd make the most of it whatever the weather. And it wasn't like the house wasn't big enough if it came to that.

'Another beer, Dad?' Eric said, breaking Terry from his thoughts. He turned to his eldest son who was pushing a bottle of San Miguel his way.

Eric was taller than Terry. More well-built too. A remnant of his rugby-playing days at school. He could also drink like a fish. No, it was a bit more than that. Terry genuinely worried about his son's habit sometimes.

'Yeah.' Terry took the beer. His third already. He'd need to slow down. Annie hadn't even made an appearance yet. If he was slurring too soon, his chances with her later were next to nothing.

He took a swig of his beer as his gaze settled on Tamara – Eric's wife – and baby Oscar on the lawn. Tamara was on her knees. Oscar wobbled around in front of her in nothing but a nappy and T-shirt. The unbridled joy on his face at his newfound skill of walking unaided warmed Terry's heart more than anything he could ever remember.

'It's not long ago you were like that,' Terry said.

'Yeah, Dad, I know. Don't forget, I had to endure watching all my baby videos in front of two hundred guests at my wedding.'

Terry laughed. 'Your face.'

'I'll get my own back on you one day.'

'Keep dreaming.'

They fell silent for a few moments. It felt unusually awkward. Terry knew why.

'How's it all going, anyway?' Terry asked. 'With Oscar, I mean. Is he sleeping better?'

'Yeah, he's fine. Look, Dad. I do need to talk to you about—'

'Not now. Not today. Please?'

Terry held his son's eye for a few moments. But what did Eric expect? This was hardly the time or the place.

'What are you two boys talking about?'

Laura.

'The wanderer returns,' Terry said as he turned to his daughter. She strode up to them, her pink floral dress bobbing around her knees. She wrapped her arms around him for a hug and he squeezed her tightly before letting her go and she placed a kiss on his cheek. 'You look amazing, as always.'

A younger version of her mother in many, many ways.

'Thanks,' she said, clearly flattered. 'Mum's nearly ready.'

So that's where she'd been. Terry nodded. 'Nice tan.'

'The weather was glorious.'

'Good for you. I don't know how you both find the time for all these foreign adventures.'

'You have to make the time.' She nudged him in the side with her elbow. 'It'd do you good to get away. You and Mum both.'

'We will. Soon.'

'You know what he's like,' Eric interjected. A little unnecessarily, Terry felt.

'Yes, I really do.'

Terry rolled his eyes. Laura laughed. Eric didn't. He needed to chill. Today wasn't about him.

'Where've you left Hamhead?' Terry asked.

Eric guffawed. Laura's face screwed up in distaste.

'Come on, Dad, that's not funny,' she said.

'I'm sorry, Where's *Hamed*.'

'He's inside helping get the food laid out. You should thank him, not make nasty jokes.'

'Anything to avoid talking to me, eh?'

'And what about you? Have you tried talking to him?'

Terry turned to look back at the house. The two sets of patio doors to the orangery extension were wide open. Several people were visible, mostly distant family members, scuttling about inside, around the dining table that was piled high for the buffet. Hamed was among them.

'It'd mean a lot to me if you made the effort,' Laura said.

As if on cue, Hamed turned and caught Terry's eye. Or maybe Laura's. He smiled and waved over. Terry took a drag from his beer. The next moment Annie appeared from the darkened interior, heading towards the patio doors.

'Ah, the belle of the ball,' Terry said, shifting forwards. But then he stopped when Annie reached Hamed and tapped him on the shoulder. Hamed turned and he and Annie hugged each other briefly.

Terry gritted his teeth as the two of them, wide smiles, began small talk. With Terry still glaring, Annie soon peeled herself away and stepped out from the orangery and onto the patio. He made a beeline for her and took her hand.

'You look incredible,' he said.

'Worth the wait?'

'And more.'

He kissed her cheek. 'What was that about?'

'What?'

'You and Hamed.'

He looked over her shoulder where Hamed was once again busying himself around the table, pissing about with napkins or something.

'Oh, come on, Terry. Don't you dare start already. They've only just arrived.'

'That's pretty much what I said to him,' Laura said as she stormed past and inside.

Annie stepped back and fixed a glare at Terry.

'What?' he said.

'You know what. Please, can we just try and be friendly for a few hours?' She then lowered her voice slightly. 'This is Laura's day, not yours. Hamed is perfectly nice if you just take your ego and your stupid prejudices out of it.'

'Prejudices? That's not what this is about and you know it.'

'Just be nice,' Annie said. Even more stern now.

She walked off. Laura and Hamed were coming towards him. Terry downed the rest of the beer from his bottle. Hamed smiled at him and reached out for a handshake. Terry obliged, doing his best to appear natural. He'd do it. As best he could. For Annie.

'Terry,' Hamed said. 'Great spread inside.' He indicated over his shoulder to the table bristling with delights.

'Been cooking all morning.'

Hamed's smile faltered slightly. Like he wasn't sure if Terry was being serious or not. Imbecile.

'Dad *can* cook,' Laura said. She was holding onto Hamed's arm like it was a precious jewel. Just for Terry's benefit? 'He just chooses not to. But believe me, his meatballs are the best you've ever tasted. I'm sure he'll do them for you one day.'

'Pork-free too,' he said with a smile. It wasn't reciprocated. 'But these days I'm too busy to cook, most of the time. You two, on the other hand, seem to have all the spare time in the world.'

'You have to make time for the important things,' Hamed said, wrapping his arm around Laura's shoulder and pulling her close.

'Indeed.' Terry held his empty bottle up. 'Oh look, I'm all out. Do you want one?' He glanced to Hamed's empty hand. 'Oh, sorry, my bad. You don't drink. Plenty of kids' pop under the gazebo, though. Help yourself.'

With that he walked past them, and into the house.

He headed straight to the kitchen and for the fridge. He opened it and looked inside. The bar he and the boys had set up outside had a decent enough selection of chilled lagers and a couple of ales on offer, but in the fridge he had a much more eclectic selection of craft ales. His own personal tipples. Not really for today, though he was tempted.

Or did he need something even stronger? A quick chaser? He looked over his shoulder to the cabinet at the far end of the kitchen where all his whiskies and liquors were stored.

No. Not yet. As much as he wanted it, he knew the more he drank, especially before everyone else, the more chance there was of this day going awry. He had to at least try.

He closed the fridge door, empty-handed. He glanced across the kitchen to the adjoining orangery, and out of the doors to the garden. Everyone in view was all smiles and giggles. Laura and Hamed were now at the gazebo. Eric and Annie were there too. Henry as well. His new girlfriend, Katy-with-a-*y* – as she'd first introduced herself and how Terry now forever referred to her – was on the lawn with Tamara and Oscar. The look in her eyes even from a distance, as she stared at Oscar, suggested she wanted a baby of her own. No way was Henry ready for that. He could barely wipe his own backside, having only left home at twenty-five.

But they all looked happy together.

Without Terry there.

'You OK, honey?'

A doddery old voice. Aunt Paula.

'Yeah,' he said, turning around.

'You don't look it.'

He peered down at her. She seemed to shrink every time he saw her. He could still remember when he was a kid and she and Uncle Frank would swing him about by his arms. Pretending he was Peter Pan. Now he wasn't sure she'd even be able to pick up Oscar for a cuddle.

'On the whisky already?' he said, nodding to the tumbler in her shaky hand.

'Whisky and water. You know me.'

She cackled before she gave him a hug, then made a doddery walk towards the doors. He was about to follow to give her a hand down the steps but the doorbell rang out. He moved out into the hall. No guests this side of the house. Plenty of opportunity to sneak back here for a bit of quiet time if he needed it.

He walked up to the door and opened it.

Hugo. Alone. Immaculately dressed as always in his overly trendy style. Loafers, no socks. Eye-wateringly tight trousers that were a couple of inches too short. What were these kids thinking? The same age as Henry, Hugo looked more like a wannabe reality TV star than the businessman he pretended to be.

'My dad's running a bit late,' he said.

'Typical,' Terry said. 'I thought you were bringing your new…'

Terry stopped himself mid-sentence as he looked over to Hugo's car. A Lamborghini Urus SUV. Some sort of overly reflective, shiny purple colour, it was as flashy and garish as its owner. The boot lid glided shut and a tarted-up woman stepped out from behind the car. She headed towards them. Terry realised his mouth was open. He shut it. He tried hard not to stare as she sauntered up, somehow walking confidently on her heels despite the gravel underfoot.

She reached them and Hugo put his arm around her.

'This is Terry,' Hugo said to her. 'Dad's business partner.'

She held out her hand. Terry took it.

'Terry, this is my girlfriend I told you about. Elle.'

Chapter 5

March

'Are you sure you're OK?' Easton said to Dani. She was sitting on the ledge at the back of the open ambulance, holding a cold wet swab of gauze to the back of her head. She pulled it away to look at the small red smudge in the middle. The mark wasn't getting any bigger. The paramedic had already confirmed she didn't think Dani needed stitches.

'I'm fine,' Dani said. 'Honestly.'

She felt embarrassed more than anything. She'd fallen awkwardly. Eric Eccles had surprised her. She'd had no time to protect herself as she fell, and had landed pretty much head first on the gravel. At least the gravel was more forgiving than concrete would have been. The lump on the back of her head was about three inches wide, but other than a little blood, and a stinging headache, she genuinely thought she was fine. No blurred vision, no confusion or dizziness. She understood Easton's wariness but she just wanted to get on with the day.

'He's still in the car?' Dani asked Easton, indicating over to the squad car.

'Yeah.'

Across the other side of the drive, Tamara was still holding onto her son, Oscar, and being gently talked to by two of the uniformed cops. She looked distraught. How much of that was down to the deaths of her in-laws, and how much was because her husband was sitting in a cop car having been arrested for assaulting an officer, Dani wasn't sure.

'We need to let him go,' Dani said to Easton.

'You're serious?'

'Come on, Aaron, his parents are lying dead in the house. He overreacted, but—'

'It took four of us to restrain him. He was like an animal. Who knows what he would have done if we hadn't had the numbers to stop him.'

'He only reacted because of the fact we *were* trying to stop him.'

'Ha. So it's our fault?'

'It's no one's fault. Let me speak to him.'

'OK, you're definitely concussed. This isn't the hard-nosed DI I know.'

She shot him a look.

'Joke,' he said.

'You go and help those two,' she said, nodding over to the officers with Tamara.

Easton didn't say anything. Dani pulled the gauze from her head and stuffed it in her pocket as she jumped down onto the gravel. She moved over to the car where Eric was stuffed into the back seat. PC Forrester was standing by the bonnet, playing with his phone.

'Let me speak to him,' Dani said.

Forrester looked dubious, but didn't say anything as he moved around and opened the passenger door.

'Eric, come on.'

Eric seemed reluctant at first, but was soon out and on his feet. He glared from Forrester to Dani, but it was

49

nowhere near as angry a look as earlier. The time cuffed in the car had hopefully caused him to see some sense, and allowed the red mist to dissipate.

'Take the cuffs off,' Dani said to Forrester.

Again he seemed unsure, but didn't say a word as he carried out her instruction. Eric nursed his wrists for a few seconds.

'You know we could take you down to a cell for that outburst,' Dani said to Eric, catching his eye now. Behind the cold exterior she could sense the grief in his eyes. Even though he had just barrelled into her, even though Dani wasn't necessarily 'feeling' the softness that she knew was needed for a situation like this, she tried to find it, because the simple fact was that Eric Eccles had suffered a massive loss.

He said nothing to Dani's words.

'We could hold you. We could charge you. But I'm not sure what anyone would gain from it. We could talk to you there, about your parents, about what's happened. Or we could start off doing it right now. No handcuffs. No lawyers. No tapes. Just me and you.'

'Am I still under arrest?' he said.

'I'd rather you weren't. I'm in charge here, and I think, under the circumstances, I can overlook what's happened, if you're willing to work with me. How does that sound to you?'

He nodded. 'Yes. Thank you.' He glanced across to the house.

'I'm sorry, but I still can't let you inside.'

'What about when they've been taken out?'

'Not until the Forensics team have finished.'

'When will that be?'

'I honestly don't know. Perhaps later today. Perhaps not until tomorrow. I'm really sorry.'

'It's definitely them?'

Dani thought about that question for a moment. She'd seen pictures of the Eccles family in the house. She was as certain as she could be that the man and woman lying dead in the master bedroom were Terry and Annie Eccles, but a formal identification – possibly by Eric or one of the other children – would still be needed. Plus, if it wasn't them, who on earth else could it be?

'I'm pretty sure it is,' Dani said.

They both went silent. Dani kept her eyes on Eric, trying to read him. She really couldn't gauge his mood at all.

'Why don't we go somewhere quiet to talk,' she said. 'I'll buy you a coffee.'

'What about them?'

Dani turned and glanced to Tamara and Oscar.

'Probably best if they head home, don't you think? Do you live nearby?'

'Ten minutes away.'

'Can Tamara drive the—'

'Yeah. She can. I'll let her know. But I'm not going anywhere. If you want to talk, we talk here.'

Dani was already shivery from the cold, and she didn't think it best for Eric to hang around waiting for sight of his parents being wheeled out in body bags. But perhaps what he was offering was about as good as she could hope for.

'Fine by me,' she said.

'What happened?' Eric asked.

He was sitting next to Dani on a bench at the far end of the lawn at the back of the house. Thick grey clouds now hung over the family home. Across the grass an ornate and glass-rich orangery stretched across the back of the house. An extension, but a sympathetic one. Dani imagined on a warm summer's day, with the doors wide open, it would be glorious out here. Today the garden, just coming out of winter, looked dull, soggy and lifeless, and the darkness and misery was thick and immovable.

'I asked what happened?' Eric said.

And Dani really didn't know how to explain it.

'They were attacked in their bed,' she said. 'Beaten.'

'With what?'

Did he really want to know the gory details?

'We'll come to all that,' Dani said. 'Perhaps it's best not to think about it.'

'You wanted to talk to me. How can I do that without thinking about it?'

'That's not quite what I meant.'

They went silent for a few moments.

'Did they suffer?' Eric asked.

'There's no indication that they did.'

That wasn't a lie, as such, but she still felt like it wasn't really a truthful answer.

'Tell me about your family,' Dani said.

'What do you mean? Why?'

'I have a colleague trying to contact your sister and brothers. But you're already here. You live locally?'

'Shenstone. It's only a few miles away from here.'

'I know it. Have you spoken to your siblings?'

'No. I…' He looked like he thought better than to tell Dani whatever he'd been about to say. 'No, I haven't.'

'You didn't try to contact them?'

'We were already on our way here when we received the call. I haven't… I haven't even had a chance.'

He seemed remorseful all of a sudden and looked away from Dani and back to the house. She studied him for a few moments. Fran had said Eric was late thirties, and his receding hairline and short greying hair suggested the same, even if the rest of his features were quite youthful. He reminded her of a slightly more rugged Prince William.

'You'd arranged to come here this morning?' Dani said.

'We had a day off. We were coming over for Mum and Dad to spend some time with Oscar.'

Every word was tinged with raw emotion – likely at that moment due to the thought of his parents playing with their grandson. It was impossible – even for Dani – not to feel his pain.

'What about the others?' she asked. 'Do they live nearby too?'

'Laura and my brothers? Yes and no.'

Dani expected him to carry on, but he didn't immediately. Dani gave him the time to think through whatever he was mulling over.

'Laura and her husband live over in Solihull. I have a feeling they're not around.'

'Her husband's name is?'

'Hamed Adil.'

'When you say they're not around—'

'Jet-setting somewhere. As ever.'

What a way to have a holiday ruined. Dani wondered if Grayling had managed to reach them yet.

'But you don't know where they are?'

He shook his head. Was that odd, not to know? And not to have contacted them already himself?

'And your two younger brothers? Henry and Will, isn't it?'

He looked unsure about her knowledge, though he now knew everything she did. Pretty basic, really.

'Henry has an apartment in central Birmingham.'

'Does he have a wife or partner?'

'A girlfriend. They live together. Kind of.'

'Her name is?'

'Katy.' He looked up to the sky, as though thinking. 'I'm not sure of her surname to be honest.'

Another odd answer?

'And Will?'

'He was in Birmingham too, last time I heard.'

'Last time you heard?'

Eric caught her eye. 'We're not on the best of terms. We haven't spoken properly in a while.'

'Any particular reason?'

'Plenty of reasons, actually.'

'Anything you'd care to talk about?'

'Not really. And before you ask, are we talking about problems which could have caused him to murder Mum and Dad? Absolutely not. But I'd rather not go into it right now.'

That was understandable, and fine by Dani. This chat was merely setting the scene. It was likely there would be plenty of more formal discussions between the family and the police in the coming days as Dani and her team delved into the lives of the murder victims to determine why someone had killed them. A potentially very painful process for the family, but an absolutely necessary one unless the identity of the killer became obvious through another route. For now, she'd stick to the basics, and not pry. Not too much anyway.

'I hate to do this,' Dani said, 'but… where were you last night?'

'Where was I?' he held Dani's eye. No agitation, or suspicion, more curiosity. As though he couldn't understand why he was being asked. 'At home with Tamara and Oscar.'

'All night?'

'Where else would I be? I got home from work around seven, seven thirty. We went to bed eleven-ish. Tamara was up with Oscar before me. From about six. I was up and out for about eight in the morning.'

'Tamara would confirm that, would she?'

'I'd bloody hope so,' he said with a slightly nervous smile.

It would be relatively simple to confirm that version of events. Dani would make sure that happened.

'What do you do?' Dani asked. 'For a living, I mean.'

He gave a confused look, one eyebrow slightly raised, as though it was a stupid question.

'I work… worked with Dad. It's a family business.'

'Eccles Property Services?'

'That's one of the businesses, but it's not the main one. Eccles Holdings Limited is the top company, but we have a series of businesses underneath it. Property Services is one of them, but not one which really takes much effort. The biggest part of what we do is development.'

'You're a—'

'Director. Shareholder. I've just got a small chunk. Dad and Peter hold most of it. Well, I mean, Dad *did*… Shit.'

He shook his head at whatever thought had just hit him, then bowed his head into his hands.

'Sorry, who's Peter?' Dani asked. 'Obviously I haven't had time to do any kind of research yet. Anything you can tell me about your parents' lives is really useful.'

He took his head from his heads, though still remained bowed, looking at his feet. 'Peter Werner. My dad's business partner. They've worked together since I was... I don't know, four or five. I joined the business as soon as Dad would let me, when I was eighteen. I was made a director five years ago.'

'What about your siblings? Are they involved too?'

Eric snorted. 'Now there's a question.'

He didn't immediately answer it, but the already-loaded statement had sent Dani's mind whirring once more.

'Laura could have been. Should have been. Probably would have been if it wasn't for Hamed.'

'How do you mean?'

A disappointed head shake this time when he caught Dani's eye. As though she should already know all this.

'Laura and Hamed have their own business together. Basically, a carbon copy of what we do.'

'A competitor.'

'They wish.'

Interesting. Scratch the surface, and it was already becoming clear that the Eccles family dynamic was far from rosy.

'And Henry and Will?'

'Henry...' Eric tailed off then sighed deeply. 'In many ways he's probably the cleverest of us all. Even if he acts the opposite a lot of the time. Dad was desperate to have him on board but he wanted to go to university. He's still studying now, for a PhD. I could never understand what the hell he's expecting to get from that. But that's Henry's way.'

'Studying what?'

'Astrophysics.' He shook his head again as though dumbfounded as to why anyone would do such a thing.

'And Will?'

'I've no idea what he's been up to recently. He helped out for a while, working for me, but it didn't work out. Me and Hugo spent more time cleaning up his messes than doing our actual jobs.'

'He got fired?'

'We went our separate ways. I know recently that Dad was trying to get him started up on other things – just buy-to-lets and the like. I honestly don't know where it all got to. The thing is, Will is… I don't know how to explain. Entitled? Privileged? Or maybe just… maybe he just never understood us, and we never understood him. I used to tease him and say he couldn't possibly be an Eccles.'

Eric half-laughed at some memory, but a morose look was soon back on his face.

'And Hugo is?'

'Hugo? He's Peter's son.'

'Quite the family industry then between the Eccleses and the Werners.'

'Something like that,' he said with a humph.

Clearly there was a lot more to the story of the business and the family squabbles, but now wasn't the time to press. It may even be entirely irrelevant, though Dani was making a mental note of everything for a later deeper dive, if that became necessary.

'I just don't know why anyone would do this?' Eric said.

He nearly broke down as he finished the sentence, but after a couple of sniffs and a rub at his eyes he seemed to grow a little. Dani could see the inner turmoil in full swing – the battle between trying to appear strong, and wanting to curl up and sob. He'd likely flip between those two states for a good while yet.

'I agree,' Dani said. 'I don't know why anyone would do this. But I do know something. Based on what I've seen, my belief is that this wasn't a random attack. It wasn't a robbery gone wrong or anything like that. I think whoever killed your parents likely targeted them deliberately. And under the circumstances, it's very likely that the killer knew your parents.'

His face screwed up again. This time with disdain. A sliver of anger even. Dani tensed. This man had already floored her once today. She'd given him the benefit of the doubt over it. Had she been right to do so?

'What are you insinuating?'

Definitely anger.

'Nothing. Nothing at all. I'm merely saying it's most likely that the killer knew your parents. Which means, possibly, they know you too.'

She could tell he was grinding his teeth now from the side-to-side movement of his jaw.

'Can you think of anyone who had a reason to do this?' she asked. 'Anyone who'd had a particularly bad falling-out with your dad? Your mum?'

'I'm not doing this,' he said.

He burst up onto his feet.

Dani flinched as she rose up too. A defensive move more than anything, though he still towered over her. Six feet three, maybe six feet four. He was bulky too. In the back garden alone with him she suddenly felt vulnerable.

His face wasn't far from a snarl as he glared at her, nostrils flaring. She wasn't sure what had got him so het up again, but she really had no need to provoke him further.

'It's fine,' Dani said. 'We can talk more another time.'

He opened his mouth to say something. Whatever it had been, it never came.

The next second he turned and stormed away.

Dani waited until he was almost at the side gate that led back to the driveway before she let out a relieved sigh.

Then she set off after him.

Chapter 6

The scene at Kibble House seemed busier than ever as night-time arrived. Dani and Easton had remained throughout, as had Eric Eccles, and Dani wondered more than once what exactly he was waiting for, and how long it'd be before he eventually gave up and went home. Did he really want to see his parents being wheeled out? Following their chat in the garden, she'd made clear to him that it was now going to be at least the morning before he was allowed in the house. Dani was determined to hold out until he'd disappeared, but she really didn't want to be at the murder scene all night.

At least the time spent at the house had given Dani extra thinking space, and also time to catch up with McNair by phone. She kind of wished she hadn't, as on speaking to McNair she'd found out that the interview with Clinton Harrison had never gone ahead. Something to do with him changing lawyers, though it was all a bit unclear. The upshot was that Dani would still be leading that, whenever the interview was rearranged.

She'd come to that tomorrow. Her primary focus remained at the Eccles house, where she'd spent a good while lightly rummaging around with Easton, trying to piece together in her mind the lives of the deceased as best she could – in particular using the information that she'd taken from her discussion with Eric. Certainly, she felt there was a lot more to be learned about the inner family pulls and struggles.

None of the other siblings had been to the house at all during the day or evening. Will, the youngest, was incommunicado. Nobody knew where he was. Was that a problem? Henry was visiting a professor at St Andrews University in Scotland and was doing his best to get back to the Midlands, but he hadn't responded to messages until well into the afternoon so now looked set to not get on a train back from Scotland until the morning. Laura had been tracked to Greece. She and her husband, Hamed, and his young daughter from a previous relationship, had flown there only that morning, and were in the process of trying to arrange flights home. Again, that would most likely now be the following day.

So Eric was all alone.

Dani did of course feel immensely sorry for him, but she also remained wary too, for obvious reasons. At least he'd had no more violent outbursts.

'What are you thinking?' Easton asked Dani as she stood staring at the thick oak desk in Terry Eccles' home office. The room was a quite bland, modern space really, not in keeping with the generally traditional and aged charm in much of the rest of the house.

'It wouldn't be the first time a businessman has been targeted like this because of a deal gone wrong,' Dani said. 'Or something similar.'

'Quite a leap.'

'It is. But unless we get anything obvious from Forensics, then the business is an area I think we need to explore. And how much is at stake because of the Eccleses' deaths?'

'Inheritance, you mean?'

'Yeah. How much are the businesses worth? The house? Cars, cash? Who gets it all? Eric is a shareholder in the family business but none of the others are. Does that mean he stands to gain the most?'

'You're saying he's number one in the suspect pecking order?'

'Not really.'

'Or does the very fact that he's the one with the biggest finger in the pot, the one standing to gain, give motive to others?'

'Jealousy?'

'Absolutely.'

Dani sighed. 'Who knows. Let's not wait for Forensics, though. Ledford already confirmed there's no obvious prints or anything on the murder weapons. Nor on those boots, or the window frame. So it's going to be a waiting game for anything useful from Forensics, DNA or the like. I think we should start looking into what we can – the family, the business – right now.'

'That might not set us off in the best light.'

'We need a motive,' Dani said. 'Right now we have nothing else.'

'You want a team in here?'

Dani nodded. 'Let's start them in this room. Get all the records boxed and out of here. We'll get computer equipment bagged up and back to the office for processing too.'

Easton looked really unsure now, but Dani couldn't do nothing.

'Get Grayling set up on CCTV in the area,' she added. 'She's always good at that.'

'Looking for what, though?'

'We have a rough timeline, don't we? They were killed sometime last night. Get her to work outward from the estate with whatever towers are nearby. Look for any suspicious movements anywhere near here during the night.'

'That's quite a spurious search.'

She ignored that comment – more subconsciously than anything, as her mind was already moving onto something else. Her focus rested on the wide sash window that led to the garden beyond. She could see nothing but her own reflection in the blackness. She felt like she was close to grasping something, but it kept slipping away.

She heard voices out in the hallway. Banging too. She moved to the door and peered out. Three workers in white suits were busy hauling a black body bag down the stairs.

'Come on,' Dani said to Easton, before she rushed out of the office and towards the front door.

Outside the house the front drive was bathed in white from two portable spotlights. The otherwise glorious front entrance looked like something from a film set. Eric was standing next to a PC Dani didn't know. Forrester and Ahmed had both already finished their shifts. Both Eric and the officer had steaming styrofoam cups in their hands, but they weren't talking to each other.

Dani wandered over. Eric already looked suspicious as she approached.

'They're coming out now,' she said to him.

He didn't say anything. His eyes moved from her and to the open front doors of the house. Dani turned and stood by him, and moments later, with the bag now on a trolley, two white suits wheeled the first of Eric's parents out of the house and towards the ambulance.

'I want to see them,' Eric said, peeling away from Dani.

'Eric, please.' Dani set off after him. Easton too.

'I just want to see them.'

He reached the trolley and everyone stopped. There was a strange silence. Eric stared at the bag. Everyone else stared at him.

'Please, can I just see? I have to know.'

Dani glanced to Easton. He was giving her a look she knew well. *Your call.*

'This isn't the right way,' she said to Eric. 'It's better to let us clean them up, do the identification properly, away from here.'

'No,' Eric said, shaking his head. He set a glare on Dani but didn't say anything more.

What was the worst that could happen?

'OK,' Dani said.

She nodded to the Forensics guy standing by the head. He didn't say anything as he reached forwards with a gloved hand and grasped the zip. He pulled it down and Dani took one glance at Terry Eccles' bloody face before she looked up to Eric. He was staring at his father. Nothing on his face at all. No emotion that Dani could read. No anger, sadness, distress. His features were frozen. He didn't even seem to be breathing.

'OK?' the man in the white suit said.

'Eric?' Dani said.

'OK,' he said. He looked back to the front entrance.

The bag was zipped up and the trolley was rolled away to the ambulance. Nothing more was said. Dani, Eric and Easton all stood in a row in silence.

A few minutes later the second trolley came out. The same routine. Trolley stopped. Zip pulled down to reveal Annie Eccles' death stare. Because of the angle of her head, it was like she was staring straight at her son, pleading, begging.

Dani again fixed her eyes on Eric. Again, he had the same stoic expression as he stared at his mother. He said nothing. His face was so passive... so at odds with the raw emotion he'd displayed earlier, and with the turmoil that was surely consuming him.

'OK,' he said, finally looking away, back to the house once more.

Annie Eccles' remains were rolled away. Dani was still staring at Eric. Waiting for something. Anything.

'Eric?' she said eventually.

He didn't respond. Didn't register her at all. It was almost as if he was in a trance.

'Eric? Was it them? Were they your parents?'

He switched his gaze to her. Didn't say a word. One side of his face was caught in the glare of a spotlight, and the shadows created were sinister and eerie. Like when a kid shines a torch under their chin to scare their friends around the campfire. Dani stared back at him, tense. Waited for something. He seemed poised. Like any second he would fly into another rage, or perhaps just break down and cry.

He did neither. After what felt like an age, he simply said, 'I'm done now.'

Then he turned and walked towards the gates.

–

Dani and Easton were soon on their way from Kibble House too. Dani had thought about going after Eric, but it had been a long and tiring day, and whatever the explanation for his strange mood at the end, she got the impression he didn't want or need her hounding him any more. She instructed one of the PCs to move out after him, to keep a distance but to see where he was going and to make sure that he was OK. Once she got word that Eric had stepped into an Uber right around the corner, she decided she was content to move on. It was time for herself to call it a night too.

The drive home for both her and Easton was short. Less than two miles to Easton's house, and hers was less than a mile from there.

'What was that about then?' Easton asked her once they were away from the Four Oaks Estate.

'Eric?'

'Odd reaction, don't you think? And he didn't even tell us if it was them or not.'

And Dani had really wanted that confirmation. She hadn't pushed for it. Why not?

'People handle grief differently,' she said.

'Thanks for the insight. I'd never have known.'

She laughed at his sarcasm. She wasn't sure if she was supposed to or not.

'He's an odd one,' Easton added.

'I'm keeping an open mind.'

And that was all that was said between them before Dani pulled up outside his home – a modest three-storey semi. A pretty big house really for a young man living alone. Young? Younger than Dani, anyway. Easton would be thirty later in the year. He'd never had a long-term girlfriend – or boyfriend, as Dani knew. A situation which had been exacerbated significantly recently by the fact that his troublesome sister and her kids had lived with him for months following the constant breakdown of her relationships with the losers she chose for boyfriends. But she had seemed to get her act together eventually, and had moved into her own apartment in the new year.

'You still enjoying the new-found freedom?' Dani asked, looking out of the window to the dark home. Nothing worse than going home to a dark and empty house. Especially after having dealt with death all day.

Easton sighed. 'Home sweet home,' he said.

She didn't quite know what he meant by that.

'Honestly?' he said. 'I do miss the kids. They were… fun. Hectic, but fun.'

'You'll have to get your own,' Dani said. She cringed at that, though she wasn't sure why.

No, that wasn't true. She did know why. Her own situation at home was the exact reason why…

'You never know,' he said. 'In fact, you might be distraught to hear that I've actually got a real live date, with a real live female human tomorrow night. I might be off the market soon.'

Dani laughed. Easton smirked. 'Good for you,' she said.

'First time internet-dating.'

'I'd offer advice, but I have none.'

'Something along the lines of, *just be yourself, Aaron,* would be fine. Or *you're quite a catch, really.*'

'OK. How about this: there's surely someone for everyone. Even someone like *you.*'

'Very funny. See you tomorrow.'

He stepped out into the night.

A couple of minutes later and Dani was parking up on her own driveway. At least her home wasn't in complete darkness. She'd never not feel vulnerable arriving home alone at night, not after the things she'd seen, and been through. She and Jason had installed a new set of security lights at both the front and back of the house late last year. The two front lights had already been triggered by her approaching car, giving a clear view of the run to the front door. Plus she could see that there was a light on in the front living room, so Jason was in, and up. Well, where else would he be at this time of night?

She got out of the car and headed into the house.

'Jay, it's me,' she shouted when she closed the front door behind her.

'In here,' came the gruff reply from the front room.

She took off her coat and shoes and moved across the lush new hallway carpet to the living room. Jason paused whatever programme he was watching as she stepped in.

'Bad day?' he said, shuffling up on the sofa. Had he been asleep?

'Pretty bad,' she said. They'd kept in touch during the day with texts, so he knew the basics of why she was late.

'You want to talk about it?'

She looked at the clock on the mantelpiece. Ten thirty. 'Not tonight.'

He let out a long sigh as he shuffled some more, like he was about to attempt to stand up. Doing so, unaided, was still an effort for him. For months after the attack in their own home by Damian Curtis – a psycho who'd nearly killed them both – Jason, now ex-police, had been wheelchair-bound. Through surgery, intense physio, and a lot of luck in terms of the natural reversal of his paralysis, he'd ever so slowly begun to walk again. He could now manage a couple of hundred steps on his own, unaided, though they were often awkward, ungainly steps. He'd get there though, back to his old self. Dani was sure of it. But he'd never serve as an active policeman again.

Looking at him now, on the sofa, his arm muscles rippling as he manoeuvred himself, reminded her of something he'd said to her not long ago. There was no doubt his body had changed shape since the attack. He'd always been big and bulky, but his legs were thin and wiry now due to the wasted muscle. His arms on the other hand had beefed up even more from all the wheelchair use, and all the times like this he needed his arms to move his body. He'd compared himself, his new physique, to the cartoon hero Johnny Bravo who had an enormous and beefy torso but tiny little legs. Self-deprecation was one of the many ways Jason had successfully coped with his trauma. It was something he excelled at, in fact. Far more than Dani did.

Still, the thought made her smile.

'What?' he said.

'Nothing.'

He grimaced as he clambered to his feet.

'You know it's still one of the marked nights,' he said, quite gingerly, like he knew he really shouldn't have said it.

She did know. Every month since they'd started this routine she dreaded these few days of the month. Not because of the time spent with him, in the bedroom. That was great. But the weight of expectation, and the thoughts of what it would all lead to, was overbearing. Choking. Terrifying.

'Yeah,' she said. 'It's just—'

'It's fine,' he said as he shuffled over to her. He put his arms around her. His weight pressed down on her as he hugged her. Not intentionally, there was just no other way for him to stay upright. 'I know it's bad timing. And there's still one more day this month.'

'I'll try to get back earlier tomorrow,' she said. 'I promise.'

Easton had his date tomorrow night anyway, so why couldn't she make a point of being home at a decent hour for once as well? It would be Friday after all.

Jason kissed her forehead. 'We'll get there, don't worry about that. We'll get there.'

Yet them *getting there* was exactly what terrified her so much. She just didn't know how to explain that to him.

But she knew she'd have to, sooner or later, because one thing was certain; she couldn't hold this lie forever.

Chapter 7

August last year

He'd had good intentions. As far as he was concerned he always did. But life often had a way of spoiling those intentions. Especially if alcohol was involved. After who knew how many beers, and a few shorts too, even Terry knew he was the worse for wear. He just couldn't do anything about it now. Nor did he really want to.

Everyone and everything around him was starting to piss him off. Like Laura and Hamhead's faces as they'd listened to Terry's brief speech earlier about how special his daughter was to him. It was supposed to have been a loving and poignant moment. Instead, he'd fielded their glares throughout. What was that about? Just because he'd tried to make a few jokes? She was the one who wanted him to make it work with her no-good husband, yet it wasn't like those two made much effort. He'd put on this bash for her, hadn't he? What had those two done?

And now this. Peter and Eric, off in the corner of the garden, quietly in discussion. They'd been there for a good twenty minutes. Had repelled the last couple of people who'd headed their way. Terry had a damn good idea what they were talking about.

He got up from the wicker chair. Ignored the looks he received. Yes, yes, just drunk Terry wobbling off somewhere. Mind your own fucking business.

He grabbed a fresh beer from an ice bucket on the bar table as he went. Brushed past distant family members and friends who were busy chatting and laughing among themselves, and headed straight for his ignoramus eldest son.

Eric clocked him when he was a few yards away and the conversion stopped. Peter turned to face Terry too and gave a disapproving look. Yeah, because he was so damn perfect, wasn't he? With his poncy pink tailored shirt, initials neatly embroidered on the cuffs in case he forgot his own fucking name. Probably had the same on his whities as though anyone gave a crap about his underwear.

'Enjoying the free booze, you two?' Terry asked. Slurred. Even he could tell.

'Not as much as you, old chap,' Peter quipped.

Terry rolled his eyes. 'You two need to enjoy yourselves more.'

'There's a difference between enjoying yourself and making a fool of yourself,' Eric said.

Who knew his balls were so big? Terry glared at his son for a few beats until the whippersnapper looked away, tail between his legs.

Soft as shit, despite his size. Was there anything he did that wasn't a disappointment?

'Come on, then. Tell me,' Terry said.

'Tell you what?' Peter asked.

'I know you were talking about me.'

'Not about you. Eric asked to talk to me for some advice about the Somerton development. And I can see why.'

Terry glared even more damningly at his son now. The little rat piece of shit.

'He had a right to know,' Eric said.

'I certainly bloody did,' Peter added. 'Half a million down the drain because you messed up on the planning?'

'Fuck off, both of you.'

Terry turned to leave but Peter grabbed him by the shoulder and spun him around again. Terry balled his fist but somehow pulled back on the urge to smash it into Peter's nose.

'No. You're not walking away from me on this,' Peter sneered. 'You might not like it much any more, but we're still partners. You can't keep shit like this away from me.'

'I didn't tell you because there isn't a problem. I'm sorting it.'

'Sorting it how? The money's already spent.'

'I'm sorting it. That's all you need to know.'

'Is it? Or is there more I don't know about?'

Peter looked from Terry to Eric now. Then Terry turned and stomped off again. Eric was soon by his side.

'We were talking about work,' Eric said. 'What was I supposed to say?'

Terry said nothing. He took a large gulp from his beer. Some of it splashed down his shirt. He couldn't care less right now.

'I think he already knew,' Eric added.

Terry stopped. Eric did too. They stared each other down.

'Sometimes...' Terry said. 'Sometimes I just wish you...'

He lost the train of thought. Or maybe just thought better of what he was about to say, even despite the alcohol.

'What, Dad?' Eric said, clearly agitated himself now. If he wanted a fight... Terry was more than up for it. 'What?

You wish it was Laura by your side? Henry? Will? Anyone but me, right? *The dumb brick.*

Terry clenched his teeth. This again. It was years ago that Eric had overheard his dad call him that. He still brought it out whenever he felt sorry for himself. And why that particular comment anyway? Terry had called him plenty of other things too.

He growled and stomped off again. This time Eric didn't follow. He downed the rest of the beer as he headed for the gazebo then tossed the bottle towards the already overflowing bin. It missed and bounced across the grass to where a group of five were sitting on plastic chairs on the lawn. A few eyes turned his way to see what was going on. Terry ignored them and grabbed a bottle of red and filled a plastic cup as far as it would go.

He spotted her out of the corner of his eye. Laura. Coming his way. This was all he needed.

'Dad, please. I think you've had enough.'

She was speaking quietly as though she couldn't bear if anyone heard.

He took a swig of the wine and put his hand onto the bar to prop himself up.

'Mum's really upset. She's inside. In tears. Will you go and talk to her?'

'There's still some people I haven't even had a chance to speak to properly.' His eyes fell upon Hugo and his girlfriend, Elle, standing on the lawn with a group of other youngsters. Elle glanced over and caught Terry's eye. He winked.

'Seriously?' Laura said.

'Put your tongue away, Dad. I think she was looking at me.'

Will.

'All right, boyo,' Terry said as he grabbed his youngest and pulled him in for a slap on the back.

Whatever could be said about Will, for all his problems, at least he had something about him.

'Bit late, aren't you?' Laura said to her brother, unimpressed as always.

'I'm here now.'

Laura rolled her eyes then headed off. Will grabbed a beer.

'You need a haircut,' Terry said, ruffling his son's locks. 'You look like fucking Tarzan. A weedy version.'

'You're just jealous.'

Terry humphed as his gaze once again wandered to where Elle was standing.

'Who is she, anyway?' Will asked.

'Hugo's new lady.'

Will laughed. Sarcastically. 'I'll give it a few weeks. Once she gets over the money and realises he's got the personality of a plank of wood, she'll be gone.'

'You may as well get in there now then,' Terry said, giving Will a nudge in the side.

'Maybe I will,' he responded with a cheeky grin.

And with that, he headed off in their direction.

Terry watched him for a moment as he inserted himself into the group and immediately had everyone's attention. Probably straight into one of his long tales of adventure, or wrongdoing. Or both. One thing was for sure, that boy could charm when he wanted to. But then that was one of Will's big problems. Everything was just a bit of a game to him. He'd never had to work hard for anything in his life, and it showed.

Terry shook his head then took a gulp of wine before he sought out his next destination. Where to? Henry and

Katy-with-a-*y* were busy talking to a group of oldies. Mostly aunts and uncles. Terry did not want to be there, even if he felt he hadn't properly chatted to Henry yet today. Compared to Will, Henry was a straight arrow. Clever, honest. A bit boring, perhaps.

No, he'd catch up with Henry later.

Annie. That's who he needed to go and see. Laura had said she was inside. He headed off that way. He stuttered over a divot in the lawn. Some wine sloshed out over the top of the plastic cup. He did his best to avoid it splashing on his trousers as it fell. Managed it just about… and almost strode slap-bang into…

'Hamed.'

He got the name right. Just.

'Terry. You look… like you're enjoying yourself.'

'You should try it sometime.'

'Alcohol? Believe me, when I was younger, I did. Just not my thing, to be honest. I prefer a clear head.'

Terry glared at him but didn't say anything to that.

'I know you don't like me much,' Hamed said with a sigh. 'And I know there's a number of reasons for that. Business, me being with your daughter. But… I'd really like to make an effort. If you would too?'

Terry still said nothing, though he found himself slowly nodding.

'Laura suggested… if you want we should grab a game of golf together. She's always telling me how handy you are…' He continued to waffle on. Something about a new set of clubs. Or a new membership at a new club. Possibly both. Terry wasn't really listening. He was concentrating on something else. '…so what do you think?'

Terry didn't answer.

'Terry?'

'Just a second,' Terry said, putting his hand out onto Hamed's chest.

'What? Are you OK?'

Terry juddered, opened his mouth wide, then spewed the watery contents of his stomach all over his son-in-law.

–

Blackness. Then, 'Terry.'

Not a happy voice.

'Terry?'

He groaned as he slowly dragged open his eyelids. Where was he? The lounge. Sofa. Annie was standing over him, hand on his shoulder. Her face was cleared of make-up. Silk robe on.

What did she have on underneath?

No. He couldn't manage that.

Or maybe…

Terry groaned again, put a hand to his head as he lifted himself up. There was a blanket over him. A full pint of water on the floor by his feet.

'What time is it?'

'Past midnight.'

'How long—'

'Long enough to hopefully make you realise what an arsehole you are.'

He pulled the blanket off him. He was still clothed. Beer and wine stains covered his shirt. A few spots of vomit too. He'd got lucky. Unlike Hamed.

What the hell had he done?

'At least I know you're all right,' Annie said. She was angry. 'Now I'm going to bed.'

She turned away.

'I'll come too.'

He went to get up. Annie turned and looked back down to him.

'No. Lover boy. Not tonight.'

She strode off.

Terry sighed deeply as he tried to push his embarrassment and disappointment aside. Instead, thoughts of his life's messes burst in his mind; Eric and the business losses they were desperately trying to recover. Peter and Hugo Werner who both acted so superior all the time but what did they really do to help any more? Laura and her arsehole husband. Henry and his simple life. Will and... Will. Finally, Terry's mind somehow settled on one person in particular. Elle.

As if he needed such a complication in his life right now. But there was no harm in just thinking about her, right?

With that thought, those images, front and centre of his throbbing mind, Terry lay back down on the sofa and closed his eyes once more.

Chapter 8

March

Friday couldn't have started any worse. Dani knew it would be a busy day, with the Eccles case, plus catching up on the Harrison case and the interview she should have led the previous day. So it was perhaps perfectly predictable that she'd somehow manage to sleep through her alarm.

She never did that.

What eventually woke her, at seven thirty, was a call from Easton. Quite why he rang, she didn't know, as she didn't answer it.

Minutes later she was racing for her car, and after a stop-start journey made it to the office not long after eight. Still an hour later than she'd intended.

So much for trying to finish early tonight.

Easton was now nowhere to be seen, and hadn't answered her calls back to him. In fact, most of the desks were unoccupied. She had a brief flash of concern as she headed to her own desk that she'd made a massive balls-up. Was there a team meeting, a press con, or something else she was supposed to be at?

Grayling was in, though. Dani hadn't spotted her at first because she was hunched down beyond her divider. Her head bobbed up and Dani was about to go over to her when McNair's door swung open. Stern face. But then that didn't really mean much.

'Can I have a word?' McNair said.

A polite way of asking. For her.

'Sure.'

Dani headed on in, coat still on, bag still in hand.

'Quite a day for you yesterday?' McNair said, as she took her seat behind the desk. Dani remained standing. She wasn't sure why. Mainly because she had so much to be getting on with, so she hoped this was brief. Hopefully, the coat would reinforce the message.

'Very,' Dani said.

'I heard you've had a team out bagging and tagging at the Eccles house.'

'We don't have any immediate ideas on suspect or motive. My gut is that the attack was personal, not random, and not a robbery. So the family's business interests, and personal problems, if there are any, seem like a reasonable starting point for the investigation.'

Dani expected some comeback from that. She was surprised when there wasn't. It only made her all the more nervous of what the purpose of this conversation was.

'Have you spoken to the press about it?'

'Not at all,' Dani said, though she had received several calls from Briana yesterday, and one already this morning. She'd also googled to make sure there was nothing in the public domain that shouldn't be. There wasn't. Some bland reports about two deaths on the Four Oaks Estate was all that was being carried in the mainstream press. Plenty of speculation on social media but nothing that caused any problems. Yet. Even if that was good news, it did make Dani a little apprehensive. She was already front and centre of the Harrison case, which was a big story in the local papers. Once the press got full wind of what had happened to the Eccles – a prominent and wealthy local couple – that would only mean even more eyes, and scrutiny, on Dani. Being in the limelight, given her past, given her relationship with Ben, had rarely turned out to be a good thing for her.

'I'm glad about that,' McNair said. 'I suggest we remain tight-lipped until we know more about what we're dealing with. I'll get an updated statement out this morning confirming the deaths of two people in Sutton Coldfield, and that enquiries are ongoing. I really don't think there's much more we can say at this stage, is there?'

'Unfortunately not. Though the longer we leave giving a more open explanation, the more chance there is of speculation growing. Both in the press and on social media.'

'Yes. I'm aware of that,' McNair said, her tone more snotty. 'So make sure you find me something soon, so we can do just that.'

Dani nodded.

'Is this something we should be worried about?'

Dani didn't answer that one straight away. 'How do you mean?'

'Have we got a madman, a mad person, on the loose, who could be a danger to others?'

Strange that McNair was asking Dani that, though Dani realised she did have more experience of such things than most people did. Was that why McNair was seeking her guidance? As though Dani was attuned to every psychopath in the area?

'No,' Dani said. 'There's nothing to suggest that.'

Apart from the battered bodies of Terry and Annie Eccles. Dani immediately doubted her own response. If this was simply a crazed killer, now on the loose and looking for their next victims, would Dani have blood on her hands if they struck again?

'I agree,' McNair said, which did mean a lot to Dani. 'Keep me updated. On everything.'

'I will.'

Dani almost managed to turn for the door.

'And then we have Clinton Harrison.' McNair sighed deeply after saying his name.

'Problem?'

'He ditched his Legal Aid lawyer.'

Dani had heard about the cancelled interview. Given McNair's tone, even before the DCI said anything more, Dani could already guess where this was going.

'Who is representing him instead?'

'Her name is Patricia Asher.'

The name meant nothing to Dani. That was something, at least. For a moment she'd feared the absolute worst – that it was that power-hungry defence lawyer who represented Ben. Who'd tried, more than once now, to get Ben's murder conviction quashed. A power-hungry defence lawyer who'd taken the gig for a vastly reduced rate not because he cared about right and wrong, or even due process, but in order to boost his own image through a very public and dirty trial and appeals process.

At least it wasn't him.

'Don't look relieved just yet,' McNair said, as though picking up on Dani's thought. 'Asher is exactly what you probably expect her to be. I've not heard of her before, but I've had a quick look, and she's everything we wouldn't want. Glamorous, sophisticated, bullish, and very, very clever. She's mainly dealt with big corporates until now. Defence of executives against fraud and corruption, corporate negligence, things like that. You can imagine the types of fees she racks up in those cases.'

Dani could. Big corporate trials were often years in the making. Legal fees could exceed tens of millions.

'So what on earth is she doing representing Clinton Harrison?' Dani asked.

They'd only just started looking into Harrison, but one thing was for sure, he was far from rich.

'Publicity,' McNair said. 'What else can it be? She's not going to make this easy for any of us, I'm sure of that.' She checked her watch. 'Which is why I think it's very important that a senior officer lead any interview she's involved in.'

'You mean y—'

'I mean you, Dani.'

Dani was as flattered as she was wary. Of course she'd planned to carry out the interview with Harrison the previous day, but in reality it usually wasn't necessary for a DI to do so, and very rare for a DCI to do so. The sergeants and constables in the team were more than accomplished in interviewing suspects and witnesses. Still, given the arrival of Asher, Dani had thought, perhaps even hoped, in this case, that McNair was telling her she was taking over. Dani was mostly glad that wasn't the case as she felt she had a vested interest already, but she also wasn't sure if this was more McNair passing on responsibility to help build Dani, or if it was simply passing the buck to wash her hands of whatever trouble she expected to follow. Plus, that same thought rumbled in Dani's mind about the extra attention she'd be getting from the press if she were the lead on both the Harrison and Eccles cases.

'Are you happy with that?' McNair said.

'Yes,' Dani said before she could talk herself out of it.

'Good. Because the interview starts at nine thirty.'

–

Dani took DC Grayling with her. Easton was still out of the office, at Kibble House, helping to sort through the office contents. He'd found nothing of note so far in his cherry-picking, but promised to call if he did. No sign of Eric Eccles or the other siblings at the house. DC Mutambe, another young, bright and keen member of the team, was now busy trying to arrange a meeting with each of them, plus the Werners. Even if there was nothing yet to suggest any of them were suspects, Dani wanted to make sure each at least had a tight alibi. And sooner, rather than later.

She snapped from her thoughts when the interview-room door opened and DC Grayling stepped in with Clinton Harrison and his new lawyer, Patricia Asher. Harrison was a big guy. Mid-forties, six feet something, probably eighteen stone of mostly muscle. An ex-powerlifter, apparently. He had a shaved head and everything about his features from his hands to his neck, to his ears to his nose, was big. Not brutish, just big. She'd noticed that when she'd first seen CCTV pictures of him on his bike. Almost like a clown on a kids' bike. He was even bigger in person. Though he somehow retained a relatively kind-looking face, even if today it was sullen and serious – for obvious reasons.

Patricia Asher, too, was sullen and serious. She strode into the room and slapped a manila folder onto the desk.

'DI Stephens, I presume?' she said.

'Yes.'

'Pleased to meet you.' She and Harrison took a seat. 'Shall we get started?'

84

'Absolutely.'

Once Grayling was seated, she got on with the formalities; explaining the purpose of the interview, reminding Harrison of his arrest, getting each participant to introduce themselves for the benefit of the tape recording, et cetera. Dani spent those few minutes scoping out both Harrison and Asher, but particularly Asher. She'd had only a few minutes to do her own research on the lawyer, and everything she was seeing here was what she'd expected.

Asher was a similar age to Harrison, but she could have passed for ten years older, or even ten years younger, depending on how she was viewed. Her clothes – a pale blue skirt suit – were overly formal, and a little old-fashioned, but her carefully styled loose and long chestnut hair and her natural-looking make-up gave her a far more youthful look. One thing was for sure. She cared a lot about her appearance. And cared a lot about her own importance. She thought she owned this room. She probably always thought that, but it would particularly be the case sitting in a poxy interview room with two female coppers, both younger than her.

Dani started the ball rolling, 'Mr Harrison—'

'Sorry to interrupt, DI Stephens,' Asher said. Dani shot her a look. She didn't look sorry in the slightest. Whatever this was, it was clearly a highly planned strategy. 'But before we go any further, can I first understand one very crucial point. Are you charging my client, or not?'

'Mrs Asher, the whole purpose of this interview, as you are very well aware, is for the police to continue to gather evidence in order for a charging decision to be made.'

'My client has been in custody for close to forty-eight hours already—'

'I'm well aware of that. Which is why we applied for an extension. And that might not even have been needed if we hadn't had the delays caused by Mr Harrison changing representation to you. We have until Sunday morning to make a charging decision, as you know. And of course our decision will be much helped by your client being open and honest with us here today.'

Asher really had no grounds for complaint there. Any protest to the contrary wasn't based on anything other than the fact she wanted to try and be in control of this interview, and she wanted everyone else to know it. Bullying tactics, and nothing more.

'And what charge is being considered exactly?' Asher asked. 'Because if you're about to tell me murder, then I think you're going to run into some pretty big hurdles pretty quickly. So how about we take that off the table and then we can move on properly and get this done.'

'Nothing is off the table. That's not how this works. This *is* a murder investigation, as you are aware.'

'I'm sorry but that's not good en—'

'Mrs Asher, you are here to represent your client, not to enter a debate with the investigation team as to how we carry out said investigation. Dylan Roberts has lost his life, and that is a very serious matter, and we will investigate the circumstances of his death thoroughly and impartially. Your client has been arrested on suspicion of murder. We need to collect as much evidence from him, and others, before Sunday so we can make the best and most informed decision with regards to charges. Now, please, can we get started?'

Asher held Dani's eye for a moment before she turned and leaned over to Harrison and whispered something into his ear. Then she returned her gaze to Dani. 'OK then.'

'Thank you. Mr Harrison, as you know we're here to discuss the incident that took place on the A38 near the Gravelly Hill Interchange on Wednesday morning of this week. Let's start with your plans that morning. You'd intended to go for a cycle ride with your son, Tyler, correct?'

Harrison set his dark eyes on Dani. He didn't say anything.

'It's the school Easter holidays. isn't it?'

Still nothing.

'Mr Harrison.'

He glanced to Asher then back to Dani.

'No comment,' he said.

Dani held in her sigh. Didn't react at all on the outside even if on the inside she was filled with frustration. She knew exactly where this was going. Asher didn't want her client charged with murder? Then why had she told him to go down this route? It was the worst possible thing for him to do as far as Dani was concerned. What was Asher's game?

'Mr Harrison,' Dani continued, 'we have various CCTV captures of you and your son travelling along the A38 shortly after nine thirty on Wednesday morning. Can you confirm this is you in these still shots?'

Grayling spread a few photos across the table. Harrison eyed them up.

'Mr Harrison?'

'No comment.'

'Where were you and your son going?'

'No comment.'

'Do you often cycle on that stretch of road with your son?'

'No comment.'

The pictures were taken away. Grayling pulled out another. 'This picture is of a blue Mercedes Sprinter van, belonging to Dylan Roberts. Can you confirm if you'd ever seen this van before the incident on Wednesday?'

'No comment.'

'Do you know Dylan Roberts? Had you ever met him before?'

'No comment.'

Dani's patience was already running low. They had so many questions to ask, but it was already clear that Harrison was determined to stick to his guns. Dani could call a day to this, or she could push on so at least there was a record of the questions being asked. Was there even a chance Harrison would slip up at some point?

Push on. Even if she did have other places she could be.

'Mr Harrison, our understanding, based on evidence from CCTV images, mobile phone footage and witness statements, is that the van driven by Dylan Roberts was involved in a collision with your son. Did you see the collision?'

A pause this time. And just the slightest wavering in Harrison's face. Emotion. Of course that had to be there. This man had been through hell with what had happened to Tyler. With what he'd seen.

'No comment,' he said, though his voice wasn't nearly as strong as before.

'Did you see how the collision occurred?'

'No comment.'

His face twitched. He was tense. Bottling up his emotion.

'What did you think, when you realised that Tyler had been knocked off his bike?'

A pause again. An eye twitch.

'No comment.'

'Witnesses suggest Tyler swerved. Did you see that?'

A shake of the head. 'No comment.'

'It's been suggested that Dylan Roberts was driving erratically. Did you see anything like that?'

Anger bubbling inside him now. Dani could tell. A vein throbbed at the side of his head.

'No comment,' he said, though it was quite forced.

'After the accident, Dylan Roberts came out of his van. Other cars stopped too. What was your immediate reaction? Did you tend to your son first? Did Roberts say anything to you?'

'No comment.'

'Did he apologise?'

'No comment.'

'What went through your mind in that moment? Seeing your son like that?'

'No comment.'

'Did you know Tyler was dead?'

He was practically shaking now. He was on the verge of breaking down. Or maybe going into a rage. Dani felt cruel. But she just wanted to hear his side of the story.

'You attacked Dylan Roberts,' Dani said. Not a question now, but a statement, and neither Asher nor Harrison said anything.

'We've reviewed countless videos from mobile phones, spoken to several witnesses, and everything we've seen and heard suggests you attacked Roberts without provocation. Is that right?'

'Excuse me, but I'm not aware of any footage which shows the onset of the altercation between my client and Mr Roberts,' Asher said.

'So you are at least confirming an altercation took place?'

'I think that's pretty well established, but—'

'Yes. You're right. It is very well established, even if your client won't now talk about it.'

'So is there footage which shows the start of the altercation?' Asher asked.

Dani looked to Grayling, though she already knew the answer.

'No. Not that I'm aware of,' Dani said.

'Good, then I'm glad we've set the record straight.'

'Great,' Dani said. 'And now it's all the more important that we get your client's response to the question. So, Mr Harrison, did you attack Mr Roberts without provocation?'

No answer.

'Mr Harrison, you attacked Dylan Roberts, correct?'

'No comment.'

'No comment? Even though we all know you did. Do you really expect this is going to help you?'

'DI Stephens,' Asher interjected, 'please—'

Dani ignored her. 'Did Dylan Roberts say anything to you before you attacked him?'

'No comment.'

'Did he do anything to provoke you at all?'

Harrison was clenching his teeth now. Anger.

Dani slammed her hand on the table. 'Clinton, you beat a man to death! We all know that! I just want to hear your explanation of *why*.'

'He killed Ty,' Harrison said through gritted teeth.

Asher shot him a look and leaned in and whispered into his ear again. He stared at Dani the whole time. The look he gave was unsettling to say the least.

'Yes, Mr Harrison, he did kill your son,' Dani said. 'Is that why you attacked him? Why you killed him?'

A pause, before, 'No comment.'

'Did you intend to kill him?'

'No comment.'

'Did you believe he deserved to die?'

His face contorted. Tension. Anger. Sadness. He wanted to speak. He wanted to break free from his shackles and tell all. The pressure of not doing so was consuming him. There was so much raw emotion inside this man, but it was all bottled up, because of Asher. Dani didn't want to think about what might happen when it all burst free. The evidence of what resulted when Clinton Harrison 'lost it' was already plainly evident from the corpse currently lying in the morgue.

'Mr Harrison, did you believe Dylan Roberts deserved to die for what happened to Tyler?'

A pause. He was shaking. 'No... comment.'

Dani sighed and sat back in her chair.

–

They managed to stretch things out for another thirty minutes, but by that point everyone in the room appeared fed up – Harrison included. Those initial slivers of emotion seemed a distant memory by the end.

Dani called it a day. They were all on their feet, Dani at the open door to let Harrison and Asher out of the room, when Asher stopped.

'DC Grayling, would you be so kind as to escort my client. I need to have a word with DI Stephens.'

Grayling looked to Dani then nodded.

'I'll be with you shortly, Clinton,' Asher said to him before he was escorted out.

'What is it?' Dani said.

'I like you, DI Stephens,' Asher said, in such a way as to indicate she really didn't. 'I've heard a lot about you. But honestly? I expected you to be cleverer than this.'

'Excuse me?'

'My client isn't a murderer. I think that's plain for everyone to see.'

'Except he killed a man in cold blood. In front of a group of other people. Who filmed it.'

'My client is not a murderer. And you'll be making a big mistake if you continue to pursue that route.'

'Is that a threat?' Dani said, undeniably irked. What exactly was Asher getting at?

'A threat? DI Stephens, please. Show some respect. I'm merely giving you some advice. My client is a sensible man, and I'm a pragmatist. We're open to offers. But if you choose the wrong path…'

'Then what?'

Asher didn't say anything as she turned and walked down the corridor.

'You want to deal?' Dani said. 'And miss out on your show-stopping trial? I have to ask, if that's what you're suggesting, then what's in it for you?'

Asher turned. She looked at Dani with a sense of disappointment in her eyes. She shook her head, like a disgruntled parent might with an insolent child. Then she carried on out, leaving Dani bubbling with anger.

Chapter 9

Dani was still trying her best to calm her anger twenty minutes later as she sat at her desk fielding the pile of admin that had built up over the last two days. She was too distracted to concentrate on anything more taxing. Asher had riled her. Deliberately so. But why had Dani taken it so to heart? There was nothing particularly revelatory about Asher's tactics, yet Dani felt personally targeted.

This was going to be a tough ride, she knew. But she'd stick to her guns, and not bow to pressure from Asher.

But what was Dani's position exactly?

Harrison had been arrested on suspicion of murder, but Dani herself was torn as to whether that was ultimately what he should be charged with. Yes, he'd killed Roberts, but Harrison had witnessed the horrific death of his twelve-year-old son, had acted in a moment of madness, consumed by conflicting emotion. Yes, he'd taken a life but...

No, Dani didn't want to think about it. Objectivity. She had to look at this without emotion.

Grayling wandered back into the office. She didn't look best pleased either.

'Problem?' Dani asked her as she walked by.

She shook her head and rolled her eyes but didn't saying anything and was soon at her desk, head down.

Dani got up and walked over to her.

'Did something happen?' Dani said. 'With Harrison and Asher?'

'Not really,' Grayling said, though it wasn't really that convincing. Dani could always tell with Grayling because whenever she was angry or offended her cheeks and ears burned red, but she never let loose and ranted or raged. Being quiet and conscientious were two of Grayling's most obvious characteristics, and Dani felt all the more angry with Asher at the thought that the lawyer had perhaps tried to take advantage of Grayling's decency.

'She's a piece of work, isn't she?' Grayling added, with just the slightest venom in her tone that surprised Dani, even if she felt it was likely warranted.

'Yeah,' Dani said. 'I think she is.'

Whatever it was, Grayling didn't seem keen to divulge. Dani hovered for a moment but Grayling was already head down again, getting back to whatever.

'Let me know if you find anything on the CCTV,' Dani said.

'I will.'

Dani looked across the office. DC Mutambe was also in, though she'd been on the phone the whole time since Dani had come back from the Harrison interview. She was free now though, so Dani headed over to her next. Mutambe was of a similar age to Grayling – though less experienced having been with the team for a little over twelve months – but was quite different in personality. Dani could well imagine the drama if Asher had offended her. The whole floor would be abuzz with the scandal by now. Dani smiled at the thought.

'Any luck with the Eccles siblings?' Dani asked after the minimum of small talk.

'Yes and no,' she said. 'I've arranged meetings, here, with Henry and Eric Eccles. Both later today. Will Eccles still isn't returning calls. Having spoken to the other brothers, no one seems to know exactly where he is.'

'Did they seem concerned by that?'

'Not really. From what I understand they haven't kept in touch much recently. I think I've found him on social media and there has been activity on his accounts as recently as last night, but it's nothing that gives away where he is or who he's with.'

'Have you tried him at his home address?'

'Not yet. You want me to send a copper there?'

'I think it'd be best. Just in case. And find out where and when anybody last saw him.'

Dani couldn't avoid the grim thoughts already swirling in her mind. Was Will Eccles lying dead in his own home, just like his parents? Or was he even on the run because he was the killer?

No. There was nothing to suggest that. Most likely he was off on a jolly somewhere with a group of friends. Why did Dani always have to think of the most extreme explanations?

Experience. That was why.

'Do it ASAP,' Dani said.

'Of course.'

'And Laura Eccles?'

Mutambe sighed. 'Still not back home. Apparently, the flight she had planned this morning got cancelled.'

'Apparently? Have you checked?'

'Well, there was one cancelled from Athens to Manchester, but I don't have any confirmation that's what she was booked on. Just that's what she told me.'

'So when is she coming back?'

Mutambe flipped her hands outwards.

'Find out. As soon as you can.'

Again, Dani wanted to be pragmatic, but her natural suspicions were always there. Laura Eccles had only flown to Greece yesterday. Had only been there a matter of hours before being called to be told her parents were dead. She'd want to get back to the UK as soon as possible, wouldn't she?

'What time's the first meeting?'

'Henry Eccles is at midday. His train's getting into New Street shortly but he wanted to go home first. Eric Eccles is at three p.m.'

Dani could get the others on the team to lead the meetings. They were simple fact-finding exercises more than anything else. On the other hand...

'Do you want to join me for them?' she asked Mutambe, who looked a little shocked to be asked.

'Yeah. That'd be good.'

'OK. Let's get our heads together about eleven thirty.'

Dani went back to her desk. She still had plenty of time before then. At least she thought she did. Except she'd only been sitting at her desk for all of ten minutes before Easton called.

'You might want to come and take a look at this,' he said.

'What?'

'Terry Eccles' will. Two of them, actually.'

Seconds later Dani was rushing for the door.

The traffic leaving Birmingham was light, and Dani was in Sutton Coldfield within twenty minutes. Kibble House

97

looked quite different to the previous evening. The outer gates were shut. A single uniformed officer stood watch there. No police tape, or anything else overt to suggest this was a major crime scene. The best way to prevent gawkers. Beyond the gates the drive was much quieter too. No ambulances, just one marked car and two unmarked, one of which was Easton's.

Forensics had finished their painstaking work during the night, so full coveralls were no longer needed, but Dani still put on shoe covers and gloves as she entered the house.

The night had been cold, but the house felt warm and stuffy. The heating had obviously been on at some point in the night or early morning. Dani would seek out the thermostat or the boiler and turn it all off. It seemed wrong to leave it on, and somehow the thick and warm air only added to the odour of death that now penetrated the fabric of the building.

Would it always?

Dani found Easton exactly where she expected. The office. Two other officers were with him, steadily cataloguing the contents of shelves and drawers as everything was boxed up to be taken away for careful analysis. Easton was overseeing that operation, but also dipping into the files and documents and belongings at his own whim, looking for anything of particular interest. Which seemed to have come up trumps.

'How was Harrison?' Easton asked.

'No comment,' Dani said.

It took Easton a couple of seconds to twig what she meant.

'Seriously?'

'Seriously. He's got himself a new lawyer. Patricia Asher. You heard of her?'

He pursed his lips to show he hadn't.

'Good for you.'

'So what are they planning?' he asked.

'That's a good question.'

'Do you need my help on it?'

She'd initially planned for Easton to more or less take the lead on that case, which had seemed relatively straightforward given it was obvious who had killed Dylan Roberts. Now Dani was feeling the exact opposite.

'No. I'd rather you were concentrating on this one. Asher is going to make the Harrison case hell, but this feels bigger. It's going to need more resource here.'

'I have to say, I agree. Particularly after what I've been seeing this morning.'

'Go on?'

'Before we get to the good stuff, I've had a couple of PCs doing house to house. To be brief, no one heard or saw anything.'

'Helpful.'

'Perhaps not. But…'

He moved over to the desk and picked up a wad of papers.

'Let's go somewhere a bit more quiet.'

They ended up in the front living room. The same one where the previous day Dani had sat with the house cleaner, Fran Willis. Dani briefly wondered how she was doing today. She'd check on her later. Twenty-four hours after the event, the shock of finding the dead bodies would still be raw as hell, but she may have taken stock enough to have thought of something else useful she could tell.

'I found two safes in the house,' Easton said.

'Two?' Dani replied. She was aware of the one in the bedroom, at the bottom of the fitted wardrobe, but another?

'Yeah. First the bedroom one, which was a simple six-digit pin device, similar to what you get in hotels. The manufacturer provided us with a reset key and we got into that one pretty simply. We found what you'd expect inside. Passports, a damn nice Rolex, some pieces of jewellery.'

'And the other one?'

'In the office. In the wall, but behind a false panel at the bottom of the tallboy unit. A similar size to the bedroom one, but more antiquated. A classic dial knob rather than PIN and electronics.'

'And you got in?'

'Well, there's the thing. I was just messing with it. Basically, just turned the dial and gave a pull. I'm not sure why really, was just taking a look. But the door came open. Either it wasn't locked properly already, or the lock isn't working.'

'Odd,' Dani said.

'I'd say so.'

'You were wearing gloves?'

'Of course.'

'Prints?'

'Someone should be out soon to go over it. Obviously it was missed yesterday because we didn't know it was there.'

Until now Dani hadn't believed the killer had been anywhere else in the house but the bedrooms. Nothing suggested anything else had been disturbed. But was this the first clue that perhaps they were wrong about that assumption?

'What was inside?'

'Nothing, except for this.'

Easton took the envelope from his pile of papers and handed it to Dani. She pulled the documents out. Thick cream paper. The name of a local solicitor's firm on the covering later, their name embossed in the top corner. Below it, in big, fancy type, it read, THE LAST WILL AND TESTAMENT OF TERRANCE ANDREW ECCLES.

Dani scanned over the document behind the covering letter.

'Dated just over two years ago,' she said.

'And very official-looking. It's properly signed and witnessed.'

'Leighton Hammersmith,' Dani said, referring to the name of the solicitor's company.

Their offices were based in nearby Lichfield, according to the letter, though Dani hadn't come across them before.

'Pretty bland stuff really,' Dani said as she continued to read.

'Yeah. In the event of Terry's death, everything was to pass to Annie.'

'Which it would as default under law anyway.'

'And there's another similar letter in there for Annie, passing everything to Terry. Read clause two point three.'

Dani took a few moments.

'OK. That makes sense too. So in the event that both Terry and Annie passed away at the same time, everything – all of the business interests, and all personal assets – were to be split equally between the children. Eric, Laura, Henry, William.'

'Correct.'

'Which doesn't lead us anywhere in particular in terms of motive.'

'Maybe not. But then there's this.'

Easton fished out another set of papers. Actually, just two pieces of paper, stapled together. White paper. Bog-standard printer paper. No solicitor's name, no embossing this time. The document was dated less than two months ago.

'THE LAST WILL AND TESTAMENT OF TERRANCE ANDREW ECCLES,' Dani said, out loud, as she read again.

In fact, much of the wording, the legalese, was exactly the same as the other version, as though whoever had written this one had simply copy and pasted. The first paragraph made reference to the previous will, clearly stating that the previous will was now null and void. So why hadn't the old version been destroyed? Wasn't that normal protocol?

Dani flicked through to the all-important clauses.

'*All interests in Eccles Holdings Limited and associated companies to pass proportionally to the pre-existing shareholders.*'

Easton nodded. 'Property assets and other personal assets were to be split differently too. Personal possessions, fixtures and fittings, that sort of thing, to be split equally between the kids. But property and stocks and cash, which is presumably the bulk of their wealth, to be distributed to a variety of charities.'

Dani moved to the back page.

'Except it's not signed or witnessed,' she said.

Though the spaces to do so were there. Just blank.

'So it's not valid,' Dani said.

'Technically not,' Easton said. 'But the existence of this might be enough to at least begin a lengthy legal dispute. And it's possible this is just a forgotten-about draft version, and that there is a signed version somewhere else.'

It was possible.

'And this document was where?'

'In one of the desk drawers. Just jumbled among other correspondence.'

'Doesn't feel right, does it?'

'Not really.'

'What are the exact shareholdings in the company?'

'I had a quick look on Companies House while you were coming over. Terry Eccles and Peter Werner hold forty per cent each of Eccles Holdings Limited. Eric Eccles and Hugo Werner hold ten per cent each.'

'So of the four siblings, Eric stands to gain the most from the new will.'

'He does, but still far less than with the old one. On the face of it, the big winner here is actually Peter Werner.'

'Why would Terry leave any of the business to the Werners, and not his own family?'

'Good question.'

'And why the change recently?'

'Another good question.'

'I know, Aaron. I'm just thinking out loud.' She realised she'd said that a little too harshly, but her brain was rumbling away. Easton didn't seem to react, though. He was more than used to her occasionally overly harsh tone. Something she still struggled to control given the lasting effects of her TBI. At least now she was better at recognising her abrasiveness, even if she couldn't stop it.

'How much is the business worth?' Dani asked.

'Hard to tell. The last set of filed accounts were to 31 December the year before last, so it's a bit out of date. They've still several months before they have to file for the year just gone. But those last accounts showed they made

103

a healthy profit. Over a million after tax. All of which was paid out in dividends. Plus big salaries on top of that.'

'We need to look into the finances more deeply,' Dani said. 'Both of the company, and also the Eccles personally.'

'We should, but… technically, given the involvement of Eric and the Werners in the companies, we're going to need a separate warrant if we want access to anything related to the business that isn't physically in this house.'

'Let me deal with that.'

The room fell silent for a few moments. Thoughts were stewing inside Dani's head. A large number of the murders she dealt with came down to one of two things, or a combination of both; love and money. Was that the same here?

'Do you want me to carry on here?' Easton asked.

Dani looked at her watch. 'Yeah, please.'

She needed to get back to the office to be ready to speak to Henry Eccles at noon. But she also had two other people to add to her list of people to meet with: Peter and Hugo Werner. Two men who were potentially a lot richer now that Terry and Annie Eccles were dead.

The question was, did they already know that?

Chapter 10

August last year

He opened his eyes with a start when a feral grunt escaped his sandpaper-dry throat. Dribble ran down his chin. He closed his wide-open mouth and winced as he tried to swallow. The simple feat was painful and near impossible, he was so parched. He looked around the room as his throbbing head caught up. Sitting room. He was on the sofa. He grimaced. From the pain in his head, but also because of the flood of hazy memories from the party the day before.

What the hell was wrong with him?

Terry leaned over the side of the sofa. The full pint of water was still there on the hardwood floor where Annie had left it for him before he'd pretty much passed out with thoughts of Elle swirling in his mind. It was morning now. Light outside. No one had woken him, though. He reached down, picked up the glass, and downed the tepid liquid. He swallowed each mouthful in an almost rabid frenzy and was panting as he finished.

He needed more.

Terry got up from the sofa. Another pulse of pain stabbed at the front of his skull. He put his hand up and pressed hard on his forehead in a lame attempt to get it to stop. Water. Paracetamol. That's what he needed.

He glanced to the clock above the fireplace as he moved for the door. Ten past ten. It was Sunday morning, but still, why hadn't Annie woken him? She'd have been up a couple of hours at least.

He really was in the doghouse.

He heard distant voices as he moved through to the kitchen, each step an effort. The front of the house had seemed calm and quiet, but the back of the house – the kitchen and the orangery – was a different story. The morning sun streamed in here, causing Terry to wince even more. Through his squinting eyes he could see the whole place was a mess. Not exactly like a bomb had just dropped, but like a bomb had dropped a couple of days ago and the clean-up was still ongoing. Paper plates and plastic cutlery and leftover food was piled high all over the table. There were piles of glasses clustered together too, on the table, on the kitchen worktops. Empty bottles of wine and beer, and spirits even, were similarly huddled close. Several black bin bags lay around the floor, brimming with rubbish.

But no one was in sight. He got it. Most likely the clean-up had been paused. Annie, and whoever else, had already worked hard to get this far so quickly, but the rest had been left for Terry.

That was fair enough.

But there was no chance he could do it yet.

He hobbled over to the sink. Filled the pint glass again, and downed the lot once more. His belly grumbled and gurgled from the sudden influx of liquid. Perhaps not a good idea. He had another flash of throwing up all over Hamed. That very thought made it all the more difficult to hold down the water he'd just drunk.

He was able to divert his thoughts away from vomiting when he caught hold of those voices again, coming from out in the garden. He moved from the kitchen to the orangery, and towards the open patio doors. The area around the gazebo was in a similar state to the back of the house. Three figures sat together on the patio, under a parasol. Annie. Henry. Will. The boys both had their backs to Terry as he stepped out. The conversation stopped when Annie looked his way.

'Look who it is,' she said.

Pissed off all right. He could hold no complaints there.

'Honey, I'm so, so—'

He stopped when Will turned around and Terry saw his son's face. Swollen lip. Bulbous nose. Blackened and swollen eye.

'You weren't the only one to have some drama last night,' Annie said, her tone as sour as her face.

She got up from her chair. Henry did so too. He glared at his dad but said nothing.

'What?' Terry said, not appreciating the look. Whatever he'd done the night before, he was still their father. Henry needed to learn to show some damn respect.

'I'm going,' Henry said to Annie. He leaned in and gave his mum a peck on the cheek. Another glare to Terry before he stomped off towards the house.

With thoughts of his hangover, and his antics at the party, quickly dissipating, Terry turned his attention back to Will.

'So?' he snapped.

'I'll leave you two to talk about it,' Annie said before disappearing.

'You look like crap,' Will said with an attempt at a smile, but the attempt was short-lived. Whether because it hurt his face to smile, or because of the death glare he received in return, Terry didn't know or care.

'Who did that?' Terry asked.

'Hugo.'

'Seriously?'

Will nodded, though he looked embarrassed now.

'That weaselly little prick,' Terry said.

He moved closer to his son, torn whether to be sympathetic or not. He could tell from the look in Will's eyes, and the way Annie had reacted, that Will was in the doghouse too. Whatever had happened, however bad his son's face looked, Terry was sure Will was far from innocent. Still, if this was Hugo…

'Just tell me what happened.'

Will sighed. 'You know what he's like.'

Terry did, but that was hardly an explanation. 'At your sister's birthday party?'

'Yeah, because you made it such a great day for her, didn't you?'

Terry ground his teeth rather than bite back.

'Anyway, she'd already left when it happened. She and Hamed went early. Pretty much because of you.'

'Whatever I did… it's nothing to do with you.'

'Yeah? That makes two of us.'

Will went to move past him. Terry grabbed his son by his shoulder. Will snapped himself free.

'Tell me what happened,' Terry said.

'Fine,' Will said, as he brushed himself down. 'I was talking to Elle, his new woman…'

Terry had a flashing thought of her once more. Jealousy was the immediate feeling that hit him.

What had Will done?

'... She's way too good for him. Pretty, intelligent, a right laugh too. I don't even know where Hugo was when we were talking. Off trying to impress someone with his shit banter and his fake tan probably. I basically told her that.'

'Are you stupid or something?'

'What? No, Dad, that's not what caused this. She was laughing with me. Laughing *at* him with me. Seems she's figured him out just fine. Quite why she's with him, I don't know. But anyway, she went off to find him, and that was that. I didn't see either of them for a good half hour. Then I'm off for a piss and I see him and Peter chatting, giving me the evils. What was I supposed to do?'

'I don't know, Will. What were you supposed to do? Go for a piss, or go and start a fight with my business partners?'

Will scoffed. 'Yeah, your business partners. Way more important than your son, right. One of the reasons I'm glad to be out from under you all, to be honest.'

'I hardly think—'

'Whatever. It wasn't me who started it. I only went over to ask them what they were chatting about. Hugo gives some piss-take answer about me... I don't know what it was exactly. But do you know what I did?'

'What?'

'I walked away. But Hugo wasn't done. He came after me, having a go, trying to wind me up. Told me how shit I am, how the business was better off without me. How *you'd* even said that to him.'

Terry had said that. At the time he'd meant it. But not quite in that way. Will was disruptive, but he was also very capable, when he set his mind to something. Terry truly believed the kid had the tools to make a success of himself.

If he applied himself. Rather than sponging. Rather than getting into stupid quarrels like last night.

'So you hit him?'

'He had it coming! He's had it in for me for ages. You know that?'

'So you hit him,' Terry said again. 'In my home. At my daughter's birthday party. In front of all those guests.'

'Can you hear yourself? Yeah, I hit him. He hit me back. He got lucky. I would have pummelled him into the ground if Peter and Eric hadn't stepped in to stop me. Always the same. You lot against me. I'm telling you, I'm fucking sick of it.'

Will turned and walked away.

'Will, come back here!'

He didn't. Terry headed after him. 'You come back here.'

Will stopped and faced Terry again. 'Or what? Our deals are off? You'll pull the plug on me again?'

Terry didn't say anything. Was he threatening that?

'I told you ages ago not to trust them,' Will said.

True, he had. Back when he'd been part of the business. When Eric and Hugo had made it clear on multiple occasions how useless Will was and how the business was better off without him. Will had claimed it was the others who were making bad decisions, costing the business money. Terry had sided against Will, despite his youngest son's protestations. Because that's all they'd been. Protestations. Too little, too late.

Or was there really more? Did Terry *want* there to be more? Dirty secrets. It would certainly help his own position right now if that was the case.

'But you didn't want to hear it then, and you still don't,' Will said. 'You know what? It'll serve you right when it all comes crashing down. I'm out of here.'

He walked off again. This time Terry didn't follow. He was left with his throbbing brain tumbling with thoughts. He did feel bad for Will. A little. As far as he was concerned, it had been Hugo and Eric's call to get rid of Will. In all honesty, Terry hadn't properly challenged that decision, because he had his own reasons for keeping the peace within the business. Even more so now.

Had he made a big mistake?

Well, yes, he had. More than one. That was plain for all to see. And what he was absolutely sure of, was that one way or another, sooner or later, the truth would out.

And when that happened, he knew all bets were off.

Chapter 11

March

Dani arrived back at the office with time to spare before the meeting with Henry Eccles. She went straight over to Mutambe's desk where she explained about the need to add Peter and Hugo Werner to their list of enquiries. And for now, Dani intended to be in on each of those conversations.

'Any luck in tracking down Will Eccles?'

'Not yet. I've arranged for an officer to go to his apartment in the Jewellery Quarter but I'm still waiting to hear back.'

How long did it take for someone to walk around there? It was all of fifteen minutes from where Dani was standing right at that moment. She glanced at her watch. She was tempted to go herself and get it over and done with. But no. She wanted to be properly in tune with Mutambe before they met with Henry Eccles.

It was just as well that Dani made that call, because they didn't have as much time as she'd thought. At quarter to twelve, the call came up from reception that Henry Eccles was already there.

No point in delaying, Dani decided.

Noon was still several minutes away as Henry, Dani and Mutambe settled down into meeting room 5 – a small, oblong room on the top floor of HQ with a table that could squeeze six around it at a push. The window looked directly out onto the glass-rich offices clustered around Snowhill Station. About as decent a view as any meeting room or office in HQ, really, which was low-rise compared to many of the more modern buildings that surrounded it. Still, this room was quaint and bright and modern in its corporate decor. A room typically used for police project teams and the like, and a far cry from the bland and sparse interview rooms further below which were used for more formal suspect and witness interviews. But Dani hadn't wanted to use those. Even if Henry would be considered a witness or suspect down the line, right now he was a grieving son, and Dani wanted him to feel as relaxed as possible.

Yet he looked terrified.

'This isn't a formal interview,' Dani said. 'We're not taping this. You have nothing to worry about. This is a simple fact-finding exercise to assist in the early stages of our investigation. Does that make sense?'

Henry nodded. An awkward nod. Dani's words of assurance weren't working at all. He was dressed casually, and was shorter and more slight than his brother, Eric. He had a slightly pompous manner about him, the kind that usually came from an expensive education, though the way he was crumpled in his chair, back hunched over, combined with his weary appearance, made him look seriously downtrodden.

'Just to clarify, you understand that we are happy for you to bring someone with you to this meeting,' Dani said. 'A friend, family member or legal representative, but you've chosen to come alone. Is that correct?'

'Yes, that's fine,' Henry said. 'My girlfriend... she's at work. I insisted she go. I couldn't stand the thought of her sitting with me at home all day. Watching me.'

'Your girlfriend is?'

'Katy. Katy Trent.'

'What does Katy do?'

'She works in marketing.'

'In Birmingham?'

'Near to here, yes.'

'And you live—'

'In my apartment near the Mailbox. Well, our apartment. I mean.'

'How long have you been together?'

'Oh, since... last year. Just over a year.'

'You own it?' Mutambe asked. 'The apartment?'

The way she asked it was more abrupt and challenging than Dani would have wanted, and Henry's face twisted as though he'd taken offence. Even as the newest member of the team, Mutambe was undeniably competent, and had plenty to offer – she was eager, a hard worker, and she had a hard edge to her that was common among detectives. But sometimes that hard edge was just a bit too hard, in a way that made her seem permanently suspicious and just a little uppity.

But who was Dani to talk about being personable...

Regardless, Dani thought perhaps Henry's reaction was something else. Perhaps he'd heard this question before, and didn't like to explain how a twenty-seven-year-old PhD student who'd never had a full-time job could afford to buy a three-hundred-thousand-pound property.

Was he embarrassed?

'Not outright,' he said. 'I've a small mortgage on it. I had a trust fund that matured when I was twenty-one.

Between that and other savings I was able to put down a decent deposit on it.'

He said all this defensively, but at least he was warming up, and his initial fear seemed to have all but gone.

'Can we talk bluntly for a moment, Henry?' Dani said. 'We believe your parents were killed, at Kibble House, sometime during Wednesday evening and early Thursday morning, when Fran Willis, the cleaner, arrived at the house. Can I ask where you were during that period?'

'I was in Scotland,' he said. 'I thought you knew that?'

'When did you go?'

'Tuesday morning. On Wednesday evening I was out at a bar in St Andrews until late. Probably half eleven, midnight.'

'Do you remember which bar?' Mutambe asked.

'I've no idea what it was called. But I could check my credit card. I paid for drinks.'

He took out his phone without being prompted, then spent a couple of seconds tapping on the screen before he turned the device around to show Dani and Mutambe. Sure enough there were three transactions in his credit card app from that day with the same description. LXTNS BAR & GRILL. No indication of time, though.

'Lexingtons,' he said. 'That's what it was called.'

Dani's eyes fell to the top of the screen just before Henry turned the phone back around, pressed the home button and set the device on the table. She caught a glimpse of the home screen too before it turned black. She glanced to Mutambe who was busy scribbling in her notepad. Had she seen?

'And after you left the bar?' Dani said.

Henry gave her a withering look. His confidence, his defensiveness, was growing. 'What? Are you actually suggesting I might have taken a six-hour trip straight back to Birmingham to kill my parents?'

Stranger things had happened, Dani knew.

'Did you?' Mutambe asked, entirely seriously. This time Dani was kind of glad she had, even if it was a little insensitive.

'Of course not!' Henry said. 'How dare you?'

Mutambe looked completely unmoved by his impassioned response. Perhaps, perversely, she was liking her colleague more and more by the second.

'So you went—'

'I went straight back to my hotel. To bed.'

'Alone?' Mutambe asked.

'I'm getting a little pissed off with this. I thought this was a fact-finding meeting. It feels more like an interrogation right now.'

'I'm sorry,' Dani said, deciding to step in. 'That's not our intention at all. But we do need to be very specific about where you were, and who you were with. Obviously, that's to help you as much as it is to help us. The more details we have, the easier it is for us to eliminate you from our investigation. I hope that makes sense? We're not trying to trick you.'

Henry seemed to think about this for a few moments. 'I went back to my hotel room alone. A Holiday Inn Express. I've got the bill for my stay, and they've probably got CCTV or something to show me coming and going.'

'OK, thank you,' Dani said.

She'd certainly make sure one of the team confirmed what he'd said, both about the bar, and the hotel.

'When did you last see your parents?' Dani asked.

He frowned as he thought. 'Not last weekend but the one before. Me and Katy went for a walk with my mum in the park.'

There was a sudden burst of emotion in his voice as reality dawned on him. That'd been the last time he'd seen his mother. The last time he ever would. The heartfelt moment reminded Dani what the purpose of this meeting was. Yes, she was determined to find who had killed the Eccles. But she had to be mindful of what the family was going through too.

'Was everything OK with her and your dad?'

'In what sense?'

'The last time you saw them, did they seem… normal?'

'As normal as ever.'

'Happy? Sad? Stressed?'

'Mum was happy enough. Dad was distracted. Work as usual. He didn't come for a walk because he wanted to catch up on emails. But I guess that was all normal.'

'He was working at home?'

'Yeah.'

'How much do you know about your dad's business?'

'Specifics? Not as much as Eric or Will, or even Laura would. I've never spent even a day working for Dad.'

'Why is that?'

He shuffled, looked a little uncomfortable.

'It's hard to explain.'

'Do you want to try?'

The frown he gave Dani suggested he didn't.

'Looking back I think… I think Dad was just *too* keen for it. Over the years his eagerness to have me working for him just put me off. I don't know what you know about my siblings, but I'd say we're all bright. We all went to a good school, got decent grades, with the exception of

Will, perhaps, but that was attitude more than aptitude. What I'm saying is, we're all clever enough to get through in life, but Dad, from when I was fourteen, fifteen, just never stopped going on about what a genius I was. Saying I *had* to work with him, how he couldn't wait, how one day I'd be able to take the business to the next level. It was like he was grooming me for it, over and above the others.'

There was a certain resentment in his voice now. And how had the other siblings felt during that time if Terry's focus had been so squarely on Henry?

'How did that make you feel?' Dani asked.

'Like I couldn't escape. Like I was trapped. A bit choked, really. I wanted to have the choice. I never could discuss it properly with Dad, he was so dogged. But Mum knew. She was happy for me to go a different path. I never told Dad explicitly… it just kind of happened in the end. I always assumed Mum had a word with him about it.'

'So you went to university—'

'Went to university, and have stayed there.'

'No regrets?' Mutambe asked.

'Plenty. But I'm not sure I'm here to talk about those.'

He said that a little more snottily than Dani felt was necessary. He didn't like Mutambe. That was fine by Dani. There was a reason good cop, bad cop was such a trope. It was effective.

'What's your relationship like with your brothers and sister?' Mutambe asked.

He shook his head – exasperation?

'I'm sensing you're thinking there's a problem here? With my family? Is that why you're asking all these questions?'

'Interesting that you think that,' Dani said. 'Were there problems?'

'All families have problems.'

Dani, of course, knew that better than most people.

'So?' Mutambe said. 'Do you get on with the others?'

A long sigh now. 'As adults, none of us are that close. We're family, so we care for each other in that sense, but we don't socialise together much. I don't think we'd choose each other as friends.'

'That's a pretty damning indictment,' Dani said.

He glared at her. 'Is it? Do you get along with your siblings perfectly well?'

Did he know about Ben?

She ignored the question. 'When did you last see your brothers and sister?'

'Is that really relevant?'

'It may or may not be.'

Another sigh now. Dani was losing him. Why?

'A few weeks ago for Eric and Laura. Will? A bit longer.'

'Why's that?'

'How do you mean?'

'I get the impression Will is a bit of a black sheep in the family,' Dani said.

'Will is Will. He does as Will wants. The last I saw or heard of him was at a bar in Birmingham. We bumped into him on a Friday night. We acknowledged each other, that was about it.'

'Was he estranged from the others too?'

'He wasn't estranged. We just didn't keep in close contact. Out of all of us, I was probably closest to Eric. Laura had a soft spot for Will when we were younger, but honestly? He wore everyone's patience down over the years.'

'How exactly?' Mutambe asked.

Henry turned his glare to her now. 'I really don't think that's relevant. Is it?'

Mutambe looked to Dani. For some reason she seemed to doubt herself now – just her natural inexperience? There was nothing wrong with her question, and in a different setting Dani would have pressed for an answer.

Not today.

'Are you aware of your parents being in any kind of trouble?' Dani asked. 'Financial difficulties, or disputes with anyone? About anything, really.'

'I have no idea why anyone would do this,' Henry said. 'If that's what you're asking? It doesn't make any sense. My mum never… she was just so sweet, kind, loving.'

His voice was shaky once again as he thought fondly of his mother. Dani waited for him to say something similarly complimentary about Terry Eccles.

'And your dad?' Mutambe asked after a few moments of silence.

A small sigh. 'He was loyal to us all, in his own way. I know where you're going. You're looking for issues. Issues that could explain this. The simple answer is, I have no clue who killed my parents. Or why. It's just so… senseless.'

He was on the verge of tears now. The rollercoaster of emotion was strikingly similar to when Dani had spoken to Eric the previous day. Not at all unusual for someone so recently bereaved, but interesting that neither of the brothers displayed simple, straightforward grief. There was clearly a lot of pent-up tension too.

'If you think of anything else…' Dani said.

She pulled out a business card and pushed it across the table.

'I'll call you,' he said. 'I will.'

—

Five minutes later and Dani and Mutambe were back in the office, wandering over to their desks.

'Thoughts?' Dani asked.

'I probably overstepped… a little.'

Dani smiled. 'I didn't mean on your own performance.'

Mutambe looked down.

'You were fine,' Dani said. 'Good, actually.'

'I know I can come across a bit abrasive—'

'Don't worry about it. It's not our job to make friends.'

'No.'

She didn't look convinced about something.

'But what I meant was, what did you think of his responses?'

Mutambe looked up again, the moment of insecurity gone. 'I mean, I don't think he's the killer or anything, but…'

'But?'

'Something didn't quite sit right.'

'Exactly the feeling I got too. And the same yesterday with Eric.'

They reached Dani's desk and both paused.

'Any word on Will Eccles?' she asked.

Mutambe pulled out her phone. 'Nothing yet.'

What was taking so long?

'Do you want me to follow up on Henry's alibi?' Mutambe asked.

'Please. The bar, hotel, train station too. Cover all bases… did you see his credit card balance when he showed us his phone?'

'Over sixteen thousand pounds.'

Dani was glad Mutambe had spotted that too. It showed she was on the ball.

'A hell of a balance for a student. Did you also notice the apps on his home screen?'

A raised eyebrow. 'No?'

'I only caught a flashing glimpse, but I'm sure there were a couple of apps I recognised for betting companies.'

'You think he has a problem?'

'I think we should consider the financial position of each and every one of them.'

Particularly in light of Easton's findings with the wills.

Mutambe's phone buzzed in her hand. She looked to the screen.

'Finally,' she said before tapping the screen and pushing the device to her ear.

The ensuing conversation was brief, and more or less one-way. Except for DC Mutambe's closing comment, that was.

'We'll be there right away.'

Moments later, she and Dani were rushing for the stairs.

Chapter 12

They went on foot rather than by car. The Jewellery Quarter was less than a mile from HQ, and by the time they got to the car park, and out, and through the city's one-way system, the car would have saved them no time. They walked at pace, but didn't run. This wasn't a 999 emergency. Yet. But Dani had an ominous feeling the whole way.

'What did he say, exactly?' Dani asked for the second time.

'Just that the neighbours haven't seen Will for weeks,' Mutambe said, her breaths as equally laboured as Dani's. 'But that there's a really bad smell.'

Of course Dani feared the worst at that, which was why they were going so quickly. Any copper who'd ever stepped into a home where a dead body had lain untouched for a long period of time was scarred for life not just from the sight, but from the smell. The smell of death in a morgue was one thing, but the stench from a putrefied and oozing, infested corpse was something else altogether.

Dani crossed her fingers as she walked, as if doing so would help alter what had already happened in some way.

Minutes later they turned off the main road onto a narrow street between two tall red-brick buildings. A couple of decades ago, this whole area had been more or less derelict, except for the multitude of small businesses that continued to operate from the largely Victorian workshops that were dotted all over. Predominantly jewellery craftsmen, badge and medal makers and the like, the businesses that had given the area its name.

In more recent times the larger and usually more decrepit workshops, long abandoned by big businesses who'd moved to more modern facilities, had been renovated into sought-after apartments. With bars and restaurants continually popping up, the Jewellery Quarter had re-emerged as a trendy spot for young professionals to live, close to the city, but the area remained uncomfortably close to some of the poorest and most crime-ridden spots in the region.

They reached the main entrance doors to Haversham Court, where PC Kendrick was standing in wait. Dani hadn't been to this street before, but the buildings either side were handsome and suited their new status in life. Neither Dani nor Mutambe knew Kendrick, and there was a brief introduction before he pressed on the intercom and a moment later the three of them were in the spacious and echoey internal atrium.

'It's on the fourth floor,' Kendrick explained as they waited for the lift. 'Honestly, you can smell it even through the closed door. I didn't know what else to do.'

He seemed slightly taken aback by the prospect of what lay beyond. Clearly this was a new experience for him.

They reached the door to 414 and stopped. Dani knocked as hard as she could.

'Mr Eccles. Please open the door, it's the police.'

A few moments of silence followed. Dani was taking short, shallow breaths, as though sucking in a big lungful was dangerous. There was definitely a pungent odour filling the corridor.

She knocked again.

'He's not in,' came a voice from her left. She glanced over to a scruffy-looking man in his forties. Dishevelled hair and beard, crumpled shirt. Shorts, no shoes or socks.

'Do you live here?' Dani asked him.

'Yeah.'

Dani didn't like to judge on appearance, but he didn't seem like the usual type to take up one of the properties in a building like this.

'Do you know Mr Eccles?'

'Know him? Not really. I've seen him about. I've banged on the wall plenty of times when he's making too much noise. But I knew something wasn't right. I've thought it for a while now. The smell, isn't it?'

'When did you last see him?'

He shrugged. 'Not for a couple of weeks at least.'

'Coming or going?'

He seemed to wrack his brain at that question. 'Going, come to think of it.'

'Day? Night? Anything unusual about that last time?'

'Nothing that struck me. Think it was a morning. Don't know the day. You know how it is?'

'OK, thank you. You can go back inside. We'll knock if we need anything more.'

He looked reluctant, but Dani stared his way until he backed down. Once the door was shut she turned back to Mutambe and Kendrick.

'Do you think we should kick the door down?' Kendrick asked. 'I thought about doing it, I just… I don't know, really.'

Dani faced the door again. Each apartment had a mailbox on the ground floor, so there was no letterbox to peer in through. She got down onto her knees, pushed her face to the coarse carpet, and her nose to the tiny gap between the door and the floor.

There was definitely a nasty stench coming from within. Even more noticeable now than before.

'OK, we're going in,' she said to Kendrick when she straightened up.

He only hesitated for a moment before he stepped forwards. He pulled his black boot up high, then crashed the sole onto the edge of the door by the handle. Another strike, then another, before the door burst open and a fresh wave of stink burst out.

Kendrick gagged and threw his arm up to bury his nose. Mutambe too squirmed in disgust as she covered her face and mouth.

Dani didn't. She carried on in.

A small hallway. Everything was dark inside. She flipped on the lights. Clutter. Rubbish. She moved over to the first door. Peered in. Bedroom. More clutter. No one inside. Mutambe and Kendrick remained loitering in the hall. So Dani moved to the open-plan living space. More clutter and rubbish. A greening milk carton stood on the kitchen counter. Dirty plates and glasses and mugs were strewn about. The remnants of food and drinks had largely turned black and green from mould growth. It smelled bad, but it wasn't the cause of the stench.

Dani moved back into the hall. The final door. Bathroom? She flipped the light on the outside. Peered in.

Just as she expected.

'Oh God, what the fresh living hell!' Kendrick exclaimed from over Dani's shoulder.

He was still cowering into his sleeve, his face twisted in disgust. But it was all a bit of an overreaction. There was no dead body here. Dani had already determined that from the first moment they'd arrived. The smell was bad, but nowhere near as bad as that smell that was so ingrained in her memory.

She stared over to the toilet bowl. Disgusting all right. The filth, the stink. Whoever had left that in there… but the problem wasn't the un-flushed faeces which had been there for who knew how long, but the leak in the toilet which meant the shitty liquid had slowly crept out onto the floor and had created a more than metre-wide puddle of thick, sticky, black sludge that was festering and alive with maggots and flies.

Grim.

Dani turned away. She'd seen enough here. No dead body. That was a good thing.

But where the hell was Will Eccles?

Chapter 13

Rain pelted down in thick droplets that pinged off the metalwork of Terry's car. He wasn't getting out until he absolutely had to. Where the hell was Akpeyi anyway?

He checked his watch. Ten minutes late. Beyond the windscreen, over which the rain cascaded down like it was a water slide, the construction site looked quiet and ominous – the rain too heavy today for the workers to pour concrete or drill piles. Dreary, dull, and decrepit-looking. Knowing how much was at stake, it was the kind of sight that sent shivers through his bones.

His phone rang. Peter.

'Where are you?' he asked.

'Little Aston.'

'Today? I thought—'

'I'm just checking up on things.'

There was an awkward silence. Awkward for Terry, at least. He'd only just managed to smooth things over with Peter about the Somerton development, after Eric had gone and blabbed behind his back. The half million wasted on that was small fry compared to what was at stake on this site. How could another development be turning to shit so soon, and in much the same way?

Did Peter already know?

'OK. Well let me know if there are any issues.'

'I will.'

Terry ended the call.

A moment later Akpeyi's Vauxhall Astra arrived outside the gates. Terry stepped out into the driving rain. He grabbed the golf umbrella from the back seat and a couple of hard hats. He put his hat on as he walked to Akpeyi's car. As he got out it was clear he wasn't impressed with something.

'Here,' Terry said, handing him the hard hat.

'Really, Terry? On a day like this you want to show me around?'

No, he really didn't *want* to. But they were here now.

'You can fit under the umbrella.'

Akpeyi shut his car door and shuffled under the umbrella. Water was already pouring off the sides like a waterfall.

'Before we go anywhere,' Akpeyi said, 'can I just ask you a simple question?'

'Go for it.'

'Have you made any amendments to the plans? Along the lines we discussed.'

'Why don't I show you around first.'

'I'll take that as a no then. I'm not sure what else—'

'Please, just let me try to explain.'

Akpeyi looked pissed off, but he agreed. They set off through the rain. And the mud. Beyond the gates it was several inches thick all over. Within a few steps their shoes were caked in claggy crap, and brown streaks rose up their suit trouser legs. This couldn't have got off to a worse start.

Despite Akpeyi's glum face, and continued protestations, Terry spent the next few minutes showing him around the site, which consisted of little more than a huge hole in the ground, with poured concrete sides and strands of rebar here, there and everywhere. It certainly looked more impressive on a sunny day.

'Why don't we go and get dry in the site office,' Terry said. 'There's coffee. And usually biscuits.'

'If we must.'

The office was empty. Not just because the site was closed for the weather, but because Terry had insisted to the site foreman that he didn't want anyone inside while he was dealing with the planning officer. The fact the site had been shut down due to the weather was an added bonus, he guessed.

Terry put the kettle on. While it boiled he watched Akpeyi mooching. What was he thinking? The guy looked really fed up. Sighing every few seconds. He checked his watch a couple of times too, like he had somewhere better to be.

'The thing is, Terry,' he said, catching Terry's eye after another sigh, 'I'm really not sure you've shown me anything, or told me anything to change my mind. The outer boundary of your dig is too close to the neighbours on both the east and south sides. Several metres closer than we agreed. I know you've poured there already but that's beside the point. The basement level… I'm going to need to see more in-depth topography. Neither of us is an expert, and the last thing you want is the site or the building sinking into the ground. Or for one of the neighbours to do that. And the addition of the top storey—'

'We're only adding a metre from the original—'

'It's not a question of *only* this, or *only* that. I get why you're doing it, trying to maximise your site, but it's not what was agreed, and if you'd submitted the plan like this it would have been rejected. It's too high. It's too big. It's too deep. The area can't take a development with this many residents. And don't even get me started on the internal plans meeting building regs.'

Terry squeezed his eyes shut and rubbed his hand across his face. How had this gone so badly wrong? It wasn't like he was inexperienced. But after the Somerton fiasco, after everything else too, he'd had to find a way to catch up, to make amends, to cancel out the losses and to try and milk this site for everything it had.

But it had gone wrong. Now he had to make it right.

Yet he really didn't want to have to do this. Was there an alternative? As he opened his eyes again and looked out of the plastic window to the sodden ground outside, he had a flashing thought of Akpeyi on his back, sinking down into the mud. Reaching up with his hand to be saved, while concrete poured down, completely smothering him. How many bodies over the years, across the country, across the world, had disappeared like that?

Would this situation come to that?

'I've known you for years,' Terry said.

'You have, but that's irrel—'

'What's it going to take?'

Akpeyi shot him a strange look. Disbelief? Or just disappointment?

'How *much* will it take?' Terry added. His heart dropped after the words left his mouth.

'Terry, I think you should stop right there.'

'Please. Just think reasonably. Think about what it could mean to you.'

'Stop. Please, just stop.'

Akpeyi looked down nervously. To the boiled kettle in Terry's hand. A part of him wanted to hurl it through the air.

'Leave the coffee,' Akpeyi said. 'I have to be somewhere else anyway.'

'I heard about the divorce,' Terry said.

Akpeyi shot him that same look again. Though this time there was something else there too. Anger?

'Expensive business that.'

Akpeyi shook his head in disgust. 'I'm out of here.'

He turned for the door. He opened it and stepped out into the rain. Terry went after him. Realised he was still holding onto the kettle…

No. He put it down. Headed out into the rain. Akpeyi was sloshing through the mud. More than once his foot slipped leaving a huge streak in the chewed-up ground.

An accident. Look at this place. An accident. A slip. He bangs his head. Falls right onto a piece of rebar coming out of the ground.

That could happen, right?

Terry set off after him. His body was shaking with tension.

He had to do something. There was too much at stake…

'Don't do this to me,' Terry shouted. Akpeyi didn't react at all. 'You're going to regret this! I'm fucking serious. You walk away and I'm going to finish you.'

Akpeyi reached his car and turned back around. He said nothing before he opened the car door and sank down into the seat.

Terry glanced across to behind his parked car.

What the hell?

There was another car there. He'd know that car anywhere. Hugo's purple bloody Urus. No one inside it.

'Please,' Terry called to Akpeyi, the desperation in his voice clear now. But Akpeyi was paying no attention. He closed his car door and fired up the engine.

Water flowed off Terry's brow. He turned and looked back to the Portakabin. He strode over. Practically kicked open the door, grunting in anger as he did so. There was Hugo. Dirty wellies on his feet. Arms folded. The kid always looked smug, but this was something else.

'I was just in the other room,' Hugo said, indicating to the partition door behind him.

The little fucker had sneaked in there. Deliberately? Had Peter sent him?

'And?'

Play it cool. This chump was nothing.

'And I heard everything,' Hugo said. 'I have to say it was nothing too surprising.'

'You've no idea what you're talking about.'

'Really? Seemed pretty obvious what was happening to me.'

'Yeah?' A pause. Nothing from Hugo. Terry really was lost as to what came next. 'So what now?'

Hugo sat down on the foreman's chair and hauled his boots up onto the desk, crossing his feet over. Thick wads of mud splashed over the paperwork there.

Disrespectful shit.

'Now?' Hugo said. 'Now we have a little talk.'

Chapter 14

March

Dani left Mutambe and Kendrick at Will Eccles' grotty apartment. There was no body there, no sign that Will or anyone else had been there for a couple of weeks at least, but having made the call to break down the door, Dani decided it was at least worthwhile to get her colleagues to properly look around the apartment to see if there were any clues as to what had happened to the youngest Eccles son.

Was his disappearance connected to his parents' death? Or had he simply cut ties and was living somewhere else now, oblivious to the fact that his parents had been brutally murdered?

Dani didn't know, though it did seem odd that if he'd cut ties, he'd done it so completely to not even be contactable.

She headed back to HQ, and three p.m. soon came around when it was time for the meeting with Eric Eccles. Earlier in the day Dani had been ready to pass this meeting off to someone else. She'd already spoken at length to Eric the previous day, but with the ever-increasing issues she was churning up regarding the family and its affairs, the meeting was taking on a whole different slant already. She hadn't firmly decided whether or not she'd bring up the matter of the wills. She'd make that call during the meeting itself. Despite Mutambe's decent performance earlier, she also decided she needed a more experienced hand by her side this time, so it was back to her and Easton.

Eric Eccles was early, just like his brother Henry had been. Easton brought him over to meeting room 5, the same room Dani had met Henry in. What wasn't the same was Eric's demeanour. Henry had been fragile, a little apprehensive, scared even, when he'd first arrived. Eric Eccles looked aggrieved, like he was up for a fight. Dani's first impression of this man, the previous day when he'd tried to bombard his way into Kibble House, had been of an angry hothead. She'd seen him calm and stoic too, but was edgy Eric the real him?

'Thanks for coming in, Eric,' Dani said.

'I almost didn't bother,' he said.

'I'm glad you did.'

He huffed. 'It'd be nice to get some peace and quiet, to be honest. I spent all day yesterday at the house. Most of this morning we had a support officer at home. Felt like some sort of cheap psychoanalyst trick. I've had to go to the morgue to identify my parents' bodies. Now this.'

'I'm sorry,' Dani said. 'I appreciate this is a really hard time for you. You and all your family.'

'Do you have any update? Any suspects?'

'I'm afraid it's very early in the investigation st—'

'You can just say no. You don't get extra points for bullshitting me.'

'OK. No. We don't. Not yet.'

He shook his head slowly. Disappointment. But in a mocking way.

'And when can I get into the house? I waited all of yesterday.'

'I know. Again, I'm sorry. Forensics have finished there now, but it is still considered an active crime scene. If you really must, then we can arrange for you to go inside, but it'd have to be accompanied.'

'That's fine. I just… I just need to do it.'

Dani could understand that.

'Have you spoken to your sister or brothers?' Easton asked.

'I went to Henry's apartment before coming here.'

'You're close to Henry?'

'He's my brother.' Defensive. Again.

'What about Laura?'

'We've spoken on the phone. We've texted. I heard she's having trouble getting back. She's… devastated.' Finally, a hint of emotion as he thought of his sister. 'I think it's all the worse because she's so far away.'

'She'll be back soon enough,' Dani said. 'What about Will?'

Eric shook his head. 'I've tried calling him.'

'We went to his apartment earlier today,' Dani said. 'The one in the Jewellery Quarter.'

'*His* apartment?' Eric rolled his eyes. 'I don't think he ever paid a penny towards that place.'

'He didn't?'

'Dad arranged it for him.' He sighed. 'It's complicated. I never fully understood what those two were doing. Dad was trying to help Will out. He set him up with some cash to start buy-to-lets last year. I thought I told you about this yesterday?'

'You did,' Dani said.

'I think that apartment was supposed to be one they were letting out. But Will moved in at some point. I don't know, six months ago maybe. I don't know the specifics.'

'Henry mentioned he'd had a trust fund that matured when he was twenty-one. He used the money for that to help buy his place at the Mailbox. Did Will not have access to money like that?'

Eric's eyes narrowed as he stared at Dani.

'What does any of this have to do with my parents' murder?'

'The thing is,' Easton said, 'we're increasingly concerned about your brother Will's welfare. You said yourself he's not returning calls. We sent officers to his apartment today. No answer. The officers broke in, and, well, to put it mildly, the place looked like it'd been abandoned.'

'You broke into his apartment? With whose permission?'

'It was a judgement call,' Easton said. 'If we fear for someone's wellbeing, or we believe a crime is being committed inside, we don't need to apply for a warrant beforehand.'

Eric didn't look convinced, but didn't say anything more of it.

'The point is,' Dani said, 'there's no indication Will has been there for some time. Do you know where else he could be living?'

'I've no idea,' Eric said. 'And to your point about trust funds? We all got broadly the same. It wasn't that long ago Will turned twenty-one. How much he got, and what he did with his money, I truly have no idea.'

'Broadly the same?' Easton questioned.

'Mum and Dad invested the same for us all. But obviously the returns weren't identical for us all. Stocks move up and down, it's all to do with timing.'

He said this as though he thought Easton was an idiot. Dani could tell from her colleague's still passive face that he'd taken it on the chin. An experienced hand. Odd, in a way, that she now thought of Easton like that. It wasn't long ago that he'd himself been the newbie.

The room fell silent for a few seconds. It felt like much longer. Dani was contemplating whether or not to bring up the wills. Was this the right time?

'Do you know if your parents had formalised a will?' Easton asked.

Dani smiled on the inside. She was happy enough for Easton to have made the decision.

Eric set his questioning eyes firmly on Easton now.

'I'm sure they would have,' Eric said. 'They were both very good with money. Dad was a businessman, but in many ways Mum kept their affairs in order.'

'Do you know *specifically* if they had a will?' Easton asked. 'As in, when it was drawn up, and with whose help?'

A short pause. 'I've no idea about specifics.'

'So do you know what your parents' intentions were with regards to their assets? Had you ever discussed inheritance?'

Another pause. 'No. Not really.'

'Not really?'

'That's what I said. Do you know something I don't?'

Now there was a question. *Yes*, was the clear answer.

'We're just trying to get to grips with your parents' situation, that's all,' Dani said. 'Why don't we move on?'

Easton glanced at her. Not a very impressed look, though to anyone who didn't know him well there wouldn't be a tell. Her answer was a lie, but for some reason this didn't feel like the right time to push further, even if she realised she might later regret it.

That thought dominated her mind as the meeting continued. Not that it really carried on with any great purpose after that. The whole affair felt a bit lacklustre, and it wasn't long before Dani suggested they call it a day.

Eric couldn't have agreed more quickly. He was out of the building within a couple of minutes.

'Why'd you do that?' Easton said, as he and Dani headed for the lifts to take them back to their floor.

'What?'

'The wills.'

'Because I want to play it cool. No point in revealing our hand too soon.'

Easton didn't say anything to that, though she could tell he didn't necessarily agree.

'He still wants to get into the house,' Dani said. 'It'll be interesting to see what he does when he's there.'

'If he goes looking in the office, you mean?'

'Exactly.'

'Do you want me to arrange something with him?'

'Yeah. Let's get it done over the weekend. And make sure we keep a PC at the house around the clock for now. I don't want any unexpected visitors.'

'OK. I'm on it. You want my opinion, though?' Easton asked.

'Go on then.'

'Of all the siblings, his alibi is the tightest.'

'Is it?'

'Didn't Mutambe confirm his account of where he was with Tamara that night?'

'She did. But Henry was three hundred miles away. That's pretty tight too.'

Easton sighed. 'I suppose. We also need to track down Peter and Hugo Werner's whereabouts on Wednesday night. And for Will and Laura, we still don't know either way.'

'Well, let's get on it then.'

As Easton wandered back to his desk, Dani headed straight over to Mutambe to discuss that exact point.

'Any update on Laura Eccles?' she asked.

'She's on a plane right now. Should be home this evening.'

That was good news. The niggling thought at the back of Dani's mind that Laura had absconded could finally be buried.

'But last time I spoke to her she wouldn't commit to coming in,' Mutambe added. 'I think she wants to meet with her brothers first.'

That was fair enough. Dani might pay Laura a visit at her home over the weekend instead, in place of a support officer in the first instance.

Dani was about to turn to go back to her desk when Mutambe stopped her.

'McNair was looking for you,' she said. 'She looked pretty angry about something. She ran out about ten minutes ago.'

That was all Dani needed. What had she done wrong now?

She went over to McNair's office. The door was closed, but Dani could see through the small window that it was empty inside. She looked at her phone. No missed calls or messages from McNair. What was it about then?

She sat down back at her own desk and opened up her emails. Ten unread messages. About usual given how long since she'd last looked. Though it was obvious, as she looked at the most recent two, both from McNair, what the issue was.

Dani opened up the first one. OK, so that explained where McNair was. In a meeting with the Chief Super. Dani needed to be there too. Before she went, Dani quickly opened the other email and clicked on the video link.

'Oh, shit,' she said after only a few seconds of watching.

She jumped up from her chair and rushed for the door.

–

Dani arrived at the meeting room just as McNair and Chief Superintendent Baxter were emerging. Both looked vexed.

'DI Stephens,' Baxter said. 'Finally. Looks like you've got a task on your hands with this one.'

She wasn't sure whether he was angry with her or not. Or whether his words were a criticism or helpful encouragement. Either way, he didn't say anything more before he turned and walked off.

McNair remained. She caught Dani's eye and shook her head despondently.

'Did we have that video already?' McNair asked.

'I don't know,' Dani said. 'I haven't even seen *that* video yet. Just the one of Asher on the news. I came here as soon as I saw it.'

'Come here,' McNair said.

They headed back into the meeting room. McNair opened her laptop up and clicked through to the grainy mobile phone footage that juddered and shook. Dani recognised the scene, but not the angle. Clinton Harrison and Dylan Roberts were both in shot. Squaring up. There was shouting between them, but the footage was too erratic and unclear to figure who was saying what.

Then Roberts stepped forwards, kind of, but the view was momentarily blocked by another bystander pitched in front. By the time they'd moved out of view again, Roberts was on the ground and Harrison was on top of him.

'I mean… it's not conclusive,' Dani said.

'Have you seen this before?' McNair asked again. Not very nicely.

'I haven't,' Dani said. 'I'd have to check with Grayling to be one hundred per cent on whether this was in our possession already, but I'm pretty sure it wasn't. The whole point was we had plenty of footage but nothing that showed anything until the fight was already underway.'

'Well, you need to be one hundred per cent. We have to be clear. And if we didn't have this already, I want to know why. How on earth did Asher get it before we did? Who's she been speaking to?'

Dani nodded. 'But… it's not conclusive, is it?'

'Of course it's not, but that's not the point. Asher is playing you for a fool. She's fanning the flames of the media circus. She's made it clear to the press now with that little speech of hers that this was nothing more than self-defence, and your journalist friend's hatchet job of Roberts as a career criminal only gives that argument further credence. Asher will battle tooth and nail against *any* charge we put forward now.'

Dani shook her head. She really didn't know what to say. The absolute worst thing to do, given Asher's hardline tactics, was to fall in line and to do battle with her, as though this were a contest. The case was about justice, not a game. If there *was* evidence that Roberts had attacked

Harrison first, then that was fine. Dani, the police, would have to consider it. But so far it felt more like Asher just wanted to win. Her way. And make the police look stupid at the same time.

'Let me look into this,' Dani said. 'I'll do everything I can to get to the bottom of this video. Who shot it, why we didn't have it already. And I'll recheck over every witness to make sure there's nothing else out there.'

'Good. You can update me on Monday morning.'

Dani sank a little at that.

'Yes. I will.'

She'd already planned to spend time on the Eccles case over the weekend, never mind finding time for her and Jason. Now this too?

McNair scooped up her laptop and then headed back to the office. A few questioning eyes poked up over the desk dividers as Dani made her way through. Once McNair was in her office with the door closed, Easton headed over, tentatively.

'Everything OK?' he asked.

Dani briefly explained. Easton's face fell as she spoke. He looked to his watch more than once.

'I get it,' she said. 'You have your date tonight. It's fine, don't miss it, because of this.'

'Are you sure?'

'Absolutely. I want you to concentrate on Eccles anyway. Grayling can take over what you were doing on Harrison.'

He looked unsure of that.

'What about you?' he said.

Dani sighed. She'd promised Jason she'd be home at a decent time tonight. After all, it was the last day marked for her ovulation cycle.

'Don't worry about me,' Dani said.

She hated letting Jason down. But honestly? She felt relief more than anything else.

Chapter 15

'I'm sorry, but that's just not good enough,' Jason said, a glower on his face as he stared at the TV. Dani was on the sofa next to him but pushed up against the far arm, away from him.

'Jason, come on, this case—'

'A convenient excuse—'

'Are you serious? It's ten p.m. I've had a shit week. I just want to relax and spend time with you.'

He rolled his eyes. She felt like throttling him. 'All you want is to have sex all the time,' she blasted. 'It's like my cycle gives you a sudden right to screw me as much as you want.'

He shot her a look.

'That's not what I signed up for,' she added.

'Don't you dare try to twist this into some sordid need of mine.'

She held her tongue at that. What she'd been about to say really wouldn't have been fair.

He sighed and reached over and put his hand on her leg.

'Dani, I *know* how it is.'

He didn't expand on the statement. He didn't have to. Dani knew what he meant. He was talking about the job. Jason was an ex-copper. Would still have been a copper now if it wasn't for the mess they'd got into… because of her. Twice he'd been seriously injured because of her cases. He'd saved her life. He wasn't just her partner, he was her saviour, both figuratively and in reality.

'I'm just disappointed, that's all,' Jason said.

Dani didn't know what to say to that. She hated to let him down, but why couldn't she just be completely honest with him? The plain and simple fact was that she was having major doubts about having kids. For a whole host of reasons.

Her mind inexplicably took her back to the interview with Clinton Harrison the other day. That look on his face as he'd held in the emotion of having seen his son knocked off his bike and killed. The sadness, the absolute despair. Could she put herself through that? Could she put herself through loving a child unconditionally, knowing that doing so could tear apart what already felt like a fragile life?

'Jason, I'm sorry.'

He caught her eye but said nothing.

'We will get there,' she said. 'I promise.'

He huffed. She moved over on the sofa and nestled into his side. Neither of them said anything more.

–

Saturday brought with it another bright, sunny, warm morning. Dani wasn't really feeling it.

Friday night had gone exactly how she'd expected given the late hour she'd arrived home, and her subsequent reluctance to have sex with Jason. Ultimately, she hadn't told him the truth, even if they'd half reconciled before they'd gone to sleep. Still, Jason had woken up grumpy. He made an excuse to get out of their previously

146

arranged early morning rendezvous with Gemma and the kids in the park, blaming aches and pains in his back. Aches and pains which miraculously hadn't been there the previous evening when he'd wanted nookie.

That was fine. Dani headed to the park alone.

The call from Briana Clark came when she was in the car. Dani sighed. How long would it take for the journalist to stop calling if Dani never answered?

For some reason she found herself reaching for the green button on the screen to accept the call.

'Good morning, Briana,' Dani said.

'Hi, Dani, is this a good time?'

'Not really. It's Saturday morning. I'm just on my way to meet my niece and nephew.'

'Oh. Oh, right. I can be quick?'

'Can we do this another time?'

'I guess so. When would be a good time to talk?'

'Monday.'

'Oh. Sure.'

'Thanks for understanding. Have a nice weekend, Briana.'

Dani ended the call before Briana could say anything more. Did Dani feel bad for the way she'd rebuffed her? Not really. She was happy to talk to the press. Happy to have a coffee with Briana every now and then. But that didn't mean she had to take time out of her weekend to update journalists.

Dani put the thought to the back of her mind as she reached the Boldmere Gate car park. Gemma, Ben's ex-wife, was waiting by her car with Harry and Chloe.

Dani stepped out of her car. Chloe, in a summer dress and cardigan, the look topped off with big green wellies, ran up and gave her aunt a loving hug. Harry, typically in a football kit, was far too cool for that kind of thing, but he was also in a bit of grump, Dani noted. Not at her, more at Gemma.

'Jason's not here?' Harry said, looking even more grumpy for the fact.

'He wasn't feeling well enough,' Dani said.

Harry sank his head further down and looked off into the distance. The truth was, Dani and Jason didn't spend anywhere near as much time with the kids as they should have done. That was due to Dani's long and unpredictable work hours, but also the fact that there'd always been a strange atmosphere between Gemma and Dani. Gemma was nice, but she'd never been a friend of Dani's. The issues, of course, stemmed almost entirely from Ben – the kids' dad, Gemma's ex, and Dani's brother.

Ben was in jail. For life. In part for attempting to murder Gemma and Dani. The kids were old enough to know the truth now. Gemma and Dani had explained it to them together last year, when the playground insinuations and gossip that Harry was hearing became too much to handle. He'd taken it well. He was a bright kid. But Dani had often wondered about the impact on the children, Harry in particular, of not just knowing their dad was in jail for murder and attempted murder, but that there was no other strong male role model in their lives. Gemma had her dad, but he and Gemma's mum had moved out of the area a couple of years ago. So the only adult male in Harry's life was Jason. Even though they all saw each other too infrequently, Harry would always come out of his shell in Jason's presence. He looked up to Jason. And Jason was such a natural with both of the kids.

He'd make an amazing father.

Dani felt a knot in her stomach. She quickly pushed the thoughts away.

'This is going to be so boring,' Harry drawled with a roll of the eyes. He kicked a stone away. It banged across the tarmac towards a parked car. Dani saw Gemma about to rebuke him but she gave her a calming look which surprisingly worked.

Harry turned away. Gemma looked worn out. Obviously, this grump went deeper than just Jason not coming out for a walk. Or a ride in his wheelchair, as it would have been.

'Tell you what, Harry,' Dani said. 'Want to hear about the most disgusting thing I've ever seen?'

He turned around now, curiosity etched on his young features. 'Yeah?' he said.

'Come on.'

She grasped his hand and set off at pace. Chloe giggled and sauntered off after them but Gemma grabbed her hand and pulled her back.

'No, sweetie, I'm not sure this one's going to be for you.'

'I've got a different story for you, Chloe,' Dani said as she turned around. 'I promise.'

Dani winked at her niece, then got started on the story for Harry; the diabolical toilet at Will Eccles' apartment.

Harry was in raptures within seconds, and throughout. They'd cleared well over a mile at a constant brisk stride by the time Dani – with a little artistic embellishment – was finished, just as they headed up the hill to the Jamboree Stone in the centre of the park.

'That is soooo… gross!' Harry said. 'How many maggots do you reckon there were?'

'Thousands,' Dani said. 'The whole floor looked like it was flowing and moving with them, like there was a sea of critters.'

He frowned – a strange mixture of fascination and disgust.

'But how do you know this was just the poo from hell?'

'How do you mean?'

'What if it was, I mean, couldn't it have been a person but the body had been completely devoured? Or an animal even. All you were seeing was just the leftovers?'

He certainly had a vivid imagination.

'I saw this movie,' he said, 'where a guy's body got completely eaten by this army of ants. Millions of them covered him and ate every last piece of him in seconds. All that was left at the end was his glasses and hat.'

Harry laughed. Dani did too. 'I think I know that one. But no, definitely no body in my story. In real life there'd be bones left at least.'

'You're sure?'

'I'm positive. This was just one hell of a big, stinking shi—'

'Auntie Dani!' Chloe called as she raced past. 'We're stopping here for some sweets.'

She looked to Harry. They both burst out laughing.

'Don't you tell your sister that story.'

'The ant one or the toilet one?'

'Either. She'll have nightmares.'

'OK,' he said, pretty unconvincingly.

As ever the area around the Jamboree Stone – a confluence of several different walking and cycle paths that trailed through the park – was busy, but they managed to find a bench to sit on. At least Dani and Gemma did, because as soon as Harry and Chloe had devoured their sweets, the sugar rush meant they were back on their feet and tearing around the place. The adults left the kids to it. Dani could sense Gemma wasn't ready to move on. Something was on her mind.

'Have you been to see Ben recently?' Gemma asked after an awkward silence.

Dani looked to her, to try to gauge where that question had come from. 'No. Not for months.'

'Oh.'

Gemma had never been to see him in jail, had vowed she never would. Dani had initially said the same, but had been drawn to him on more than one occasion in search of answers to his crimes, and also when her work had at times led her inexplicably in his direction.

Yet even now, even though she hadn't seen him for months, Ben was never far from her mind. Dani generally put that down to trauma, the aftermath of the problems that he'd created, that riddled the lives of Dani, Jason, Gemma, them all. But was it different for Dani? Was the sticky bond of brother and sister something else?

'Why do you ask?' Dani said.

Gemma was looking over at the kids, but it felt to Dani like she couldn't face her.

'I guess there's no easy way to say this. We're moving.'

Another knot in Dani's stomach. She didn't say anything. The silence hung in the air until Gemma turned to her.

'Sorry to spring it on you like this, but I didn't know how else to tell you.'

'Where to? When?'

'In a few weeks. I'm going to rent the house out to start with, but Mum and Dad found me something near them. A small cottage by the lake.'

'Up in Cumbria?'

'Yeah.'

They only lived a few minutes' walk from Dani right now, and she still hardly ever got the chance to see the kids. What would it be like when they were two hundred miles away?

'The truth is, I've been thinking about it for ages. I've got no ties here. No family. A few friends, but…'

No family? Dani felt like saying. What about her?

'I understand,' she said instead.

'You do? God, I was so worried about telling you. I know you love them… and it's going to be hard not having you to call on.'

'It's fine, really. You don't call on me that much anyway.'

She hadn't intended that to sound as accusatory as it did.

'I'll miss them,' Dani added. 'All of you.'

'They'll miss you too. And Jason.'

Dani hadn't expected the news to hit her so hard, but tears were welling and she did her best to keep them from falling. She swallowed hard. Gemma seemed to notice her discomfort and quickly looked away as though that would help the moment pass.

'There's a really good school for them up there too, and one of my old university friends lives nearby.'

'Gemma, you don't have to explain. Honestly.'

'We'll come and visit. And you should come up north too.'

'We definitely will.'

They fell silent again. The kids were still racing around happy as anything, but Dani just wanted to go.

'There is another thing,' Gemma said.

Dani turned to her again. Gemma was looking really worried now.

'What?'

She let out a long sigh. 'I'd really appreciate it if you could tell Ben. You know I can't see him. But he has a right to know. About the kids.'

Dani closed her eyes for a few seconds. Had she been looking for an excuse to go and see him anyway? Not exactly. Not really. In an ideal world she'd be rid of him for good, but there was no doubt that even after everything, Ben still had a pull on her. Yet it felt a bit of a cheap thing for Gemma to put pressure on like this.

'Do you think you can?' Gemma said.

'I will,' Dani said.

Gemma leaned over and gave Dani a brief but pretty emotionless hug.

'Thanks so much. I really owe you one.'

'Don't mention it.'

'I might be out of line here,' Gemma said, 'but… with Harry and Chloe further away, maybe it'll make you pine that little bit more for the patter of tiny feet in your own house. You know?'

Gemma spoke light-heartedly enough. She couldn't have known the background to what she'd just said. Dani smiled but said nothing.

'You two would make great parents,' Gemma added. 'I really mean that.'

'Thanks,' Dani said.

But inside her head throbbed with thoughts of her murderous brother, and the idea of facing him again, and her heart ached for the hurt she knew she would have to cause Jason sooner or later. Even as she watched her niece and nephew so full of joy and life, once more she had to fight back the tears.

Chapter 16

October last year

Terry sat in his car looking out over the boarded-up houses beyond. On this section of Birmingham Road, each of the Victorian semis was three storeys tall, plus basement, and had long but narrow plots. Big, grand houses really. Though the fact the plots were so long, meant the back gardens were ripe for redevelopment.

All along here, over the last decade or so, land grabbers had been persuading homeowners to part with large portions of their gardens to allow the building of new houses. Terry wasn't a land grabber. This was a serious development. Not just squeezing in a couple of new homes at the back of the existing houses, they were planning to bulldoze the entire multi-home site. Where once eight buildings containing sixteen dwellings had stood, they planned for fifty-four homes as part of a mixed-use development. It was one of their most ambitious projects yet, and stood to make them a substantial sum. Enough to solve all of Terry's problems and to put the problems with the Somerton and Little Aston developments way behind him.

If he could just get it off the ground.

The biggest problem in achieving that was 104 – the left-hand semi in the second to last of the eight buildings;

104 and the now derelict 106 were the only buildings that remained. Only recently refurbished – and to a damn high standard, all told – 104 remained occupied. Rented out to a family by a local landlord who owned dozens of properties in the area. Omar Mansoor. Terry knew him. Terry didn't like him. Hence why he needed to think more strategically if he was to overcome this hurdle.

His phone vibrated on his lap.

Annie.

'Hi, honey, you OK?'

'I'm fine. Is she there yet?'

'Laura? Not yet.'

'OK, well, tell her I said hi.'

'Will do.'

'Ask her if she wants to pop over to see me after.'

'I will. Was that why you called?'

She'd already said pretty much the same thing when he'd left the house half an hour ago.

'Not quite. I just spoke to Henry,' she said.

Terry sighed. He already knew what this was about. 'And?'

'I've said we'll send him an extra ten.'

'Ten thousand!'

'Come on, Tel, he needs it. His fees—'

'It's his bloody choice to be there!'

'It's just to tide him over for the rest of this year.'

'Yeah, of course it is. I'm sure he's going to spend it on nothing but essentials.'

'No need to be pissy. He's our son. We can't just—'

'Just what? Let him starve? He's hardly on the bread-line.'

'You're such an—'

156

Terry didn't really hear the insult that came next. He was already pulling the phone away to end the call. Partly because the conversation was going nowhere. Partly because a car had just pulled up in front of him.

Not Laura's Jaguar, but a Tesla Model 3. As if Hamed gave a shit about the environment.

He got out of the car. Hamed did so too.

'Morning, Terry,' Hamed called over. 'You're looking better than the last time I saw you.'

Terry rolled his eyes. 'Yeah.'

Hamed looked like he was waiting for Terry to say something else. What? He wanted an apology? No chance. The party had been ages ago. Terry had moved on, even if the two men hadn't seen each other since.

'So how can we help?' Hamed said.

Both of them remained by their cars. As though this was some sort of Wild West stand-off.

'Where's Laura?' Terry asked.

'She had something else on. She asked me to come. She thought it would be good for you and me to discuss business together.'

Terry balled his fists to try and channel his frustration. Hamed was really loving this. Terry had gone to Laura holding an olive branch in his hour of need. He hadn't expected her to do this to him. To humiliate him like this.

'She showed me the plans,' Hamed said, as he looked off to the boarded-up houses. 'Quite a development.'

'Out of your league,' Terry said.

'Really? Then why are you asking for our help? Our money?'

'I proposed an idea to my daughter, that's all. I've always wanted her to work with me.'

Hamed smiled now. Or was it a smirk? Terry wished he could wipe that look off his face for good.

'Come on, you don't need to be so tough and proud, Terry. We want to help you. Honestly? The plans for this place look amazing. I'd be thrilled to partner with you on it.'

Terry's nails were digging into his palms painfully, he was squeezing his fists so hard. But… the simple fact was he needed them.

'So that's the one?' Hamed said looking over to 104.

'That's the one.'

'Have you met Omar before?'

'A couple of times,' Terry said.

'My uncle is actually very close to his brother. Small world, and all that. Anyway, take it from me, he's not an unreasonable man. You just need to make this worth his while.'

'I already offered him more than it's worth.'

'I know. He said. Two hundred grand more than you paid for 106.' A really smug look on his face now as he glanced back to the houses again. 'I spoke to him last night about it.'

So this wasn't a spur-of-the-moment thing. Why hadn't Laura mentioned it to him?

'And?'

Hamed shrugged. 'He feels his hands are tied. His tenants are on a two-year lease, more than eighteen months left. They're adamant they don't want to move. Unfortunately, they have rights.'

'I understand the law, thank you.'

'The other issue is Omar himself. He knows what you're trying to do here. I think, quite honestly, he wants in.'

'No go,' Terry said, shaking his head. 'Absolutely not.'

'I'm glad you said that. Because I don't really want my profits diluted either.'

This guy. Terry wanted to rip his head off. Hamed and Laura's business was already going to take fifty per cent of the profit here based on what he'd discussed with Laura. Terry hadn't properly explained that to Peter yet, but the fact was they couldn't afford to get this off the ground without help. This was the only way. Hamed knew it. And he was loving it.

'So what's it going to take?' Terry asked.

'Well,' Hamed said, 'the key question is, how far are you willing to go?'

'Money wise? I'm already at the limit. And that's the truth.'

'There are other ways to solve these problems, Terry. Money isn't everything.' He paused and held Terry's eye. 'So I'll ask you again. How far are you willing to go?'

Chapter 17

March

After the walk in the park, Dani made a quick trip home before she set out for the rest of the day. She hadn't mentioned anything to Jason about Gemma moving away, or about how she'd been asked to go and tell Ben the news. She wanted to think it all over first. Though as she drove away from the house, a niggling thought at the back of her mind grew; why was she seemingly so comfortable keeping things from Jason now?

She'd had a message from Easton earlier. He was busy in the office looking through the documents taken from Kibble House. He was also planning to arrange for Eric to go there, perhaps later in the day. Dani might even try and get there for that.

After a short drive through Sutton Coldfield, and across the M6 to Castle Bromwich, Dani came to the cluster of grey rendered homes called Yenton Crescent – a circular 1970s development with a small recreation ground in the middle that was overgrown and had a children's play area that was rusted and decrepit. The basic houses that encircled the area were identical in their design, though quite different in their condition. Some looked bright and had neat front yards with colourful pot plants. Others had a clean yet sparse appearance, their front yards with new tarmac or paving. A few of the properties were in a terrible state, yards overflowing with weeds and rubbish, windows and doors that looked beyond repair.

This wasn't one of the worst areas in the region, but it was far from the wealthiest either. Unemployment here was high, as was petty crime.

Dani parked in one of the spots on the road and looked out to 33a. The house Dylan Roberts had lived at. Kind of. He hadn't owned it, hadn't paid any rent on it. His on-off girlfriend and her five-year-old son, by another man, lived there. DC Grayling had already spoken to her – Carrie – the day Roberts had been killed. Dani had listened to some of the tape of the conversation, which had only confirmed to her what Grayling had suggested about the interview. That Carrie seemed almost relieved that Roberts was gone. With everything they were finding out about Dylan Roberts, to say he was unsavoury would be a kind way of putting it.

Not that that meant he'd deserved to be beaten to death.

Dani got out of the car. A group of kids were whizzing around on their bikes in the near distance, circling around, on and off the kerb. Other than that the area was quiet. She headed up towards 33a. She was nearly at the front gate when there was a whoosh behind her and she turned to see two of the boys on their bikes ride by. They circled and came back to her, stopping a few yards away, right in the middle of the road.

'There's no one in,' one of them shouted over, without looking at Dani. Within seconds there were four of them together, all at a stop, hanging off their handlebars and staring at Dani as though she didn't belong. They were all of ten years old, perhaps twelve at most. Despite their young age, Dani was wary.

Sad really, to feel like that in the presence of kids. But she'd learned the hard way.

'How do you know?' Dani asked.

'She's not been there for a couple of days. Some guy came and took her.'

'And you are?'

'We live around here,' another of the boys said. The one on the left. He was the biggest of them, in every way, with a rounded face and puffy cheeks. 'She's gone. Not sure she's coming back.'

'Who did she go with?'

A shrug. 'Never seen him before.'

'Who are you anyway?' another of them piped up.

'A detective.'

They turned to each other. A couple of them laughed. The big kid looked angry.

'Told you she was,' the kid on the right said. Even though he wasn't the biggest, he looked the roughest. Toughest. Likely the leader of their little gang.

'Fuck off,' the big one said to his mate.

Or maybe not.

'Excuse me?' Dani said.

'What?'

'Mind your language.'

'Why? It's none of your fucking business what we do.'

Dani sighed. What could she say to that?

'I knew you was police,' said the wiry kid in the middle who'd first piped up. 'Can tell by your shit clothes. And your shit car.'

'Plus you're ugly,' said the leader with a nasty glint in his eye.

Cackles from his friends.

'She's not that ugly. I'd do her.'

'Very mature,' Dani said.

As if they even knew what 'do her' meant. Most likely at least one of them had an older brother, which was where they'd heard such things. She took a couple of steps towards them. They cowered as though they weren't quite sure of her intentions. She fished her notepad out, pen too, and put the pen to the paper as she looked over them.

'Right, so I'll just start with your names and addresses then. So I can add you to the list of people we're interested in related to the murder investigation I'm running.'

Silence now. Until the big kid huffed.

'You can't do that.'

'Can't do what?' Silence again. 'So?'

They looked at each other. All a bit less confident now than before.

'Or,' Dani said. She put the pen and notepad away and took out her purse.

'Fiver for anyone who can describe the man. Another fiver for anyone who can give me the reg of his car.'

She took the money from her purse and held it aloft. They all looked at each other. again. Then Puffy Cheeks piped up. 'Money first. We're not stupid.' He held out his hand.

'Neither am I. You don't want it? Fine.'

She put her hand down and moved towards her car. She was almost there when, 'All right. I'll tell you.'

Dani turned back to them.

'He was big. Old. Bald head.'

'Old?'

'Forty. Fifty. I dunno.'

'White? Black?'

163

'White. Had tattoos all down his arms.'

'Tattoos of what?'

Another shrug. 'Like a cloak. You know? Covered his arms.'

'And the car?'

'Better than yours.'

A couple of guffaws.

'Corsa. Silver. Fuck–off–loud exhaust on it.'

'Reg?'

Shrug. 'Not new.'

'Anything else?'

No answer.

'Thanks.'

Dani opened her door and sank down into the seat.

'Oi! What about my money?'

She fired up the engine, then wound down the window.

'Oops.'

She pushed the accelerator and her car shot away leaving the foursome cussing and waving their fingers about.

'Little shits,' she said under her breath when she turned the corner to the next street and they were out of sight.

Despite their nastiness, she didn't know whether to feel sorry for them or not. Were they simply victims of their own circumstances? Either way, she soon put them out of mind, and instead turned her thoughts to what they'd said about Carrie heading off with a man. Was there something to that? Dani really didn't know. She parked the thought and headed to her next destination.

The road Clinton Harrison lived on with his wife and two kids in Tyburn was a slight upgrade from Yenton Crescent, but not by much. The houses here were all 1950s three-bed semis, not much smaller than the one she and Jason lived in, though with tighter plots both at the front and the back, and overall the houses here were at least fifty per cent cheaper than in nearby Sutton.

Interestingly the houses had a similar broad range of upkeep to over in Castle Bromwich, though the key difference here was that all of the properties were privately owned – either by the occupants or private landlords – compared to the majority council-owned Yenton Crescent. Harrison and his family were homeowners. He was a mechanic at a local car repair shop. His wife worked part time in a nail salon. They were far from wealthy, but they both had employment and the impression Dani had got from the investigation so far was that they were… pretty normal.

Dani found a parking spot on the road a few doors down from where the Harrisons lived. The street was jam-packed with cars, bumper to bumper, both sides, with barely enough room for vehicles to pass each other in the space that was left. Dani headed up to the Harrisons' door and rang the bell. She waited thirty seconds. No answer. Dani sighed. This wasn't going to plan at all. She pressed the bell again, but still there was no answer. As she turned around her eyes fell on the upstairs window of the house opposite. She was sure she saw the curtain beyond the glass twitch. No sign of anyone there, though.

Becoming increasingly frustrated with her day, she headed back to the car. One last destination before she'd park the Harrison case for the day and go to Laura Eccles' house instead.

The garage was four miles from where Clinton Harrison lived. Set behind a row of shops that were mostly empty, or takeaways, the building had a simple corrugated steel shell that looked like a workshop you might find in a tinkerer's garden, except several times larger. There was a rusted gate topped with barbed wire at the edge of the forecourt. Dani parked there and headed in on foot.

Several cars were parked up, some clearly there for repairs, others not. Dani carried on towards the main building from where voices drifted over. The doors to the building were half open. Four men inside, clustered together.

Dani took her phone from her pocket and tapped into the camera app, then she brought the phone back down to her waist, holding it casually, albeit with the lens facing the men.

'Good morning,' she said as she stepped into the open.

The men jumped in surprise. All of them turned around. Two of them peeled away. Dani tapped on the phone screen.

'See you around, yeah?' one of the departing two said to the others.

A few grumbles of acknowledgement. The two moved towards Dani and the exit. She stepped aside and smiled at them as they passed, though they were trying their best not to make eye contact.

'Can I help you?' one of the remaining two asked.

'DI Stephens, West Midlands Police.'

Their faces soured.

'I'm investigating the deaths of Dylan Roberts and Tyler Harrison. Tyler's father, Clinton, works here, doesn't he?'

'Yeah,' the younger but more gruff-looking of the men said. He was short and stocky with a bushy beard and a dirtied vest. He looked exactly how Dani expected a mechanic to look. The other man was taller, slimmer, older. He was dressed in blue overalls and not nearly as grubby.

'How can we help you, Detective?' the older guy said.

'Who owns this place?'

'What does that have to do with your investigation?' the younger one replied.

Dani looked at him, eyebrow raised.

'It's fine. I own it.' The older guy again.

'So you'd be Nelson'?' Dani said, referring to the signage outside which read NELSON AND SON.

'Eddie Nelson. And this is Trey. Trey Wallace. He works for me.'

'What sort of work are you doing here?'

'Whatever you need. MOT. Service. Body repairs.'

'Modifications?'

Nelson shrugged. 'Sometimes. Exhausts. Wheels. A few body trims. Trey mostly does that sort of thing. I'm more your old-school service-and-repair guy.'

'What about Clinton?'

'Clinton worked for me,' Trey said.

Interesting. Because Dani would have guessed Trey, despite his beard, was only in his late twenties. Clinton Harrison was forty.

'I let Trey sort out his own guys,' Nelson said, 'even though I'm boss of it all.'

The explanation didn't really seem necessary.

'How did Clinton get to work here?' Dani asked.

'He applied,' Trey said. 'That's how these things work, isn't it?'

'I guess so. How long ago?'

'Four years.'

'Was he a good worker?'

'I've certainly had worse.'

'I don't mean to be rude,' Nelson said, 'but why are you here?'

Dani didn't answer. She turned off to the side and took a couple of steps, mooching.

'Have you ever worked on a silver Vauxhall Corsa?'

She turned back to them. They both looked nonplussed.

'How do you mean?' Nelson asked.

'A silver Corsa, with a modified exhaust. Does that ring any bells?'

'None,' Nelson said. 'But I've been here for twenty-five years, so I've seen thousands of cars. You'd have to help me out a bit more.'

Trey, though, looked more nervous all of a sudden. Didn't he? Or was Dani reading too much into that?

'It's someone I'm looking for,' Dani said. 'Someone who has a connection to Dylan Roberts. Forties or fifties, bald, arms covered in tattoos. He owns a silver Corsa with a modified exhaust.'

Trey and Nelson exchanged a look now.

'Honestly?' Nelson said. 'That doesn't sound like anyone I remember. Bit of a long shot this, isn't it?'

'And you, Trey?' Dani asked.

'I've worked on a lot of Corsas. Pretty cheap, second-hand, ain't they? A lot of young kids want them, and they bring them here to make them sound like fart cans. Whatever, I do that for them. But no, don't know what you're talking about with that guy.'

'Do *you* know Dylan Roberts?' Dani said as she held Trey's eye.

He pursed his lips and shook his head.

'I never heard of him until I saw what happened on the news,' Nelson added.

'You're both sure about that?' Dani asked. 'Better to tell the truth now than to be caught in a lie later on.'

Trey scoffed. Nelson folded his arms and glared. 'We don't know him. I've no idea why you think we do. Now is there anything else we can help you with?'

'If there is, I'll let you know.'

Dani turned to walk out.

'He didn't deserve any of this,' Nelson called.

Dani faced him again.

'Clinton was decent, and a good dad to his boys. What happened to Tyler was a tragedy. No father should have to see that. But just think about what Clinton's still got left. A wife. Another young boy. They need him now more than ever. Clinton should be at home with them, not in jail.'

'Everyone knows that,' Trey added.

Dani didn't say anything more. She walked back to her car. Took snaps of the car registrations in the forecourt for good measure. She sat back down in the driver's seat and sent all the pictures across to Grayling together with an explanation. If there was a connection between Harrison and Roberts, they'd find it. If there was more to Harrison than him being a decent, family man, she'd find it.

Yet Dani's mind sloshed with Nelson's parting words.

They need him now more than ever. Clinton should be at home with them, not in jail.

And even as she sat there doing what she could to dig into Harrison's life in the hope of finding dirt that would keep him behind bars, a large part of her agreed entirely with those words.

Chapter 18

It'd been a frustrating morning for Dani, all told. She called Easton on her way to Solihull. Other than having enjoyed his Friday night date, he had nothing particular to update her on. To be expected, really, given how Dani's day was going. Easton hadn't made any headway in confirming evidence in the Eccles murders, and was still to hear back from Eric Eccles as to when he'd like to go to Kibble House. Was that odd, given how keen he'd seemed previously?

Laura Eccles was Dani's next stop. She'd arrived back in the country last night, and had so far been reluctant to agree a time and date to come to HQ to speak to Dani. So Dani was taking matters into her own hands. Hopefully a visit to Laura's home would see her more relaxed anyway.

Solihull was, in many respects, similar to Sutton Coldfield, in its size, its demographics – a large borough that was directly attached to Birmingham, but had its own well-funded council. Its public spaces, shopping centres and the like were all the better for it. Not everyone in the area of over 200,000 was wealthy, but there were certainly a lot who were.

Laura Eccles and her husband, Hamed Adil, lived on a quiet cul-de-sac of ten houses, each of them unique in design, even if the common elements of dark red brick interspersed with Tudor-style timbers were uniform.

Their house took up a wide plot in the corner of the cul-de-sac, with dense trees out front and stretching around the separate double garage to the garden beyond.

Dani parked on the drive, behind a Tesla. Only one car there. She was already feeling downbeat as she stepped out. She headed up to the door. Curtains were drawn in the front downstairs windows. Same up top.

Were they still in bed?

Dani rang the bell then knocked on the door and waited.

No answer. Bloody typical.

She rang again. Why not?

'Can I help you?' came a voice from behind her.

Dani turned to see a grey-haired woman standing at the edge of the drive. She looked to be in her late seventies or early eighties, short and hunched over.

'I'm looking for Laura Eccles and her husband,' Dani said.

'You're with the police,' the woman replied.

The second time today that a random stranger had deduced that so easily. Did she really reek of copper so much? She'd have to have a think about why that was.

'Yes, I am.'

'Terrible thing that happened.'

'It was,' Dani said, figuring the woman was referring to the deaths of the Eccles. 'Truly awful. Do you know where they went?'

'They?'

'Laura and her family.'

'I haven't seen the husband or the girl,' the woman said. A little snottily. Like she didn't approve of Hamed, or perhaps his daughter, for some reason.

'How do you mean?'

'Laura was back here last night. But not the others. Then I saw her driving out not long ago.'

'Any idea where to?'

'Sorry, I haven't a clue.'

And with that she turned and trudged off, back to the neighbouring house where the front door remained wide open.

Dani sighed as she looked around the street. So Hamed hadn't come home from Greece? Dani thought through her conversations with Grayling. She realised she'd never specifically been told he was coming back with Laura, Dani had just assumed that would be the case. Why hadn't he? It certainly seemed odd that a loving husband wouldn't accompany his wife after her parents had been murdered.

Regardless, there was little else she could do. Minutes later she was back on the motorway heading north to Sutton Coldfield and home. Or she could detour west and go into the office…

A call came through on the car's dashboard. Easton.

'Please give me some good news,' Dani said. 'Or at least some exciting news.'

'Er, yeah. I can.'

She perked up. She could tell from the background noise that he was in his car.

'I just had a call from Kibble House,' he said. 'From the PC there, I mean.'

'Eric turned up?'

'Not Eric. Laura. She's demanding to be let inside. I'm on my way there now.'

'See you there.'

Easton beat Dani to it, but only by a few minutes. The scene on the driveway of Kibble House was reminiscent of Thursday morning when Eric Eccles had angrily tried to barge his way into the house, except this time it was his younger sister, Laura, who was swearing and gesticulating to Easton and, once more, PC Forrester, who was likely sick to death of standing around the Four Oaks Estate by now.

Dani headed over to the three of them. There was a temporary lull in the stand-off. Laura turned to Dani. She'd seen the Eccles daughter in plenty of pictures in the house, and she nearly always looked vibrant and well-dressed. Today she wore leggings and a baggy jumper, and her face looked puffy and worn. Perhaps understandably so, given the trauma.

'She's here now,' Laura said, glaring at Dani. 'So can I finally go in?'

She turned back to Easton. So did Dani. Easton still looked perfectly calm.

'As I was explaining to Miss Eccles,' Easton said. 'She *can* go into the house, but she needs to be accompanied. And I simply requested she put on some shoe covers and gloves. She didn't like that idea, so I suggested perhaps she wait for you to arrive.'

'And now you're here,' Laura said, glaring at Dani again.

'I am,' Dani said. 'And I'll happily escort you through the house. If you could just follow what DS Easton has asked for.'

Laura threw her hands up in the air. 'This is ridiculous.'

'It might seem inconvenient, but I can assure you it's not ridiculous. We're simply trying to do our best to preserve the crime scene, as well as we can. Doing so will undoubtedly help in the long run, in catching whoever is responsible for killing your parents. You do want that, don't you?'

Laura put her hands to her hips. Then she slumped ever so slightly, as the fight finally left her. 'Well, if he'd just explained it to me like that in the first place…'

Easton looked like he was about to say something to that, but he did the right thing in bottling it up.

'Shall we go?' Dani said.

Easton came too. The three of them put on their shoe covers and gloves by the front door, then Dani stepped inside first. Chilly. That was the first thing that Dani noticed. She'd turned the heating off the last time she'd been inside, and the house was several degrees cooler now, despite the sunny spring day. It meant the lingering smell of death didn't seem anywhere near as bad as before, though somehow in its place was an unsettling eeriness.

Dani glanced to the spot where the discarded bloodied boots had been. Hopefully by Monday some of the Forensics results would start to come back and they'd find some clues as to who they belonged to. Laura took a sharp inhale of breath as she stepped in and Dani turned to her. Her irritation was now gone. She looked mournful. Trembling? Just a bit.

'Where do you want to go?' Dani asked.

No answer. Laura looked about the place, her body rigid.

'Is there something in particular you're looking for?'

'What? No. Not really.'

Then awkward silence once more. Laura's eyes had settled on the staircase where the bloodstains were still evident on the carpet, on the painted walls, on the hand-rail, although the marks were now black.

'It happened upstairs?' Laura asked.

Dani nodded. 'In their bedroom.'

'I… don't know if I want to go up there.'

'You don't have to.'

'I thought I did. I thought I wanted to. I thought it would help to see. But now… I really don't know.'

'Just take your time. There's no rush.'

She continued to fixate on the stairs. She shook her head. What was she thinking?

'No. I do want to see.'

She moved forwards.

'Are you sure?'

'Yes.'

Dani turned to Easton and mouthed, *wait here*. He nodded.

Dani set off after Laura. They took slow, contemplative steps. By the time they reached the top, Laura's breathing was deep and a little erratic. She paused on the landing, then moved towards the open door to the master bedroom. She was a couple of steps from the threshold when she gasped and whipped her hand up to her mouth in shock. But she didn't stop moving. She carried on inside, Dani right behind her, and within moments they were both staring at the bed, the bloodstained mattress on top of the wooden frame.

Laura sniffed and wiped at her eyes with her sleeve.

'Do you think… do you think they knew what was happening?'

'It's hard to say,' Dani said. 'But I'd think it unlikely. I saw no evidence to suggest they tried to fight back at all.'

Dani winced at her own words. Couldn't she just have kept it simple and said *no*?

They both remained on the spot for what felt like several minutes, not a word spoken between them. Then Laura turned to Dani. Her face had taken on a certain strength that hadn't been there before.

'OK,' Laura said. 'I've done it. Now we can go.'

'You're done in the house?'

'No. I'm done in here.'

Laura turned and walked out, back onto the landing. She moved to the adjacent bedroom. This time she didn't go in, but remained standing right by the entrance.

'This was my room,' Laura said with a flicker of a smile. 'We only moved here when I was a teenager, so I didn't have it for long, but... I always loved it. Such fond memories. My first boyfriend, my first kiss. My first... you know.'

She tuned to Dani, her cheeks flushed. Dani didn't say anything. There was nothing left now to show this had once been a teenage girl's haven. Now it was a plush-looking guest room. Far nicer than the two rooms at the back of the house that had belonged to Will and Henry which had been left sparse and simple since the boys had left home. But then that had happened more recently.

Laura sighed deeply. 'You don't have any suspects.'

'Not yet.'

'But... how did they even get inside the house? Did they break in?'

'We don't know for sure, but it looks like through a bedroom window. In Will's old room.'

Laura shot Dani a look. A strange look. Shock?

'Whoever came in, they were very careful,' Dani said. 'There was no obvious sign of anything having been disturbed in the bedrooms, or anywhere else.'

Laura didn't say anything now as she looked across the landing to the door to Will's room. She seemed unsettled, as though the culprit were still there, behind the door.

'I always told them to get better security,' she said after a few moments. 'They had an alarm, but… it wasn't the best. And the windows…'

She turned to Dani. Now distressed. 'Oh God, listen to me. I sound like I'm blaming them. I'm not. I just…'

She never finished the sentence.

'I need to check a couple of things downstairs. Then I'm done.'

'OK,' Dani said.

She followed Laura down. Easton remained by the front door, playing on his phone. He looked up and smiled meekly. Laura ignored him and turned the corner to head along the hall. She looked like she was going to the back of the house, but then turned right and into the front living room. She paused there, as she had done upstairs.

'So many things,' she said.

What did she mean? Pictures? Ornaments?

'I don't even know how this works. But when… when do we come and clear it all out?'

'Honestly? I can't give you a specific time yet. Soon, I hope. For now, if there're particular items you want, that's fine. We can log it. Just let me know.'

Laura looked around the room again, as though trying to decide if there was anything to take now. In the end she turned and moved out, and back along the corridor. To the office.

She took one step in.

'What the hell? What happened in here?'

177

It was the first time Dani had seen it like this too. The furniture remained, but other than that it was clear this room had been entirely emptied of its contents.

'We've taken some things away for the investigation,' Dani said.

'Taken things away? You've cleared this place out! How dare you!'

'Laura, I can assure you there's nothing—'

'What are you even looking for? This is crazy!'

She looked more upset than angry. As though she felt her parents had been violated in some way. Dani could understand that. There was nothing nice about delving into the private affairs of the deceased. But it was absolutely necessary.

Laura turned and stomped across the room to the desk. She opened and closed the drawers, shaking her head in disbelief as she did so. She went to the tallboy. Did the same thing.

'Everything,' she said without looking to Dani. 'Everything is gone.'

'It's not gone,' Dani said. 'We have it all.'

Laura shot Dani a look. 'That's not what I meant, and you know it.'

Laura turned back to the unit. She reached inside. Dani stepped forwards, peering closely. Was she going for the panel, to reveal the safe? Did she know that was there?

Before Dani could see, Laura pulled her hand back out and turned around. Dani jumped back. A little too suspiciously, as evidenced by the glare she received from Laura in return.

'If there are any documents you need,' Dani said, 'anything that related to you specifically, for example, you can let me know and we'll find those for you.'

Laura didn't say anything. She stood up straight. She looked contemplative now.

'Is there anything?' Dani asked.

'No,' Laura said. 'I think I'm done.'

Dani nodded. 'OK. But, before you go, could we just chat briefly?'

Laura didn't look as if that idea appealed to her. But still, she agreed, and with Dani and Easton she headed back to the front living room once more. Dani and Easton sat together at one end, Laura at the other. It was almost the same arrangement as when Dani had been in there with Fran Willis.

'We've spoken to Eric and Henry already,' Dani said.

'Yes. I know. They told me about you.'

Dani wasn't sure how to take that.

'We haven't been able to get hold of Will, though.'

'That's because no one has a clue where he's gone,' Laura said, in such a way as to suggest whatever problem there was, was with Will.

'Are you not concerned?'

'Concerned? Will has always been like this. He's… in many ways he's not even part of the family. He doesn't care for any of us, so why should we care for him?'

Harsh words. Even more strongly spoken than Eric and Henry's.

Dani explained about the abandoned apartment in the Jewellery Quarter.

'I've never been there,' Laura said. 'I knew he had that place, but that's about it.'

'And you don't have any ideas as to where else he is now?'

'None.'

'How was your relationship with Eric and Henry?'

'I get what Eric meant now.'

'Excuse me?'

'He said you were – and these are his words not mine – a nosey cow.'

Dani raised an eyebrow.

'I'm sorry, but that's what he said. I can understand why. You do realise my parents were murdered, don't you? We're sitting in their house right now. Yet you're going around our family, one after the other, trying to… to do *what* exactly? Look for any fault in our familial relationships?'

'We're trying to find a killer,' Easton said. 'To do that we have to look for evidence of motive, among other things.'

Laura scoffed at that. 'Do you really think one of us did it?'

'I don't think either DI Stephens or myself suggested that,' Easton said. 'But it's interesting you did.'

'OK, OK,' Dani said, hoping to calm the meeting. 'Our intention is not to antagonise any of you. I'm sorry if that's how you and your brothers have felt. I can only assure you our intentions are simply to do the right thing by your parents. To help us, we just want to understand them, and by extension you and your siblings, a bit better.'

Laura didn't say anything to that, though her expression seemed to relax.

'You and your husband are in business together,' Dani said.

'We are. I wondered how long it would take to bring him up.'

'You did?'

'Hamed's always made to be the scapegoat.'

'In what sense?'

Laura rolled her eyes. 'How do you think? His brown skin. His Pakistani family. His religion. The fact he has a daughter by another woman. The fact our business… our business…'

'Was a competitor to your father's?' Easton suggested.

Dani wished he hadn't. She wanted to understand what Laura had been trying to say.

'I guess so, yes,' Laura said.

'How long have you known Hamed?' Dani asked.

'Seven years. We've been married two. And yes, I'm sure you can do the maths. His daughter is seven. He met me while his ex-wife was pregnant. Don't worry, I've heard it all before. And no, his parents didn't shun him for it, even if mine did.'

'And Hamed is still in Greece?' Dani asked.

A flicker of something in Laura's eyes. Hurt?

'We were visiting Hamed's cousin and his family. Poorna hasn't seen them for a couple of years. She doesn't know my parents that well, but Hamed's family are close. She was really shaken to hear what happened here, but she would have been devastated if we brought her home after less than a day of a holiday she's been looking forward to for months.'

Was that a reasonable enough explanation for why her husband had chosen to stay thousands of miles away?

'Why did you never work for your father?' Dani asked.

She realised she was pushing things with that question, given Laura's defensiveness so far, but she had to at least try.

'You never met him. Let's leave it at that.'

'Did he want you to?' Easton asked.

'He wanted all of us to, in a way. Somehow, in the end, he got lumbered with the lummox.'

She almost laughed at that. The lummox. Eric. Not the first time it had been insinuated that he wasn't the brightest of the kids, yet he was the one enmeshed in Terry's business. He was the one with a share of that business.

'Did your father, your mother even, have any enemies?'

Laura opened her mouth then shut it again. Then finally spoke after a sigh. 'There's no point in hiding it, but yes, my dad did. He was a tough businessman. It would be hard to deny that there is a long line of people who he's screwed over the years. That was his style. But you know what? I don't think he *meant* to hurt people. He just didn't care enough about the impact he had on others. Did he have enemies? Plenty of people disliked him, put it that way. Do I know of anyone who hated him so much they'd kill him, and my mum? No. I don't.'

The room fell silent as Dani took that statement in, not just the words, but the feeling behind them. Laura had shown plenty of conflicting emotion so far in this house – she'd been up and down, just like her brother had been. But that statement, about her father, was delivered so coldly. A surprise to Dani.

The conversation didn't last much longer after that. Dani knew she was already wearing Laura's patience down, and there was no point in riling her so much that she became uncooperative for whatever was to come. Dani didn't see herself as a nosey cow. Just a detective trying to do her job.

She'd back off. For now. A little.

Perhaps.

The three of them headed out to the driveway, where Dani and Easton waited on the gravel until Laura had disappeared off in her Jaguar SUV.

'Friendly,' Easton said.

'Tell me about it.'

'So basically, anyone who ever knew Terry Eccles is a suspect. Is that what she said?'

'Unfortunately that was the case already, if you think about it.'

'True.'

'And her husband staying in Greece? What do you reckon?'

'Odd.'

'Odd. And probably worth taking a look at extradition protocols, just in case.'

A step too far, too soon perhaps? 'Better safe than sorry,' Dani said regardless.

'Has Eric agreed yet when he's coming over?'

'Not yet.'

'Odd, again.'

'A little. So… did she go for it?'

'What?'

'Laura. In the office. Did she go for the safe? Or through the desk drawers where the other will had been?'

'Possibly. She was certainly more keen to search that room than any other. And more angry when she realised we'd beaten her to it.'

'Do you think she was looking for the will? Either of them?'

'I really don't know.'

Easton smiled. Smugly. 'I reckon we might have a motive after all.'

'I reckon we need to keep our options open.'

Dani moved off to her car.

She made it home within a few minutes. It was early evening and the sun was disappearing beyond the trees at the back of the house. All told it had been a long and tiring day, though at least the meeting with Laura Eccles had exposed a few additional threads to tug on.

Dani was exhausted and distracted as she stepped onto the driveway. But not so distracted as to not have spotted the car off to her right, parked just beyond the entrance to her driveway. She jerked in surprise though when the figure stepped into view from behind the car. Tall, broad. A man. Dani tensed. The man pulled his hoodie down from over his face as he moved towards her.

Despite his dishevelled appearance, the cuts and bruises to his face, Dani recognised him. Will Eccles.

'DI Stephens?'

'Will, what on earth are you doing here?'

He looked around himself nervously as he approached.

'Will, where have you been?'

A car whizzed past behind him. Dani hadn't heard it approach, and by the nervous flinch Will gave, it looked like he hadn't either. He turned his head to follow the car, and when he faced Dani again he looked all the more worried.

'Will, what's going on?'

He didn't answer. He looked back over his shoulder, to where the car had just gone. Another was approaching from that direction. More slowly. Will backtracked.

'Don't trust them,' he shouted over. 'Don't trust anything they say.'

Dani moved towards him. As she did so he looked even more nervous. The question she really wanted to ask, the one that meant the most to her in that moment, was *how do you know where I live?*

Instead, 'Will, please, let me help.'

'Ask about Elle.'

'What? Elle who?'

But he was already turning and moving quickly for the driver's door.

'Will, how can I contact you?'

He didn't answer. He was only looking at that approaching car as he ducked into the driver's seat of his VW Golf. The engine started and he glanced briefly at Dani who was rushing towards him, before he floored the engine and, tyres screeching, shot off.

Dani reached the edge of her drive. The other car went past her without stopping or slowing. Dani didn't know which way to look.

To Will. His Golf was speeding away. The taillights flicked on as he got ready to turn. Dani had just enough time to catch the plate.

She turned the other way. But the car that had gone in that direction was already out of sight.

She stayed there for only a couple more seconds. Then she spun on her heel and rushed towards her house, pulling her phone from her pocket as she went.

Chapter 19

Annie was already in bed when Terry finally made it home from the office. Another day of firefighting. Another day of dealing with idiots like Hugo, Hamed, and Eric. Couldn't he find just one person to work with who wasn't an imbecile and didn't need their hand held throughout life?

Well, there was Peter. But then, in Peter's presence, Terry had had the opposite problem recently. Often *he* felt like the fool. Which perhaps explained why he was spending less and less time around his business partner, and why he was keeping more and more from him. What had once been a solid business relationship built on friend-ship and trust and loyalty was now teetering on total collapse. Terry despised Peter all the more for it, because he knew full well that Peter blamed Terry for anything and everything that went wrong these days.

But if he could just get the Little Aston and Birm-ingham Road developments properly off the ground, everything would be back in line. Soon. It would all be sorted soon.

He locked the house up and headed for the stairs. In their bedroom, Annie was sitting up, reading in bed.

'Hey, honey,' he said.

'Hi,' she replied, without looking from her book. Even with that basic two-letter word he could tell she was unhappy with something.

Something. He knew what really.

He washed and brushed his teeth and stripped down to his boxers before he jumped into bed and scooted over to her, pressing his body up against hers.

She tutted. He ignored her and kissed her on the neck, lightly, teasingly. She closed her eyes and her mouth turned up in a slight smile. So he carried on. Placed his hand on her thigh and slowly drew it up her body, under her nightie, towards her breast.

'What happened to the money?' she said.

Terry stopped kissing her and pulled back.

'What money?' he said, rather lamely, even to his own ears.

'You know full well. Thirty grand taken out of the savings account yesterday.'

'I had to put it into the business account. There were just a few big one-offs we needed to cover before month end. It'll come back in a week or two.'

'Bullshit.'

He sat up now. Trying to act offended.

'You knew I needed that money for Henry.'

'And you knew I wasn't happy that we've become his personal charity.'

'He's your damn son, not a charity.'

'If he's that desperate he could take out a loan.'

'He could. That's not the point. I *promised* him.'

'You did. Without agreeing with me.'

She glared at him but didn't say anything.

'Suppose the money did come back...' He puckered up again and went to kiss her.

'Are you kidding?' she said, pushing him away. 'What is this? Pay for favours? You do something for me, I give you sex in return? Jesus, Terry.'

'Fuck's sake, I was just trying to lighten the mood.'

'You want to lighten the mood? Put that money back.'

'And if I don't, what? You won't sleep with me any more? This is ridiculous.'

'Damn right it is. Put the money back. Please.'

'I'm going to sleep.'

He turned over and shut his eyes. He expected her to say something else. To come back to compromise.

She didn't.

–

Terry woke early with his alarm. He had a busy morning ahead. Site visits to both Birmingham Road and the Somerton development which, after Peter's intervention, they were hoping to complete at only a minimal loss despite the previous planning issues.

Could he get some good news on just one of those fronts today?

Annie was still in bed while he ate breakfast alone, and after last night's spat, he really couldn't be bothered to go and wake her. He also had no intention of moving the money back into their savings just so she could palm a chunk of it off to Henry, never to be seen again. And his reasoning for that wasn't just because his son was a freeloader.

He was on his last mouthful of toast when his phone rang. Henry. Of course.

'Dad, I don't know what's going on—'

'Good morning, son.'

'Dad, just listen to me. That money, I really need it. Mum said—'

'Sorry, Henry. We just can't do it right now.'

'Bollocks. You've got it—'

'Have you ever considered getting a job to pay your way? Or maybe stop wasting what you've been given on alcohol and gambling.'

'You're an arsehole.'

Henry ended the call. Whatever. One day the kid might actually get it. If he'd joined Terry in the business several years ago he could have been something by now. Talk about wasted talent. Maybe the hardline approach would finally get him to see sense.

Terry was in his car, heading towards Birmingham Road when the second call of the day came through. Hugo.

Couldn't he just have a bit of peace?

'What is it?' Terry asked, even though he knew exactly why Hugo was calling.

'I thought we had a deal?'

'A deal is where two parties agree on something. What you made was a demand.'

'A demand which you haven't met. You've got until the end of today to pay me. Don't play games with me, Terry. I know you don't respect me, but perhaps this will make you realise you should.'

'You really think blackmail is going to earn my respect?'

'You've got until the end of today.'

Hugo ended the call.

These kids. How the hell had he and Peter gone so wrong as to be left with these pieces of shit?

All he needed now was for Laura to call, complaining about the mistreatment of Hamed, then Will, babbling on about his latest failed venture, and his offspring failure bingo card would be completed before it was even ten a.m.

Thankfully those calls hadn't come before Terry arrived at Birmingham Road, where Hamed had agreed to meet him. Terry was early. Yet his day wasn't about to get better, he realised, when he stepped from his car and looked over to 104 and 106, squeezed in between the new perimeter boards they'd put up around the rest of the site.

Terry's mouth hung open as he stared at the building. Not a home any more. Now 104 was nothing but a shell. Huge swathes of black rose up on the brickwork above each of the empty window openings. There was nothing left of the roof structure except the charred and still-smoking embers of a small number of joists. Even the front garden hadn't escaped the inferno, the grass and shrubs all around were frazzled and scorched brown.

'Awful, isn't it?'

A voice from behind him. He turned to see an elderly man with an elderly looking Jack Russell that was sniffing a lamppost like it was emitting a heaven-sent fragrance.

'What happened?' Terry asked.

'Who knows? Fire engines turned up about six last night. The whole thing was already ablaze by then. They worked through the night to put it out.'

Terry had no words.

'I guess you could say it's lucky the neighbouring buildings were already demolished, otherwise who knows what would have happened?'

'What happened to the family?'

He shrugged. 'Some ambulances came. I read online they got out. All except the dog. Terrible.'

He shook his head in sorrow, then walked off.

Terry looked at his watch. Where was Hamed? He waited another ten minutes, most of that time spent staring in disbelief at the house. There was still no sign of Hamed.

He bit the bullet and made the call.

'Where are you?' he said, unable to hide his irritation.

'Over in Walsall.'

'Are you serious? We agreed to meet—'

'No, I think what I said was you should head over to the site for ten a.m. You're there now, are you?'

'Yes, I'm here now, you fucking prick. What the hell have you done?'

Hamed actually laughed. 'It's all good, Terry. You wanted help with your problem. You got it. I'm meeting with Omar later to renegotiate.'

'Are you out of your mind?'

'You ask me, I think we'll get a pretty decent price after all.'

This time it was Terry's turn to hang up.

He stared back over to the charred remains. What on earth had he done?

Chapter 20

March

Dani's brain was on fire Sunday morning. It felt like everything in her life was coming to a head in one frenzied moment. There were only hours left before a charging decision had to be made on Clinton Harrison. She was neck deep in the Eccles investigation, with Will Eccles' bizarre appearance outside her home the previous evening playing heavily on her mind. Not to mention all the issues with the other siblings, the wills… the list went on. Then there was her personal life, Jason and her doubts over them starting a family. No, they weren't doubts, it was far more serious than that. And finally, Gemma, and Ben.

No. The last thing she wanted to think about right now was him.

She shook her head then pressed her fingers into her temples as though that would help clear her head, as though it would help to get rid of her pounding headache.

It didn't.

Should she try to wriggle out of one of her cases to give her some breathing space? Easton was surely capable of taking the lead on at least one of them…

'Are you ready?' McNair said.

Dani opened her eyes and looked up. McNair was hanging over her desk.

'Yeah,' Dani said.

'You look… like you haven't slept in days.'

'Thanks.'

'I wasn't saying it to be mean. I said it out of concern. Are you OK?'

Dani pulled her papers together then stood up from her chair.

No. She wouldn't palm anything off. That wasn't how she worked. She'd get the assistance she needed. But she was determined to crack both cases.

'I'm fine,' Dani said. 'Just a bit tired.'

Which was surely understandable given it was eight thirty a.m. on a Sunday morning and here they were back in the office again.

McNair gave Dani an odd look but didn't say anything more. Despite her words, Dani felt that McNair was criticising her, rather than showing genuine concern.

They headed up to the top floor to the meeting room where Chris DeMario from the CPS was already waiting for them. Coat still on, he was standing by the tall window looking to the city beyond, takeaway coffee cup in hand. He looked like he didn't think he was staying for long.

McNair lightly knocked on the door as she headed in to get his attention.

'Ah, ladies,' he said, turning around with a big, wide smile on his face.

'Good morning, Chris,' McNair said, shaking hands before they went through some obligatory banter about the sacrifices they'd made to be in the office on a Sunday morning.

They were soon all seated, DeMario's coat now removed. Dani had met him on a few occasions, but this was the first time at a weekend, and he was clearly making a point with his unshaved face and his casual clothes. Minimal changes, really, but it created quite the contrast to his usual clean-cut, supremely aloof appearance.

'Where are we at?' he asked, to Dani, more than to McNair.

'Following Asher's stunt on Friday, it's quite clear that she's going to use the media as much as she can,' Dani said. 'Whatever charge we put their way, I think they'll plead not guilty and go self-defence.'

'Off the back of a single video?' DeMario said, screwing up his face.

'As far as we know, it's just that one video, yes.'

DeMario sighed. 'But I thought you told me the other day that Asher was willing to consider a deal?' he asked, switching his focus to McNair now.

'That was the impression we originally had.'

'And have you spoken to Asher since to clarify that?'

'I tried. Several times yesterday. She's not answering calls. She knows the clock is ticking. She's forcing our hand.'

'And what about that video?' McNair asked. 'Why did Asher get it before we did?'

'I don't think there was anything underhand about it. We had a list of witnesses, and list of car registrations we were working on tracking the occupants of to gather statements and video footage. Asher got to a small number before we did.'

'How embarrassing,' DeMario said, shaking his head as he held Dani's gaze, as though staffing and funding levels of the Police Force were Dani's remit.

Dani said nothing.

'Has anything else come out of the woodwork?' DeMario asked.

'No,' Dani said, perhaps more conclusively than she should have. 'If there's anything else now, it's not because we were beaten to it, it's because we've been lied to or not given everything we've asked for.'

'So there is still a possibility, then.' A statement from DeMario.

'Possibly, but at this stage unlikely that there's something that will drastically alter the picture, I'd say.'

DeMario seemed to consider this for a few moments. 'Then it's a simple choice, isn't it?' he said.

'Is it?' McNair responded.

'Clinton Harrison killed Dylan Roberts. I'm not sure that's in dispute?'

'No.'

'And from what I've seen, no Crown lawyer in their right mind would jump to self-defence and allow him to walk away charge-free based on what we have, and that one video which casts doubt but is hardly conclusive. Unless there's something else obvious here, to suggest his actions weren't intentional, I can't see why we're even still debating it. We charge him with murder.'

'Asher will fight that hard,' McNair said. 'They'll fight for acquittal and drag everything through the press.'

'I expect so. And that's fine. But, to put it simply, the courtroom is the proper place to fight these things. We charge him, and we all get our chance in court.'

'Leaving aside an acquittal,' Dani said, 'their two routes of defence to a murder charge would be diminished responsibility and loss of control. Wouldn't—'

'Thank you, DI Stephens. I'm aware of that. Are you aware of any kind of medical condition that Mr Harrison is suffering from that could have impaired his judgement, or contributed to or prompted his actions?'

'None,' Dani said. 'He hasn't been assessed by a psychologist since his arrest, but his mental state hasn't been raised as a concern. There's nothing in his medical history to suggest he has a condition, and it's not been raised by Asher either.'

'Perhaps he *should* have been assessed.'

Dani and McNair said nothing to that. They'd certainly have to carry out a thorough assessment before any trial, but it simply hadn't been a priority to try and force that in the little time since Harrison's arrest.

'So if we take that away for now,' Dani said, 'it comes down to loss of control. On the face of it, wouldn't you say it's going to be hard for us to fight against that?'

'Because?'

'Because of the circumstances. Clinton Harrison had just witnessed his son being killed, being crushed and torn apart in front of him by a van.'

Dani shuddered at her own words. Had DeMario seen those horrific videos himself?

'I'm not saying it wasn't an awful situation for Mr Harrison,' DeMario said, 'but it really is for his defence to bring that argument. I don't mean to sound heartless, but unless you have specific evidence to show me, that negates that Clinton Harrison murdered, and intended to murder, or at least to cause serious harm to Dylan Roberts, then the charge is murder.'

'If anything, I think it's to the contrary,' McNair said.

DeMario raised an eyebrow. McNair looked to Dani and indicated for her to talk.

'You probably saw the newspaper article the other day highlighting Dylan Roberts' criminal past,' Dani said.

'I did,' DeMario said. 'Very unhelpful.'

'We've also done a lot of work unpicking Clinton Harrison's past.'

'And it doesn't make for comfortable reading,' McNair said. 'Two cases of assault and affray when he was a teenager. A dropped charge of sexual assault against a former girlfriend. A dropped charge of GBH, three years ago.'

'This wasn't picked up straight away?' DeMario asked, his tone showing his incredulity.

'It's not always as simple as typing a name into the system and hitting enter,' Dani said.

Not a great explanation for the failings of cross-Police-Force collation and storage of information, but DeMario didn't challenge her further.

'The GBH charge?' he said.

'A dispute with a former work colleague,' Dani explained. 'He was living in Manchester, working as an installation guy for a satellite TV company. He got into a dispute with a colleague and, allegedly, battered him with a wrench.'

'But the charges were dropped?'

'We haven't got to the bottom of why,' Dani said. The information she'd received had only been pulled during Saturday, by Grayling, and Dani was still working her way through all the documentation. 'But it looks like it was because the colleague actually provoked the attack. He'd been having an affair with Harrison's girlfriend, and not only goaded Harrison, but threw the first punch.'

'Self-defence,' DeMario said with a roll of his eyes.

'Both of them accepted charges for affray. Both were given community service, although Harrison got twice as much.'

'Is there any evidence yet to suggest Harrison and Roberts knew each other?'

'DI Stephens has been working on that,' McNair said.

'Nothing. Yet,' Dani said.

A sigh from DeMario. As though Dani's clarification was unsatisfactory.

'Whichever way you look at it, though, our man has a history of violence,' DeMario said. 'As tricky as it is to use that past behaviour to help our case in court, I don't think we need to discuss this any further. Do we?'

McNair nodded. 'So we're all agreed? We're charging him with murder?'

DeMario nodded in turn. Dani didn't. All eyes turned to her.

'DI Stephens?'

'Yes, I agree,' Dani said.

'Very good,' DeMario said. 'Then I'll leave it to you two to give the news to Mr Harrison.'

With that he got up, grabbed his coat and coffee, and left.

'Are you OK with this?' McNair asked Dani. That same look of concern on her face again.

'Like he said, I'm not sure we have another option right now. But I'm just not… I don't know.'

'Do you want me to do it? I can see you've got a lot on your mind.'

'Yes. Please.'

'Very well.'

McNair scooped up her things and headed for the door. Dani remained in place. Why did this still feel so wrong?

–

After a few minutes of quiet contemplation in the meeting room, Dani was back at her desk soon enough. The fact they'd come to a decision on Harrison did at least lift a slight weight off her shoulders. Now she needed to try and forget about Harrison, and concentrate on the Eccles murders.

The office was as busy as Dani had ever seen it on a Sunday morning. There was little chit-chat, everyone who was in had their game face on and was head down.

Dani went over to Easton. He had a broad smile on his face.

'Another date?' Dani asked.

'Not yet,' he said.

'So why the look?'

'We got the warrant approved. For Eccles Holdings.'

'Nice,' Dani said, giving him a high five.

'I'm heading there in a few minutes. You want to come?'

Dani kind of did. But bagging and tagging really was just that.

'No. I'll leave it in your capable hands,' she said.

'I spoke to the solicitor too,' Easton said. 'Bill Hammersmith. He remembers the Eccles family, though the will was the only matter he'd ever dealt with for them.'

'What about the rewrite?'

'News to him. Was never something he advised on, and certainly not something he had witnessed.'

'So where does that leave us?'

'Hoping we find a signed version somewhere else.'

'And if we don't?'

'Then the new will isn't valid.'

'But even if it's not valid, it was still drawn up for a reason.'

Easton didn't say anything to that.

'Any news on Eric going to Kibble House?'

'He's still not come back to me.'

Was there any point in chasing it? Probably not.

'Let me know if you find anything at the office?'

'Will do.'

Dani moved back over to her desk, but Mutambe stuck her head up over her divider before she got there. 'Do you have a minute?'

'If it's good news, you can have two.'

'It could be.'

Dani wandered over.

'I think I found who Will was referring to when you saw him yesterday. Elle Martic. Hugo Werner lives in Edgbaston. I was checking on the electoral roll for all of the people close to the Eccleses, and this came up.'

She showed Dani the piece of paper. Both Elle Martic and Hugo Werner were listed on the electoral roll at 32b Bridlington Terrace in Edgbaston.

'So she's Hugo's girlfriend?' Dani said.

'Possibly. Or flatmate. Or something.'

She'd wanted to speak to Hugo and his father Peter anyway, so this was certainly an interesting turn. Why had Will Eccles mentioned Elle's name to Dani? Why had Will gone to Dani's house at all?

'I've done a few more searches for her name. I found a profile on Instagram that is almost definitely her.' Mutambe tapped away on her keyboard to bring up what she'd found. 'There're no recent posts on here, she certainly wasn't a prolific poster anyway, but there are a few pictures from around the Midlands area. A few references to spending time with her *bae* and the like. No actual pictures of Hugo to properly confirm this is the right person, though.'

'Pull that picture up,' Dani said.

Mutambe did. The picture filled the screen. Elle on a sunny day, standing in front of a fountain in Florence. Greenery all around her. A short summer dress exposed her long, slender legs. Designer handbag, shoes. She was more than glamorous, she looked like a supermodel. And by the flicker in her eye, and her stance, she knew it.

'Judging by her name, and some of her posts, I'm not sure she's British, but I can't find any kind of employment history, or immigration documents or anything like that.'

'OK. Well, it's a start.'

'You also asked me to look into Will's car?'

Dani had. She herself had performed a few basic searches. Had found that the registration appeared genuine, but that the car was currently registered to a second-hand dealership in Sandwell.

'I called the dealership and they confirmed they'd sold it to a William Eccles a few days ago. He paid in cash.'

'Did they take any details from him?'

'The order form listed Kibble House as his address.'

Which wasn't very helpful in finding him.

'What on earth is he up to?'

'A good question. And I might be able to help with that. I used CCTV and ANPR records to see if I could track his car around the area. I found it twice heading into a Tesco in Sandwell this past week. I've tracked the movements from the store and narrowed down where he might be staying to a cluster of about four roads.'

'Unless he slipped through a black spot in the cameras?'

'I don't think so.' Mutambe brought up a map of the area. 'Here's the Tesco store. Here are the streets where I think he's possibly staying, about one and a half miles away. There are cameras covering all the main roads the other side, so if he was simply driving through I would have picked him up.'

'What about that one,' Dani said, pointing to the screen.

'It's one-way. So, unless he was specifically trying to fool us, by travelling the wrong way down a one-way to avoid cameras…'

'It's possible, though.'

Mutambe looked disheartened.

'I guess so.'

'But you're right, probably unlikely. We'll check out those streets. See if we can spot the car.'

Mutambe perked up again. 'Now?'

'Not quite. First we're going to go and pay a visit to Hugo Werner.'

'You want me to come.'

'Absolutely.'

Mutambe beamed.

Chapter 21

Edgbaston was only a short drive from HQ. Most famous for the international cricket ground of the same name, the historic area also contained the city's Botanical Gardens, as well as being home to some of its wealthiest people. That said, it was very much an area of clashing cultures, with its boundaries bordering on some of the most deprived parts of the city, and, depending on exactly where the boundary lines were considered to be, also containing one of the city's most frequented red-light districts.

Not that Dani expected Hugo Werner to live near there, even before Mutambe gave her thoughts.

'I know Bridlington Terrace,' she said as Dani navigated the myriad of traffic lights heading out of the city centre towards Hagley Road. 'Me and Gael lived in a flat over the road from there when they were building it.'

Dani had heard of Gael before in passing, though realised as they drove now that she'd never met him, nor did she really know much of Mutambe's private life really. Mutambe had been with the team for a little over twelve months, and the fact was that Dani had rarely worked closely with her, one on one. And, the other fact was, Dani really wasn't that good at getting to know her colleagues on a personal level. Was that just another example of how her TBI had changed her personality, made her less sociable and less empathetic? Or had she always been like that? There was a reason, she guessed, why many had long thought of Dani as the next hard-nosed DCI within the team.

'Gael's a paramedic?' Dani said. She thought she could recall someone saying that.

'Yeah. At Queen Elizabeth. We met when he was training there.'

'A paramedic and a detective. Like ships passing in the night.'

Mutambe laughed, though the angst in her face suggested a certain strain. 'Something like that. At least with his shifts you get to plan ahead. Kind of. With our job, you just never know.'

'Yeah.'

Dani had a flashing thought of Jason. More than likely he'd be sitting at home now. TV on, watching sport, or perhaps in the back room – the sun-trap room – listening to music. Sunday morning, alone. She suddenly felt immensely bad for him. They'd barely spoken all weekend. They really needed to tonight.

'Anyway, my point was, I know Bridlington Terrace. I remember looking at the units coming on the market when it was going up. Virtually nothing there was less than eight hundred grand. The top properties were in the millions. I checked out 32b earlier. Wanna know how much Hugo Werner paid for it?'

'We're assuming he paid for it.'

'Yeah, true; after all, how can people afford a 2.5 million property when they're in their early twenties? That's how old he was then.'

'Two-point-five?'

'Yep.'

204

'As you'd expect, I've heard it's popular with footballers and the like. Particularly those coming to the area from overseas. You don't even get a garden for your money.'

A couple of minutes later the development came into view through the gaps in the trees. All set behind at huge red-brick wall, Bridlington Terrace consisted of a cluster of buildings, three to eight storeys tall. All modern, all glass-rich. A mixture of high-end apartments and town-houses. Dani pulled off the road and into the entranceway where they were met with a huge pair of wrought-iron security gates. A CCTV camera was perched on top of the pillared columns either side.

Dani was about to open her window to press on the intercom when a Porsche approached from the other side. The gates slowly swung open. The Porsche rolled out. Dani turned to Mutambe and shrugged. Then slipped inside as the gates closed.

Beyond the gates it became more clear what the residents were getting for their money. No private gardens, but a hell of a lot of beautifully landscaped and mani-cured grounds, with pergolas and patios and seating dotted around the place. Everything about the buildings, their design, highlighted that they were high end.

They headed around the twisting paths, a little aimlessly to start with, until Mutambe pointed.

'That's his car,' she said, referring to the dazzlingly bright purple Lamborghini Urus.

'You have been doing your homework,' Dani said. Mutambe looked flattered.

'I saw it on Instagram. Custom paint job, apparently.'

'Looks more like an accident to me. Like the swirls you get from an oil slick.'

Dani took the parking space two away, giving plenty of room so as to not nick the far more expensive motor. As she stepped out she glanced around, looking for a clue as to where 32b was.

'Over here, I think,' Mutambe said, pointing to the eight-storey block in front of them – the tallest, and most grand of all the buildings there.

They moved over and sure enough, 32b was one of only eight buttons on the intercom panel. Dani pressed it and waited. She noticed there was a small camera within the fixture.

'Yeah?'

A smooth male voice. Dani looked to the camera.

'Hugo Werner?'

'Yeah. Who is it?'

'DI Stephens and DC Mutambe from West Midlands Police. Can we come in?'

A short pause.

'We just want to talk to you about Terry and Annie Eccles.'

A longer pause. Mutambe and Dani shared a look.

'There's not a back entrance, is there?' Dani said, quietly, and facing away from the camera.

'I don't think so,' Mutambe whispered in return.

But then why would Hugo run off in the first place?

Finally, 'Come up.'

There was a buzz and a click as the locks released and Dani pushed the door open. They walked into a sump-tuous inner atrium. Glitzy marble floor, water feature, strip LEDs all over. A single elevator. They headed inside. Floors one to six were labelled. Dani guessed on six. When the doors opened, and they moved into a tiny corridor, she realised 32b was the only apartment on this level. Given there was another storey above them, that already gave a clue as to just how big the home was likely to be.

The door opened as Dani and Mutambe approached, to reveal Hugo Werner. In his late twenties, his skin was bronzed, his hair neatly coiffed on top, trimmed almost to the skin on the sides. He wore leg-hugging trousers and a tight white shirt that had three buttons undone to reveal even more bronzed skin. He looked like he wanted to be an Instagram model, though it was all a bit forced, and his face looked more than a little weary.

'Why are you here?' he said.

Not suspicion, more nerves. For some reason Dani had expected more confidence, more bravado. He looked more like a child about to be reprimanded by a school teacher.

'Perhaps we can explain inside?' Dani said.

Hugo seemed to mull this over, before eventually nodding, and stepping aside.

Dani had to admit, 2.5 million got more than just an apartment. Hugo Werner's home was huge. Probably as big on the inside as Kibble House, though far more modern, and quite clearly a bachelor's haven. Who knew how many bedrooms it contained on the top floor of the duplex – or indeed why Hugo would need that number – but the open-plan living and dining space he took Dani and Mutambe to was sleek, plush and gargantuan.

Dani and Mutambe settled on a corner sofa that could have seated seven. For all its looks, though, it was uncomfortably low, and soft. Dani may as well have been sat on the floor. Hugo perched on the edge of the opposite sofa – a carbon copy, except lacking a corner.

Between them was a sleek black glass-and-chrome coffee table. Nothing on it except for a glass of water, though there was a big wipe mark streaked across the glass top, not yet fully dried. Clearly Hugo had spent the minute or two that it had taken Dani and Mutambe to get up in the lift cleaning up something.

Interesting.

'Mr Werner,' Dani said, 'are you on drugs?'

That seemed to knock him. His worried face dropped for a second – dismay – before he battled whatever inner turmoil was going on in his head to try and put on a brave and confident exterior again.

'Excuse me?' he said.

'Your behaviour. The way you're rubbing your hands together like that. Tapping your foot. You look like you're sweating, and it's pretty bright in here but your pupils are—'

'I've got a fever,' he said. 'I've taken a few paracetamol.' He pointed over to the kitchen counter where indeed there was a packet of pills. 'And I'm nervous, that's all.'

'Why are you nervous?'

'Because I've got two police officers in my home. That's not normal, is it?'

'Perhaps not.'

'I'm not on drugs,' he said again.

'I wasn't suggesting you were in trouble if you were. It would just be an important point for me to note.'

'I'm not. What do you want to talk about?'

'I can only presume you've heard about what happened to Terry and Annie Eccles.'

He shook his head in apparent despair. 'Of course. It's horrible.'

'We've obviously been keen to speak to family members, but seeing as you and your dad were business partners with Terry, we wanted to speak with you too.'

Hugo nodded, but didn't say anything.

'How long had you worked with Terry?'

'Since I was eighteen.'

'What's your main role in the business?'

'Role? I guess, I'm, well, me and Eric run specific projects. We help out with finances too. That sort of thing.'

'But you're a director, aren't you? A shareholder?'

'Yeah. Me and Eric both are.'

'So you're pretty senior.'

'I guess so.'

'You guess so?'

'I am senior. That's what I mean.'

'But you don't have a specific role. A specific job title.'

His face soured now. It was good to see something other than rabbit-in-headlights. 'Commercial Director. That's my title.'

'Fancy. How is the business doing?'

'We have challenges.'

'Such as?'

'Sorry, I thought you wanted to ask about Terry and Annie.'

'That's what I am doing,' Dani said. 'I'm trying to understand about the business Terry ran. It was obviously a big part of his life. Yours too.'

'Yeah. It is.'

'How did you find working with the Eccles?'

'Honestly?'

'I like honesty.'

'Terry was all right. Old-fashioned, in his outlook, in his methods. But he knew what he was doing. He was good to work for, if a little erratic.'

'Erratic?'

'Just… he did things his way. That's all.'

'And Eric?'

'Eric's fine too.'

Though the way he said it suggested Eric wasn't fine.

'Didn't Will Eccles work for you at one point as well?' Mutambe asked.

'He did. It was a disaster.'

'Because?'

'Because Will Eccles is even more unhinged than his brother.'

As soon as he said it, his body tensed, like he couldn't believe the words had actually come out of his mouth.

'Unhinged?' Dani said. 'You think both Will and Eric are unhinged? Can you explain that?'

'No. That's not what I meant. Not really. Will is a troublemaker. That's all. And Eric… he's got good intentions. I think all he ever wanted to do was to make his dad happy, and proud. A bit of a kiss arse, really. Unfortunately he just… he just…'

'Makes mistakes?'

'He means well.'

Hugo's phone vibrated in his pocket. He lifted it out – a huge wedge of a phone, clad in a shiny gold shell. He stared at the screen then cancelled the call and put the phone on the table.

'Sorry. You were saying?'

'Does Elle Martic still live here?' Mutambe said, looking around the room.

Dani certainly hadn't noticed anything feminine about the place. No designer shoes or handbags lying around, which she imagined someone like Elle certainly would have. No pictures of her even.

'Why are you asking about Elle?' he said, looking genuinely confused.

'Does Elle live here?' Dani asked again.

'She never did.'

'She's on the electoral roll,' Mutambe said, 'registered at this address.'

The look on his face suggested he didn't know this.

'I don't know why. We dated for a few months. She spent a lot of time here, but… she never lived here. I never asked her to, anyway. I've no idea why she'd be registered here.'

'So you're not seeing her any more?'

'I haven't seen or spoken to her for a few weeks at least.'

'Why's that?'

'Because we split up. It's not a big story.'

'Do you know where she is now?'

'I haven't a clue.'

There was a click and then a bang from behind them. The front door opening and closing? Heavy footsteps coming down the hallway. Hugo got to his feet first. Dani and Mutambe did so in unison, just as a red-faced man burst into view.

'What the hell is going on?' he slammed.

Similarly dressed to Hugo, although in a style more in keeping with his age, equally well-groomed and with the same tanned skin, the man was short and just a little overweight. Dani recognised him. Peter Werner.

'Mr Werner, I'm—'

'Don't even start. You don't come here, speaking to my son—'

'I'm not sure what you think we've done wrong?'

'Don't take the fucking piss, lady. I know you. DI Stephens. Right? I know all about you. Even before I got a call from my lawyer this morning to say there's a warrant giving you and your colleagues full access to *my* business. And now you're coming after my son? Who the hell do you think you are?'

OK, so perhaps the warrant explained why Peter was so het up.

'I don't know what your game is—'

'Then perhaps let me explain,' Dani said, raising her voice sufficiently to hopefully get him to listen.

He paused. Looked seriously pissed off. But he also didn't bite back.

'You obviously know my name, and this is my colleague DC Mutambe. We're detectives investigating the murders of Terry and Annie Eccles. Particularly brutal murders, I might add. We're taking this matter incredibly seriously, and as a matter of course we're reaching out to anyone who knew the couple well. Clearly, you and your son have a close relationship with the Eccles family, so it's perfectly obvious that we'd want to speak to you both as part of our investigation.'

'You think? Then perhaps you should have done that before concocting your damn warrant to get access to my business records, as if that's got any relevance? You might have found us a bit more open.'

'I apologise if our timing offended you, that wasn't the intention.'

'I couldn't give a fuck about your intentions. You messed up. You want to speak to me and my son? You do it properly, with our lawyer present. Or you don't do it at all.'

Dani turned to Hugo.

'Don't you look at him,' Peter shouted. '*I'm* telling you.'

'I'm sorry,' Hugo said to her.

'It's time for you to leave,' Peter said.

And Dani knew she really had little choice.

Chapter 22

'Do you believe what Hugo said?' Mutambe asked Dani as they drove away from Edgbaston and towards Sandwell. The low sun in front of them glowed with warm orange light that crept through tree branches and through the gaps between buildings. Dani pulled the visor on the windscreen down to shield her eyes.

'About which part?'

'About Elle. About her never having lived with him. About her having simply left one day?'

'No. Not really.'

Hugo had given them a phone number and email address for her, but he'd already suggested she was using neither any more.

'Can you set up something with Missing Persons and see if Elle has been on their radar at all? Otherwise carry on some further enquiries to see if we can figure out where she is. The fact Will Eccles tipped us off about her suggests there's a story here that we've not yet been told.'

'Let's hope we find Will then.'

'Indeed.'

'And you were right about the drugs.'

Dani glanced over at Mutambe. Her face was passive as she stared out of the windscreen.

'I've seen it enough to know the look,' she said. 'The behaviour traits.'

Dani wondered what she meant by that. Personal experiences? She decided not to ask.

'You think he's a big user?' Dani asked.

'There were no needle marks or anything like that, so probably not heroin. My guess would be coke.'

'My thought, too. Let's keep an open mind. Do what we can to find out without alerting him we're looking at him closely. I don't think Peter Werner would take it too kindly, and I'd rather at least try to keep him onside while we go through the business records.'

'Judging by my first impression of him, perhaps it's already too late for that.'

'Perhaps.'

Five p.m. had come and gone by the time they reached Sandwell. The Tesco car park seemed as good a place as any to stop, and they made their way on foot towards the four streets Mutambe had marked out earlier.

Sandwell was nestled between Birmingham and Wolverhampton city centres, and the housing in the area was typically modest in price. The majority of homes around them as they walked were either traditional two- and three-bed terraces, or blocks of flats and apartments largely from the 1960s and 1970s. There were a few newer apartment blocks too, but they were affordable rather than luxury.

'Not quite as nice as his place in the Jewellery Quarter,' Mutambe said.

'Yeah,' Dani agreed. So what had brought Will out here?

They spent more than twenty minutes walking around until they finally spotted the car, parked on the road outside one of the newer apartment blocks in the area. Ten storeys tall. A combination of engineered red brick, grey aluminium, and larch cladding that was only just starting to weather.

Across the other side of the road was a run of terraces, the ground floors occupied by a mishmash of small businesses and takeaways, the top floors either storage rooms for the businesses or poky flats.

'My guess is the apartment block,' Dani said, looking up at the building.

'What do you want to do?' Mutambe asked. 'There's a cafe over the road. I'm happy to sit and stake out.'

Dani thought for a moment. 'Possibly. What we don't want is to spook him. We want to speak to him, not arrest him. The aim of being here is to find out where he's living so we've a means of contacting him.'

'So?'

'So he knows me. He came to my house. He wants to talk. But he's clearly wary, on edge about something. I'm worried that if he sees me here, if he realises we're tracking him, he's just going to run.'

'But he hasn't seen me before.'

Unless he's watching us right now, Dani thought. She shivered slightly.

'No. He hasn't, as far as we're aware. I'm happy for you to stay and keep watch for a while.'

'I'm happy to stay,' Mutambe said.

Dani thought about it for a few moments. But really what was the worst that could happen? Mutambe was offering to give up the rest of her Sunday to help out.

'You'll get home OK?' Dani asked.

Mutambe laughed like it was a silly question. 'I've been stranded further afield than this before.'

Another interesting comment from Mutambe that Dani really wanted to probe a bit more. She didn't.

'Thanks,' she said. 'But keep in touch.'

'I will.'

Mutambe headed off to the cafe. Dani took one more look around her, one more look up at the apartment block, then turned to retrace her steps to the car.

–

The journey back to Sutton Coldfield went in a flash. Largely because Dani spent the entire time on the phone. Grayling, then Easton. Grayling had nothing new to report on Harrison and Roberts. Despite all the digging she'd carried out into the various people Dani had spoken to or taken pictures of, and the vehicles at the garage Harrison worked at, plus the efforts in trying to figure out where Roberts' girlfriend had gone and why, Grayling had turned up nothing new of note. Both Harrison and Roberts had troubled pasts, the police now knew, but there was still no hint of a link between the two men, and nothing to suggest that Harrison's attack on Roberts was anything other than a moment of madness fuelled by severe grief.

Was the answer that simple?

Even if it was, Dani still didn't know how she felt about the situation, how much she wanted to fight for the murder conviction, how much she wanted to fight whatever Asher was planning to throw the police's way.

The call to Easton was slightly more positive. He'd been at the office of Eccles Holdings Limited, helping a team to box and bag up documents, computers and anything else they saw fit. That had surprisingly gone

217

without a hitch. Peter Werner – hot-headed – had initially been there, before he'd abruptly left. No doubt because of a message he'd received from Hugo to say the police were with him. Cheeky bugger. Dani hadn't realised Hugo had done that until his dad had turned up at Bridlington Terrace.

It was telling that Peter had deemed it more important to race across the city to pull the police away from his son than to stay at the office during a police raid, but also that Hugo saw his dad as his guardian. Hugo was a grown man. A wealthy grown man, yet apparently, he couldn't fight his own battles.

Or was there something else?

Dani didn't know the answer, although she was determined to figure it out. As she arrived home, though, she tried her best to put all thoughts of work to the back of her mind. The weekend had gone by in a blur. Poor Jason had been sat in the house alone for most of it, which would have been shitty for him even if there hadn't been the angst between them already. If she could at least switch off from work for the rest of the evening, before it began in earnest again on Monday morning...

She stepped out of her car. A strange sense of déjà vu washed over her when movement caught her attention at the edge of the driveway.

No. Not déjà vu. This really had happened before – last night when she'd arrived home.

She whipped her head around. A darkly dressed figure bore down on her, wearing a hood that covered their face. Behind the figure a car door shut. The car. A black BMW. Another figure next to it. Rushing Dani's way too.

She back-pedalled, reaching into her bag as she went. Reaching for what? Her phone? The spray she'd carried for years but never once used?

She fumbled. Went to turn to rush for the front door instead.

She had no chance.

Dani turned again as the nearest of the two swung a baseball bat up behind his shoulder. Dani cowered and threw her arm up to protect her face...

The second man barged into her. The force sent her scuttling and she lost her footing and clattered into her car and to the deck.

The bat came down. Her arm went up.

SMASH.

Dani screamed in pain. But the scream didn't last long because a foot launched into her chest and pushed the wind from her lungs. Another two shots to the gut and Dani was doubled over in pain, face down on the tarmac.

She tried to move and took another blow from the bat to her back.

'This is just a warning,' came a gruff male voice. 'You ask too many questions, you stupid bitch. You need to stop.'

Another boot to her side. Dani writhed and groaned.

'You won't get another warning.'

'Do you understand?' said the second man.

'Dani!'

Jason.

'Get the fuck away from her!' he shouted.

What was he doing? As much as she needed help, she willed for him to back down.

Where was he? Her brain was so fuzzy she couldn't even focus to see him.

There was a horrible laugh. A cackle.

'What you gonna do, you fucking cripple?'

Dani squeezed her eyes shut. Pleaded in her head for Jason to just go back inside.

'Police,' she heard Jason say before giving the address.

She still couldn't see properly but she could hear the man close to her, could feel his breath on her skin. He was crouched down right by her side.

'Remember what I said.'

He was close. Completely unfazed by Jason.

Then she heard footsteps. Heading away. Car doors opening and closing. Engine on. Revs.

Then silence.

Dani sighed.

They were gone.

Chapter 23

An ambulance came. Two squad cars. Easton. They all wanted to help. Dani just wanted to be left alone.

She was angry, scared, ashamed. More than anything she was embarrassed.

Aside from Easton, the other police officers were all outside, doing who knew what. Dani had moved inside, to the lounge, with one of the two paramedics. The last thing she wanted was the neighbours gawking.

Well, they were already gawking, but at least inside the house she was out of their sight.

'You'll need an X-ray to confirm if there's a stress fracture,' the paramedic said, letting go of Dani's swollen limb where there was already a lump the size of a tennis ball protruding from her forearm.

'No,' Dani said. 'I'm not going to hospital now.'

The paramedic didn't look impressed.

'If it doesn't feel right in a few days, I'll go then,' Dani said.

Easton came into the room with Jason by his side.

'One of the neighbours confirmed the car reg Jason got,' Easton said. 'I've checked and that reg actually belongs to a BMW 1 series registered to a guy in Glasgow. His car is on his drive, exactly where it should be. A local copper confirmed it. So that doesn't really leave us anywhere, other than the car here is running fake plates. Most likely it was stolen.'

Dani shut her eyes. She really didn't want to put herself back in the moment of the attack, but if they had any hope of finding those two cowardly bastards then she had to. She tried to picture the scene, tried desperately to think of anything useful. Anything about the appearance of the attackers. Their voices. The words they used. She'd already gone over this twice over with Easton, but had she missed something?

No. She really didn't think so.

'I just need to be alone now,' Dani said. 'With Jason.'

Both Jason and Easton looked unsure about that.

'I think I'm done then,' the paramedic said, finishing packing up his things.

'Thank you,' Dani said.

He headed on his way. Jason sat down next to Dani. Easton remained hovering.

'Seriously, Aaron, there's nothing else you can do here.'

He still didn't look sure. 'I can arrange for a squad car to stay outside the house—'

'No,' Dani said.

'Thanks, Aaron,' Jason said. 'I think that'd be useful.'

Easton looked from Jason back to Dani. 'I'll speak to you tomorrow.'

Then he walked out.

'You didn't have to do that,' Dani said to Jason, more bitterly than she'd intended.

'It's for both of us,' he said. 'I'm hardly good security for you any more.'

A burst of emotion threatened to derail her at those words. Dani had always thought of herself as a strong and capable woman. She didn't *need* a male guardian. Yet, in many ways, Jason had been just that for her in the past. He'd put himself in harm's way more than once – complete disregard for his own wellbeing for the sake of her. She loved that about him.

To see the doubt in his eyes now, the realisation that he no longer was physically capable of defending her how he wanted to... it was heartbreaking.

'Just for tonight,' Dani said.

Jason nodded. He sat back on the sofa and sighed. Dani did the same. They both turned to look at one another, their faces only inches apart. There was a strange vibe between them. God, how she missed just sitting with him, talking, not talking.

'Who was it?' Jason asked.

'I really have no idea. But it feels like I'm stumbling onto something big, doesn't it?'

He sighed. 'When I heard you scream... I just didn't know what to do.'

He put his hand onto her leg. She placed her hand over his.

'You did what you could,' she said. 'You stopped them attacking me. You called the police.'

He looked away from her.

'How many more times do we have to go through this?' he said.

He was right to question it. They'd both been through so much in their pursuit of justice over the years. Dani had been nearly killed by her own brother. Jason had twice nearly been killed as he stood by her side – first at the hands of serial killer Ethan Grant, secondly, and more recently, in their old home in Harborne at the hands of Damian Curtis.

Jason – likely to be permanently disabled because of that encounter – would carry the weight of that attack for the rest of his life. He'd saved Dani that day. But at what cost? They'd moved from that house soon after because the memories were too raw and painful. Tonight's attack was far less severe, but had it changed how Dani felt about their new home too?

'You've had a rough few days,' Jason said. 'Why don't we get away for a couple of nights? Maybe you need time to clear your head, and who knows if you've heard the last of—'

'I can't do that,' Dani said without even thinking.

He caught her eye again. He had a hard look on his face now. 'You *can*. But you don't want to. And that's what I don't understand.'

'I can't. Not while there's so much going on.'

'Dani, look at you. You were lucky tonight, but this was so close to going horribly wrong. What does it take?'

'But it didn't go horribly wrong. I've got a sore arm and a sore chest and a bruised ego, but—'

'Would you listen to yourself?' He was angry now. 'This isn't just about you. It's not about your damn cases. It's about us. Our lives.'

'What do you want me to do? I can't just drop everything—'

'Why not? You just drop me whenever you're busy.'

'That's not fair.'

'Isn't it? Where've you been the last two days? Where've you been the last few nights? Not just physically but mentally too.'

'Jason, I'm not doing this right now.'

He huffed and pulled himself to his feet.

'Yeah. And that's the problem,' he said, glaring down at her. 'It's never the right time for us any more, is it?'

Dani opened her mouth to bite back at that, but Jason was already moving for the door.

Chapter 24

November last year

The Birmingham Road blaze had made it onto the local news. Terry wasn't sure why, it wasn't that remarkable, really, and a small part of him wondered whether the prominence being given to the story was due to someone having called the incident in to the paper. Someone trying to deliberately make his life uncomfortable. Hugo, perhaps? But then Hugo had something to lose too if the development was scuppered.

Omar?

That was more likely. Hamed had since confirmed that Omar had agreed to sell after all. For the original valuation. Not a bad price for the landlord considering what he was selling was, in the end, nothing more than a brick shell. He was also having to fork out to rehouse the now dog-less family, though Terry had no doubt that Omar would get his recompense through insurance.

Terry and Hamed had not only saved themselves more than two hundred thousand, they now had the opportunity to push forward the development with gusto, as long as Terry could get the final plans over the line with the council.

Was any of that even the point, though? What about that poor family? Yes, Terry had been desperate for them to move out, but he'd wanted it done amicably, not by putting their lives at risk.

Their lives, and *his*. What if the police tied the blaze back to him? He hadn't yet had the chance to speak explicitly with Hamed about how far removed he was from whoever had set the house alight. Most likely a bunch of kids, he assumed. They'd better keep their damn mouths shut.

Did Laura know anything about Hamed's ways of doing business?

Terry needed to think carefully about how to broach that with her. Was there even such a way he could do it so as to drive a wedge between the married couple? A way to bring her back closer to him, and leave that shady bastard out on his own, where he belonged?

Terry crossed his fingers on the steering wheel as he drove, as though that would help the thought become reality.

Laura and Hamed would have to wait. So too would Henry. Terry had a more pressing concern to deal with now. Hugo Werner. Following the youngster's ambush at the Little Aston development the previous month, he'd laid bare his demands for his silence. Twenty thousand a month. The little shit. Terry would never have considered such an attempt at underhandedness in the past... but now? If it meant keeping everything afloat? Did it?

He arrived outside the gates to Bridlington Terrace just before two p.m. He was here unannounced. For more than one reason.

He slipped in through the open gates behind another car, and was similarly lucky with the door to the building that housed 32b. Apparently, the wealthy residents around here had more money than security sense. Oh well.

Terry headed up to the sixth floor in the lift. He hated this place. He'd been a couple of times before. Yes, he and Annie lived in an expensive house in Four Oaks, a house that was worth over 2 million pounds, but theirs was a house with class, a family home where they'd brought up four kids. This place? Terry saw few redeeming qualities either in the properties, or the residents.

Though he would admit he was envious of the developer who'd been lucky enough to pull this place off. Given the eye-watering prices of the properties, they'd no doubt made millions out of the development.

Birmingham Road would be Terry's equivalent. His crowning glory before retirement. He was so close to finally getting it moving…

But Birmingham Road wasn't why he was here. Hugo had no idea of the issues with that development. Thankfully. Otherwise he would surely have found a way to squeeze Terry over that too.

Terry stepped out of the lift and over to the apartment's front door. He knocked on the solid oak fixture and waited. He briefly wondered what he'd do if there was no answer. How he'd love to get inside and go through Hugo's space. He was sure he'd find something to hold against him, to even the playing field a little.

But no, Terry could hear the tap, tap of footsteps the other side. The clunk of the door handle being pushed down. Then the door opened.

And there she was. Elle.

The other reason he'd wanted to come here.

She wore gym gear. Figure-hugging. Figure-accentuating. Gym gear? Could have been beach gear. The top was nothing more than a bra, cleavage and all.

The shorts… short was the right word. Her face? Well, she hardly looked like it had been a strenuous workout.

All in all, she looked incredible. Irresistible.

'Terry! How nice to see you.'

'Elle, you too. Is Hugo in?'

His heart was pounding, like it had when he was a teenager speaking to a hot girl. *Get a grip, moron*, he told himself.

'Hugo? No, he's at work.'

'You expecting him back any time soon?'

'I don't think so. Probably not until five or six. Unless he said he was meeting you here?'

'Not exactly.'

She glanced at her glitzy watch.

'But it seems silly that you came all this way for nothing. I'm not busy if you want a quick drink?'

The look she gave him… What on earth was that look? He knew what he wanted it to be. He could feel the movement in his trousers.

'Yeah,' he said. 'Why not.'

Chapter 25

November last year

Nothing untoward had happened that first time Terry had been alone with Elle in Hugo's apartment. *Hugo's* apartment. Because although she was living there, it was very definitely still his space, not hers. Though he supposed she couldn't grumble – she was living there rent-free after all. But that wasn't to say her time in the plush abode wasn't without issue.

Nothing untoward had happened between Terry and Elle the second time he'd been there, alone with her, either. Though bloody hell had he wanted it to. They'd sat on the same sofa. For over an hour. Closer to each other than the first time.

What would it take?

When he received the call from her, several days later, to say she really needed some company, he didn't even hesitate.

Third time lucky, after all.

No, he couldn't think like that. He wasn't a damn teenager experiencing puppy love, he was a grown, married man.

Yet he still rushed over there at her beck and call. But only because this time she'd sounded upset on the phone. What was that about?

He was at Bridlington Terrace less than thirty minutes later. Rain pelted down. It'd been bright and sunny first thing and he'd gone out in nothing but his shirt and trousers and a light jacket even though it was November. Dark clouds had closed in before lunch, and since then it'd been the classic sunshine and showers with blue skies one minute, and thick clouds the next dumping an inexplicably large volume of rain. He was caught in the latter as he rushed from his car to the building entrance. His shirt and the front of his trousers were already soaked through by the time the door was unlocked.

He headed up in the lift, taking the few seconds in there to shake himself down and make his hair look less like it'd been plastered to his scalp. He just about managed it.

Elle was waiting at the open front door of the apartment. Joggers. A tight strappy top. Even such simple clothes and she looked sublime. Though it was clear by the lines etched on her usually perfect face that something was wrong.

'You OK?' he said.

She didn't say anything. She moved forwards, head down and sank her head into his chest as she wrapped her arms around his waist.

'Elle, what happened?'

She sniffled, but still didn't say a word. Terry slowly brought his arms around her waist too. Then they stood there as the moments passed, Terry torn as to what he should say or do next.

Eventually she pulled back from him. The make-up around her eyes had smudged. She'd left a dark patch on his chest.

'I'm so sorry,' she said, cupping her mouth with her hand. 'And look at you, you're soaked through.'

'I got caught in a downpour.'

She looked down at herself and laughed. 'And I'm soaked too.'

She wasn't. She was barely damp.

She caught his eye and smiled.

'Thank you, Terry. I really needed that.'

'Are you OK?' he asked.

'It's just been a horrible day.'

'Do you want to talk about it?'

She nodded. 'But first, let's get you dried off.'

She held out her hand to him. He didn't hesitate in taking it.

—

Was he disappointed? Not really. Was he relieved? In a way. He'd never had an affair before, had never cheated on Annie even with a kiss. But he'd never met anyone quite like Elle before either.

No, he wasn't disappointed that, after her invitation for him to remove his shirt, that they ended up back on the sofa once more, albeit he with one of Hugo's shirts on as a replacement. Honestly, he was just glad to be there with her.

'He's just so… unpredictable,' she said as she wiped at her face with a tissue. She'd already cleared up the smudges, but she looked like she was on the verge of becoming teary once more. 'One minute he's up, the next minute he's down.'

Terry nodded, but didn't really know what to say.

'When I say down, I mean really down.'

Her voice mesmerised him. Her accent, so soft, almost perfect English but just with the slightest lilt to show she wasn't native, but which made everything she said sound all the more intriguing. He could listen to her all day.

He shook his head to remove the thought. He was supposed to be listening properly, not just gawking at her.

'I've seen some of the signs myself,' Terry said.

Her ears pricked up. 'You have?'

'I'm no expert, but his mood swings worry me. I've tried to speak to Peter about it, but he just says Hugo's under pressure.'

'Aren't we all?'

'You got that right.'

'It's not just mood swings. I think... it might be more serious than that. I was reading up about bipolar disorder, and... I really think that might be it.'

They both went silent for a few moments, holding each other's eye contact. Bipolar? Terry didn't know about that. What he did know was that Hugo had a long and dark history with alcohol and drugs. Peter had always played down his son's problems, but did this show that the young man's lack of control was on a downward spiral?

'It could be that,' Terry said. It could, couldn't it? Though what did it say about him that he was begging for the truth to be that Hugo was troubled. How in that moment he was thinking how it would be so good for his own position for Hugo to have a real-life condition, whether mental illness or addiction or both. 'Have you talked to him about it?'

She scoffed. 'He's too manly to talk about feelings. Even if there was something seriously wrong he wouldn't admit to it. I don't know what to do.'

She looked genuinely scared all of a sudden.

'You don't have to worry,' Terry said. 'I'll be here for you.'

'I know you are. Now. But… what if that's not enough?'

'How do you mean?'

She looked away and gently rubbed at the skin at her throat. 'This morning… he was so angry. I don't even know why.' She returned her gaze to him. 'I hadn't done anything. We hadn't argued. He just started to get mad. He got so mad at me. I didn't even know how to react, and that just made him even more angry. He grabbed me, around my neck.'

Terry clenched his teeth now as anger bubbled up. Hugo really was a sorry excuse for a man.

'I didn't know what to think. I was so scared.'

The tears were definitely welling once more.

He shuffled over on the sofa, and she shuffled closer to him. He wrapped his arm around her and pulled her close and she nestled her head on his shoulder. Her hand went to his thigh, then they sat like that in silence for minutes. Not a word spoken. No words needed.

Eventually Terry tilted his head to look down at her. She tilted to look up at him. Then she reached forwards and planted her lips on his.

He didn't resist. How could he?

How could he ever say no to *her*?

Chapter 26

March

Dani slept horrendously. Another unfortunate consequence of Jason's physical frailty was that he always slept flat on his back. It was the only position he could remain in comfortably for a period of time. Which meant he snored. A lot. Dani had grown used to it, and at other times, when she was less stressed, less troubled, she could ignore the noise and sleep through regardless.

Not last night. They hadn't spoken properly since the lounge argument. Jason had gone to bed first, and had still been awake when Dani had gone upstairs. They'd not had a proper reconciliation, hadn't cleared the air, though Dani had given him a kiss good night and thanked him for helping her.

He'd fallen asleep minutes later. Dani suspected it may have been due to some of his high-strength painkillers, which could knock him out for hours on end. Dani was left wide awake, her brain whirring despite the toil of the day.

Come Monday morning she felt horrific. Looked horrific too, with big bags under her eyes, pale and blotchy skin.

Despite that, she was dressed and in her car on the way to the office by seven thirty. She would make a point of reconciling with Jason later. She had to. For a large part, he was in the right, she was in the wrong. She got that. She just had a hard time saying it out loud. But she couldn't continue to push him away. She needed him.

Her arm remained painfully swollen. She did need to get an x-ray. But not just yet. She had work to do. Not least doing what she could to find out who had attacked her and why.

Was there a parallel between Will Eccles coming to her home one night, then those two goons the night after? Will had been edgy, paranoid. As though he was expecting trouble. Were the same people he was scared of the people who had attacked Dani?

Or was the attack nothing to do with the Eccles case at all, but the Harrison case?

Or something else altogether?

Her head hurt from trying – and failing – to find the answer.

She was all of a mile from her home, travelling up Birmingham Road, when she glanced across the street and her foot – almost involuntarily – slammed onto the brake. The car rocked to a halt. There was a chorus of beeps from behind her. Dani ignored them. She indicated then pulled her car over to the side of the road. Continued to ignore the cars that went past, driver's gesticulating angrily at her.

She dialled into Easton. He answered on the second ring.

'You OK?' he said. He sounded genuinely worried.

'I'm fine, I'm fine.'

He sighed. 'Dani, I thought—'

'Listen. You know that development that's going up on Birmingham Road.'

'Development? You mean the hole in the ground by the shops?'

'Yeah, that one. Did you know that Eccles Holdings is behind it?'

'Kind of. I know from what I've seen in the accounts already they had something planned there, but it's not even off the ground yet, is it?'

'No, not really. I just noticed their name on the boards this morning. I hadn't paid much attention before. But you're right, there's nothing much here. But do you remember there was a fire there a while ago… before Christmas, wasn't it?'

'Shit,' Easton said, as though he was just putting the pieces together. In much the same way Dani just had. Why hadn't she thought about this before? She passed this place virtually every day? 'Yeah, I remember getting stuck in traffic the day after. The fire engines were still there.'

'That's exactly what I remember too.'

'What are you thinking?'

'I'm thinking I want to find out a bit more about that.'

'Gotcha. I'm only five minutes from the office. I'll get onto it.'

'OK, I'll see you there shortly.'

–

Dani made it twenty minutes later. Easton, the only other person in, came over to her desk before she'd even sat down.

'Here's the story from the paper the next day,' he said, putting the printout on her desk.

She picked it up and scanned over it.

'A lucky escape for the family, by all accounts,' Easton said. 'Though their dog never got out. Horrible.'

'It is,' Dani said. 'Suspected arson?'

'The family were renters. Their landlord moved them to another property across town.'

'And the landlord is?'

'Not Eccles, if that's what you were thinking.'

It was. And Dani was a little disappointed.

'Who then?'

'Omar Mansoor. He lives in Aldridge.'

He put another piece of paper down onto the desk. A profile of Mansoor. Fifty-four years old. Shareholder and director of OM Properties Ltd.

'A competitor of Eccles, do you think?' Easton asked.

'Why don't we go and find out?'

—

They were back on the road minutes later. Easton was driving. He'd insisted. As though Dani couldn't manage herself. On another day she would have picked Easton up on that, but she decided to let it slide. It really wasn't worth the aggro.

'Were you OK last night?' Easton asked.

'A bit shaken, that's all.'

'If it's any consolation, the fact someone sent those two—'

'I don't really want to talk about it.'

'Sure.'

The cabin fell silent. Though Dani could tell Easton wasn't quite finished yet.

'Is everything OK between you and Jason?'

Dani sighed. The obvious answer was no. Really, she knew it would do her the world of good to rant to Easton – anyone – to explain what was going on. Even if she couldn't quite grasp the answers in her head herself, it would surely help to lay it out for someone else. But then she'd never done that before with Easton. He'd asked now, but did he really want to be party to all of the details and all of the problems? Would it have a negative impact on what was currently a perfectly sound working relationship?

'I'm sorry,' Easton said. 'It's just that... I could sense something going on. I know it wasn't the best timing last night, but I just felt—'

'We're fine,' Dani said. 'We'll work it out.'

'I'm here for you, you know?' he said. 'Even the indestructible DI Stephens must need a friend every now and then.'

Dani sighed. She was hardly the most open person in the world. In fact, she was probably one of the least open people she knew. Yet Easton always had a good read of her. They spent enough time together, after all.

'I appreciate the thought,' Dani said, trying to sound a bit more friendly. 'But it's really not something I want to talk about.'

'Fair enough.'

'How was the rest of your weekend anyway? Weren't you seeing your date again?'

'It was pretty damn good actually,' he said. He looked over and winked at her.

'Too much info for a Monday morning,' she said.

'That's what she said,' Easton replied.

Dani tried, but failed to stop the smile.

-

Omar Mansoor lived on a quiet, leafy road on the outskirts of the town of Aldridge, nestled between Walsall, Lichfield and Sutton Coldfield. Some of the houses in the town were as big and as handsome as the prime residences in Sutton, though came at a considerable discount given the extra distance to Birmingham.

There were no cars on the driveway of the Mansoors' home, and a quick knock on the door confirmed no one was in.

'The address of his company is in the centre of town, less than two miles away,' Easton said as they settled back into the car.

'Let's go then.'

They parked up on the street next to a recreation ground and walked the short distance towards the town centre that largely consisted of 1960s and 1970s low-rise rows of shops.

The address they arrived at was part of a three-storey, flat-roofed terrace. There was no frontage here, just a door that was flanked by a charity shop on one side and a nail salon on the other. There was no indication on the door of what business lay beyond.

Dani rang the buzzer. No answer once again. This was becoming an increasingly frustrating theme.

She sighed and stepped back from the pavement to look up at the building. No sign of anyone in the windows above, and it wasn't even clear which windows belonged to the property.

'What do you want to do?' Easton asked.

'Go home and take a long bath with a bottle of cava.'

Easton laughed. 'You've not even made it to nine a.m. on Monday morning.'

'It's going to be a long week.'

'We'll arrange another time to visit.'

Dani turned around. The street was quiet. Other than the shops there weren't many other businesses here –

offices or factories – and it was too early for many shoppers to be out and about.

But twenty yards ahead, there was a convenience store where a man emerged carrying a small paper bag. He brought the bag up to his mouth to take a bite of whatever early morning treat he'd bought himself – pastry, cake, sandwich.

Dani nudged Easton in the side, and indicated with her head.

The man looked up at them both, mid-bite, the paper bag covering his mouth. Even with the bag to his face she thought she recognised him from the picture Easton had showed her in the office.

The next second Omar Mansoor dropped the bag, spun on his heel, and ran.

Chapter 27

Dani and Easton both ran too, though within a few strides Easton was already pulling away. Dani was no slouch. Normally. Perhaps the after-effects of yesterday's attack, and the poor night's sleep, had taken more out of her than she realised.

They took the left turn to follow Mansoor. Headed away from the shops and back towards where they'd parked their car at the recreation ground.

'Stop! Police!' Easton shouted out for the second time.

Mansoor took no notice. It wasn't clear if he was ignoring them, or hadn't heard.

Within yards, Dani and Easton were closing. The streets were quiet enough, but somehow the few people out and about all seemed to get in Mansoor's way. An old lady pushing a trolley bag. Two mothers pushing prams. A young guy head down solely focused on his phone rather than the world around him. All of them hindered Mansoor's escape. That together with the fact that he was at least a couple of stone heavier than Easton, and considerably older too.

'Stop!' Easton shouted again as Mansoor scaled the small fence that ran around the recreation ground, to head onto the dewy grass.

Easton galloped over the fence. He was only a couple of yards away. Mansoor looked over his shoulder. Eyes wide with fright and surprise. He obviously hadn't expected Easton to be so close. He tried to shimmy right to avoid the inevitable. Too little, too late. Easton leaped forwards. He grabbed Mansoor around the waist and the two of them crashed to the ground.

Dani, head spinning, chest heaving from exertion, caught up a few seconds later, by which time Easton had rolled off his prey and seemed caught in two minds as to what to do next.

'Omar Mansoor?'

He groaned and moved onto his side, clutching his knee. At least he wasn't putting up a further fight.

'We're from West Midlands Police. DI Stephens, DS Easton.'

'The police?'

'Why the hell did you run from us?' Easton asked through laboured breaths as he got to his feet and wiped himself down. The legs of his trousers and the side of his jacket were sopping.

'I didn't know you were police!'

'Then who did you think we were?' Dani asked.

Mansoor shook his head and pulled himself up. 'What do you want with me?'

'To talk. But perhaps not out here.'

He looked dubious. Hesitant. Nervous. Just a bit annoyed, too, though that certainly wasn't predominant.

Who exactly was he scared of, to have bolted like that? It wasn't as though Dani and Easton were particularly menacing. Were they?

Mansoor looked around himself. For what?

'OK, this way,' he said, and set off back towards the town centre.

'Office' was a kind word to describe the place. Essentially it was a one-bedroom flat, above the nail salon. Poky bathroom, poky kitchen, lounge and bedroom. Although the bedroom had a desk with a computer on top, the room was clearly mainly used for storage, with boxes and files crammed on shelves all over. The lounge, a slightly larger space, had another two desks, a few less boxes. No one inside except Mansoor, Easton and Dani, so quite who else worked there was anybody's guess.

The room still retained patterned wallpaper, curtains, carpet. Not even a basic makeover had been carried out before Mansoor had turned this from a dwelling to his office space. Yet from seeing his house, he clearly wasn't short of a few pounds.

Mansoor sat at the leather chair behind the desk by the window. The chair was probably the plushest thing in the whole room. Dani and Easton remained standing. There weren't two other chairs in the room anyway.

'What is this about?' Mansoor said.

He was sounding more confident than before…

'We're from the Homicide team,' Dani said.

…until she said that, then the nerves were back.

'We're investigating the murders of Terry and Annie Eccles. You know them?'

He nodded, though it was a strange gesture, almost involuntary, like he hadn't meant to and regretted it. 'I knew Terry, but only a little. I never met his wife. I read about what happened.'

'Can you explain how you knew Terry?'

'I didn't really know him. Not personally. We're in a similar line of business. I'm a landlord. I have properties all over the region. Over a hundred. Terry and his partner, Peter, were more into developments, really.'

'Like the one on Birmingham Road?' Easton said.

Mansoor squirmed in his seat.

'What do you know about that?' Dani said. 'You own one of the buildings right next to there, don't you?'

'The one that had a fire late last year,' Easton added.

Mansoor shook his head. 'It's not what you think.'

Dani and Easton shared a look.

'What isn't?'

'I had nothing to do with that fire.'

'No one suggested you did,' Easton said.

Mansoor was still squirming. He needed a better poker face.

'No. We didn't,' Dani added. 'But clearly you know something.'

Mansoor looked like he might clam up. But then he decided to talk. 'I've dealt with Terry before. Peter too. Quite honestly, they're both arseholes.' He closed his eyes and shook his head. 'Sorry, that was uncalled for. Terry… we never really liked each other. Perhaps because we'd gazumped each other more than once. And I knew he was desperate to buy that house off me for the development.'

'The house was supposed to be part of the development?' Dani asked.

'Yeah. But I had tenants. They have rights. Plus, I didn't want to make it easy for him. You know?'

Dani didn't but she could imagine. 'So what happened?'

'I had a price in my head. I knew he'd go that high eventually. He couldn't afford to have the development scuppered.'

'And then the fire happened?' Dani said.

'Yes and no.'

'How do you mean?'

'That wasn't me. And it wasn't Terry. Or Peter. I honestly believe that.'

Dani looked at Easton. He looked as confused as she was.

'He nearly killed those people. Forced my hand. I lost nearly two hundred thousand because of him. And that poor family.'

'Because of who?'

Mansoor looked at her as though she was being dense.

'Hamed. All of this only happened after Terry brought Hamed Adil on board. I know it was him.'

'Hamed Adil?'

Mansoor nodded. 'He did this. I'm sure of it. That man… believe me, he'd do anything to get what he wants.'

Dani looked to Easton. He nodded.

It was time to go and pay Laura Eccles another visit.

Chapter 28

Dani and Easton had been intent on heading straight over to Solihull to find Laura Eccles, whether at home or the office that she and Hamed Adil worked at. Would that be a similarly odd set-up to Omar Mansoor's place of business?

Either way, they got sidelined. In a good way. Laura could wait. The call from Saad Tariq from Forensics came only a couple of minutes after they'd left Aldridge. He was in Birmingham. About equidistant to Sutton Coldfield from where Dani and Easton were. Kibble House was the logical place to meet to discuss the findings.

'Are you not going to say anything?' Easton asked after a few minutes of silence.

'What?'

She'd been miles away. If her head had anything more crammed into it, fighting for prevalence, her brain would surely explode.

'About Mansoor?' Easton said. 'What are you thinking?'

'I don't think he was lying. About having nothing to do with that fire. He had nothing to gain.'

'He's pretty rattled. Do you reckon that's just about Hamed Adil?'

'Possibly. It does make sense that he'd be wary of Adil if what he said is true. Hamed Adil very nearly caused the deaths of a whole family. Why? Simply so he could get a good deal on that house? A couple of months later and Terry Eccles and his wife are dead. Now we have Mansoor running scared, Will Eccles too. Heavies coming to my home threatening me. Is it unthinkable that the events are all connected?'

'Not at all. Plus Hamed Adil is still conveniently out of the country.'

'Which worries me more and more each day.'

–

They arrived at Kibble House before Tariq. There remained a PC stationed outside. PC Shaw, a young female copper who Dani hadn't met before.

'Anything happening?' Dani asked her after they'd parked up on the drive.

'Nothing at all. The only person I've seen is the postman.' She sounded seriously downbeat. Perhaps she should look on the bright side. There was a balance between boredom on the job, and putting your life on the line. Dani often came far too close to the latter for her liking. Perhaps a few days standing outside an empty house was exactly what she needed.

'So Eric Eccles still hasn't come back to you about meeting over here?' Dani said to Easton a few moments later as they stood in the hallway with their gloves and plastic boots on.

The house was chillier and more dank than ever. Dani really wouldn't want to be here alone at night now. Not that she believed in ghosts, but still…

'I haven't heard back from him,' Easton said.

'Odd.'

'A little,' Easton said with a shrug.

Dani mooched while they waited, though Tariq arrived within ten minutes with a big briefcase full of papers. He scuttled into the house in his typical foppish manner, falling over his own feet, tussling with his briefcase. With the glasses that he was forever pushing back up his nose, he couldn't have been a more stereotypical geek if he tried. All that was missing was him falling head first and chucking reams of paper everywhere.

That said, when he spoke, once he got in his stride, he was articulate and engaging. Especially if he was talking about crime scenes. He was equally impressive on the witness stand, Dani knew.

They congregated in the front living room. Dani and Easton sat together. Tariq sat adjacent, fumbling away as he did. Perhaps it was all an act, to make people doubt his intelligence.

'Did you see the PM results?' he said, with the obligatory push of the glasses. Dani held back her smile.

'I haven't read the reports yet,' Dani said. She'd seen that the results had appeared in her inbox while they'd been in Aldridge, but she'd been too preoccupied to open the documents yet. 'Anything useful?'

'Useful? That depends,' he said with a sigh as he fished some papers out of his case. 'You'll need to speak to Ledford directly if you want to follow up on anything, but from my reading there's nothing startling in there.'

Dani took the report off him, he handed another copy to Easton, then they both took a couple of minutes to leaf through.

'Blunt force trauma,' Dani said as she read out loud. 'Internal haemorrhaging. Blood loss. All pretty consistent with what we thought about the attack, and the injuries were consistent with the bat and axe found at the scene?'

Tariq nodded. 'I'd say so. Ledford didn't indicate any particular concerns.'

'Drugs in Annie's blood?' Easton said.

'Yes,' Tariq said. 'Prescribed drugs for a heart condition. Expected levels; so nothing to suggest they were forcibly administered or caused her to be unconscious before or during the attack.'

'And the same for Terry,' Dani said. 'He'd been drinking, but that blood alcohol level isn't far over the legal driving limit.'

'It might have caused him to fall asleep a little more quickly,' Easton said, 'but again hardly enough for him to pass out.'

'So the conclusion is they were most likely attacked when they were asleep,' Dani suggested.

'The way I read it, they possibly woke up during the attack,' Tariq said, 'but the attack was likely so quick, and so debilitating that they had no chance to defend themselves.'

'Which isn't far off what we always thought,' Dani said, though it was absolutely necessary to have it concluded through Ledford's analysis of the corpses.

'What about Forensics results?' Easton asked.

'This is where it gets more interesting,' Tariq said, 'but also potentially more confusing.'

Dani raised an eyebrow as she and Easton handed the PM reports back. 'What do you mean?'

'Let's start with the bedroom. Do you want to go through it here, or upstairs?'

Dani already had a vivid image in her mind of the gruesome scene she'd witnessed several days ago. She'd also returned there with Laura. She didn't need to be up there again unless absolutely necessary.

'I'm fine here,' she said.

Tariq took another moment to ready himself as he scanned the document in his hands. He didn't offer a copy to Dani or Easton this time.

'We found multiple trace fibres around the room. On the bodies, on the murder weapons. Mostly fabrics of various types that are possibly from the perp's clothing.'

'Anything useful?' Easton asked.

'Not on its own. The traces are too small to be definitive of an origin such as brand make or anything like that. But if you do find a suspect, then we can try a sample match, of course.'

'What about DNA?' Dani said.

'Nothing of note in the bedroom. No bodily fluids, no blood that didn't belong to the victims.'

'Not much at all then,' Dani said, sounding more disheartened.

'Nothing that's going to get you directly to your murderer,' Tariq said. 'Though I think there's plenty useful in here still.'

'Such as?' Easton asked.

'Traces of latex fibres on the murder weapons.'

'The murderer wore disposable gloves?' Dani said.

'I would say so, yes. And we also have latex traces elsewhere. Plus smudges and prints from the gloves which, after the attack, were most likely covered in blood.'

'Where?' Dani asked, feeling more upbeat.

'Latex residue on the window frame in bedroom four. That's the one at the back right-hand corner of the house.'

Will's room. Just as Dani had always thought.

'And on the drainpipe outside. Plus there's a blood print on the handrail coming down the stairs.'

'If there was blood on the outside of the gloves, would that leave an impression of the perp's actual fingerprint?' Easton asked.

'Yes and no.' Tariq flicked to a page and turned it around to show Dani and Easton. 'There were two cases where we can see certain patterns in the blood marks, but honestly I think it's quite unclear.' Dani stared at the scaled-up images on the page. Did they look like fingerprint fragments? Kind of. But they could have been several other things too. 'Again, if you had a suspect, you could look for consistencies in the patterns, but I'd have a hard time persuading a judge and jury that it was one hundred per cent an accurate match based off just this.'

'What about the boots?' Dani asked.

'A curiosity, for sure,' Tariq said. 'No DNA in there, which to my mind is quite unusual.'

'It is?'

'Think about your footwear. How long you wear shoes or boots for. You get a lot of transfer through socks. Oils, sweat, dead skin cells. Not just from your socks actually, but from your lower legs too. But we found nothing usable in those boots, nor on the floor around them to give a clue as to where the killer went after they took the boots off.'

'Do you think they were worn by the killer at all?'

'They definitely had the victims' blood on them. And there was a scuff mark on the drainpipe that had a consistent tread pattern to the boots.'

'Then what other explanation is there, for the lack of transfer?' Easton asked.

'Honesty, it could be a lot of things. Thick socks. Multiple pairs of socks. Leggings, stockings.'

'What size were they?'

'Nines.'

So most likely a man's, though that wasn't a certainty.

'Anyway,' Tariq said, clearly ready to move on. Dani would come back to the boots in her own time. 'The tiles in the hallway are old, but relatively clean. I understand from the notes that the family cleaner actually found the bodies?'

Dani nodded.

'Poor lady. But my point is that tiles like those are really good for capturing not just shoe prints, but also footprints from socks, where the body's oils and sweat pass through the thin sock fabric. We do have several impressions on the tiles, both from shoes, and from either socks or even bare feet. We've eliminated what we can from the victims' own feet, and from the footwear we found for them in the house, but there are still several other samples remaining.'

'Shoes or footprints?' Easton asked.

'Both actually.'

'What about specifically around the boots?' Dani asked. 'Isn't that what you were getting to?'

'Yes, sorry. Nothing stood out. In that there was no obvious trail away from those discarded boots. Either to the front door, or anywhere else. Were traces of the killer's steps left on those tiles? Very likely, but at the moment we don't have enough information to draw a conclusion.'

Dani sighed. This really wasn't adding anything at all.

'There is one thing, though, that we haven't yet touched on,' Tariq said, as though picking up on Dani's mood.

'Yeah?'

'We know the killer took those boots off before they left the house. We also know they wore gloves before and during the murder, but I don't think they left with those gloves on.'

253

'Because?'

'Because the latch on the front door was wiped clean. Or wiped clear, I should say. The smudges were quite obvious, but whatever fingerprints would have been there were removed.'

'So the killer took the gloves off before they left the house?' Dani said. 'Then wiped clean the latch. I'm not sure where that leaves us?'

'I'm sorry, it's because I'm telling the story a bit backwards. Yes, I think the gloves were removed before the killer left the house. But not before they'd been into the home office.'

Now he had Dani's attention.

'There were several latex traces found inside the office,' Tariq said.

'That makes no sense,' Easton said. 'The gloves had blood on them. You already said that?'

'Perhaps the killer switched gloves,' Tariq said.

'Possibly,' Dani said. 'But there are at least two other options, too. One, the killer went to the office first, then killed the victims after. Or, there was more than one of them.'

'I have to say there's nothing to suggest more than one attacker.'

'Where specifically were the traces in the office?' Dani asked.

'A few places. Doorknob. On the desk drawers. The tall cabinet, and on the door to the safe.'

Dani and Easton looked at each other.

'The safe door wasn't properly locked,' Easton said. 'When I first helped clear that place out.'

'I remember,' Dani said. 'So the killer was inside the safe at some point.'

'Looking for what?' Tariq asked.

Dani didn't say anything. Though she felt she knew exactly what the answer was.

Chapter 29

'The wills?' Easton said as he and Dani strode across the gravel towards the car. 'Do you think that's what the killer was looking for?'

'That was my immediate thought,' Dani said.

They both sank down into their seats.

'Which raises one very big question,' Dani added after Easton had started the engine.

'Which is?'

'Did they find what they were looking for?'

Easton looked confused now. 'Except the will was still there, wasn't it? Plus the more recent, unsigned version was in the desk. If the killer went through the office, and those were left, what were they looking for? Or are you suggesting one of those items was planted?'

Dani frowned. He was right. Her immediate leap was that the killer being in the office, in the safe, was linked to the wills, but did that really make sense. Or was it something else altogether. 'I really don't know.'

'But it does, on the face of it, bring us back full circle.'

'It does,' Dani said. 'I think Terry and Annie Eccles were killed by someone they knew. And the most obvious explanation is that it was to do with money.'

Given that hypothesis, there remained only a small group of people who Dani had on her radar. Now she just needed to find out which one of them was the murderer.

Dani contemplated whether to go to the office first or not. Grayling and Mutambe were in. Dani needed to speak to them both on multiple fronts. Grayling continued to dig into Harrison and Roberts. Harrison remained in custody having been charged with murder and awaited a court hearing to determine if he'd be granted bail or not. Mutambe's stake-out in Sandwell on Sunday afternoon had ultimately been unsuccessful. She'd seen no sign of Will Eccles. Dani had decided against putting surveillance outside the apartment block full-time – they didn't have endless resource – instead opting to put an alert out across the Force for any sightings of either Will or his car on the move. In the meantime Mutambe continued to dig into the Eccles children from afar, as well as the Werners, and was now also assisting Easton in reviewing the documents taken from Eccles Holdings Limited.

Dani felt that everything they needed to crack both cases was at their fingertips, if they could just find the right threads to pull.

Noon had passed by the time Dani and Easton arrived in Solihull, and the weather had changed too. The bright and dewy morning had turned into a cloudy and blustery afternoon, with sleety showers. A harsh reminder that they were still only in the early throes of spring.

Dani's belly grumbled with hunger. They'd been in and out of the car most of the morning. She was whacked already and needed a break.

Not yet.

'She'd better be in this time,' Easton grumbled as they battled against the wind across the driveway to the front door. There were two cars on the drive at least. A Jaguar and Tesla. Did that suggest at least Laura was home?

'Do you think the elusive Hamed is actually back now too?' Easton said just before they reached the door.

Dani didn't answer. She rang the bell and knocked. Within a couple of seconds she spotted the shadow of movement beyond the frosted glazing.

The door opened. Laura.

'Miss Eccles—'

'Detectives,' Laura said, already sounding and looking disgruntled. 'What a surprise.'

'Can we come in?' Dani asked.

Laura looked over Dani's shoulder, as though it was of concern whether there were neighbours watching. This a woman whose parents had been murdered a few days ago, but who was more concerned with nosey neighbours?

'I have a client appointment to get to, but I can spare a few minutes.'

'That should be fine,' Dani said.

Laura showed them in. She took them through to an airy, bright lounge at the back of the house that overlooked a long and gloriously green garden. Carefully tended, that was for sure. So who was the green-fingered one? For some reason Dani wasn't sure she saw it as being either of the homeowners.

Dani and Easton took a seat next to each other on a cream leather sofa. The whole room was decked out in creams and beiges, with luxurious and sumptuous fittings. Not particularly modern, but nice. What was strange was that the room, and everything Dani had seen so far, was very child-free. No signs of Hamed's daughter at all. No toys, books in this room. No slides or scooters outside. One photo of her and Hamed and Laura on the mantelpiece, but that was the only indication of her existence.

'Is your husband back home yet?' Easton asked.

'They're due back in a few days,' Laura said.

Dani decided not to say anything more about that. Yet.

'Have you actually got anything specific to discuss?' Laura said, perching herself on a chair arm, as though indicating she wasn't getting too comfortable. 'Like I said, I do have somewhere to be.'

Except she was dressed in jeans and a sweatshirt. Was that really the attire she chose for meeting with a client? Perhaps it was.

'We have initial Forensics results back now,' Dani said.

Laura's ears seemed to prick up, though Dani also thought she looked a little more nervous.

'There is an odd thing, actually,' Dani said.

'There is?'

'We think it very likely that the killer spent time going through your parents' office. Either immediately before or after they'd killed your parents.'

Laura screwed up her face. 'How do you... what do you mean?'

'Among other places, we believe the killer gained access to the safe in there.'

Dani let that one hang. Laura didn't say anything.

'Do you know what the killer could have been looking for?' Easton said.

'I have no idea,' Laura said, perhaps too defensively, though she quickly tried to compose herself. 'Do you think they took anything?'

'There's the thing,' Dani said. 'We really don't know. We have the documents we *did* find in there, but we can't be sure if there was anything missing.'

'Do you know what that safe was used for?' Easton asked after another short pause in the conversation. 'What your parents kept in it? That might help us to determine if something has been taken.'

'To be honest, I didn't even know there was one in there,' Laura said.

She looked at the floor as she spoke. Something about the tone, the stiff body language, told Dani it was a clear lie. After all, when she'd been in the office with Laura she was sure she'd gone to that tallboy unit to check the safe. Why?

'Did you ever discuss inheritance with your parents?' Dani asked.

Laura frowned. Anger. Agitation, just below the surface, though it was obvious she was trying to keep it from showing. 'I feel like you've got something you want to say. I'd really appreciate it if you just said it, rather than weaving around like this.'

'I'm not trying to weave around anything,' Dani said. 'It's an important question.'

'No. I didn't. I don't know if any of my brothers did.'

'We found a copy of your parents' wills,' Easton said. 'In that safe in the office.'

Another statement that was left hanging. Laura's discomfort was obvious now. Fidgeting, eyes flicking between Dani, Easton and around the room.

'And?' she said.

'Nothing particularly startling,' Dani said. 'You'll have to pick this up formally with a solicitor, but essentially everything, their assets and the business holdings, were left equally between you and your brothers.'

Laura nodded but said nothing. She still looked seriously uncomfortable.

'That will was dated a couple of years ago,' Easton said. 'Do you know if they had updated it at all?'

'I already said I never discussed inheritance with them.'

'You did,' Dani said. 'I do wonder what the killer was trying to find in that safe.'

Laura was silent again. Dani wondered whether to mention the second will or not. Laura looked cornered already, and they hadn't even yet moved on to discuss Hamed and that fire.

'The strange thing is,' Dani said. 'We did find a second will, too. A more recent version than the one in the safe.' She paused, but Laura wasn't about to add anything. 'In that will, the business holdings were treated differently, and were to be distributed to the current shareholders. So Peter Werner would take the lion's share of the business, together with Eric and Hugo.'

Dani deliberately didn't mention that that will was technically invalid. Right now, that fact was beside the point.

Laura's face twitched. 'I really… I really don't know what to say,' she said.

'Plus most of their personal assets would be given to charity rather than to you and your brothers.'

Laura's mouth was open but she said nothing.

'We're particularly interested in understanding why the wills were changed,' Easton asked.

'I just don't know. But you say Peter would have been the main beneficiary under the new will?'

She was growing in confidence now. Because she had someone – Peter – to palm the pressure off onto? Convenient.

'That's what it looks like,' Easton said.

'Do you have any idea why that would be the case?' Dani asked.

'I really don't. But I don't like the sound of it at all.' On her high horse now. She was a good actor. 'And that's not just from my own selfish perspective. It simply doesn't... it doesn't sound like something they would do.'

'Why do you say that?'

'It's... hard to explain.'

And she didn't try to, even though Dani and Easton gave her the time to attempt to find some words.

'This is just what we've found so far,' Dani said. 'Of course we'll be looking into this very closely indeed. As you say, it seems a strange decision for your parents to make, especially as it happened not long before they were killed, so we want to make sure we fully understand the implications.'

'You think this has something to do with their murders?'

'It's a line of enquiry we're following very seriously,' Easton said. 'It's the clearest suggestion of motive that we have.'

Laura looked a little confused by that statement but didn't say anything more. Behind the confusion, Dani could practically see the cogs turning. She felt the pressure was off her. Pressure on Peter, Eric and Hugo instead?

Time to change it up again.

'So Hamed will be back later this week?' Dani said.

'Yes.'

'Good. Because we do need to speak to him too.'

'About?'

'For one thing, about the development he was working on with your father, on Birmingham Road. Do you know about it?'

Laura sank down again.

'Vaguely. It's not something I've been directly involved in.'

'Why not?' Easton asked.

'Because that's not the way we run our business. We each focus on different projects.'

'I got the impression from you last time, and from your siblings too, that your father didn't get along very well with Hamed?'

'It wasn't like that.'

'What was it like, then?'

Laura sighed. 'Yes, they had some issues. Mainly because of my dad's outdated views of marriage and… you know, religion, race, whatever. But they were both professionals. They both wanted success and to make money.'

'That may be, but it just seems odd to me that the two of them got together for that development, rather than say, you and your dad.'

The sides of Laura's jaw pulsed. She was clenching her teeth. A sign she was feeling rattled now.

'You'd have to speak to Hamed about that,' she said. 'I know they hit a few delays with planning and then the builders, but I honestly don't know the full details of it.'

'Well, of course, we'd like to find out more,' Dani said. 'But Hamed's not here, is he?'

No response to that.

'So I suppose you don't know anything about the fire either?' Easton asked.

'What fire?' Laura said after a short pause. A pretty lame attempt at a throwback, Dani thought.

'We've heard your husband was responsible for a house fire that very nearly led to the deaths of a family living in a house on the site,' Dani said.

'What are you—'

'A house your father had been trying to purchase to move the development into the construction phase.'

Laura was all aghast now. It was hard to tell whether it was an act or real.

'I've really no idea what you're talking about,' she said.

'We spoke with Omar Mansoor earlier today. He was the owner of the property. He was very clear in his belief that Hamed was responsible for that fire. And we will be investigating his claims as far as we can. He insists that the purpose of the fire was to force his hand in selling the property, and at a cheap price, so that the development could go ahead.'

Laura shot to her feet.

'I'm sorry, I'm not doing this.'

Dani and Easton remained where they were.

'I don't know anything about what you're saying. And I find it incredibly disrespectful – unprofessional – for you to come to my house unannounced and drop these scandalous claims onto me. Claims about my father, about my husband, when neither are here to defend themselves.'

'We're just trying to find out what you know,' Easton said.

'But that's a good point you make,' Dani added. 'Hamed isn't here, is he?' She looked to Easton and shrugged.

'I'm sorry, but I need to go,' Laura said. 'It's time for you to leave.'

'That's fine,' Dani said. She and Easton both got to their feet. 'Perhaps we'll pick this up again when Hamed is back home.'

Laura put her hands to her hips but didn't say anything.

'And if you do speak to him before then,' Dani added, 'please tell him how keen we are to talk to him.'

'Just go,' Laura said.

Dani and Easton did exactly that.

–

Following the very uncomfortable conversation – uncomfortable on Laura Eccles' part, at least – Dani seriously considered asking Easton to stay behind in Solihull and follow the Eccles daughter wherever she was going. She was one hundred per cent sure Laura knew more than she was telling. Given that what she was telling was pretty much bugger all.

She decided against it. For now. She hoped that was the right decision.

'That was eye-opening,' Easton said, as they headed along the A45 back towards the centre of Birmingham.

'What was?'

'All of it, really. But I'm glad you brought up the wills like you did.'

'Yeah,' Dani said.

'And the fire. She's a shady one, all right. You know what I think?'

'What?'

'Regardless of whether she knew about that fire, I think she knows exactly the type of businessman that Hamed is.'

'Perhaps she does. The question is, what type of businessman was Terry Eccles?'

They both went silent. Dani tried to go back over in her head everything Laura had just said. Every reaction that had been slightly off, evasive, combative. There was a lot to take in.

Another downpour of sleet pelted onto the car as they headed along. The cars in front all slowed. The wipers whizzed back and forth on the windscreen like they were on acid. Watching them made Dani's head pound even more than it already was and made the seemingly simple task of thinking of the meeting from all of ten minutes ago more difficult.

'When we mentioned the safe, do you know the strangest thing?' Dani asked.

'What?'

'She never asked how we got inside.'

Easton seemed to ponder that one for a few moments.

'You think she already knew we had?' he said. 'From that first time she was in the office with you?'

'Possibly. She did look in the tallboy. It's odd she didn't ask. To anyone who just found out the safe was ransacked by an intruder, which is basically what we told her, surely the first thing to think is how on earth did the intruder get into a locked safe?'

'So you're suggesting she was the one who left it open in the first place?'

'Not necessarily. Maybe just that she knew, from previous experience – a conversation with Terry perhaps – that the door was temperamental, and that's why it was open when you found it. Or maybe it's something else. Like she *knew* the attacker would go there.'

Easton huffed. 'That'd be convenient. What are we going to do about Hamed Adil?'

'A good question. Let me pick it up with McNair. I'm nervous about what we've been told, that's for sure. Let me see if we can get any kind of dialogue open with the Greek police to keep tabs on him. I don't want him disappearing.'

'Seems sensible. Unless he's not even there at all.'

Dani really hoped that wasn't the case.

She took her phone out. She'd felt it buzz a couple of times when they'd been with Laura, and on the way back to the car she'd noticed both calls had come from the office, but had been too preoccupied to deal with them straight away. She listened to the voicemail. She expected it to be Mutambe or Grayling. Not McNair.

She already felt nervous as she listened to the rings as she called back.

'Finally,' McNair said. 'I've been trying to reach you.'

'What's wrong?' Dani said. A whole host of horrible thoughts and images flashed.

Jason. Please don't let it be Jason.

'I took a call from the Governor at Long Lartin this morning,' McNair said. 'I don't know the details. I've just been told you need to call them urgently.'

Long Lartin. The prison where Ben was locked up. What on earth?

Dani rang through to the switchboard. Spent a couple of minutes persuading whichever admin or prison officer she was speaking to that she really was worthy of the Governor's time.

Eventually she won the argument.

'DI Stephens?' came a smooth male voice. Dani had never spoken to him before. In the past whenever dealing with Ben it'd been the Deputy Governor who she'd seen or spoken to. She didn't like the implications of this at all.

'Yes.'

'I'm calling about your brother.' Background noise suggested he was driving, or outside. 'Detective, I need you to come over as soon as you can.'

'To Long Lartin? I'm—'

'No, Detective, not the prison.'

'Sorry?'

'You need to go to Worcestershire Royal Hospital. There's been... look, I'll explain all when you arrive. Please, come soon.'

And with that, he ended the call.

Chapter 30

January

'You look nice,' Annie said as she wandered into the room.

Terry was standing in front of the mirror, doing up his tie. He didn't usually go the whole hog with suit and tie these days, but whenever he did it made him feel that extra bit important. Nice to know Annie noticed the difference too.

He also realised, as he looked at himself in the mirror, that he looked far more fresh than he had done over recent months. He thought he knew why that was. *Who* it was that had given him this new lease of life.

Annie, still in her silky dressing gown, sauntered over and placed her arms around his waist. He stared at her in the mirror.

'Last night was fun,' she said, catching his eye.

He smiled.

'I think we both needed that,' she added, before giving him a kiss on the back of his neck. 'You smell good too. Who are you trying to impress?'

He turned around to face her. 'You, of course.'

She pulled away, playfully. 'Don't go getting any funny ideas.'

'Just try and stop me.'

He hoped and expected she might carry on the game, but she didn't. She turned to the wardrobe and began fishing for something to wear.

'You meeting someone important today?' she asked.

'The bank,' he said.

She stopped what she was doing and faced him again.

'Don't give me that look,' he said.

'What look?'

'Everything's fine. We're just trying to re-arrange a few things.'

She held his eye for a moment, the doubt clear in her face, but she didn't question any more.

'What about Henry's money?'

He moved over to her now. Put his fingers under her chin to lift her head. 'This meeting is really important. Once the details are ironed out with the bank, the money for Henry will come straight back. I promise.'

'You said that weeks ago,' she said. 'It was before Christmas when he asked for it.'

He pecked her lips. She barely responded. The look of doubt was still there.

'See you later,' he said.

'Yeah.'

'I love you.'

'Love you too.'

Though both of the statements were etched with unease.

–

Eric was in the office, but there was no sign of Peter or Hugo. That was good. Terry had mentioned the meeting to them both, though he also knew that Peter didn't really understand the full importance. Essentially because Terry had told him explicitly it wasn't that important. That it was just routine. If Peter had known otherwise, he almost certainly would have been involved too, and would likely have taken over and done anything he could to undermine Terry. That seemed to be Peter's goal at every turn recently. As it was, matters were down to Terry and Eric.

Eric should have been pleased about that. Pleased that he was being given a chance to step up and show some real business leadership skills for once.

So why, when Terry arrived in the office, did his son's face look like a slapped arse?

'We've still fifteen minutes before they arrive,' Terry said as he fixed himself a coffee, his third of the day, from the Nespresso machine. 'If there's anything you don't understand, let's try and get on the same page now.'

Eric had his eyes set on a folder in his hands.

'Eric? Did you hear me?'

'What the hell is this?'

'Excuse me?'

Eric wandered over and pointed to the sheet in his hand. Terry only needed a second to realise what it was.

Shit.

'Where'd you get that?' Terry said, glaring at his son.

'Where I got it isn't the point, is it? Why the hell have we got 5 million owed to HSBC? From a loan they gave us six months ago? I've never seen that money in the accounts.'

'Obviously you didn't look properly.'

Now it was Eric's turn to glare. 'I know you think I'm stupid, Dad, but I understand how basic bookkeeping works. Where's that money gone? And this loan account isn't even part of the refinancing we're discussing today? Do Lloyds know about it?'

'Of course they do.' Though the words weren't particularly convincing even to his own ears.

'We lump together everything with Lloyds today,' Eric said, 'take out the additional 10 million you've asked for, and we're—'

'I understand my own company's financial position,' Terry said. 'How the hell do you expect us to finance something like Birmingham Road without cash?'

'*Your company?* Except it's not just *yours*, is it? It's mine too. Peter's. Hugo's.'

'You need to drop that tone.'

'Do I? Or what?'

Terry gritted his teeth rather than say anything to that.

'Do Lloyds know about the HSBC loan?' Eric asked, like he was some sort of bloody morality detective all of a sudden.

Terry didn't answer this time.

'Dad? Do they know?'

'No.'

Eric shook his head in disbelief. 'So you're expecting me to go in there and lie on your behalf?'

'I'm expecting you to go into the meeting and do what is best for this company. *Our* company.'

'No. Sod this.'

Eric turned away. Terry reached out and grabbed him around the shoulder.

'You're not bailing on me.'

'Damn right I am,' Eric said.

He tried to shrug Terry off, but Terry renewed his grip on his son's jacket.

'You do this… see where it ends for you.'

Terry didn't see it coming. Eric snapped out of Terry's grip, spun around, lifted his hands and thrust them into Terry's chest. He was sent scuttling back into the countertop. The Nespresso machine wobbled. Stacked cups fell and clanked.

'You little…'

He very nearly went for his son. Somehow he found the will to stop himself.

'This is your mess,' Eric said, jabbing a pointed finger to Terry's face. 'You sort it out.'

'You walk out now—'

'And what?'

Terry was about to say exactly what, but once again he held back.

Eric shook his head in disappointment then carried on towards the exit.

'Eric, you can't tell Peter,' Terry called. He squirmed at the desperation in his voice. 'I'll never forgive you. I mean it.'

Eric paused.

Then headed on out without saying another word.

Chapter 31

January

The meeting with Lloyds went about as well as could have been expected. They'd agreed to the new facility, which meant several overdrafts and other loans that were due to be repaid over the next twenty-four months were now refinanced into a single lump-sum loan from HSBC that would run for six years. No capital repayment for the first two to give them extra breathing space. The interest rate was horrendous, and in the long run they'd be paying a fortune, but Terry saw no other way to keep them afloat – they simply didn't have the cash to settle the other outstanding balances month on month, never mind complete their ongoing projects.

They needed this. With this cash break Terry could finally get things moving again.

Eric was the first person Terry called coming out of the meeting. Partly to give him the good news. More to try and reconcile with him, before he went and did something really stupid.

What would Peter do if he knew about the HSBC money?

Eric didn't answer. Terry left him a voicemail. An upbeat, friendly voicemail that completely glossed over their earlier argument. He felt like a complete fraud afterwards.

What else could he do?

He supposed he could double-down and keep the pressure on Eric, to make sure he stayed onside. But he wasn't sure he wanted to do that.

A call came through on the car's dash. Henry. He'd been expecting this. Henry had called at least twice a day recently. Always about one thing and one thing only.

Terry thought about ignoring the call. Like he often did. For some reason this time he didn't. Perhaps because he did feel a bit bad about the run-in with Eric earlier.

'Henry.'

'Dad. I really need to see you.'

'If this is about—'

'Please. We need to meet. I need to tell you the truth.'

–

Terry had suggested he meet Henry at his apartment by the Mailbox in Birmingham city centre. Henry had suggested he couldn't do that because Katy-with-a-y was in, and he couldn't talk properly around her.

So many secrets. So many lies. The sad and unfortunate truth was that each of them really was his child.

Instead they met in a pub in the city, not far from Victoria Square. An underground cavern that had a more extensive array of beers from around the world than Terry had ever seen. It was barely noon, he was driving, but he still opted for a feisty Belgian beer. He got the impression he was going to need it.

Henry got the same. Waited silently and pathetically at the bar until Terry offered to pay.

'Thanks, Dad.'

They took seats at a table in the corner next to a battered old bar billiards table. There was only one other patron in – an old soak at the other side of the room, who was nursing a half.

'I know I should have come to you sooner,' Henry said.

No point in small talk, apparently. Terry said nothing.

'I'm really sorry I didn't.'

He was only sorry because he hadn't yet got the money he so desperately needed. And he only went to Annie first because he'd assumed she would be a light touch. Which she was, of course, in the nicest possible way.

'Henry, you're twenty-seven,' Terry said. 'Sooner or later you're going to have to start taking care of yourself. You've got Katy too. I know she's working part-time, but between the two of you, you have to find a way to be self-sufficient.'

Henry looked at Terry like he was an idiot. 'That's not it at all.'

'Listen to me, Henry, I know Mum agreed she'd send that ten grand, and you've been waiting on it a long time now. You've managed without it, right? And the thing is, she didn't speak to me before she agreed with you, which is why there's been a mix-up.'

'Dad, listen—'

'I'm not sure I would have said yes, but I understand why she did. You can have the ten grand. It'll take me a couple of days. But after that, no more. And I really mean it.'

Henry shook his head, took a big swig of his beer.

'The thing is… I owe someone money.'

Terry's grip on his glass strengthened. He willed for Henry not to take the conversation where he thought it might be headed.

'What do you mean?'

'You know…' He paused, then sighed, sank lower in his seat. 'If I'd just had the money Mum promised already, this wouldn't even have happened.'

'What have you done, Henry?' His tone was hardening with each word. Henry wouldn't make eye contact.

'There's a casino. On Bristol Road.'

'That dodgy fucking backwater place!'

'Dad, please?'

As hard a task as it was, Terry buttoned it. He knew exactly which casino Henry meant. About the dodgiest around. A privately owned affair that it would be crazy to think ran as an entirely legitimate business. Full-scale Mafia? Perhaps not. Dodgy as hell, and somewhere to avoid like the plague? One hundred per cent.

'I've been going there a while. They gave me a credit line. I'm one of their biggest customers.'

'Yeah, every casino loves their biggest customers. VIPs? Biggest losers, more like.'

Henry closed his eyes a moment rather than bite back to that. 'It was just a bit of fun, and I've always done all right.'

Terry shook his head in disbelief. 'Henry,' was the only word that came out of his mouth.

'But… I've been going there more and more. Perhaps I wouldn't have needed to if I'd had the money off you sooner. I know what you're going to say, but you don't know what it's like.'

Terry couldn't speak now. He really didn't know what to say. He was just praying this wasn't as bad as he feared.

'I needed the ten grand to clear my account. I promised Katy I would. She hates what's happening. I told her I'd stop, and I've really tried… but I had to pay off the money first.'

'What have you done?'

'I persuaded them to increase my credit.'

'Well, of course they're not going to say no, you moron! Not once they've got their claws in.'

Henry squirmed but seemed determined to carry on. 'There was a poker game. The guys there are normally complete novices. What was I supposed to do?'

'How much?'

Henry hung his head even further. If that was possible. He muttered under his breath.

Terry slammed his fist onto the table. 'Look me in the fucking eye and tell me how much!' The old soak and the barman both looked over. Terry couldn't care less.

'A hundred.'

'A hundred grand! Are you actually an imbecile?'

Henry didn't answer that.

'How long have you got?'

'These guys aren't messing, Dad. They gave me a week. After that they'll double it, then double it every week after that. And that's if they're being kind. I'm sure you know what I mean by that.'

Terry downed his drink. He got up from his chair.

'Dad, please?'

Henry looked up at him now. Tears in his eyes.

But Terry said nothing more before he turned and headed for the exit.

Chapter 32

March

Dani had never been before, but the Worcestershire Royal Hospital simply reminded her of every other hospital she'd ever stepped foot into over the years. Clinical, cold. Scary. Just the smell as she walked through the entrance doors sent her head spinning. Dani herself had spent months on a ward following the attack – by Ben – that had nearly ended her life, and had led to her permanent brain injury which had forever changed her. She'd got a life back since then, not the same life, but a good life nonetheless, yet it was an understatement to say she was scarred from her experience of that attack. Not to mention the fact that only last year, Jason himself had spent considerable time in hospital.

Now Ben.

Was Dani cursed in some way?

There were so many reasons why she hated being in hospitals. She especially hated that she was coming to see her brother. How was she supposed to feel about that? She wanted to feel aggrieved and angry, but she felt more like a fraud.

She was directed to a quiet ward adjacent to A&E, where a confident-looking consultant was busy in conversation with a short, plump, bald man in his sixties who was smartly dressed in a pinstripe suit. Governor Jackson, Dani assumed. Both men looked her way as she reached them. Jackson stepped towards her.

'DI Stephens,' Jackson said. He offered a hand. Dani didn't take it.

'Where is he?'

Jackson glanced to the consultant – his name badge read Pickering – as though seeking his guidance.

'Your brother was attacked this morning,' Jackson said. Kind of blurted. Like he just wanted to get the uncomfortable moments over and done with.

'How?' Dani asked.

Jackson's eyes flicked anywhere but to Dani. 'I don't yet know the full details, but you can be certain we'll do everything we can to find out. And to bring appropriate measures against those responsible.'

The way he said it irked Dani. Very corporate. Very defensive. He was already thinking about potential lawsuits and the like.

'Can I see him?' Dani asked Pickering.

Now he looked to Jackson for an answer.

'Yes,' Pickering then said. 'He's stable, but just to warn you, he's in a coma. He can't communicate with you at all.'

'I understand,' Dani said.

It wasn't anything she hadn't dealt with before.

–

There was a young uniformed officer seated outside Ben's room. After a couple of routine checks by a nurse, Dani was left alone with her brother, though Jackson remained on the outside, looking through the glass, as though he didn't trust either Ben or Dani or both.

Dani remained standing, by the bedside. Not too close. She didn't really know *what* to do.

The crumpled man in the bed in front of her had nearly every inch of skin covered by sheets and bandages. Only the skin on one hand, into which a cannula was attached, one eye, and his mouth, which had a breathing tube sticking out of it, were visible.

There was barely anything to even recognise this man as Ben, her brother. Her twin brother. Someone she'd grown up with. Her best friend through most of her child-hood. A close companion until early adulthood, when their lives had slowly begun drifting apart. Eventually they'd drifted apart completely, during the period of time when both their parents had suffered ill health, and even-tually passed away. After that, brother and sister hadn't spoken for years, even though the two of them were all that remained of their family.

Until Ben's life spiralled out of control with his second marriage – to Gemma – failing. That episode had culmin-ated in Ben launching a violent killing spree of hate and revenge, which had ultimately seen him try to kill both Gemma and Dani.

She'd often wondered how he'd fallen so far. What defect of his personality, his mentality, had led to his crimes? Whether she too, her DNA so closely aligned to his, had those same defects. As a child, as a teen-ager, as an adult even, there'd been no indication of his dark side. They'd both come from a stable family back-ground with two loving parents, had suffered no traumas or hardships. The death of their parents as young adults had affected them both, but at what point exactly had those killer instincts in Ben come to the fore? Could they have remained buried if aspects of their shared lives had followed different paths?

Or had it always only been a matter of when, not if?

She hated him so much for what he'd done. She also remained inexplicably drawn to him.

Which was why she was standing here now.

She hadn't even begun to process the implications of whatever attack had taken place in the prison. Who the perpetrators were, why. How much Ben had suffered. Nor what would come next.

Did she want him to recover?

She really didn't know. She didn't even know why she was here.

'It's me,' she said, after a long period of silence. 'Ben, it's me. I don't know if you can hear me, but...'

She didn't know what she was trying to say. She looked out of the internal window, embarrassed. Jackson caught her eye and didn't look away. His being there was hardly going to make her more comfortable.

Yet she tried her hardest to block him out. To block everything out. And when she looked back to her brother... all she saw was Ben. The real Ben. The one she'd known growing up. Her Ben.

That was when she sat down. And then she started to talk.

Chapter 33

'Harrison killed Roberts,' Dani said. She'd been talking to Ben for ten minutes already. Word after word, sentence after sentence in free flow. All to no response. It didn't matter. She kept on going.

'Harrison killed Roberts, but I just… I just don't know if he's really a bad person. A good person can kill for a good reason. Self-defence. You know? But can a good person kill for a bad reason? One simple mistake. I'm not saying that doesn't mean he shouldn't be punished, but…'

But what? She really didn't know. And what about Ben? Would he not say something similar? That he'd been a good person too? A son, brother, husband, father. He loved his kids, Dani truly believed that. He'd loved Gemma at one point. He loved Dani, didn't he? He'd made horrible mistakes, but was he really a monster?

Dani slammed her fist onto her thigh. Anger. At herself. How could she even think that? Ben had destroyed lives. He'd destroyed *her* life.

She glared at him now in silence as her brain rumbled.

'Jason wants us to have a baby,' Dani said.

She paused, as though waiting for a response. None came. Not even a twitch.

'Perhaps I've never really been the maternal type. I've never cooed over babies or anything like that, but that doesn't mean I didn't want it. It doesn't mean I wouldn't do it for Jason. I love him. I've put him through so much and all he's ever done is stand by me. I know, I know, that isn't the right reason for having a baby, but do I owe it to him? Then again… what if they turned out like you?'

That was possible, wasn't it? If Ben's DNA made him a killer, and if it was inside Dani too, then could she pass it on?

'Or what if something terrible happened? Look at me? At Jason? Will we ever achieve a life of safety and security? Can I, with good conscience, bring a child into our world?'

Or was that all just a convenient excuse? Was the real issue something much more selfish?

'The truth is, Ben, I'm scared.'

And in that moment, despite herself, despite everything, she wished he would open his eyes, get up from his bed, and walk over to hug her. Her Ben. Her brother.

Her only kin.

—

Dani stayed by Ben's side for more than an hour. She spent the vast majority of that time in full one-sided conversational flow. She'd talked openly about all of her personal problems, both at work and at home. Yet she hadn't told Ben that Gemma was moving away with his kids. Even if Ben was in a coma, Dani had shied away from bringing it up with him. Would Gemma even reconsider now?

Regardless, when was the last time Dani had ever spoken to anyone for so long? She wasn't sure.

Catharsis. She knew that's what it was, and that she'd needed it. That for weeks, months, perhaps years, she'd kept events and emotions bottled up inside. She hadn't opened up properly to anyone, not Jason, not even herself.

Yet she came out of the hospital feeling all the worse for it. Because the one person she'd turned to, in her time of need, was Ben. She felt ashamed. Not just because of opening up to him – a murderer – but because she'd chosen that moment for her own therapy, rather than to support someone – her closest relative – who had very nearly been beaten to death.

She was so confused.

After she came out of the room, she spent five minutes with Jackson as he tried to explain what had happened. How two men had jumped Ben during his exercise hour. How, once again, he would get to the bottom of how it happened. Dani wasn't really interested. Not at that moment. She still had far too much else going on in her mind.

She was nearly in tears as she sat back down in her car.

Had Ben been able to hear her? Did she want him to?

She checked her phone to try and take her mind off it.

No calls or messages. Often that would be a relief. This time it was a major disappointment.

She called Easton. No answer. She called Mutambe. No answer. Grayling… she answered, but had nothing new to share.

She didn't call Jason. Why not? What would he say if he knew she'd been with Ben? If he knew the things she'd just shared with the man who'd tried to kill her?

Dani sucked it up and drove the rest of the way back to Birmingham in silence, failing miserably to take Ben off her mind. When she got back to the office it was quiet inside. McNair was in, but her door was shut which meant she was busy. Grayling and a few others were in, but no sign of Easton or Mutambe.

Dani settled down and tried her best to use the vast amount of data that had been loaded into the HOLMES system for the Eccles case to distract her troubled mind. It worked. Kind of. At least in the sense that it was a distraction, but she pulled nothing of use from her ad-hoc review.

Finally, after what felt like several fruitless hours, but had actually been less than one, Easton and Mutambe wandered back in. No coats on. They hadn't been outside. Just in a meeting?

They both came straight over to Dani's desk.

'Are you OK?' Easton asked.

'I'm fine.'

Easton didn't look sure about that, but he obviously read the signs clearly and didn't push further.

'If you've got a minute, we've a couple of interesting developments.'

That was exactly what Dani needed to hear.

–

They headed back upstairs to a meeting room. Mutambe was clutching a file like it was the Crown Jewels. Dani's sense of expectation was high. She hoped she wasn't going to be disappointed.

Once they were all seated, Easton nodded to Mutambe. She smiled before she put the file down on the table.

'I've been doing a lot of searches on the various family members, plus the Werners. We've turned up a few oddities.'

Both Easton and Mutambe looked to Dani as though expecting her to say something.

'OK?'

'First up there's Henry Eccles. It's a bit of a long story, but, to put it simply, we think he may have a serious gambling problem.'

Dani looked to Easton, then back to Mutambe.

'You *think*?'

Mutambe was acting more nervously now. What was that about?

'I was looking through the transactions in the Eccles Holdings accounts, and I noticed a couple of recent big lump-sum transfers between the business and the Eccleses' personal joint account. It doesn't mean much on its own, but when I looked in the personal account, which we got the records for this morning too, there was a payment of forty thousand pounds to Henry Eccles not long ago, plus other big lump sums going back in time.'

'But you said gambling?'

'I also got access to Henry Eccles' bank account.' Tail practically between her legs as she talked.

Dani frowned. 'How?'

'I got McNair to fast-track a warrant. Given the importance of the case.'

Dani bit her tongue. Mutambe hadn't broken a law, or regulation as such, but she had broken the chain of command. A decision like that – to request personal banking details of someone, especially someone who was only on the periphery of the investigation – should have gone through Dani. She was the SIO. She looked over to Easton.

'DS Easton didn't know either,' Mutambe said. 'I'm sorry, but… it was a hectic weekend, right? There was so much going on and McNair was right there in her office when I was putting this together, and I knew you two were both so busy.'

Dani sighed. 'We have protocols in place for a reason. To protect you as much as anything else.'

Mutambe nodded.

'The point is,' Easton said, 'putting aside procedure, it was obvious within minutes of receiving Henry Eccles' bank records that he's got a problem. For months he's been bleeding cash to several online gambling companies, his account continually topped up by his parents, but also a couple of other accounts of so-far-unknown origin.'

'I'm working on figuring out who those accounts belong to.'

'Any idea how much?' Dani asked.

'Not exactly,' Mutambe said, 'but large lump-sum withdrawals and payments to online gaming companies are well into six figures this year alone.'

'When you put it together with the idea we have around the inheritance being a potential motive, it does add an extra dimension,' Easton said.

It did indeed.

'OK,' Dani said. 'Continue to scrutinise the cash accounts, both of the company, the Eccles parents, and Henry. Was it just Henry's accounts you got access to?'

'He was the only one who I saw being paid like that by Terry and Annie.'

Which was another interesting fact.

'Let's leave it at that then, unless we get a particular reason otherwise.'

'There is another finding,' Easton said. He nodded to Mutambe again.

'Don't ask me exactly how I got onto this, because I'm not entirely sure, but I was looking into Hugo Werner's past, and… perhaps it's best if you see for yourself.'

She pushed the file across the table. Dani took it and spent a few minutes looking through, trying her best to keep her jaw from dropping to the floor.

'Money can buy you anything, right?' Easton said.

'None of this was in HOLMES or any other database?' Dani asked.

'None of it,' Mutambe said. 'Otherwise it would have popped up immediately. I've had to go around the houses with other departments and Forces to get this far, and there's still plenty we don't know.'

'In two of the cases the charges were dropped by the police before trial,' Easton said. 'In the third case Hugo was arrested but released without charge. A civil case followed but was settled out of court.'

'So nothing stuck,' Dani said, 'but what I'm seeing is that Hugo Werner has been accused of assault and serious sexual assault on three separate occasions, by three different women?'

'Correct,' Mutambe said. 'One case of common assault against a girlfriend when he was nineteen years old. Charges dropped pre-trial due to insufficient evidence, which – from what I've been able to find on the sketchy files that are available – was in part due to the girlfriend refusing to testify. In the second case he was origin-ally charged with several instances of sexual harassment and sexual assault against a university peer. Again, those charges were dropped pre-trial, though it's a bit less clear why and I'm still trying to find out more details. He dropped out of university after that, and came back to live around here. In the third case – the only one which took place in the West Midlands – he was arrested on suspicion of raping an ex-girlfriend. He was released without charge. A civil lawsuit was filed following that, but it was settled out of court within a couple of weeks and we have no information what that settlement looks like.'

She shook her head in both disbelief and disgust. Hugo had never been convicted of any of the allegations, but that didn't mean he was innocent either.

'What we do know,' Dani said, 'is that Hugo Werner has a history of women accusing him of violence and sexual predation.'

'It certainly looks that way.'

'Which really begs the question, what the hell happened with Elle Martic?'

Chapter 34

February

Several days had passed since Terry had seen Henry in the pub. He'd sent the forty thousand, but nothing more, and had heard nothing more. He understood his son's predicament. Not understood from personal experience – he'd never owed a debt to a casino-running loan shark – but he firmly believed that Henry's situation really was as dire as he made it out to be. But a hundred thousand? He didn't have access to that kind of cash right now. Certainly not until everything with Lloyds was properly cleared, and even then he'd have to find a way to extract it from the business accounts without anyone noticing. Not that he hadn't had to do that before, but right now it felt like Eric had an eagle eye on him.

Henry would have to wait, or find another way. He could remortgage his apartment. Sell it, even. There was certainly enough capital there. Though he'd have to persuade his creditors to hold fire on doubling his debt – or breaking his legs – to make that work.

Terry was sure his son would be in touch, grovelling once more, soon enough, but today it was Will's turn to complain about his position on the Eccles gravy train.

Where did all of this end?

Terry arrived outside the development in the centre of Wolverhampton before his son. Terry had rarely ventured this far west in his own business life, which was perhaps one of the reasons why Will had. He was determined to make his own way. To make his own mark. Despite the trouble he'd caused in his teens, Will was still a young man. Young enough and bright enough to make a decent life for himself if he really wanted to. Yet, it seemed, he still had to rely on Terry and Annie financially.

Terry spent a few minutes looking across the building site from the outside while he waited. Two tall cranes lifted steel girders up high. Ten, twelve storeys at least. The pictures on the hoarding enclosing the site showed various glammed-up shots of the apartment block that was to come. Nice and modern, though nothing overly spectacular.

Will arrived on foot a few minutes later.

'Where'd you come from?' Terry asked, a little surprised.

'The Metro station's half a mile that way,' he said pointing behind him. 'It's one of the reasons this place is so good. It's sandwiched between transport links, the university, the city centre.'

Terry looked back over to the site. It seemed OK enough, nothing that got his juices flowing, though.

'Do you want to have a look around?' Will asked. He sounded about as upbeat as Terry could remember in recent years. Was the kid finally getting his shit together? 'They've got the sales office open now.'

Terry could see that. 'I don't need to,' he said. 'Nothing I haven't seen a hundred times before.'

Will looked disappointed.

'So what's the deal?' Terry asked.

'Do you know the developer?' Will asked.

Terry had heard of them, but had never had anything to do with them before.

'Not really.'

'The main guy's called Bob Hunter. The thing is, I got to know his daughter pretty well.'

Will said this with a twinkle in his eye. Typical Will.

'Did you now.'

Will laughed. 'It's not like that. I mean, it kind of is, but she's really decent. We just had a bit of fun. Nothing serious. Anyway, she introduced me to her dad. I told him all about you, all about us and what we're planning. He's definitely the kind of guy we could work with.'

Terry sighed. He could already sense where this was going. 'And?'

'And they're looking for a cash injection. Just to get this place finished off. They'll turn a profit after they've sold only half of the seventy-five units here. They're selling off-plan now. A dozen have gone already, but they expect the final ones won't go until it's finished. They're expecting that within the next six months, but they want it finished ASAP to get them all sold this financial year.'

Terry shook his head. 'How much?'

'This is a proper cushy deal, Dad. Bob agreed to sell ten units to me, twenty-five per cent off asking price. Twenty-five per cent up front. Seventy-five on completion. We can then keep them and rent them, or he'll work it so we can sell them on as new if we want. They'll even market them for us.'

Terry sighed but didn't say anything.

'It's four hundred grand down,' Will said, 'but we'll make a profit of half a million if we resell. Basically for doing bugger all.'

Terry still didn't say anything.

'Dad?'

'You kids'll be the death of me.'

'What's that supposed to mean?'

'Every single one of you is the same. You've all had it way too easy in life. And what? You think Mummy and Daddy will just bankroll you through every step of adulthood too?'

He went to turn away towards his car.

'Are you serious?' Will said.

'I'm not giving you two hundred thousand, Will,' Terry sneered. 'Three hundred, four hundred, whatever the fuck it is you're asking from me.'

'Seriously?'

'No deal, son. I'm not your damn personal ATM.'

'Fuck you, Dad. Is that what you thought this was? Shows how much you think of me.'

Terry was confused.

'I didn't ask you here because I need your money,' Will continued. 'I asked you here because I wanted to do you a favour. I wanted to help you out and see if you wanted a slice of this.'

Terry tried to think of something to say to that in return, but he couldn't find the words. Or figure out whether he was more angry, or disappointed. With himself.

'I heard you were having a hard time of it,' Will said. 'And I know the mess Henry is in. I was trying to do you a favour.'

'Who the hell has been telling you what?' Terry asked, his hackles raised. As far as he was aware, Eric, Henry and Laura didn't speak to Will at all.

'Sod off,' Will said. 'You don't want this deal? Fine. The offer's gone.'

He turned and walked away.

'Will, wait!' Terry shouted out, but his son was already storming up the road. Should he go after him?

He didn't even know what bothered him the most. The fact he'd misread his son's intentions, or the fact that he was desperate to know what Will knew, and how.

Will turned around, mid stride.

'Oh, and say hi to Elle for me,' he said with a mischievous wink.

The little bastard. Terry felt like launching himself towards him. Instead he remained rooted, watching his son stride away, as he wondered in vain just how much trouble he was in.

Chapter 35

February

It'd been days since Terry had spoken to any of his sons. Laura too. Partly because he was trying his best to stay away from them all, for various reasons, but did it work the other way too?

Henry and his gambling issues. Laura and her no-good husband. Dumbass Eric and what he knew about the loans. Will...

Was he Terry's biggest problem now? Will had been speaking to someone about Terry, that much was clear. He wouldn't rule out that Will even knew something about the deal with Hamed, and how Laura's terrorist husband had resorted to arson to get their way.

But the situation that concerned him the most was the possibility that Will knew about Elle. How on earth would he know that?

Of course there was no way that he would ask Will directly. He wasn't going to prompt a discussion about it, even if he was fearful about what Will would do with the information. If there was one thing that could be said for his youngest son, it was that he often used his wits to get exactly what he wanted.

So what did he want?

Regardless, Terry wouldn't confront Will. But he would ask Elle. When the time was right.

Today. He'd ask her today.

They hadn't seen each other for a couple of days. Hugo had been keeping a tight leash on her. Quite literally. Barely letting her out of his sight.

But today Terry knew that Hugo was with Peter at the Somerton development.

Hence why he was travelling over to Bridlington Terrace.

Somehow it made him feel all the more powerful – and smug – that he wasn't just having an affair with Hugo's girlfriend, but that he was screwing her in Hugo's home.

Terry smiled to himself.

He'd often wondered exactly why Elle was with Hugo. She bad-mouthed him all the time. Other than his money and good looks, Hugo simply wasn't good enough for her in any way.

Her attraction to Terry? He firmly believed it was because he offered everything Hugo couldn't. Yes he was older, but no less capable. Elle wanted a real man, not a spoilt boy.

He arrived there in good time. With any luck they'd have at least a couple of hours together before Hugo was finished with his meetings. Terry was already bursting with excitement as he travelled up in the lift. Her voice on the intercom… fuck, did she know how to get him going.

He could already imagine her. The look in her eyes. Her body. Her smell. Her touch.

The doors to the lift opened. He tried to calm himself as he approached the front door. He rapped the wood with his knuckles.

Barely a second later and the door swung open.

Terry's face dropped as his heart faltered.

'You piece of shit,' Hugo said.

Then he grabbed Terry by the scruff of his neck, yanked him inside, and tossed him to the floor.

—

Moments later they were all inside. Terry stood motionless in the lounge area. Why? Why was he just standing there like an idiot?

The look on Hugo's face, in his bloodshot eyes. That was why.

Hugo was high. Out of control high. Strung-out. The white powder remnants were spread across the coffee table. Hugo was sitting on the edge of the sofa, credit card in hand, as he played with the bits, pulling them together for another hit. The bottle of scotch on the kitchen counter showed it wasn't only the coke that was coursing through his system, and causing his erratic behaviour.

Elle was sitting on the opposite sofa. Curled up. Her eyes teary. Her make-up a mess. Her bottom lip swollen and bloodied, her cheek red.

Terry just stood there, watching them both. Numb.

'I knew I couldn't trust her,' Hugo said, his body trembling as he spoke. 'I see the way every bastard looks at her. Do you know what kind of power trip that gives? But somehow I knew it'd come to this… I really fell for her. I couldn't stop it.'

Which was exactly how Terry had felt.

Hugo caught his eye.

'But you?' he said, with pure revulsion. 'Look at *you*. I just don't get it.'

He leaped up from the chair. Elle cowered back.

'What the fuck is wrong with you!' Hugo screamed, leaning over her while waving his arm towards Terry. 'He's old, weak, pathetic. He's a piece of shit.'

'I'm sorry,' Elle sobbed.

Quite who she was speaking to, it wasn't clear.

'Hugo. Just let her leave,' Terry said, trying to sound as calm as possible. The truth was, he was scared. For himself, and for Elle. The state Hugo was in, who knew what he was capable of. 'She doesn't want to be here. Look at her.'

'Look at her? I'll look at her if I want. You? You don't get to. Not ever again.'

'We don't have to do this,' Terry said.

Hugo burst forwards. Terry couldn't react quick enough as Hugo grabbed him around the neck and lifted him up off the floor and pushed him against the wall.

'This is my house! She's my woman! I'll do whatever the fuck I want! Got it?'

Terry couldn't have choked a response even if he'd wanted to. Hugo's grip went tighter still. He was grimacing so hard from the effort.

Across the room, Elle got to her feet. She looked shocked. Petrified. She moved over.

'Hit him,' Terry tried to say.

Really it sounded nothing more than a splutter. But the effort, and the aversion in his eyes, caused a momentary lapse in Hugo's concentration. His grip loosened. He flicked his gaze over his shoulder.

Terry went for it. He hauled his knee up into Hugo's groin. Snapped Hugo's arms away. Then delivered a thunderous hook to Hugo's jaw to send him sprawling to the floor.

'Hugo!' Elle shrieked with concern.

She rushed to him. Knelt down by his side as he grog-gily tried to prop himself up. Blood dribbled down his chin. Much the same look he'd given Elle.

She cradled Hugo in her arms. Tears streamed down her face.

Terry was gobsmacked. She glanced up to him.

'Just go!' she shouted.

What was she doing?

'You heard her,' Hugo croaked.

Terry was so shocked he found himself backing away, towards the door.

'If I see you around her again...'

Hugo left the threat dangling. Terry turned for the door.

'And I want my money!' Hugo shouted out. 'You pay me what we agreed. Or I'm gonna make your life hell!'

Terry didn't respond. Didn't look back at all. Unsure what to think, he simply opened the door and walked out.

Chapter 36

March

The meeting with Mutambe and Easton was exactly what Dani had needed to push thoughts of Ben from her mind. She drove home that evening with a head full of murder and scandal instead. Hardly upbeat, but what she needed in that moment.

To her mind, the pool of likely candidates for who had murdered Terry and Annie Eccles remained small: those who were closest to the victims. Yet the shadiness, the misdemeanours, the criminality, the motives, for each of those people seemed to grow all the time.

Dani arrived home at seven p.m. Positively early for her, but she'd felt like crap most of the day, was still feeling the after-effects of the attack the previous night, and wanted to at least try and spend something that came close to quality time with Jason.

She'd called ahead to say she was coming. Jason was standing by the lounge window when she pulled onto the driveway. Her protector. In his own way.

Thankfully, it was unnecessary this time. As cautious as she was as she stepped out of the car, there was no one in wait for her. Not Will Eccles, not any goons. Just Jason.

'How was your day?' he asked once she was inside and had collapsed onto the sofa.

'Horrendous,' she said.

'Do you want to talk about it?' he asked, hovering over her like he expected her to say no, and was ready to leave the room to do something else. Her mind took her back to the hospital. The conversation with Ben. The confusion she'd felt afterwards, but also the sense of relief for finally spilling her guts to someone else. Ben hadn't responded at all. He couldn't. But here was Jason, ready and willing, as ever, to help her through.

'Yeah,' she said. 'I think I do.'

He smiled and sat down next to her.

–

A good night's sleep. Finally. Was it pure exhaustion that had won out, or was it the mental relief from the two hours she and Jason had spent chatting on the sofa? Not about anything too deep really. A little about the cases, but most of the rest of it was banal and… fun.

There was a glaring omission from their chatter; family matters. Both in the sense of them starting a family, and Ben. Dani simply hadn't been able to bring herself to open up about either of those. Nonetheless, she felt like a weight had been lifted off her shoulders as she stepped – rather than dragged herself – out of bed on Tuesday morning.

Jason was already up. Already in the kitchen. Breakfast made.

'Well, this is nice,' Dani said.

He didn't say anything, just smiled at her.

Dani sat down at the table. He brought her over some toast, buttered and jammed. She wouldn't say it was perfect or bliss or anything as over-the-top as that. But it was certainly nice to feel more at ease, see a smile on his face, and to feel closer to him once again, even if she knew their issues remained far from fully resolved.

She was one mouthful in when her phone rang.

They looked at each other.

'It's fine,' he said.

It really wasn't. She got that. But she answered anyway.

'Aaron, what is it?'

'I'm on my way to Kibble House,' he said.

'Again? What for?'

'Henry Eccles is going there at eight thirty.'

'I'm on my way.'

–

Easton beat Dani to it. Even though she lived close, she'd tried to at least enjoy her breakfast before she'd left. Jason seemed to appreciate that. She hoped so at least.

Dani shivered as she got out of the car at Kibble House. With an overcast sky and a blistering wind, it felt more like mid-winter. Still, Easton was standing outside the house, ignoring the cold, chatting to PC Shaw, who'd been there the other day too. Chatting? More like flirting, Dani thought, given the way the two were smiling at each other. Easton certainly thought of himself as a charmer these days.

Minutes later she and Easton were inside, warming through, even if the house was only a few degrees warmer than outside.

'You two looked rather cosy together,' Dani said.

Easton smiled coyly. 'Yeah, Jess is all right.'

'First-name terms too?'

Easton didn't respond.

'You've moved on from your weekend date already?'

He didn't get a chance to answer that one. Dani caught the sound of a car engine outside.

'Early,' Easton said.

'Convenient,' Dani responded to that.

Henry Eccles was alone. And he didn't look too happy when Dani opened the door to him. Had he expected only Easton? As though he were a soft touch compared to her?

'Wow, the cavalry's out in force,' he said with a sly look on his face as he stepped inside.

'We both live locally,' Easton said, as if a justification was needed.

'And apparently have nothing better to do. Like catching a killer.'

Dani very nearly bit back at that, but held the response in her head.

'What can we do for you today, Henry?' Dani said.

'I'm guessing you're going to tell me I'll have a couple of shadows following me around the house.'

'Is that a problem?'

'Yes, actually. Between meetings with you, liaison officers, and whatever else, I'm finding it hard enough to get space and time to grieve. What I want is to be left alone so I can take this all in.'

'I understand,' Dani said. 'We won't stand in your way. Take a look around. Do what you need to do. The only thing I ask is that if you want to take anything, you tell us. Yeah?'

He looked a bit unsure. Like it was all a trick.

'OK,' he said. 'That's fair enough.'

And off he set. Dani waited until he was upstairs, out of sight, before she met Easton's eye. She was aware he'd been staring at her for several seconds.

'Did I miss something?' he asked.

'No?'

'So what's the game?'

'No game.'

Easton didn't look convinced, but what was the worst that could happen now? They'd already had Forensics scour the house. Dani herself had looked top to bottom, as had Easton. They'd cleared out the office and the safes. What could Henry possibly do now, without them knowing, to jeopardise the investigation?

But mostly she wanted him at least a bit onside for when they had a 'chat'.

Henry mooched for only ten minutes. About a minute of that was spent in the office. He didn't look at all surprised when he came out that it was empty in there. Had Laura already told him?

'Did you find what you needed?' Dani asked when he resurfaced in the hallway and came over to them.

'I really don't know,' he said.

A bit of a strange answer.

'Do you think we could talk to you for a few minutes?' Dani said.

Henry sighed. 'I guessed that was why you were here. Come on, this way.'

They moved through to the kitchen and dining area where the back of the house opened out into a gorgeous Georgian-style orangery. That said, on a cold, gloomy day, without the heating on, the vast amount of glass in the space made for a chilling atmosphere.

All three of them retained their coats.

They seated themselves around the slab-like dining table. A relatively modern affair given the generally traditional decor, it reminded Dani more of an oversized butcher's block than a dining table. For some reason that thought brought with it a flash of blood and gore. Dani shook it away.

'So come on then, fire away,' Henry said.

Where to start? Dani thought.

'Did you ever discuss inheritance with your parents?' she asked.

Henry's fist was on the table. He clenched it a little at the question, before quickly pulling it onto his lap.

'Laura warned me you were going to ask about this.'

Of course she did. What else had she pre-warned Henry about? Dani would press on regardless.

'Was that a yes or a no?' Easton asked.

'No. I didn't. Was I aware there was a will? No, I wasn't. Am I surprised Dad made out a will that left his shareholding in the business to Peter, Hugo and Eric but not me or Laura or Will? A little.'

'But you didn't know about that?' Dani said.

'I thought I already said that. I didn't know about it. I don't know why he would do that. I'm only taking your word for it that he did, because I haven't seen that will, and as far as I'm aware neither has his solicitor.'

'His solicitor?'

'Bill Hammersmith. Dad used him for everything.'

Did he? Hadn't Hammersmith said the will was the only interaction he'd had with the Eccles family? Dani would check that with Easton after.

'You've spoken to Mr Hammersmith about this?' Dani asked.

'I think Laura has. To get to the bottom of this will you talked to her about. Apparently, he had no knowledge of it at all either.'

'So according to this new will,' Easton said, 'you got none of the business, and most of everything else would go to charity. Peter Werner, on the other hand, gets forty per cent of Eccles Holdings. How do you feel about that?'

'Feel? You two are really something. I've only just started to think about funeral arrangements with my family, and you're onto this.'

Dani supposed that was a fair point.

'The way I see this,' Easton said, 'there's a pretty big motive—'

'You two are so bloody obvious,' Henry said. 'Why don't you just come out and say it? You think one of us – perhaps even me – killed Mum and Dad. Why? To get hold of their money? Did you see what was done to them?'

'I did,' Dani said. 'It was horrible.'

'You think I could do that?'

Neither Dani nor Easton answered that question. The lack of response only seemed to rile Henry further.

'Tell us about your gambling?' Dani said, well aware that the prompt would only piss Henry off even more.

He gritted his teeth like a snarling dog.

'We know your parents were bailing you out,' Dani said. 'How long has it been a problem for you?'

'I'm not doing this.'

'Doing what?'

'Whatever my problems are, they're absolutely nothing to do with you.'

'Actually, that's the problem,' Easton said. 'Because we're investigating your parents' murder, and in doing that we're looking for motive—'

'You want motive? What about the rest of them? Laura and that twat of a husband of hers. Setting a fire that nearly killed four people—'

'You knew about that?'

'It was bloody obvious. I'm not directly involved in the business but I get to hear what's going on. Dad didn't know what to do, it was basically like blackmail. And it's not the first time.'

'First time what?'

'That Hamed has resorted to underhand tactics. Apparently, he's known for it.'

'Like what?'

'Like... I don't know. It's your job to investigate these things, but Eric said there are rumours all over. And what about Eric?'

'What about him?'

'You talk about inheritance and my gambling as though the two are connected. What about the others? They all lose out the same, if not more than me, from that will.'

'Except you're the only one with a desperate need for cash,' Dani said. 'Aren't you?'

'And what about Hugo and Will?' Henry said.

'What about them?' Easton responded.

'Hugo and that woman, Elle.'

'You know about Elle?' Dani asked.

Henry shook his head in disgust. 'She was a piece of work.'

'In what way?'

'You don't know?'

'Apparently not.'

'Hugo ditched her. Because she was having an affair. Not just that but spreading gossip around the place.'

'Having an affair with your dad?' Dani said, as she began to put the pieces together.

'Dad? What? No, he… he would never do that. But Dad found out about it. That was the problem.'

'So who then?'

'Will,' Henry said, as though it should have been obvious. 'Will was having an affair with Elle. Dad found out. He exposed it. Will and Hugo both hated him for it. You're asking me about motive? You're looking in the wrong place.'

Chapter 37

Dani and Easton waited on the gravel as Henry Eccles drove away.

'So basically he's accusing his siblings, their business partners, his brother-in-law of murder,' Easton said. 'How loving.' Rather too tongue-in-cheek given the real-life situation.

'What a mess,' was all Dani could come up with.

'If Will really was having an affair with Elle... I'm not sure I get the motive.'

'It depends exactly what Terry did when he found out. Will could have blamed him for bringing the affair to light. Hugo because... shoot the messenger? I don't really know.'

'Unless Henry is lying. What if the affair wasn't with Will, but with Terry?'

Which was what Dani had thought Henry's reveal was going to be. She turned that idea over in her head for a moment.

'Lying, or he doesn't understand the full truth,' she said.

'About the murders?'

'About any of it. But I was thinking more about the situation between Hugo and Elle, and Will and Terry.'

'You think there's more to it?'

'I'm almost certain of it. But Hugo's not going to talk to us. Terry is gone. So we have to find Will or Elle.'

'I'll make it a priority.'

'Thanks. See you back in the office?'

They both had their cars there. It'd be simple to drop one of the vehicles off and head to Birmingham together. Save the planet, and all that. But given the last few days, Dani really didn't know what the rest of Tuesday would bring.

'Yeah,' Easton said. 'I'll see you there.' He glanced over to his companion standing by her squad car. 'I've just got a couple of things to sort out here first.'

Dani smirked. His cheeks flushed. Perhaps he hadn't realised how obvious he was.

'Subtle, Aaron. Really subtle.'

–

The bizarre conversation with Henry Eccles continued to dominate Dani's mind as the hours rolled away. She spent much of the time staring at her computer screen, sifting through the reams of data on the HOLMES systems for the Eccles case, including the financial records for Eccles Holdings Limited which was a minefield all on its own, and which was why they'd already brought in the Force's in-house Forensic Accounting Team to assist them.

She hadn't even got around to considering where everything was at with the Harrison case. At least with him now charged and in custody, they had some breathing space.

First, she needed a break.

No. Instead, she went over to Mutambe.

'Any luck getting hold of the Bridlington Terrace CCTV?' she asked.

'I was promised the files today. Still waiting on it.'

Security at the development was outsourced to a private company. Among their duties, they were responsible for operating close to fifty CCTV cameras around the grounds, and in the communal areas of the buildings. Dani hoped getting hold of those recordings would at least provide some clues as to what had happened between Hugo and Elle, when she'd last been with Hugo, and potentially even if she'd had any other visitors – like Will Eccles – to add credence to Henry's accusation.

'Let me know when it arrives,' Dani said. 'I'll help you get into it.'

'Absolutely.'

Dani was about to move over to Grayling for an update from her, but her phone, vibrating on the desk, put paid to that. Dani jogged over, lifted the phone up just before it rang out. A number she didn't recognise. She answered.

'DI Stephens,' she said.

'DI Stephens? This is Sergeant Colter from Traffic. You have an alert out—'

'Two actually,' Dani said. One for Will Eccles' car, one for the car belonging to the men who'd attacked her.

'Black BMW 1 series.' He read the registration out.

'That's the one,' Dani said, already reaching for her coat with her free hand. 'You stopped them?'

'No. I've got eyes on it. No one inside. It's parked by the shops on Angleton Road in—'

'Castle Bromwich,' Dani said.

'Yeah.'

'I'm coming now. Try to stay out of sight. And if the car goes anywhere, follow it.'

'Yes, Ma'am.'

Dani was there within twenty minutes. She parked a couple of hundred yards away from the location Colter had given her – trying to be discreet – then dialled his number.

'I'm here,' Dani said. 'Anything?'

'Nothing yet,' he said. 'But the on-road parking here is only for an hour at a time so unless they're quick we'll at least have that.'

Dani stepped out of her car and looked down the street towards the shops. 'I don't see you,' she said.

'Side street. Green Road.'

'I'll be there in a minute.'

Dani slowly walked along, head down, trying to keep her nerves in check, though her heart rate was steadily building. Two days ago two men had turned up at her house and beaten her. Two men who very possibly could be within yards of her now. She was wary of them, scared of them.

She was also absolutely determined to catch them.

As she approached the shops – a row of Victorian terraces either side of the road that contained everything from coffee shops to butcher's to bars to hair salons to a furniture store – the pavement became busier with pedestrians, though there were hardly throngs of people jostling. Dani spotted the BMW in the near distance, other side of the street, parked directly outside a barber's that was nestled between a bank and a pizza takeaway. She reached Green Road and looked left. Colter's BMW 3 series was parked a few cars down where there was a BP petrol station. Dani headed over to him, looking over her shoulder every couple of steps, back towards the shops.

When she reached Colter's car she moved to the passenger side, opened the door and climbed in.

Her heart was thudding as she shut the door again.

'Nice to meet you,' Colter said.

Dani looked over at him and smiled, trying to compose herself.

'You too,' she said.

Colter was young, probably late twenties, but he was hefty. Tall and hefty. His head was an inch from the roof of the car, and with his uniform on, all tooled up, he spilled out around his seat. She could tell from the bulge in his arm that his size was largely muscle rather than fat. Primal instincts made her feel that bit more secure all of a sudden.

'What's the deal then?' he said. 'You're Homicide, aren't you?'

'I am. Two days ago I was attacked. At my home.'

'That explains the banged-up lip.'

'Among other bruises and scrapes. There were two men in that car.' She indicated over to the 1 Series. 'They jumped me, threatened me about my investigation, then ran.'

'But you don't know who they are?'

'Not yet.'

'Description?'

Dani thought about that one for a moment. Yes, they'd both been wearing hoods, but why could she not pick out anything at all about their faces? In her mind there was nothing. Just the hoods, the dark figures rushing towards her, then crowding over her as they delivered blow after blow.

'I don't know,' Dani said. Though she was sure she'd at least recognise their voices.

At least she hoped she would.

'What were you doing around here anyway?' Dani asked.

Her question sounded accusatory. She hadn't intended it to. The look on Colter's face showed his confusion.

'I was just filling up. On my way to the M6.'

'Thank you. For looking out, I mean. This could be really important.'

He nodded but didn't say anything.

'How long have you been here now?' she asked.

'Nearly forty minutes.'

'Let's get some back-up sorted. Another car. But get them to keep it discreet. They can park the other side from here, out of view.'

'I'm on it.'

Colter got speaking into his radio that was attached to his broad chest. He only had to duck his head a couple of inches to speak into it. Dani's eyes remained glued to the car across the road.

Then her gaze flicked to the barber shop when the door opened. Two men stepped out. Then three.

Dani didn't recognise the first two. The third… it took a moment, but she placed him.

The men were clustered in a triangle, right next to the 1 Series, chatting, smiling.

'That's them,' Dani said, hand on the door handle.

'Wait, what are we doing?'

'I'm going over there.'

'There's three of them.'

'We've got back-up coming.'

'They're a couple of minutes away.'

'They'll be here soon enough. Tell them to come in on blue lights. Sirens. You're coming with me.'

'Wait, that's not—'

Dani didn't wait to hear what he had to say. Most likely something about how he was a traffic cop. How it was more sensible to follow the car and wait for the back-up.

Dani wasn't waiting.

'Stay apart until we close in on them.'

Colter didn't say anything else. Dani stepped from the car and strode towards the three men. She crossed to the other side of Green Road. Colter was a few steps behind her on the other side. Out of the car he was even bigger. Six feet five or six. About as inconspicuous as an elephant. Hopefully, he could move quickly if he needed to.

Dani reached Angleton Road. The men were still chatting. Two of them were smoking. A fourth man came out of the barber's and joined the group. Shit. Four against two now. But Dani didn't stop moving. She stared at the new arrival. She knew him too. Her heart was beating even faster than before as adrenaline surged. But it was also mixed in equal measure with anger.

She looked left and right, then dashed across the road. The BMW was all of twenty yards away.

A siren in the distance. The men took no notice. Too confident. Cocky. They couldn't care less.

Dani reached the pavement they were on. The men were ten yards from her when the one furthest to the left looked her way. He did a quick double-take before his eyes flicked behind her. To Colter, no doubt. He nudged his friend. One of the two Dani knew.

He looked over. There was a strange moment as he stared. Dani stared back, closing in all the time. There it was. Recognition complete.

That was when he turned and ran.

Chapter 38

Dani ran too. As did the other three men. As did Colter – Dani could hear the pounding on the ground behind her.

'Stop, police!' she screamed. Several pedestrians turned to see what the commotion was. Would any of the bystanders be brave enough to help?

One of the men dashed for the car. He grabbed the driver's door and yanked it open. The other three pelted away down the street. Dani burst forwards and kicked the car door shut, grabbed the man and tossed him onto the bonnet.

'You take him,' Dani shouted to Colter.

She set off again at a sprint. Further ahead the blue lights came into view. The three men took their chance to split up. Two went left, across the road, the third, the one Dani had her sights set on, went off to the right, down a side street.

She'd have to rely on the coppers in the squad car to pick up the other two.

Dani sprinted down the street, her breaths heavier by the second, her legs already aching from lactate build-up. She wouldn't give in. Not until she was spent.

The street was residential. Modest semis, cars parked bumper to bumper on both sides of the road. The runner darted across the street without looking. Dani did the same. The end of the road was less than a hundred yards away. A T-junction. Beyond there, Dani had no idea. Sirens filled the air. The man looked over his shoulder. Fear, Dani thought, rather than anger.

He went to dart back across the street again. What was he doing?

Then a police car came screeching to a halt at the end of the road. Did that mean the other two had got away? No. Dani was sure she could still hear a siren behind her too. There was more than one police car.

Two coppers jumped from the car in front. The man skidded to a stop. Turned. To face-off with Dani.

But Dani wasn't stopping. She drove forwards. The man looked shocked. Like he had no clue what to do.

Until the knife came out of his pocket.

Too late for Dani.

With a guttural roar she barged into him. He tried to stab the knife into her side, but the momentum of her hitting him sent his aim off and the blade nicked her skin. Painful, but it'd take more than that to stop her.

Dani crashed him up against the side of a van. The metalwork boomed. The van wobbled on its suspension. Dani grabbed the man's wrist. Turned it inside out. He screamed as the knife came free.

She carried on twisting, using momentum, and the hold to bring him down on the tarmac. She dug her knee into his back.

'Cuffs!' she shouted to the officers hurtling nearer.

Seconds later the man was secured.

Dani grabbed his shackled wrists and pulled him to his feet. She spun him around and looked into his defeated eyes.

'Nice to see you again,' Dani said. 'Remember me?'

He didn't say anything.

'Trey, right? Trey Wallace? You're under arrest.'

—

Two hours later and Dani didn't know whether to be smiling or fuming. There were four men in custody. None of them had got away. That was good. And a relief for Dani as events could have turned out quite differently if the back-up hadn't arrived just in time.

One of the four men in the cells was Trey Wallace, the young guy from the garage where Clinton Harrison had worked before his arrest. Two of the other men, Dani now realised, she'd seen that day in the garage too – the ones who'd left just as she arrived. The fourth man she had never met before, but having run his prints, and the others' prints, all had records for a variety of offences from driving while disqualified to assault to drug possession and even one count of supply. They were all lowlifes. And Dani firmly believed that given the connection to both Clinton Harrison, and the car, that among the four were the two who had assaulted her outside her own home. She still had some work to do in proving that, but for now the assessment was clear; the men were all known associates of Clinton Harrison. Dani had been attacked not because of the Eccles case, but because of her digging into Harrison. For some reason that surprised her, though she wasn't sure why.

And that wasn't the only finding. It hadn't gone unnoticed to Dani that one of the men bore a striking resemblance to the man described to Dani by that group of boys in Castle Bromwich. The one they'd seen Dylan Roberts' girlfriend leave her home with.

As far as Dani was concerned, the circle was complete, and she and DC Grayling were on their way to interview

Clinton Harrison to confront him with their findings, and to get to the bottom of it all.

Dani wasn't quite sure what kind of response she was expecting from Asher and Harrison. She'd spoken to Asher on the phone to arrange the interview, and had very deliberately slipped to the lawyer what had happened in Castle Bromwich earlier, who the four men in custody were, and their apparent relationship to her client. Doing so was a bit of a gamble on Dani's part as it would have been nice to spring that all on the two of them in the interview, but Dani wanted to give them both the opportunity to do the right thing.

Still, Dani was surprised when she and Grayling arrived outside the interview room to find Asher standing by the closed door on her own.

'Detectives,' she said, her face as sour as her tone.

'Where's Clinton?' Dani asked.

'He's waiting for you,' Asher said, indicating to the door.

'Is there a problem?'

'For me there is, yes.' She paused, as though Dani was supposed to know what that meant, and should respond to it. 'Unfortunately, I'm no longer able to represent Mr Harrison.'

As far as Dani was concerned, there was nothing unfortunate about that at all.

Asher's decision was exactly what Dani would expect from a lawyer like her. Asher had only become involved in the case for one clear reason: to boost her own public profile. She hadn't cared about doing the right thing. Clearly Harrison hadn't told her the truth about his relationship with Dylan Roberts up front, otherwise she'd likely have retracted her olive branch much sooner.

How would Asher's departure, and the reasons for it, be captured in the press? Dani wondered. Asher was surely unlikely to hold a big, bold TV conference this time. The police had evidence that her client's close associates had assaulted a detective to divert the progress of the case. That was ammunition that could destroy Asher's career. Dani wasn't sure she wanted any of that ammunition made public – to keep herself out of the limelight as much as anything else – but was Asher complicit in those events, even if in an indirect way? Was further action from the police warranted? Asher's overly quick and quiet departure would suggest she herself believed she was worried about her position.

Dani would quietly consider that point. But for now, she had Harrison to deal with.

The prisoner was sullen. Dani and Grayling took their seats then Grayling opened up the interview formalities before handing over to Dani.

'Mr Harrison, I understand you are no longer being represented by Mrs Asher?'

He grunted in response.

'Mr Harrison, is that correct?'

'Yeah.'

'And are you happy to carry on this interview without representation?'

'What choice do I have?'

'Sorry?'

'I can't afford a lawyer.'

'A lawyer can be provided for you—'

'Just get on with it.'

Dani stared at him for a few seconds. He glared back. Why did she feel sorry for him again?

'OK, Mr Harrison, I'm going to show you pictures of four different men. I'm going to ask if you know each of them, and if you do, what the nature of your relationship is with each one.'

Grayling handed Dani the photos and she slowly flipped them over and placed them in a row in front of Harrison.

'Mr Harrison, do you know this man?' Dani said, starting with the picture of the man named Greg Pollard. The man who potentially knew Dylan Roberts' girl-friend.

Harrison looked from the picture, to Dani, back to the picture.

'His name is Greg Pollard,' Dani said.

Harrison held Dani's eye now. His lips were pursed. The look in his eyes, the way he held his face – he looked so different to the grieving father Dani had seen the last time she'd spoken to him.

'Mr Harrison, do you know this man?' Dani said, her tone harder as she tapped the picture with a fingertip.

'I want a lawyer,' Harrison said.

'You don't—'

'I want a lawyer,' he repeated. 'And I'm not saying another word to you until I get one.'

Chapter 39

Dani wasn't quite sure what she expected when she and Grayling headed back into the office. A standing ovation from her colleagues?

The abandonment of Harrison by Asher, together with the four men in custody – two of which were likely the men who had attacked Dani, and one of which had a direct connection to Dylan Roberts – certainly felt like a major victory. Didn't it?

Perhaps a standing ovation was a bit too Hollywood. Yet what Dani hadn't expected was for McNair's stony face to appear in the door of her office and for the daggers to be thrown Dani's way.

'In here, please,' she said, before Dani had a chance to do or say anything.

The 'please' seemed a bit unnecessary given the tone. And no standing ovation. More like being sent to the headmistress's office.

Dani skulked over. She closed the door to the office then remained standing while McNair glared up at her from her desk chair.

'Quite a morning,' McNair said.

'It certainly has been.'

'You're pleased about Asher?'

'Aren't you?'

'Ordinarily I would be, yes.'

'But?'

'But I've just had a call from the hospital to inform me that Trey Wallace has a broken arm.'

'What! I—'

'He's already asked about the procedure for making an official complaint against you for use of excessive force.'

'That is ridiculous.'

Dani thought back to the moment. Wallace had been bombing away from her. She'd had to catch him somehow. Then he'd turned back to face her when the cop car had arrived. Had drawn a knife as Dani closed in on him. The blade had nicked her. Not a bad cut, but it could have been. Yes, she'd thrown him to the ground, had twisted his arm forcefully to do so. It was broken? She'd very nearly suffered a potentially fatal stab wound. His choice.

'No,' Dani said, shaking her head. 'I'm not having this. It's ridiculous. He could have killed me. And there were two officers who witnessed everything. I did nothing wrong!'

McNair sighed. 'That might be the case, but a complaint is a complaint. It has to be dealt with properly and fully. And the problem, Dani, for you, for me, is that it's not the only one.'

'The only one what?'

McNair lifted up a piece of paper from her desk. 'I've had a formal complaint this morning from the law firm representing Peter and Hugo Werner. They allege unfair harassment of their clients, and also detail their belief that the warrant covering Eccles Holdings Limited was not only frivolous but potentially damaging to both the business and the personal reputations of the Werners. They're seeking as yet unspecified, but substantial damages.'

'That warrant wasn't even me—'

McNair slammed her fist on the table. 'Whoever requested that warrant – whoever signed off on it – is beside the point, Dani. The point is that you're personally named in this complaint, and are the sole focus of the complaint I expect to receive from Trey Wallace.'

Dani's shoulders dropped. 'So what are you saying?'

This certainly wasn't the first time complaints had been made about her. It wasn't the first time she'd been the subject of investigations. She'd even been suspended in the past pending the outcome of investigations. Not that she ever felt her conduct had fallen below what was required, but sometimes it was as though criminals had more protection than the police officers who were trying to keep law and order.

'I'm afraid this puts me, and you, in a very tricky position,' McNair said.

Dani slumped even further. It was pretty obvious what McNair was about to say. And at such a crucial point in the Eccles and Harrison investigations too.

Why did Dani put herself through this?

'But I can't afford to have you off work at this time,' McNair said. Dani's ears pricked up. She caught McNair's eye. 'We both could have done without this added pressure and scrutiny, and you need to have a long, hard think about your actions… but I want you to carry on as SIO on both of these cases. You need to get some answers for me. That's going to be the most clear-cut way to shut down these baseless claims.'

Dani couldn't believe what she was hearing. Was McNair on something?

'Is that clear?' McNair said.

'Yes.'

'Good, then get back to it.'

Dani said nothing more, even if she had felt like going up to McNair and hugging her. Instead she walked out of McNair's office with her head held high. There weren't many times she'd done that. Even her colleagues looked surprised.

She sat down at her desk. Her brain was swimming. Not just with the news from McNair about the complaints, but about everything that surrounded them. Trey Wallace surely had nothing on Dani, but the process would have to be seen through. Strangely, what irked more was the complaint from the Werners. Heavy-handed to say the least, particularly when put together with the way Peter had shut down the conversation between the police and his son the other day.

Which begged one very big question: what exactly were those two trying to hide?

Time to find out.

Chapter 40

The only question for Dani was where to start. There was still so much about Eccles Holdings that she didn't know but wanted to. She had a team of accountants working on that too, but that didn't mean Dani couldn't make inroads herself. Then there was the vast swathes of CCTV data they now had for Bridlington Terrace. Mutambe was too busy chasing up on Elle Martic's whereabouts to take the lead on that herself. Grayling was still swamped with the Harrison case and pulling out anything and everything she could for the four men they had in cells. Easton was... where was Easton?

'Hey,' Dani shouted across the room to Mutambe, who stuck her head up over the divider. 'Where's Aaron?'

Mutambe shrugged. 'Haven't seen him for a couple of hours. But...'

She got up from her chair, looked around her as though she wasn't sure she wanted anyone else to hear what she was going to say. She wandered over to Dani.

'I'm getting nowhere with Elle Martic.'

'In what sense.'

'I don't know. I don't know whether the lack of anything useful is actually a really bad sign. I mean, she's so elusive. Other than a bit of a social media profile, and the electoral roll record, her life is like a closed book. No employment record, no bank account. The mobile number we had for her is a prepaid SIM and there's been nothing from that number for a couple of weeks.'

'When did she first get that SIM?'

'That's the thing. Not long ago. About six weeks. I'm still trying to figure out what number she had before that but I haven't managed it yet. Perhaps she does have an older number. Perhaps she has a new one.'

'Hugo Werner would know the answer, I'm sure,' Dani said with a sigh.

'Indeed. I tracked her parents. They're Lithuanian. They haven't spoken to her for six months, and couldn't provide anything useful. It sounds like there's been strain there for some time. I've found a couple of friends from social media who live around here, both of them Eastern European too, but neither of them was good friends with her. Both claimed she was private, as elusive as she was aloof. They haven't heard from her for a couple of weeks but neither was too concerned. They just assumed she'd moved to a different city having broken up with Hugo.'

'So they knew she'd broken up with Hugo?'

'I think... kind of, yeah. Both suggested she was seeing someone else.'

'Will Eccles?'

'I mentioned his name but they both said no.'

'Get a picture of Will in front of them both. See what they say then.'

Mutambe nodded. She looked like she wanted to say something else. She didn't. Instead she wandered back to her desk, a little disconsolately, Dani thought.

That made Dani's mind up. CCTV. She was determined to get to the bottom of this story.

There was a whole cache of files uploaded to the HOLMES system from the security company that oversaw

Bridlington Terrace. Each file was labelled with a confusing sequence of numbers and letters. It took Dani several attempts to figure out the meaning of it all. Location, date, time. That kind of made sense, except they were all out of order chronologically.

There was only a small number of cameras that she believed would be relevant. Given that the file names began with the camera location reference, she was able to immediately reduce the pool of files to review drastically.

Dani worked through the list. They had two months' worth of records, ending two days ago when they'd made the request, which was the extent of readily available data, though the security company had indicated that there was far more backed-up which could be made available within a few days if required.

Dani hoped they'd get what they needed way before then.

She scrolled through the videos at speed, stopping anytime she spotted Hugo Werner or his glaringly obvious car on the screen. She also spotted herself and Mutambe from their visit on Sunday, though the first file she stopped to properly scrutinise was from two days before that. Last Friday morning. Not much more than twenty-four hours after the murders. A day Dani had spent mostly in and around HQ, including a visit to try and track down Will Eccles at his apartment in the Jewellery Quarter. Except Will Eccles hadn't been there. Where he had been, at eight minutes past three that afternoon, was Bridlington Terrace.

The camera Dani was concentrating on had a clear view of five parking spaces and the main door to the building where Hugo lived. As the video rolled, Will Eccles came onto the screen on foot. Dani would have to find another camera angle to see how he arrived. He headed up to the building's main door where he waited for several seconds having pressed the intercom. With no sound it was hard to know if he was speaking to Hugo through the intercom or not, but after a while he took a couple of steps back from the building to look up to the top floor. He then went back and pressed the intercom again. Finally, Hugo appeared the other side of the door. But Will didn't get invited in. Instead Hugo came outside, and it was quite clear even without audio that the two men were involved in a slanging match.

Then Hugo grabbed Will by the scruff of his neck and shoved him back. Will stumbled. Burst back towards Hugo. And took a stinging hook to his jaw from Hugo which sent him to the floor.

Hugo looked like he was about to attack Will as he lay prone, but then looked up, off-screen. Was there someone else there? He didn't communicate with them if there was. Next he gesticulated to Will before he stormed back inside the building.

Will, groggy and nursing his jaw, pulled himself up. It looked like he was debating whether to go back to the door or not.

No. Moments later he turned and walked away and was soon off-screen.

'What the hell,' Dani said out loud.

The video at least clarified why Will's face had looked battered when he'd appeared outside her house the other day.

She continued to work at speed, going in and out of files looking for any other sightings of Will. Anything at all of Elle. Working through the files in out-of-date order, she made a series of notes of the days and times she'd covered.

Finally, a sighting of Elle. Hand in hand with Hugo. Date? Five weeks ago. So everything looked rosy enough back then.

Dani's desk phone rang.

'Yeah?'

'It's me,' Easton said.

Dani carried on scrolling. 'Where are you?'

'With the accountants. I've been going through this stuff for hours. My brain is a mess.'

'But you've found something really juicy, right?'

He laughed. 'Yes and no.'

'OK?'

'I'm pinging you a spreadsheet. Take a look.'

Dani minimised the video that was playing and opened her emails. The message with the file came through the second the new window popped up.

'What am I looking at?'

'To put it simply, not everything was as it seemed with Eccles Holdings.'

'No?'

'Have a look for yourself.'

Dani opened and then scanned over the first sheet in the file that was labelled RESTATED P&L. Her brain wasn't really in the zone to take this in.

'And?'

'And the team here think someone at Eccles Holdings was, for want of a better phrase, cooking the books.'

'Seriously?'

'There's loads of transactions, bank payments, receipts and loans, that we've found records for, but which don't appear in the main accounting system. There were even separate spreadsheets which seem to track some of it.'

'Whose machine specifically are we talking about?'

'We're looking at server data currently. We'd have to do a separate cross reference to see if the same files were on any of the devices to figure who was actually responsible for these. Our guys will perform that analysis, but for the moment they've been working on restating the financial position rather than figuring out who the files belonged to.'

Dani was listening, but she was also distracted. She closed out the window and went back to her own search as Easton talked. Seconds later she was watching another video where a familiar figure wandered into view. Two actually. One after the other.

'You're kidding me,' Dani said out loud.

'Am I?'

'Sorry, I didn't mean you.'

'Were you even listening to me?'

'I was, but… no, not really. The thing is, guess what I'm looking at?'

'Something more important than my spreadsheet apparently.'

'A video from Bridlington Terrace. Seven weeks ago. I've finally found Elle. But she's not alone.'

'Will Eccles?'

'Not Will. Terry. And the two of them look pretty cosy together.'

Dani made a note of the date then carried on searching.

'So Terry Eccles really was having an affair with Elle?'

'An affair? I couldn't say based only on that, but if I was Hugo Werner I wouldn't be impressed with how the two of them were together like that.'

'But no sign of Will Eccles with her?'

'Not yet.'

'So was Henry lying about Will having an affair with Elle?'

'I really don't know. But there is something else.'

She explained about the scrap.

'Dani, this is serious,' Easton said. 'Together with what we've found in the accounts—'

'Which were what again?'

Eason sighed. 'There's nothing left. No money at all. There's a hole of more than ten million pounds. That's how much the company owes that wasn't recorded. The business has been bleeding money for at least the past three years, propped up by nothing more than ever-increasing debt. Basically, as a business, it's absolutely worthless. It should have folded months, if not years ago.'

Dani didn't know what to say. Partly because she remained seriously distracted.

'That inheritance issue?' Easton said. 'I don't even know how it can be an issue. Eccles Holdings is basically bankrupt. No one's going to get anything.'

'No,' Dani said.

'I know, it's just—'

'Sorry, Aaron, I didn't mean about that. I mean what I'm watching now.'

'How do you mean?'

'I'm ticking off the dates as I scroll through. This file, it's just over two weeks ago. Elle's on it. She doesn't appear on anything later than this. I think this is the last time she was with Hugo.'

'So that's when they split up? Two weeks ago?'

'I don't think they split up.'

'You don't?'

Dani rewound the ten seconds that Elle spent on screen and watched it a second time. At two a.m., on a stormy-looking night, she came out of the building first. Head down, arms folded. Jeans, sweatshirt. She looked cold, shivery. Scared. Hugo came next. He grabbed her arm and pulled her along. She resisted only slightly before they moved off-screen.

Dani blitzed forwards on the feed. In the middle of the night it was quiet. No one else came into view at all until nearly two hours later when Hugo returned.

Alone.

'She left that night,' Dani said. 'With Hugo.'

There was still two hours of video left until the next day's file, which Dani had already reviewed. She continued to scroll forwards at speed to see if Elle reappeared.

Nothing. Nothing. Nothing. Then…

'It's Hugo again.'

This time he came out lugging a suitcase and a holdall.

'Dani? What's going on?'

'She disappeared that night,' Dani said. 'She left with Hugo and never came back.'

'Are you saying what I think you're saying?'

'For her sake, I really hope not.'

Chapter 41

'You're very quiet,' Easton said. He was driving. Dani was watching the world blur by.

'I've got a bad feeling about this,' she said.

'You think he killed her?'

'I really hope not.'

'You think this is all connected to what we found in the accounts too? To Terry and Annie's murders?'

Dani didn't answer immediately. Did she think that? That Hugo had killed not just Elle — because of an affair? — but Terry and Annie Eccles too? The motive for Elle would be clear, but what motive for killing the Eccles parents, unless pure revenge against Terry if he really was having an affair with Elle? But then none of that seemed to relate at all to the mess in the company accounts. Surely that was relevant too?

Dani's head hurt from trying to figure it all out.

'What if he won't let us in?' Easton asked.

'We'll get inside one way or another.'

Thankfully he didn't ask what she meant by that. She wasn't sure herself.

'What if he's not there?' Easton asked.

Dani took her gaze from the outside and glared at him. He seemed to understand the look. 'Sorry.'

She picked up her phone. Dialled Mutambe. Before they'd rushed from the office, she'd already set her colleague up to pull as much further CCTV from the night Elle had disappeared as she could, to see if they could trace the movements of Hugo's car. But she'd just had another thought too.

'I think we should organise some basic surveillance on Will Eccles.'

'Sure. I can make that happen.'

With what they'd been told by Henry about Will and Elle having an affair, plus the argument she'd seen between Will and Hugo on the CCTV, finding Will was now more important than ever. Ever since he'd turned up outside her house, it had been apparent that Will knew far more about what was happening around his family than anyone else.

But was it just finding him, or protecting him, that they needed to do?

They arrived outside the gates to Bridlington Terrace. Easton opened his window. Dani stared through the wrought-iron bars to the grounds beyond.

'His car's there,' Dani said.

Easton pressed on the intercom. They waited. No answer.

'He could have gone for a walk,' Easton said.

Dani gave him another glare. Easton sighed and pressed the intercom again. No answer. He pressed again.

'As soon as he knows it's us here he'll be straight onto Daddy,' Dani said.

'Then what do you suggest?'

'What do you want?' came a groggy drawl through the speaker. Definitely Hugo, though it sounded like he had marbles in his mouth.

'Delivery for you,' Easton said before turning to Dani and shrugging.

'Delivering what?'

'How should I know. A box. For Hugo Werner.'

There was a click from the speaker – Hugo ending the conversation? Then the gates slowly swung open.

Easton and Dani looked at one another. Was he expecting her to say something? Would that element of deceit come back to bite them? Not that she hadn't been thinking of a similar ruse to get inside if necessary.

Easton drove on through.

'My biggest worry is not getting the chance to talk to him before Peter or the lawyer turns up,' Dani said.

'Agreed.'

'He doesn't know you. If he comes down the stairs and recognises me—'

'I know, I know. He'll be on the phone before we can stop him. So what do we do?'

'Let me out here. I'll walk around, out of sight towards the entrance. Park as close as you can to the door. Pretend to rummage in your boot while I sneak up. If he opens the door… bingo.'

Easton raised an eyebrow. 'Can we not just ask him nicely to speak to us?'

'We will.'

Dani opened her door to force Easton's hand. The car came to a stop and she jumped out then quickly moved off to the side. Easton moved off again then parked up, on double yellows all of three yards from the entrance door. Dani continued to move at pace. As Easton got out of the car he smiled and waved towards the building. So Hugo was there, though Dani couldn't see him because of the angle.

She scuttled across to the building as Easton opened up the boot to his car and stuck his head inside. Dani pulled up against the wall of the block then edged closer to the still closed door. She was several steps from it when she heard a click. Then it opened.

Dani dashed forwards as Hugo Werner emerged. He clocked Dani and went to step back inside. Dani stuck her foot into the closing gap between door and frame just in time.

'Hugo!'

He stopped halfway across the atrium. Turned to face her. Bloodshot eyes wide, with thick bags underneath. His skin was blotchy and pale. His baggy clothes made his figure look gaunt and bony rather than slim and athletic.

He looked ill. He looked scared.

'What do you want?' he slurred.

He was drunk. High too?

'Just to talk,' Dani said, trying to appear and sound calm.

Hugo glared from Dani to Easton, who was now standing over her shoulder.

'This is DS Easton,' Dani said. 'Please, Hugo, why don't we go inside? It'd be better for all of us.'

'We told you last time—'

Dani held her hands up in resignation. 'Call your lawyer if you need to. Or your dad. But think about the endgame here, Hugo. Help us. We'll help you.'

Dani could see the torment in his eyes. This young man was troubled. Better for her to play to that than to antagonise him.

Dani heard a car engine behind her. She glanced over her shoulder to see a Mercedes pulling into a spot just past Easton's car. Not anyone that she recognised, but when Dani turned back to Hugo he looked even more uncomfortable, embarrassed.

'Come on, let's do this upstairs,' Dani said. 'It's best for all of us.'

Hugo said nothing. Then he nodded.

Dani and Easton moved inside. They followed Hugo to the lift. Dani kept her eyes on his hands the whole time. Not just in case he had his phone and was trying to summon help, but in case he had any kind of weapon on him too. It wasn't an unthinkable scenario.

They travelled up to the top floor in silence. Hugo led them out, opened his front door and carried on walking. Dani followed him step for step. She looked to Easton for the briefest beat and mouthed, *Take a look around*.

She wanted to make sure they really were alone.

Hugo led her through to the living space where he slumped on the sofa. Dirty glasses, cups, crockery lay here and there. Empty bottles of wine and spirits were clustered in a pile on the kitchen counter. This man was alone and on a downwards spiral. Dani almost felt sorry for him. She was more wary, though.

'You looked troubled, Hugo,' Dani said.

He didn't meet her eye. Just stared at the floor in front of him.

'I just want you to talk to me.'

'About what?'

'About whatever it is that's making you like this. What's happening to you, Hugo? What are you trying to achieve? You want to drink yourself to death?'

Now he glared at her. There was a certain fire in the look which hadn't been there so far which made Dani all the more nervous.

Easton came back into the room, he nodded to Dani. Hugo was alone.

'Can we sit down?' Dani asked. She wanted Hugo as relaxed as possible. Having two detectives hanging over him was unlikely to do that.

'Knock yourselves out,' Hugo said. 'Help yourselves to a drink if you want. Order a fucking pizza or whatever.'

Dani ignored that comment. She and Easton took the sofa opposite Hugo.

'Tell us what happened to Elle,' Dani said.

Hugo held her eye, held his tongue.

'Hugo, don't make his harder on yourself. You need to think very clearly about what happens next. If something bad happened to her, if you had anything to do with what happened to Terry and Annie Eccles, now is the time to tell us.'

'Terry Eccles?' Hugo said, practically spitting the name. 'Fuck him, and fuck his wife too. Fuck their whole family, in fact.'

Easton shuffled slightly next to Dani, as though readying himself for a confrontation. There was certainly something unsettling about Hugo's mood.

'Elle was having an affair,' Easton said.

Hugo was looking at the floor again.

'Is that right?' Dani said. 'She was sleeping with someone else?'

No answer.

'Did you love her?' Dani asked. 'I imagine that really hurt you, to know she was with someone else.'

No answer.

'So who was it?' Easton asked. 'Who was she sleeping with? Terry? Will? Both of them? Is that why you killed Terry and his wife?'

Hugo looked over to Easton. His eyes narrow, his face twisted with hate. But still he was silent.

'Hugo, talk to us,' Dani said. 'We're worried about Elle. Where is she?'

'I would have done anything for her. I would have given her everything I ever could.'

'She hurt you,' Dani said. 'She hurt you in the worst possible way.'

Hugo was mute once again. His whole body quivered. He was mad. He was sad. He was lost. In his state he was about as dangerous as a person could be.

'What happened to Elle?' Dani said. 'We've got video of you two leaving here. Third of March. The middle of the night. You came back that night. She didn't. She hasn't been seen since. Where did you go?'

He shook his head. His eyes were welling.

'Please just tell us.'

'I didn't… I didn't want to hurt her.'

He almost broke down with that sentence. Dani balled her fists. Dug her nails into her palms. Both in anticipation but also in anger. What had he done?

'Where is she?' Dani asked.

Hugo didn't say anything. He was so close to opening up. But he also looked about ready to explode.

'You killed her,' Easton said. 'Then what? A few days later you went over to Sutton and killed Terry and Annie Eccles too? Why? Because he'd been sleeping with her?'

Hugo didn't say anything to that.

'You killed her,' Easton said again. 'We all know it. You don't even have to say the words. We just want to know where she is. You say you loved her. That you'd do anything for her. Tell us where she is. She deserves it. Her family deserves it.'

'No,' Hugo said through gritted teeth. 'She got exactly what she deserved already. And so did Terry fucking Eccles.'

Dani had sensed it coming. Still, she was too slow to react when Hugo leaped up from the sofa. Well, not quite up, but across. He dove forwards, over the coffee table, heading straight for Easton.

Easton rose up from his position but in doing so only moved closer to Hugo who barrelled into him and the two of them crashed to the floor in a frantic grapple.

Dani jumped up from her seat. Reached into her pocket for her phone. The two men groaned and roared. Fists, elbows flew.

Then Hugo pulled himself free and was back on his feet. Easton went to clamber up too, but Hugo dove back onto him and they both crashed down to the coffee table, the top of which shattered into thousands of glass shards.

Dani hurriedly shouted into her phone for the back-up they needed. Hugo delivered a thunderous head-butt to Easton before pulling himself back to his feet once more. Easton writhed but remained on the floor among the glass.

Hugo, snarling, chest heaving, looked to Dani.

'You don't have to do this,' she said, putting the phone down.

Hugo dashed towards her. Dani had barely any time to react. But she wouldn't just cower and hope for the best. Instead she stood her ground. Shimmied so that Hugo couldn't barge into her like he had with Easton. He righted himself and threw an arcing punch. Dani easily blocked it. And the next. Then she went on the attack herself. She ducked down and rushed forwards and grabbed him and slammed him into the wall, knocking the wind from him. She tried to use the moment of confusion to grab his wrist to get him into a hold. Just as she had with Trey Wallace.

She managed it.

But Hugo was a different beast from Wallace altogether. Wired on drugs and alcohol and adrenaline and hatred and primal survival instinct, he wasn't stopping. Dani twisted his arm around but it was like he didn't even care. She could have broken his bones there and then and it wouldn't have stopped him. Instead, as she battled to subdue him, she took an unexpected uppercut, right under her jaw, which caused her head to jolt backwards. There was nothing she could do to stop herself stumbling back and falling to the floor.

Her head crashed off the carpet and the room blurred.

She was prone on the ground. She knew it, but she could do nothing about it. Easton was down too. Hugo could do whatever he wanted.

No. Fight. She had to fight.

'Aaron!' Dani screamed, as though the strength of the shout would cause a wave of clarity to rush through her mind.

Not quite. But it helped her focus a little bit better at least. She blinked a couple of times to reset her vision. She expected Hugo to be right there.

But he was nowhere to be seen.

A bang. A clunk. The front door.

'Aaron, he's gone. Come on!'

Chapter 42

Dani hauled herself up. Easton did the same. Dani's jaw, the back of her head, both throbbed. Easton looked as groggy as she felt. Blood cascaded down his cheek and neck from somewhere on the side of his head.

'I'm fine,' Easton said, sounding anything but as he wiped at the crimson patch.

As soon as they could, they both rushed towards the door. Didn't bother with the lift, taking the stairs instead. More than once Dani teetered and nearly lost her balance and tumbled forwards. Somehow she made it to the bottom unscathed.

As they came out into the atrium there was a rumble outside. A raucous rev of an engine. Hugo's garish Lamborghini blasted past on the road.

'Come on!' Dani urged, as much to herself as to Easton. They made it outside. Hugo's car was already at the gates which were still opening, the gap not quite wide enough for him to get out. He didn't wait. His car shot forwards and there was a crunch as the front passenger side caught on the gate. It didn't stop him. He carried on out, heading right. 'Shit!'

Dani and Easton jumped into the car. Easton's far more puny engine whined into life and he reversed back onto the road then bombed forwards towards the gate that was already closing.

'Don't stop!' Dani shouted.

Easton let out a desperate cry. Dani shut her eyes as they raced through the impossibly narrow gap. Completely unscathed. Dani laughed in relief. Easton didn't say a word. He was in the zone. Or was he just out of it from the blows he'd taken?

Dani's phone was against her ear again. She gave the details. Explained the direction they were headed. She needed blue light support on the ground, helicopter support in the air. Where the hell was Hugo going?

'I see him,' Easton said.

'He's heading for the dual carriageway.'

'We'll never keep up with him.'

No. They wouldn't. Nor would any of the Force's cars. They needed to stop him any way they could.

Dani hadn't been involved in a high-speed chase for years. She was glad about that. Her whole body was rigid with fear. She grasped the seat with one hand, the dashboard with the other. White knuckles on both hands. Easton weaved in and out of traffic barely taking his foot off the accelerator.

Soon they were approaching the turn for the dual carriageway. Somehow still not a scratch.

'No,' Easton said.

It took Dani a couple of seconds to realise why he'd said it.

'What is he doing?'

Going down the exit ramp, was what he was doing.

'Follow him,' Dani said to Easton.

He didn't hesitate. He swung the car right and they were racing down the ramp heading directly into any oncoming traffic. With an open stretch in front of them, Hugo's Lamborghini pulled away, but within seconds they

345

were facing a cluster of vehicles. Horns blared. Lights flashed. Tyres screeched.

At least he was clearing a path for them.

On the opposite carriageway, Dani saw blue lights flashing. Two cars raced along, almost side by side with her and Easton. Unfortunately they could do nothing from there.

'This is bad,' Easton said. 'Really bloody bad.'

Hugo's car swerved left and right and back again to avoid the oncoming vehicles. Easton tried his best to follow. Then Hugo pulled hard right and was riding half on the tarmac, half on the verge to avoid a sudden build-up of traffic that covered both lanes, with a string of lorries on the near side. The Lamborghini was pulling further ahead again. They blasted past one lorry. Then another, and another. Each time the turbulence sent Easton's car rocking. Dani winced with every vehicle they passed. How had they made no contact? Yet they were losing Hugo with every second.

'We need someone further ahead,' Easton said. 'To head him off.'

Dani said nothing, but had her phone to her ear again.

They cleared the last of the lorries and the carriageway opened up once more. The perfect scenario for Hugo. Easton was doing ninety-five. Hugo must have been flooring well over a hundred.

Up ahead a solitary lorry closed in on them. Hugo moved into the opposite lane to go past it. The lorry flashed its lights and blared its horn.

Hugo was about to blast past…

Why didn't he?

His car suddenly swerved right. The lorry driver had no chance.

There was a horrific smash as the Lamborghini slammed head-on into the multi-ton beast.

Debris flew. Tyre smoke billowed. There was an awful screeching sound as the mangled car and the lorry scraped across the tarmac to a stop.

Easton and Dani both stared aghast, speechless. Their car rolled to a stop. Dani stepped out, unable to take her eyes off the twisted, steaming wreckage just a few yards in front. Other than a strange hissing there was a serene silence, until the sound of not-too-distant sirens punched through the air.

Dani moved forwards to the wreck, her legs weak. Beyond the glass of the lorry's cabin, the driver stared down, dumbfounded.

Easton was by Dani's side as she came to a stop.

Neither of them said a word. There really was nothing to say. The Lamborghini was all but sliced in half, its top taken clean off with the supercar wedged beneath the cabin of the lorry. There was no sign from where they were standing of Hugo, and Dani really didn't want to get any closer to find him.

She didn't need to in order to know that Hugo Werner was already dead.

Chapter 43

The response to the devastating crash was swift and thorough. Ambulances, several squad cars, a fire engine. The dual carriageway was closed and would be for some time. Dani and Easton both remained on the scene, and both did their very best to rebuff the attempts of paramedics to see to them.

Dani had barely moved from the spot in front of the wreck. She watched as the fire fighters continued to cut through the metal frame of the Lamborghini to try and release it from underneath the lorry. A ghostly-looking paramedic had already confirmed Hugo was beyond saving, though hadn't revealed details of exactly what she'd seen of him. Dani didn't want to know, even if she was still staring at the wreckage.

Easton wandered over to her. He'd spent the last few minutes trying to console the distraught lorry driver. Even if he'd done absolutely nothing wrong – which Dani firmly believed to be the case – then this crash, and Hugo's death, would weigh heavily on his mind for a long, long time.

'Hugo was desperate,' Easton said. 'We had him. Not just on Elle, but on the Eccleses too. It was the only way out he saw.'

Dani didn't say anything. Hugo hadn't admitted to what he'd done. Not directly. But it was clear to Dani he'd killed Elle that night. And the Eccles parents? He'd said Terry too got what he deserved.

Was that a confession? Everything fitted, didn't it?

So why the niggle in her mind?

'We'll find out what he did to Elle,' Easton said.

What he'd done to her? He'd killed her. Elle was dead. Dani couldn't see any other explanation. Hugo had killed her in a fit of rage, or revenge, or whatever it was called when a partner finds that their lover has been screwing around with someone else and reacts in the worst and most extreme way.

Strangely, Dani was thinking about the similarities to Clinton Harrison. A lover's quarrel hadn't caused him to kill, but the extreme emotion of being wronged had. The sense of something special being taken away that could never be retrieved. The sense of loss, of betrayal, could stir up the most primal of behaviours in all humans. That's what had happened to Clinton Harrison when he'd witnessed his son being killed, and it had happened to Hugo Werner too when he found his girlfriend was having an affair. Blind rage had caused both men to kill.

But had Hugo stopped with Elle, or had Terry and Annie Eccles borne the brunt of his vengeance too? Annie Eccles, who was perhaps the biggest victim of them all.

Dani still couldn't get her head around that.

'Let me take this,' Easton said as he turned and walked away with his phone to his ear.

A few seconds later and Dani's phone was ringing too. Mutambe.

'Are you OK?' she asked.

'Kind of,' Dani said.

'I thought you'd appreciate this update.'

'Always.' She could certainly do with the distraction.

'I've made some progress on tracing Hugo that night. The third of March. Not to a final destination yet, but he headed east, out past the motorway and into Warwickshire.'

Not much of a finding really.

'I'll keep searching and see what else I pick up,' she continued. 'But he can't have gone too much further than that, given what time he reappeared at his home.'

'OK. Let me know if—'

'Sorry. That wasn't all. There's something else too.'

'Yeah?'

'The officer we have outside Will Eccles' apartment has been updating me for the last half hour. Would you believe Eric Eccles turned up outside the building? He went inside. Invited, by the sound of it.'

'Eric? But...'

Dani really wasn't sure what she'd been about to say. How did Eric even know where Will was?

'Is he still inside?' she asked.

'No. That's why I was calling. He came out again just a couple of minutes ago. With Will. This is second-hand, obviously, but it didn't sound like it was a particularly friendly reunion. Will was practically tossed into Eric's car.'

'Do we still have eyes on them?'

'Yeah.'

'OK. Stay on the line. I'm coming.'

Chapter 44

Dani looked around. Easton was talking to a couple of uniformed coppers. She raced up to him.

'We need to go.'

'What?'

'Eric Eccles just turned up outside Will's place.'

The look on his face suggested he didn't understand the significance.

'Dani,' he said, 'Peter Werner just turned up *here*.'

He indicated beyond the police car they were standing by, to where three more officers crowded around an irate Peter Werner. He spotted Dani and glared over.

'Damn it. That's the last thing we need.'

'Tell me about it.'

'Still, I need to go,' she said to Easton. 'But maybe you should stay here.'

He looked at her like she was… it didn't even matter.

'Just give me your keys.'

He did so. Dani raced back along the road to his car. She spent the next couple of minutes painfully navigating through the myriad emergency vehicles before she was finally on the clear stretch of dual carriageway beyond the crash.

'Talk to me,' she said after putting the phone on speaker.

'Sergeant Cartwright is still following. They're heading north on the A34. They're nearly at the Scott Arms junction.'

'Where the hell are they going?' Dani said, as much to herself as to Mutambe.

From their position they were all of a mile from the M6. From there they could race away from the Midlands, heading either north, east, south or west. Dani was miles away from there.

'Wait, they turned off the A34 at the Scott Arms. Heading east on the 4041.'

'Which means they're heading straight for Sutton Coldfield?'

Dani felt she knew where they were going. What she didn't fully understand was why.

'Can you try and get hold of the officer at Kibble House? Let her know to expect some visitors.'

No answer.

'Hello?'

She picked up the phone from her lap. Dead.

She was running blind. She just hoped her hunch was right.

—

Dani's mind was a mess the whole way. Earlier, in Hugo's apartment, it had felt like the whole case had finally fallen into place. Hugo had killed Elle in a fit of rage. He'd later taken his revenge a step further by battering Terry and Annie Eccles to death in revenge for Terry and the affair.

That all made sense, didn't it?

No. That was the problem Dani had. It didn't make full sense at all. Not when put together with everything about the crime scene, the Forensics findings on the safe, the wills, the fact the intruder likely had an intimate knowledge of Kibble House. That wasn't Hugo.

Less than fifteen minutes later, Dani turned the car off Lichfield Road and onto the Four Oaks Estate. Everything was quiet. Serene. Eerie. The latter probably only because of the sickly feeling Dani had in the pit of her stomach.

Kibble House was a hundred yards in front. A Ford Fiesta was parked up on the verge outside the gates. Sergeant Cartwright's car?

Dani slowed as she approached. There were no sounds, no sights of anything or anyone.

She stopped just behind the Fiesta and stepped out. Absolute calm, except for the boom of her heart and her deep breaths. She walked around to the driver's side of the Fiesta. No one inside.

Dani carried on to the closed gates. On the drive was Eric Eccles' car, and PC Shaw's squad car. On the gravel, by the police car…

'No!'

Dani wrenched open the gate and sprinted through. She crunched across the gravel to the lump on the ground. Shaw. Her body was stretched out. Blood streamed down her face. The small rise and fall in her chest showed she was breathing, but she looked in a bad way. Dani carefully tried to rouse her.

No luck. Shaw's radio was no longer on her jacket. Dani couldn't even call for help. Unless she ran out of there…

A bang and call of pain shot through the air. Coming from the house. The sudden noise was followed by angry shouting.

What else could she do?

Dani rose up and proceeded with caution towards the front door, eyeing up the substantial house and its grounds as she moved, looking from window to window. She saw and heard nothing more.

She reached the front door. It was closed, but not locked. She ever so carefully opened the door so as to not make a noise. It was all of a foot open when she spotted the heap on the floor by the foot of the stairs. Dani looked up to what she could see of the landing. No sign of anyone else. She slipped inside. Up to the body on the floor. No blood, but the man wasn't moving. Sergeant Cartwright?

'Nice to see you again,' came the voice off to her right. Dani jumped in shock and whipped around to face the figure in the office doorway.

She wasn't surprised at all at who she saw.

'What are you doing, Eric?'

He said nothing.

'Where's Will?'

Eric laughed. 'Now, how many times have I heard that damn question through the years? Will, bloody Will. Who'd have thought everyone's lives would come crashing down because of him?'

'No, not because of him,' Dani said as everything fell into place in her mind. 'Because of you.'

Eric glared at her.

'Show me your hands,' Dani said. Both of them were held behind his back.

'Or what?' he said as he took a step towards her. 'You're going to arrest me?'

Dani shook her head. 'Whatever you do to me, or to Will, or to anyone else, there's no way out of this for you now.'

Again, he didn't respond, but she could see the emptiness in his eyes. He must have known the game was up. That was why Dani was so petrified.

Cartwright groaned and shuffled on the floor. Dani instinctively looked down to him.

'Don't touch him!' Eric screamed. He took another two steps forwards. Dani stepped back, holding up her hands.

'I won't,' she said.

Eric brought his right hand out from behind his back. It was wrapped around a cricket bat. Blood streaked the end of it.

'I'd ask why,' Dani said. If she could keep him talking. If she could keep him at bay… it had to be the best shot she had. 'I'd ask why you killed your parents. Why you've attacked, possibly killed your own brother. But I think I already know.'

He glared at her with pure hatred, as though she was the cause of his life's problems.

'What could you possibly know?'

'You hated your dad.'

He shook his head. 'No. I loved him so much.' His voice trembled. He looked like he was about to break down, but he was just as likely to go berserk. 'I loved him so much, but he ruined my life.'

Another step forwards. Dani took another back-step towards the door.

'Have you any idea what it's like to be *fifth* best? At everything!' He laughed now. Dani really couldn't understand why. 'OK, so perhaps fourth at some things. Nobody really liked Will much, but at least Dad saw something in him. Me? He called me the idiot. Did you know that?'

Dani said nothing.

'He belittled me constantly. For years. All through my childhood, all through my adult life. The idiot. The dumb brick. Too stupid. Not sporty enough. Not funny enough. Everyone else was the best at something. I was only the best at disappointing him.'

'Eric, it's not—'

'But he was wrong. There was something I was the best at. I was the most loyal.' He pumped his fist with each statement, like a politician on a podium. 'I stuck by him no matter what. All I ever wanted was to work with him. To show him I was good enough. I'm the only one who had a stable family life, who gave him a grandchild.'

'You did. And what about them now? What about your wife and son?'

'I gave everything to Dad, all the times I covered for him.'

'You knew about him and Elle.'

'And I said nothing. Nothing to my brothers or sister, my mum—'

'Your mum. Eric, why did you have to hurt her?'

His anger faltered. Remorse now.

'She was a mistake,' Dani prompted. 'Did you not mean to? Was it too dark? Or did you just figure you couldn't allow her to live after what you had planned for your dad? How could you ever have looked her in the eye again?'

He seemed like he was about to break down. Dani had hit something of the truth. But then in a flash he rose tall again and his face turned once more. 'No,' he snarled. 'She's just as much to blame as he is. She was so weak. She stood by him, all those years, all through the abuse I got. She did nothing to help me. She's as much to blame as he is. My dad was my hero. I would have done anything for him. But in the end, it meant nothing.'

It made sense to Dani now. It had always been right there in front of her. 'The will?' she said.

Eric's face twitched.

'Everything I gave to Dad, and I wasn't even going to get my fair share of the business that *I* helped build.'

'That's why you were searching the office,' Dani said. 'The safe. You knew about the new will.'

The old will had been left behind. Easton had found an unsigned version of the new will in the desk drawer. But Eric, the night he'd killed his parents, hadn't looked in the drawers. At least there was nothing in the Forensics reports to suggest he had.

Which meant…

'You took the signed version of the will,' Dani said. 'Did you plant that old version back in there? You only realised you'd made a mistake when we started confronting you and your sister about what we'd found.'

He said nothing. How he'd found out about the change, Dani had no clue. Had there been a final confrontation between father and son that had sent Eric over the edge? Had that even happened the very night that Terry and Annie had been killed?

'Except I think you made a big mistake,' Dani said.

He glared but didn't ask what she meant by that.

'He changed the will, but I'm not sure it's for the reason you think.'

Still nothing, but Eric was fuming again.

'I never met your dad, but I think he changed the will as a *screw you*. Not to you, Eric, but to the Werners. There was no money left. The business is gone.'

That twitch again. Confusion. Anger. Hatred. He hadn't known the dire situation the business was in. Somehow Terry had kept it from everyone. Dani was sure she was right.

'Where's Will?' Dani asked again. 'Where's your brother?'

Eric inched forwards. Dani took another step back and brushed up against the door. What was the plan? Turn and run?

'And the award for sneakiest piece of shit goes to... Will Eccles.'

Eric swung the bat above his head in some sort of weird mock moment of triumph.

'I already knew Dad was shagging Elle. But Will? Jesus, what a filthy bitch she was. You could ask why. Why would she do that? But we won't get an answer any more.' He cackled as though having made a tremendous joke. 'But that's Will for you. He never could resist causing problems for others. He knew about Dad and her.' His face screwed up in disgust. 'Can you imagine? Having sex with the same woman your Dad is? Enter Will. And it wouldn't even surprise me if he let slip to Hugo somehow about what Elle was up to. Why? Because why not? He loved chaos. He loved causing trouble for all of us.'

'He also knew about you,' Dani said. 'He knew you were the killer. You've been trying to find him.'

'Because I knew he'd never do the right thing. He had no intentions of being a hero. He only wanted to better his own position.'

Except he had tried to reach out to Dani, hadn't he? Why the change of heart?

'Blackmail?' Dani asked. 'He was blackmailing you?'

Eric smiled. 'You could say it all worked out in the end, though. The way I see it, none of this is on me. Hugo Werner flipped. He killed Elle. She's dead, isn't she?'

Dani said nothing to that. How long had Eric known?

'Then he came here to take his revenge. First on Mum and Dad. Then today, on Will.'

His smug look broadened, as though his was the plan of a rational genius. Although until half an hour ago, Dani had been in exactly the same camp in thinking that Hugo was responsible for three murders. Had Eric planned this all along, or was it simply one last desperate ploy? Given the mess, Dani would have betted on the latter rather than the former.

'There's just one big problem in that,' Dani said. 'Hugo's dead.'

Another twitch of confusion on Eric's face.

'And soon, you will be too,' he said.

Then he burst forwards.

Dani turned and grabbed the door. Swung it open. She bound down the steps. Stumbled onto the gravel and took several teetering steps before she righted herself.

Too long. Eric was already on her. She could sense him without even looking. She didn't see how he did it. A reaching swipe with the bat? Full-on dive? Or was it nothing more than a tangle of bat and limbs. Either way Dani lost her footing and fell face first into the gravel which burst up around and onto her.

She had no time to recover. The blow to the back of her head made sure of that.

Within seconds, the world around her turned to black.

Chapter 45

How long had she been out for? Not long. She was in the office. Tied to Terry Eccles' plush leather chair. By the door lay the crumpled body of Will Eccles. Unmoving. Was he already dead?

What about Cartwright and Shaw? No sign of them.

The stench of petrol filled Dani's nose, the smell almost strong enough to cause her to gag. But not so over-powering as to mask the deeper smell of smoke.

From where?

'Welcome back,' Eric said coming into the room. His face was hard with determination.

He tipped up the petrol can in his hand and splashed several glugs of oily liquid over Will's body.

'Eric, this isn't the way,' Dani said, though her speech was slurred.

She had a painful flashback to her time in hospital, after suffering her TBI. As well as her physical ailments, she'd worked for months to rebuild seemingly simple elements of her life like her speech. Had that blow to the head on the driveway set her back?

Did it even matter? She simply had to find a way out of this alive.

She pulled on her wrists. Rope. Her ankles too were shackled to the chair.

Eric came over to her. He stopped the other side of the desk and held her eye. He lifted the can up as if deliberating what to do with it.

'Eric, please. This isn't you. I see it in your eyes.'

Except that last part was a lie. Right now? Right now his eyes were bursting with rage. But the point stood. 'You're not a psycho. I don't believe that. You were just desperate. You're a family man, Eric. Think about your family.'

He ignored her completely.

'Wow, Hugo Werner really is one sick bastard,' Eric crowed. 'Elle, Mum and Dad, now you lot. And burned alive. Horrific.'

'Eric,' Dani said shaking her head in despair. 'Hugo's already dead. Even if I die in here, this isn't going to work for you.'

'Why? You think I'm too stupid to pull this off?'

'That's not what I said.'

'But it's what you think.'

He pushed the can towards her, tilted it and a splash came out of the spout and landed by Dani's feet, before he had a second thought and pulled back.

'You know what—?' He paused. What on earth was he thinking? 'No. You deserve no help from me.'

Then he thrust the can back towards her and tilted it up again. Another splash came out, covering Dani's legs. But only drips after that.

'Damn it!' Eric shouted before tossing the empty can at Dani's face. It bashed off the side of her head as she turned away and clattered to the floor. Her eyes stung from the drops of liquid that landed on her face. By the time her sight cleared, Eric was back by the doorway, looking over at her.

'Good luck,' he said with a wicked smile.

Then he struck the match in his hand, and tossed it down onto his brother.

Chapter 46

Flames leapt up within a heartbeat. Will's body and the carpet all around him was ablaze with ferocious columns of orange and yellow.

Eric jumped back, gazing down on his brother with a look somewhere between astonishment and horror. He twisted his head to look over to Dani. Then laughed before he turned for the door.

He never made it. A flaming arm reached out from Will's body and grabbed hold of Eric's ankle. He tripped to the floor, cracking his head off the doorframe as he went.

A cascade of flames erupted from the trail of petrol between Dani and the desk. She pushed back on the wheeled chair as much as she could with her legs secured to the bottom. The chair shifted back merely half a foot. Not nearly enough to move away from the petrol trail, or to stop the flames from licking up onto her shoes and lower legs.

Dani screamed, even before there was any sense of pain. She lurched forwards, onto her feet, the chair suspended behind her, but with her ankles tied she could do nothing but shuffle inch by inch. No use. She'd never make it to the door before she was consumed by the inferno.

She jumped up, awkwardly, but with as much effort as she could, and propelled herself backwards. She crashed to the floor and screeched in agony from the painful contact, the chair wedged between her and the floor. It felt like her back had snapped in two. The chair didn't exactly fall to pieces, but it cracked and smashed enough for Dani to yank her limbs free from the ropes.

She patted at the flames that were inching up her legs. Enough to keep the fire at bay, but what she needed was to get out of the room. Behind her the thick drapes around the windows were in full flame. She had no clue if the frames were locked shut. The desk in front of her was fully lit now too. She could barely make out the doorway beyond.

Still, she chose to go that way.

She pushed her head down, arms up, as she jumped over the flames by the desk. Will was still there, on the floor. His arm still outstretched, his body unmoving now. His last stand nowhere near enough to save himself.

Where was Eric? No sign of him.

Dani took a slow but deep breath, then rushed for the door, head down, through the flames. She made it into the hall, lifted her head a little.

She'd hoped to see a clear space. But every room was alight. The walls, the stairs. Black smoke billowed along the hallway ceiling. The heat was so intense Dani felt like her lungs were cooking. She thought she'd smelled smoke earlier. Was the office the last room lit?

As she searched for a way out, Dani only saw the shadow flicking off to her right at the last moment.

She ducked and spun. Eric. Bat in hand once more. But his blistering swing missed. The bat smashed into the wall, sending his arm juddering. Dani didn't hesitate, she bolted towards the door.

'No!' Eric screamed.

She didn't turn around. Focused only on the door in front of her, which was about the only place she could see that wasn't in flames.

Her trailing foot caught midair. Had he grabbed her? She was heading for the ground once more. At least this time, with her hands already up to protect her face from the flames, she had a better landing. But Eric still had hold of her ankle as she hit the deck. She tried to wrestle free. Tried to kick him off. He was on the ground too, flames rising up from him now. His face contorted in anger and agony and hatred.

Dani screamed in desperation and tried to kick him off. The pain in her legs ratcheted up each second as the fire tore through her clothing.

There was a calamitous crash from above. Dani glanced up to see the rafter from the landing break loose and swing down like a pendulum. The burning wood smashed onto Eric's back. His body shuddered. His head bowed.

His hand remained gripped around Dani's ankle.

She screamed again with effort as she finally wrestled free. Rolled across the ground to do everything she could to stop the fire consuming her trousers and the skin underneath. She did enough. She pulled herself to her feet. Dashed for the door. A quick glance to the foot of the stairs. Cartwright was still there. Still not moving. But he wasn't on fire either. Dani couldn't leave him.

She grabbed him by the shoulders and roared as she pulled him to the exit. She yanked open the front door. The superheated handle scorched her hand. She fought through the pain. A waft of cool air billowed in. The roar of the flames behind her intensified further with the influx of oxygen.

With one last burst of effort, she dragged Cartwright out, down the steps.

A few yards onto the driveway, Dani collapsed onto the gravel. She rolled onto her back and she looked up to the sky that was filling with wispy dark smoke.

Above the din of the fire that was rapidly consuming Kibble House, and everything and everyone in it, Dani heard the sound of sirens, quickly closing in.

Chapter 47

One week later

Dani closed the browser window on her phone and set it on the kitchen table then took a mouthful of toast.

Jason hobbled into the room, propped himself against the kitchen island, and picked up his coffee.

'You OK?' he asked.

'Just reading the news.'

'About Elle?'

Dani nodded then swallowed hard. The story had broken last night and was now a major headline across the country. Elle's body had been found in a shallow grave in a small woodland near to the town of Berkshill. CCTV and then sniffer dogs had been enough to find the location where Hugo had dumped her. Dani had been one of the first there. She still couldn't get Elle's hollow death stare, her muddied, lifeless face, out of her mind. Initial indications were she'd been strangled. With Hugo dead, perhaps they'd never know for sure exactly how her death had played out after she'd left Bridlington Terrace with Hugo at two a.m. on the third of March.

'Are you all set?' Jason asked.

'Almost. Just need to pack my toiletries.'

'What time do you think you'll be done?'

'Hard to say.'

He didn't look particularly impressed with the non-committal answer.

'You really need this,' he said to her. 'We both do.'

'I know.'

He came over to her and kissed her lightly on the cheek before sitting down. She finished her toast then headed out, and to the bedroom where the open and full to bursting suitcases were on the bed. She looked at them and sighed.

Yes, they needed this, but was it the right thing to do now?

–

Dani made it to court a few minutes before the hearing was due to start. It wasn't particularly busy. The Clinton Harrison case had very much fallen by the wayside over recent days given the high-profile scandal in the news over the Eccles and Werner murders, together with Dani's determination to keep herself out of the press's eye as much as possible. Plus, the sheer fact that Harrison could no longer be viewed as the paternal hero meant that his case simply didn't have the draw any more, so she wasn't particularly surprised when there was no gaggle of reporters to accost her about the case.

The only calls she'd had from the press the last few days had all been from Briana Clark, and Dani was sure the reporter was interested in the Eccles case rather than Harrison. Dani was still yet to return any of those missed calls. Not that Briana had been deterred. She and her press colleagues were having a field day on the Eccles case. Clearly Briana had plenty of other sources within the Force. Strangely Dani felt sad, and a bit used by that.

DCI McNair and Chief Superintendent Baxter were standing outside the courtroom. They both turned to Dani as she approached. Baxter gave her probably the warmest look she'd ever had from him.

'Look who it is,' he said. 'The talk of the town.'

Dani blushed. How childish? Her embarrassment only made her cheeks redden further.

'No need to look like that,' Baxter said. 'You're a hero. It's one thing to catch the bad guys, but singlehandedly saving the lives of two officers too?'

'Natural instinct,' Dani said.

'Natural for you, but not for everyone. That's what makes you so special.'

Dani had nothing to say to that. McNair was looking at her strangely. A mixture of jealousy and pride.

'How are the legs?' Baxter asked.

'Fine,' Dani said. 'All things considered. The hand too.'

She'd likely have a little bit of scarring around her ankles, but overall the outcome was far better than it could have been, and certainly far better than it had been for poor Will Eccles. Eric, somehow, had been pulled from the inferno alive, though the burns and other injuries he'd suffered were so severe it remained unclear if he'd make it. He remained in an induced coma, in a critical condition. Dani had visited his bedside once, though wouldn't again unless he became lucid enough to talk. She had no sympathy whatsoever for the state he was in, though for the sake of his victims, she hoped he did pull through. She had so many questions for him, and his parents and brother deserved answers.

She glanced at her watch.

'Where is everybody? Where's DeMario?' she asked.

McNair and Baxter looked at each other, it clear that they knew something Dani didn't.

'He's with Harrison,' McNair said.

'Speak of the devil,' Baxter added, looking beyond Dani.

She turned to see DeMario and one of his assistants striding across the polished tiles. DeMario had a satisfied grin on his face. His assistant headed off and DeMario came over, waving a piece of paper in his hand.

'Good news, I take it?' Baxter said.

DeMario said nothing but handed the paper to Baxter who scrutinised it for a few seconds before passing it to McNair. Dani was left as the odd one out.

'Anyone?' she said, looking from one to the other.

'Let's just say Harrison's new lawyer is a lot more sensible than his last,' DeMario said.

'You've done a deal?' Dani asked.

'I'm not sure it's much of a deal on Harrison's part,' Baxter said with an overly smug look on his face.

'He pleaded guilty to murder,' DeMario said to Dani. 'Sentencing still needs finalising, but he'll get life. A minimum term of perhaps only ten or twelve years, but—'

'But this is a great result for all involved,' Baxter said.

There were a couple more minutes of self-congratulation, through which Dani largely stood in silence, not sure what to think. Since the arrest of Trey Wallace and his cronies, two of them had confirmed that Roberts and Harrison did in fact know each other. That they'd had a long-running feud over a drugs debt owed by one to the other – which way around that debt went depended on who was asked. Harrison had never given any comment over the whole thing, despite the mountain of evidence in front of him. The two men who had attacked Dani were both still on remand, awaiting trial for the assault. Though given the text messages the two had shared with each other, along with Trey Wallace, where they'd explicitly discussed the need to keep 'that bitch from the police' quiet, in order to protect Harrison, their cases were likely a slam dunk too. Roberts's girlfriend had been found too. She was fine. Harrison's cronies had taken her away to make sure the police couldn't talk to her, but she'd never been in danger. Dani was relieved about that.

Even if they would never know for sure if the collision that killed Tyler Harrison was a true accident or not, the case had come to a relatively clear-cut end, all things considered. Far more so than on the Eccles case where so much still hung in the balance, from the possible involvement of Peter Werner in helping his son to cover up murder, to the shady dealings of Hamed Adil, to the substantial and illegal debt that Henry Eccles had purportedly owed to a local gangster. Was there anyone in that family who'd come out from the mess unscathed?

Dani's head hurt thinking about it all. Which was one of the very big reasons why she absolutely needed the break she and Jason were taking.

'DI Stephens?'

Baxter's voice wrenched her from her thoughts. McNair and DeMario were walking away.

'Sorry, I was somewhere else.'

'I could tell. I just wanted to say...' He paused and sighed. 'I heard about your sabbatical. Six months?'

'Time to get my head straight. It's been... difficult.'

'I'm sure, and I'm not trying to get you to change your mind at all, but...' Another pause, another sigh. 'You're very highly thought of in our Force. By McNair, by me, by many others. To put it simply, there's an opening for a new DCI. I can't think of anyone we have internally who'd be better suited for the role.'

Dani gulped. She didn't know what to say.

'Your relentless attitude is an example for everyone,' Baxter said. 'The problem is, the role needs filling now, not in six months' time.'

Dani simply had no words. After everything she'd gone through, after everything she and Jason had discussed about their future together. Talk about lousy timing.

'What do you think?' Baxter asked.

'Can I think about it?'

He looked disappointed. 'I'll give you until the end of the day. Once again, great work. On Harrison, on Eccles. On everything.'

He tapped her on the shoulder then walked away.

Chapter 48

Dani didn't even want to think about the reasons for her being at Worcestershire Royal Hospital again. She'd expected to be tied up in court for far longer than she had been. Had planned to spend a couple of final hours in the office after that in order to wrap up everything she could, and pass off anything she couldn't to the team, before she walked out for the next six months.

Instead, she found herself sitting on an uncomfortable plastic chair in a hospital, next to her murderous brother, who remained in a coma.

She wasn't talking much today. Not like the previous time she'd been here where her outpouring had surprised even her.

'I don't know what I'm doing,' Dani said after what had felt like a painfully long silence. 'I don't even know what I want any more.'

No, that wasn't quite true. What she wanted was Jason. There was no doubt about that. But did that mean she wanted him at any cost? She knew she wanted to spend the rest of her life with him. She knew he'd make the most amazing father. Were the sacrifices that she'd have to make worth it?

Was that even the point? How could Dani just walk away from her job now? Regardless of the offer of a promotion – which Dani hadn't even been going for –

she felt a duty to her job. To her colleagues. To the Force. To the victims of the most despicable crimes who needed her help to bring murderers – like Ben, like Hugo Werner, like Eric Eccles – to justice.

'I only ever saw you as a killer,' Dani said as she stared at her brother's withered face. 'I could reason why you did it. I thought for hours on end about it. Over and over, asking myself why you. What is it about you? What defect? Do I have it too? But you know what? I think I finally figured it out.'

She paused, as though letting the words sink in. As though he would suddenly open his eyes and look at her and ask her what the hell she was talking about.

'There never was anything different about you. Just like there was nothing different, no mental defect, in Harrison, in Hugo, in Eric. They were all just otherwise normal people, put into extraordinary circumstances.'

Did that make her understand Ben's actions more? Not exactly. She sincerely hoped she'd never be capable of such a heinous crime as murder. But then she'd never truly been put in such a pressured situation as any of those others.

Her phone vibrated. She looked at the screen. The office. She let it go. Seconds later a voicemail pinged through. She listened to it straight away as she stared at her brother.

'Baxter told me he had the conversation with you,' McNair said. 'I just wanted to let you know you have my full support either way, Dani. But, in my view, the Force will be missing out big time if you're not a DCI here. Speak soon.'

Dani's hand trembled as she pulled the phone back from her ear. Largely with anger, though she didn't quite know why.

'I need to go.'

—

An hour and a half later, Dani was finally approaching home. The traffic on the motorway had been horrendous, and the aggravation only added to her sullen mood and ongoing confusion.

She parked up and headed inside. The packed suitcases were sitting in wait in the hallway. Jason was in the lounge, perched on the edge of the chair. How long had he been sat like that, waiting in expectation?

'Everything OK?' he asked.

'Yeah.'

'How was court?'

'Never happened,' she said. 'Harrison's done a deal. Pleaded guilty to murder.'

Jason shook his head – disbelief. 'Another one bites the dust. There really is no stopping you, is there?'

Apparently not. Though, even after everything, she still wasn't sure how she felt about Harrison spending the next decade or more behind bars. In particular, she felt immensely sorry for his wife and son. Yet despite her misgivings, she'd fought hard for the murder conviction. She was responsible.

'I went to see Ben again,' she said. Jason's face dropped. 'I just…'

'You don't need to explain it,' he said.

'Don't I?'

She hadn't told him straight away after the first time. Hadn't told him about the attack in jail at all until a few days later. Partly because of the cases all blowing up at the same time, partly because she felt ashamed about having gone to see Ben in the first place. Jason had, naturally, taken it all in his stride. Like he did with virtually every facet of life. What had she done to deserve someone so calm and grounded?

'There's a bond between you and Ben that can never be broken,' Jason said. 'A blood bond. It may sound silly, but there's no other explanation, and it'll always be there, no matter what.'

It was that same blood bond that had led to so many problems in the Eccles family. For Clinton Harrison too, who had, in essence, defended his son's honour in the strongest possible terms.

'Come on, are we ready to go?' Jason said.

He grimaced as he hauled himself to his feet. He remained by the sofa as he stared over at her.

'Dani?'

Baxter's words rattled in her mind. McNair's too. She'd never been so confused. Jason moved over to her and gently took her hands in his. He gazed into her eyes.

'Don't ever feel like you can't open up to me,' he said. 'Whatever's going on in your mind, you can tell me. I'll always want that, whatever it is.'

'I know,' she said.

'So. Do you want to talk?'

'I do,' she said. She glanced at her watch. Three p.m. Not the end of the working day yet. She still had time. 'But let's hit the road first. We've got a long ride ahead of us.'

He smiled. She did too. She stepped into the hallway and picked up the largest and heaviest of the suitcases. She looked down at the others. Perhaps they wouldn't need so much luggage after all.

'After you,' Jason said to her.

She smiled at him again, then headed for the door.

They made it all of twenty miles before her phone rang. The office. She looked to Jason.

'It's fine,' he said.

She slipped the bud into her ear and pressed on the dash to take the call. McNair.

'I've just had a call from the hospital,' McNair said. 'Dani, he's awake.'

Her heart stopped. This couldn't be happening. Not now.

'Who?' Dani asked. Ben? Or Eric?

'Who? Your brother. Ben's awake.'

Dani pounded the brake.

Her heart thudded. Her brain swam.

She looked over to Jason. He hadn't heard the answer, but he was breathing deeply, holding onto the door handle in shock as he stared at her like she was crazy.

'I'm sorry,' she said.

He didn't say anything. Didn't ask a thing. Just nodded.

'We have to go back,' she said.

And that was exactly what they did.

A letter from Rob

Thank you for reading *The Bonds of Blood*, the fourth instalment in DI Dani Stephens's dramatic life story! I really hope you enjoyed it. Thanks too – as always – goes to the great teams behind the scenes at both Canelo and Hera – without them you wouldn't be reading this now!

Dani Stephens is one of four different series that I have written, and I often wonder just how far I can take each of those series while keeping characters and plots relevant, exciting, but perhaps above all believable. With *The Bonds of Blood* I decided to do something a little different with Dani – I mean, how many serial killers can she keep coming across in the West Midlands of England?! *The Bonds of Blood* was my take on a somewhat simpler case for her. A dysfunctional family. A single horrendous crime. A whole host of potential suspects. A classic whodunnit, if you like, albeit in my own style. Hopefully as a reader it simply came across as a thrilling read, but perhaps you did notice this slight change in plotting, and that it has left you wanting more!

I wonder what might get thrown at Dani next…

If you have any thoughts, you're more than welcome to let me know!

Once again, thank you for taking the time to read my work. I'm always grateful for reviews, if you could spare a few minutes to write and post one online. I also welcome direct comments and feedback, and you can reach me via my website (where you can also sign up to my newsletter), and on social media, links as follows:

Website: www.robsinclairauthor.com
Twitter: @rsinclairauthor
Facebook: fb.me/robsinclairauthor

All the best
Rob Sinclair